Susan Carlisle's love affa[...]
when she made a bad grad[...]
Not allowed to watch TV until the grade had
improved, she filled her time with books.
Turning her love of reading into a love for
writing romance, she now pens hot Medicals.
She loves castles, travelling, afternoon tea,
reading voraciously and hearing from her
readers. Join her newsletter at SusanCarlisle.com.

Tessa Scott is a lover of animals, nature and
happily-ever-afters. She lives in Northeast
Connecticut, surrounded by lots of trees, wildlife
and a menagerie of pets. A copywriter by day, she
enjoys that magical moment when the characters
she creates come to life and help take the story in
new and exciting directions.

A KISS UNDER THE NORTHERN LIGHTS

SUSAN CARLISLE

HEALING THE BABY SURGEON'S HEART

TESSA SCOTT

MILLS & BOON

First published in Great Britain 2025
by Mills & Boon, an imprint of HarperCollins*Publishers* Ltd,
1 London Bridge Street, London, SE1 9GF

www.harpercollins.co.uk

HarperCollins*Publishers* Macken House, 39/40 Mayor Street Upper, Dublin 1, D01 C9W8, Ireland

ISBN: 978-0-263-32495-2

01/25

This book contains FSC™ certified paper and other controlled sources to ensure responsible forest management.

For more information visit www.harpercollins.co.uk/green.

Printed and Bound in the UK using 100% Renewable Electricity at CPI Group (UK) Ltd, Croydon, CR0 4YY

A KISS UNDER THE NORTHERN LIGHTS

SUSAN CARLISLE

MILLS & BOON

To Finnley.

One of the greatest pleasures in my life.

CHAPTER ONE

A KNOT HUNG in Beatrice Shell's throat. She searched the land below for the town that should be at the end of the northern Iceland fjord. The stretch of blue water grew closer as the pilot of the single-engine plane prepared to land. Ahead she could just make out a single runway of black asphalt with piles of gray stone alongside it, extending into the water. She'd never seen anything like it. Yet that wasn't a huge surprise. Coming to Iceland had been her first real trip anywhere.

The large airliner she had taken to Reykjavík had been scary, but exciting at the same time. Getting into the small plane had created a different sensation all together. Terror. The six-seater plane was nothing like the jet, the only similarity being it soared through the air. This flight had kept her hair standing on end and her heart palpitating in her chest. She would see if there was a boat out when she left. No more swooping and dipping for her. Small plane transportation wasn't her idea of a good time.

Her fingers gripped the well-worn seat as the wings tipped one way, then the other. The pilot lined up with the runway. If he missed it, he would put them in the water. She glanced at the beautiful snowcapped mountains and shivered. Into the cold water.

She brushed her finger across the small scar on the top of

her hand, then forced herself to open her eyelids. Isn't this what she'd been wanting to do since she'd learned of her rare skin disorder as a teen? To have a connection. Belong.

She'd experienced a blistering skin rash. Her foster mother had taken her to the doctor. After much discussion and other doctors being called in for their opinions, she had learned she had a skin disease called hepatoerythro-poietic porphyria disease or HEP. What intrigued her the most about the disease was it was genetic, particular to people with Nordic ancestry. Until then she'd had no hint of her background.

She recovered completely with little scarring from the flare-up of the disease. She would always carry the gene, but the illness would become nothing more unless she spent too much time in the sun or was prescribed the wrong drugs. The positive thing that came out of the experience was the knowledge of her Nordic lineage. When she had saved enough money, she'd had a DNA test done, which had led her to Iceland.

With a squeak of tires, the plane touched the asphalt, bounced, then settled to coast to a stop. She let out the breath she'd been holding. At least they weren't in the water.

When the opportunity arose to work in a clinic in Iceland for a year, she'd applied for the chance. She was tickled when she won the position. Now she could care for people with the same genetic background as herself. They might not be direct family, but they were closer than anyone else she had known.

She dared a look out the window. Another plane sat parked in front of a white block building, and they coasted beside it. The sign on the wall read Welcome to Seydisf-jordur.

Gathering her purse and her small duffel bag, Trice

climbed out of the side door the pilot had opened. He offered his hand, and she accepted it. The last thing she needed was to arrive at her new job with a busted nose from falling on her face. That wouldn't encourage the town's faith in her medical abilities.

She glanced around at the buildings lining a single road following the curve of the fjord. The town was located in the end of a narrow green valley. A gentle-looking river lead into the mouth of the fjord. The backs of the town structures hovered against a wall of rock creating the fjord. In the sunshine, the stores and houses glowed white, pink, yellow and light blue with a few having red roofs. If anything, the place was picture-perfect.

Her heart beat faster. She'd dream of coming this far north for years but never thought it would happen. Now she was here. This place she could call home. Excitement built. This could be her chance to find a link to family. No matter how distant.

"Miss, your suitcase is right here. The clinic is over there." The man pointed around the water toward the only piece of land wide enough to have a center street with buildings on both sides. "It's the white building with the red cross sign."

"Thank you." She pulled the handle up on her case, assuming she was expected to walk the half a mile. She was thankful for her warm socks and her down vest. Her new hiking boots maybe not so much. They had been a going away gift from her best friend, Andrea. "I appreciate the ride in."

The man with a beard lifted and lowered his chin and went back to the plane.

Taking the suitcase handle, she rolled it toward the small terminal building that sat securely on land. At least this part of the airport wasn't surrounded by water. Unable to see a red cross from that distance, she followed the road toward the village.

The sun shone bright, and the air was brisk. Thankfully the place wasn't covered in snow. People often mixed Greenland up with Iceland. Greenland was icy and Iceland was green.

Trice had been offered the job at the last minute because another doctor had backed out. She'd jumped at the opportunity despite the short notice. In less than forty-eight hours, she'd wrapped up her personal business, stored her few belongings and stepped on a plane bound for the far-off north. Andrea had thought she was crazy and wished her well.

She had not even had a chance to break in her new boots between yesterday and today. After a hurried last two days, a long plane ride, and the altitude, she didn't care much about the time zone changes.

Trice surveyed the area past the airport away from town. In that direction, there was some type of business located in a large red metal building next to the water. Just how much could happen in this tiny place? Compared to living in metropolitan Atlanta, where she'd spent her entire life, this town was no larger than a neighborhood. No doubt she would have culture shock. She wasn't sure if that would be a good thing or a bad thing. She was too busy trying to keep her mind off the ache of her toes to worry about how she would make this work.

Around the curve of the bay, she saw the white clapboard house. Outside it hung a small sign with the red cross on it. She headed that way.

Trudging on, she promised herself with every step she would remove her boots as soon as she had a chance. The impeccable view of the vibrantly painted wooden buildings, the vivid blue water, the green of the valley, and the white of the snowcapped mountain filled her. Here she had a chance to find her lineage and through that herself. She could feel that in her bones, just not her toes.

Drake Stevansson noticed the woman for two reasons. First, he didn't know her. Having been born and raised in Seydis-fjordur, he knew everyone. Second, even from a distance, something about the woman intrigued him. Maybe it was her vivid-colored yellow coat or the hot pink suitcase she pulled. Whatever it was, she was eye-catching.

She followed the long curve of the road into town. He handed the envelope to his aunt, the postmistress, and started in the stranger's direction and toward the medical clinic. What could possibly land this fascinating creature here? He had seen plenty of people come from a cruise ship, but there wasn't one in port. She must have been on the plane.

The woman continued on but slower now. She had a rather haggard look. Every once in a while, she stopped and shook a foot. What was that about? The road wasn't muddy. Did she walk like that all the time?

She would square her shoulders, raise her chin and start again. Something about this woman screamed, "I won't be defeated." That spoke to him. That was an Icelandic mantra. His gut said she had the determination, the grit needed to live through so many hours of darkness in the winter, not to mention the cold. Why that should matter to him he had no idea. He would be leaving soon with the possibility of not returning except to visit.

As a boy, he had watched his grandfather die because there wasn't anyone close who could do a simple appendectomy. He'd promised himself then that he would become a surgeon. He would fix people's bodies. He had gotten far enough in his training that he could do the procedures, but he still need the practice hours. He had been working on those when he was called away.

Drake had returned to Seydisfjordur for the funeral of his mentor and friend, Dr. Johannsson, to learn there was no one to oversee the practice. Drake had made arrangements for a break from his surgery work so he could provide the town medical care. Locating someone to take his place had turned into a frustrating ordeal. Finally, someone had agreed to come for a year. The mayor had taken almost two years to find someone. The man was expected any day. The mayor would continue to look for someone else beyond that. In two more weeks, after settling the new person in, Drake would leave.

The only issue tugging at him not to go was Luce. She was getting older, frailer. Because of circumstances, he had become responsible for her. Yet she encouraged him leaving. "Don't worry about me. Go follow your dream." The new doctor had better be good enough to care for Luce.

Drake reached the medical clinic. He stood outside and watched the woman approach. She made the same actions once again with her feet before she reached him.

Her look focused on him as she crossed the short distance. He found her even more interesting up close. Her blond hair was as fair as any person he knew. She controlled it by twisting it on the back of her head with a sparkling hair clip. She wore a bright red shirt, baggy black pants, and had a yellow, red, orange and black scarf around her neck. An orange bag was slung over her shoulder. Everything about her screamed confidence.

"Hello. Can I help you?"

She came to a stop in front of him, again lifted a foot and

shook it from side to side "Oh, good, you speak English. I'm afraid my Icelandic is nonexistent."

"You are in luck. I happen to be one of the ninety-eight percent of the people who speak English in Iceland. I'm going to use it now." Drake leaned down so they were at eye level. He wished he could see her eyes, but they were covered by sunglasses. "Are you okay? Lost? How can I help you?"

"My feet hurt. New boots." She moaned.

With a compassionate smile, he said, "I've been there. I can help with that."

"That's okay. I just need to get them off. Mind if I sit on your step?" She was already moving to do so.

"Not at all."

She pushed the pull handle of the case down. "I just need to get my tennis shoes out." She moved to picked up the bag.

"Let me have that." Drake lifted the case. "Come inside. You'll be more comfortable here."

"Thanks. I appreciate that." She followed him inside the small wooden building. She flopped into one of the plastic chairs in the waiting room with a sigh, resting her feet on her heels.

"Here, let me help." Drake went down on his haunches.

"You don't need to do that." She pulled her feet back.

He looked into her blue eyes that reminded him of the fjord with the sun shining across it. When the few other single men in town found out about her, they would be scrambling to her door. He wouldn't be around long enough to do that. Something about this woman made him suspect he would be missing out. He reached for her foot and began unlacing the boot. "I'm a doctor. It's my job to help those who hurt."

"So you are the doctor here." Her look met his as she studied him.

"I am for at least another two weeks."

She winced as he removed her footwear.

He dropped the boot to the floor. "Easy. You must have really done some damage to your feet."

She wiggled her foot. "That at least feels better, but I have no desire to put another shoe on."

"Let's remove the sock and see what's going on." He slowly rolled the sock off. Her foot was red and swollen with blisters on both sides. "You did a job."

"I should've known better. But they were a gift, and I wanted to wear them when my friend was the one taking me to the airport." She lifted her foot with the intent of rubbing it.

"Don't do that. Then it will really hurt. Wait right here. I have just what you need." He stood.

"I'd rather take care of them myself," she called after him.

"As the medical professional here, I'd rather you let me make sure you're okay." He headed down the hall without giving her time to respond.

Soon he returned with a square plastic container and Epsom salts. He poured a generous amount of salt into the pan.

She pushed a straight length of hair that had escaped her clip away from her face. "I can do this at the place where I am staying."

He gave her a direct look. "You can't even walk there. Let me at least get you comfortable enough to do that. I'll get the warm water."

"If you insist." She grinned.

He glanced back at her. "I do. Around here we take any

injury seriously. If it gets out of hand, we have a long way to go to get treatment."

When he came back this time, she had the other boot and sock off and was leaning back in her chair with a look of acceptance.

He poured the water into the pan. "Ease your feet in. You don't want them burned on top of being blistered."

She dipped an unpolished big toe of a slim, delicate foot into the water with a sigh. Slowly her feet went into the liquid. "This feels wonderful. Thank you."

"You keep those in there for a few minutes. I'll be back with a towel." He returned with a bottle of oil. He poured a generous amount into the water.

"What's that? It smells good." She inhaled.

Drake watched her neck lengthen. He was tempted to run a finger down the length of the smooth, creamy skin. "It is something I mix myself. It's fish oil with some local herbs. I use it when hikers come by for help. We get a number of those this time of year."

"So this isn't your first time to help out like this." She fluttered her feet in the water.

"No, I see abused feet more than I'd like to."

She curled her toes. "This will be the last time you will see mine."

He took the chair beside her. "Famous last words."

She leaned back beside him. "This is amazing."

He liked this flamboyant woman's attitude. "Do you have some nice warm socks and some substantial shoes that are not brand-new?"

She nodded. "I've got my tennis shoes in my suitcase, but the thought of putting them on makes my feet hurt even more."

"I have something you can wear that will make your

feet happier." Drake went to his office and located the soft boots his grandmother had given him for Christmas. He had brought them to the clinic thinking he might like to wear them when he was doing paperwork. Finally, he would be putting them to good use. He added a pair of clean socks.

This time he found the woman with her head back and eyes closed. Was she asleep?

Seconds later her eyelids opened.

He handed her the socks. "These are made of natural fibers and will help your feet avoid getting infected." He placed the boots beside the pan.

She sat straighter. With a hand, she pushed another stray strand of hair away from her face. Raising her chin, she looked at him. "You know, I don't even know your name."

He offered his hand. "I'm Dr. Stevansson. Drake."

She jerked to an upright position. "You are? Well, now I'm completely embarrassed."

"Why?"

"Because I'm here to take your place. I'm Dr. Beatrice Shell."

That he hadn't expected. She would be his replacement. He should've thought of it first thing, but nothing about her looked—he glanced at her petite build and soft face, then her flashy clothes—like someone he would expect to live in Iceland. Or that would survive a Seydisfjordur winter. And he'd been told by the mayor that a man had been hired for the doctor position.

Drake had stayed out of the search process for his replacement, both by his own choice and the mayor's. Drake had feared that if he was involved, he would never think anyone was qualified enough to have the position. The mayor's reasoning was that since Drake didn't care enough to stay, he shouldn't have a say in who took his place.

"But I guess I'm at the right place," Beatrice said, "and you are just the person I was looking for."

Drake liked that idea too much. Still, she was coming, and he was going. Nothing would be happening between them. Just his luck. The first woman near his age and not related to him who had shown up in town in years and he'd be leaving soon.

She offered him her hand. "I'm Trice to my friends. I was expecting somebody much older."

He chuckled. "I get that quite a lot." In fact, he heard it enough for it to grate on his nerves. Dr. Johannsson had been the town doctor for years. He'd delivered Drake and most of the adults in town. Compared to him, Drake was young.

Drake had worked for Dr. Johannsson as a teen and through high school, then gone off to medical school. The old doctor had encouraged Drake to consider taking over the practice, but Drake's dream was surgery. He felt like he could help more people using those skills. But it meant leaving Luce, which he didn't like doing. She had no intention of moving from her home. Unfortunately, there was no surgery clinic near Seydisfjordur. That was an entirely different issue.

He gave Trice a good long look. No, he hadn't expected this woman with her sassy attitude, flashy clothing, and full-of-confidence outlook. She appealed to him, too much so. The last woman he'd liked couldn't leave Seydisfjordur fast enough. Trice acted thrilled she was there. "I was expecting…a man."

Her shoulders went back at that statement. "Women now make up more than fifty percent of doctors." Her brows drew together. "No one told you? The doctor who was coming backed out at the last minute. I only found out I had the job a couple of days ago."

He hadn't been told on purpose would be his guess. Drake put his hands up in defense. "That wasn't a sexist statement. It's just that we don't get many women who want to live in such a distant and hostile environment. I'm just surprised, that's all."

"I'm tougher than I look." Determination showed clear in her eyes.

His mouth quirked. "You'll need to be."

Yes, he liked this woman who seemed excited about being in his hometown. Would she still feel that way this winter? What was she looking for? Or running from? Too bad he wouldn't be around long enough to find out.

Trice gingerly put her feet on the towel Drake had placed on the floor. "Now that I have thoroughly embarrassed myself, could you point me in the direction of where I'll be staying?"

"I'll do better than that. I'll show you. I'm sure you are tired."

She chuckled. "Yeah, that would be an understatement. After two plane changes and then a prop plane to get here, I could use a rest."

"Where did you start out from?"

"Atlanta."

He whistled. "Bright lights, big city. Seydisfjordur will be a big change for you."

"So far it looks wonderful." Her eyes were glowing with anticipation. "I can hardly wait to get to know everyone."

"It won't take you long. Many will line up to see you."

That she wasn't used to. Most of her life she had gone unnoticed. It would be nice to have people actually want to meet her. She pulled on the soft, thick socks. With some trepidation, she pushed her foot into the first shoe. It felt wonderful around her abused toes. With less concern, she did the same with the other foot. "Thank you. I dreaded putting on even my tennis shoes. I promise to return them all clean."

"It's not a problem." He stood.

"I'm sure the last few minutes make me look unqualified to take over here, but I promise to have my act together tomorrow."

"Everybody makes mistakes about footwear at times. I certainly have." He smiled.

Trice doubted he had made any mistakes. He looked and sounded like the perfect guy. Kind, understanding, gentle, caring, and best of all, male. Too bad he would be leaving. Something about Drake made her believe he was different from the last guy she had dated. She stood and hobbled toward her suitcase. For some reason, she sensed this man was careful with women's hearts.

"I'll get that. You can hardly make it to the door. You can't handle the case too."

She managed to get down the steps only by holding the rail with two hands.

Drake quickly came up behind her. He placed her case on the ground, then bent in front of her. "Get on."

"You have to be kidding. You can't mean to carry me through the street on your back!" She couldn't think of a less dignified way of making a first impression than parading through town on this man's back.

"Would you rather be cradled in my arms?"

Her pride refused to let him do that.

He looked over his shoulder. "If I don't carry you, how do you plan to get there?"

She glanced around.

Drake's look held hers. "You could stay here at the clinic if you wanted."

She considered sleeping on the examination table after having been on an airplane the better part of the day. The idea didn't appeal. "Okay."

"Wrap your arms around my neck. It's just a couple houses down."

She did as he said. His arms looped under her knees. Her front pressed against his back. Heat washed through her. This was far too familiar for someone she didn't even know, but what choice did she have? Walking wasn't a good suggestion.

He pulled the handle up on her suitcase and took off at a steady stride.

She voiced next to his ear, "I can get my suitcase later."

"I believe I can handle both of you at one time. Neither of you is very heavy." He threw the words over his shoulder without any exertion indicated in his voice.

Trice couldn't help but appreciate the movement of his muscles as he walked. His broad shoulders made her confident he wouldn't drop her. This was a man who knew how to care for people and took pleasure in doing so.

They made their way down the road lined with houses and businesses no taller than two floors. Curious faces met them along the way. A few people stepped out of the buildings to watch them.

"Is everyone going to know?" She started to hide her face but thought better of it.

"Pretty much. There are only around one thousand people who live in this area, and most of them are related to me. I would bet that in an hour, everyone will have heard of your arrival."

"Good to know." She smiled at one of the ladies, who waved.

He chuckled.

People continued to stare. A few spoke to Drake as they went. He responded with a grin in return.

One older man joined in beside Drake and asked, "Who you got there?"

"The new doctor. You can meet her later. We're kind of busy right now."

The man glanced at her. "Why is she on your back?"

Trice buried her face in his shoulder. She felt more than heard Drake's laugher. His body shook.

"Isn't she a little old to need to ride that way?" The man sounded perplexed.

"Gustaf, we'll talk about it later."

Trice groaned as Drake moved on. "I'm going to have to work extra hard to earn people's respect after this show."

"You'll find people here are warm and forgiving." He stopped in front of a pink house trimmed in white.

He set the case to the side then let her legs go. She slid down his back. Heat she'd not felt in a long time washed through her. Mercy, the man had a nice body. She'd had one serious relationship, but his body wasn't as defined as Drake's.

Nor had been his strength of will. Her ex had been from a society family, and his mother made it clear Trice's background was not suitable. A foster child with no family would never do. Her boyfriend couldn't stand up to his mother, so he and Trice parted ways. A marriage between them probably wouldn't have worked anyway. Her sense of adventure and sense of humor hadn't always been appreciated. Her boyfriend had been far too serious. Worse, he had been under his family's thumb. Trice wanted a man who stood on his own two feet.

Even with her and Drake's short association, she didn't

think those were issues for him. But she shouldn't be making these observations. She had no interest in becoming involved in a relationship. She wouldn't take the chance on being second choice again. There had been enough of that in her life.

Something about Drake appealed to her. Maybe it was the fact he had been willing to carry her as he had. He seemed to enjoy the absurdity in life.

Drake's strong grip held her arm, letting her get her feet under her. He knocked on the door but didn't wait for an answer before he opened it. "Luce?"

The scrape of chair legs and shuffling of feet came from the back of the house. He carried the luggage inside. She followed, closing the door behind her. A petite stoop-shouldered woman with a weathered face entered.

"Drake, what do you mean coming into my home bellowing?" The woman's voice was gruff but held a tender note.

"I'm sorry, Luce. I brought your new boarder. This is Dr. Shell."

The woman, who must have been close to a century old, gave Trice a long look. "From America, I hear."

"Yes ma'am, I am." Was that a good or bad thing?

"Nice manners too."

Somehow Trice believed that was high praise. "Thank you. It's nice to meet you. I appreciate you giving me a place to stay."

"You have come to take my Drake's place."

There was a tone of sadness to that question. "I have come to take care of the people here for a year and do some research."

The older woman studied Trice a moment, her eyes landing on her feet. "She is wearing your Christmas present." Her accusing look shifted to Drake.

"She is. By the way, Luce is my grandmother." Drake hung his head as if in shame.

Trice liked the idea a man as large as Drake could be intimidated by this tiny woman. She had certainly called him on the carpet.

"She's just borrowing them. I had them over at the office to wear if my feet were cold while I was doing paperwork. Dr. Shell's feet hurt."

"They are very nice," Trice assured the woman. "Thank you..." She looked at Drake.

"You may call me Luce. Everyone does." The woman gave a sharp nod and said to Trice, "I'll show you where you will stay."

Trice, with Drake carrying her case, followed the older woman through the small, dim home and out the back door. In the backyard stood an even smaller cottage.

Luce opened the door. "You have everything you need in here except a full kitchen. There is a microwave and a toaster oven, but if you want to do more, you're welcome to use my kitchen anytime you please. All you have to do is to come in the back door."

Luce pushed the cottage door open. "Come in and I'll show you around."

Trice joined her. Drake entered behind her, setting the case out of the way. With him there, the place went from small to tiny. After that ride on his back, she was too aware of him. He seemed to surround her.

Luce explained everything in detail. Which wasn't much. A solid wooden bed sat in one corner. In another was a bookshelf filled with books, a chair and small table with a floor lamp beside it. Nearby rested a TV on a substantial-looking dresser with drawers. Across from that side of the room was a kitchen area that consisted of a cabinet, a table and two chairs. A small bath took up the back corner. A hoop rug created out of pastel colors lay on the floor.

As far as Trice was concerned, she'd found heaven. After growing up with little she could call her own, this would be a treat. "This really looks wonderful. I know I'll enjoy staying here."

"If you need anything, you just ask me or tell Drake. He helps take care of things around here when he's not busy seeing patients." The old woman flashed him a look. "At least, until he leaves."

"Luce, you said you wanted me to go. To be happy." He put an arm around the woman's shoulders, looking at her with a teasing grin.

"I do want you to follow your dream. I will miss you. Enough of that. You aren't gone yet. Let's let the girl settle in." She nudged him toward the door.

Drake went while looking over his shoulder at Trice. "See how I'm treated around here? No wonder I want to return to my work in London."

That far away? Why did that idea bother her? She had just met the man. Those thoughts she must squelch. They led to disappointment and pain.

"When you get ready for a tour of the clinic, you come on over. I'll be there until five o'clock. Better yet, why don't we just let that wait until in the morning?"

"Thanks for your help and for letting me borrow your shoes. And of course for the ride."

He grinned. "My pleasure."

It had been hers as well.

CHAPTER TWO

DRAKE LOOKED UP from his paperwork when the door of the clinic opened early the next morning. He saw Trice's blond hair before the rest of her. His heart did a little dip and jerk before it settled. Something about the woman charmed him. Why here and why now? He needed to keep his interest under control. There wasn't time for them to get involved. It wouldn't be fair to either of them if they did.

"Good morning," he offered as she closed the door. He pushed away from his desk that sat in the small area doubling as a waiting room.

"Hey." She looked around the area as if taking in all the details.

"How'd you sleep last night?"

"Good," she said as if in afterthought, her attention still on the space.

"I'm not surprised after the day you had." He stood. Once again she was dressed in a vivid colors. Her shirt was sunshine yellow, paired with jeans. Her hair was pulled on top of her head and bound by a piece of cloth the same shade as her shirt.

She fingered the sign-in clipboard. "I appreciate the coffee and pastry. That was very sweet of you."

"I just figured after the day you had yesterday, you wouldn't bother with buying food."

"It was nice to wake to a hot cup of coffee waiting. Along with the wake-up knock."

His chest expanded with pleasure. He felt overly pleased she had been glad to receive his gift.

She looked down the hall. "I'm ready for the tour. I need to appear professional when someone comes in after yesterday. I should try to redeem myself some."

"You have nothing to be embarrassed about." He had to have fielded at least thirty questions about that show. On the phone and in person.

"I think that piggyback ride through the middle of town might qualify under embarrassment. Too close to a Lady Godiva ride."

He chuckled. "Except you were fully clothed."

She grinned. "Thank goodness."

Drake liked she didn't take herself too seriously. He enjoyed this woman a little too much for comfort, especially since he would be leaving. His life had been on hold for so long that it felt good to trade quips with Trice. "How're your feet this morning? Do I need to give them a look?"

"They are fine. Thanks. I'm even returning your shoes." She held them up by two fingers.

"I would tell you that you are welcome to keep them, but I would suffer the wrath of Luce."

She smiled. "We can't have that."

He took the shoes from her. "Come on. I'll give the half-cent tour while I put these away. You'll know where they are if you need them."

"You're not taking them with you when you go?"

He started down the hall. "Nope. I won't need them. It's much warmer in London."

"So, what is it you're going to London for?" She slowly followed him, stopping to glance into the rooms they passed.

"I'm returning to surgery training." Drake could hardly wait. He had missed it.

"What happened, you didn't finish?" She sounded genuinely interested.

"Dr. Johannsson died. I returned for his funeral and didn't go back." He just couldn't leave.

"Why not?"

He stopped and looked at her. "After Dr. Johannsson died, the town needed a doctor. I couldn't leave them without medical care. It has taken the mayor two years to find someone to replace me. By the way, why did you decide to come here, of all places?"

"Because I've wanted to come to Iceland for years. I'm also interested in researching HEP."

His brows narrowed. "That answer I hadn't expected. Hepatoerythropoietic porphyria is an interesting condition for an American to study. Why that of all things?"

"Because I carry the gene."

His brows rose. "Really? So your family is from here?"

"My DNA test says Iceland, and other Scandinavian countries by smaller degrees."

"What have your parents told you?"

"Nothing. I went into foster care when I was three. I remember little about my mother and never knew my father. I was too young to remember anything my mother might have said. Which I doubt she did. I understand she died of a drug overdose when I was five."

His eyes filled with sympathy. "I'm so sorry."

Trice shrugged. "It is what it is. Before you ask, no, I wasn't adopted. People want babies, and I was almost six by then. It didn't happen for me. I was passed from foster home to foster home." She paused as if making a decision, then continued, "After I learned I had the HEP gene and it was explained to me how only certain people had it, I then started reading everything I could find on the subject. I made excellent grades, and that led me to medical school. I have a general medical degree, but I'm interested in research as well. I wanted to come here because it offered me a chance to do both."

Drake knew everyone in town and was related to most of them. The idea of not knowing his family was a foreign concept for him. The chance to be alone was part of the appeal of returning to London. Too often they had been involved in his business. "I didn't mean to pry."

She shrugged. "I had often wondered what my background was, and finding out I had HEP gave me a link."

He watched Trice. Her eyes had brightened. Then he understood. "You're looking for some bridge to your family."

"Yes. No. I don't know. I don't think I'll find my grandparents or anything like that, but I am interested in the people who share the disease with me."

The woman became more interesting by the minute. "That sounds reasonable. But patient care can keep you pretty busy around here."

"I can handle both. Patient care will always come first."

He liked hearing that. After all, these were his family and friends.

Trice looked at him. "You're having a hard time giving up being responsible, aren't you?"

Was he that transparent? He hung his head. "A little bit."

"That's understandable. I'm sure I will feel the same way when it's time for me to leave. It's natural."

Somehow this conversation wasn't making him feel any better. "Let me finish showing you around."

The tension in her body eased. "Thanks, I would like that."

"We aren't that busy on a daily basis. There are clinic

days for regular checkups and days for shots. Otherwise there will be those who come in to see you with the usual illnesses. Then there are the emergencies. Which reminds me, I need to call the air ambulance about an issue."

"How are emergencies handled?" She looked around the examination room as if taking stock of where everything was stored.

"I stabilize the patient the best I can. If I can't handle it here, then I call the air ambulance. If the weather is fine, then a fixed-wing plane is dispatched. If the weather is bad, which is usually in the winter, then a helicopter will be used. In the worst-case scenario, a coast guard helicopter will be sent."

Drake couldn't help but be proud of the little clinic. He had made a number of improvements during his time. "Come along this way."

She started up the hall toward the front. "I did notice you have a couple of beds here where people can stay overnight."

"I do, but that happens rarely. Most wish to go home, and I stop in to see them." Many times he shared an evening meal with the patient's family.

"So you make house calls?"

"On occasion. I also do a monthly well-child clinic and another one for the geriatric patients. On those days, a nurse flies in to help."

"That sounds straightforward." She wandered into one of the two examination rooms.

He had to give her credit. She was self-assured if nothing else. Or was she just putting on an act. Where did she get all that confidence?

"Until it isn't." He stopped in front of the open door.

She followed him down a short hallway. Doors led off to the right side.

"Back here is a small kitchen, lab and supply room. You're welcome to bring in anything you like and set it up."

"A coffee machine is all I need." She looked into the cabinets.

"Got that, but if you need special beans or flavored syrups, you'll need to bring it. Plain Jane coffee is what I have here."

She looked at the setup. "I never developed a taste for the fancy drinks. There wasn't money for that. It looks like you stay well supplied for medical work. How often do you order?"

"Once a month. Supplies come in by ship. I'll show you where all that information is."

He started back up the hall, speaking over his shoulder. "We have telecommunication with the hospital. If we can't resolve problems here, then the ambulance is called. But as you can imagine, that's only as good as the weather allows."

Trice covertly studied the handsome, tall blond man with a shadow of a beard as he showed her around. His pride for the place was evident on his face. He looked like the Nordic Vikings whose blood ran through his veins. It didn't take much for her to imagine him standing on the front of his long boat, a foot on the gunwale, his hair flying in the wind as he led his men on a raid across the water to England. His chest would be thrust out beneath a breastplate, strong legs holding him steady. Everything about Drake said he was in control of his world.

She didn't need anybody in control of her world. After years of being told where to live and what to do, her life was finally her own to oversee. Now was the time for her to find herself and what she wanted. Where she belonged.

The door opened, taking her attention away from Drake.

A boy of about eight entered, followed by a woman whose forehead was wrinkled with worry. The boy's hand was wrapped in a dish towel.

Drake stood. "What's the problem, Stavn?"

The woman spoke. "Stavn cut his hand trying to open a package with a knife." She glared at the boy. "He knew better. I'm afraid it's large enough to need stitches."

"I was trying to open the package without using my teeth." The boy sounded near tears.

Trice went down on her knees to eye level with the child. "Sometimes those things happen. I'm Dr. Shell. I'm going to be taking Dr. Stevansson's place. It's nice to meet you, Stavn. Do you mind if I have a look? I promise not to make it hurt."

Stavn hesitated, then slowly offered his hand.

Trice unwrapped the rag gently while holding pressure to his artery at his wrist, stopping the flow of blood. "Yep. That's a pretty deep and long cut. You must have been pushing really hard on the knife."

Stavn nodded, tears glistening in his eyes.

"Then I guess we better get you into an examination room and stitch that up." Drake directed Stavn and his mother down the hall. "Take the first room."

Trice accepted the hand Drake offered her. He pulled her to standing with seemly little effort.

"One of us better go make some pretty stitches." Trice grinned.

He left her to follow their patient. "I'll get the supplies while you settle Stavn."

Trice entered the examination room. "Stavn." Trice pulled a couple of plastic gloves from a box on the counter and tugged them on. She then rolled a small stool over beside the boy, who sat on the gurney. "May I see your hand again?"

The boy was quicker to let her see it than the last time.

She turned his hand over, palm side up. "Dr. Stevansson and I are going to clean it, then stitch it closed. Do you know what I mean by stitching?"

He nodded. "Yeah. Like my mother sews up my pants when I tear a hole in them."

"That's exactly right. We'll make it so it'll doesn't hurt. If it does, all you have to do is tell us, and we'll give you more medicine. There is one more thing you should know. We will have to give your hand a shot, so that might hurt for a sec. Then it'll be gone. You can hold your mother's hand, and it'll go by real fast."

Drake entered the room with a handful of supplies, making the space even smaller. He had a way of doing that. He looked at her. "You stitch and I'll bandage."

Was he testing her? "Sure." Her attention went to Stavn. "Is that okay with you?"

The boy agreed.

She took Stavn's hand once again. "I need a pan and saline."

Drake handed her the bottle. He held the pan under Stavn's hand.

She opened the bottle top. "We're going to pour this liquid over your hand. We have to wash it out really good."

Stavn sat still and rod straight as they worked. Done, Trice picked up a towel and patted the area around the wound dry while Drake set the pan aside.

"All right, let's see what we've got here." Drake pulled back the cover of the suture kit. "Stavn, if you start to feel sick in your stomach, please tell us."

His mother said, "He has a pretty strong stomach."

"Famous last words," Trice mumbled. "All right, Stavn, I need you to lie on the table. Your mom can keep holding

your hand, but she should move to the head of the bed."
Thank goodness the mother followed her advice.

Trice helped Stavn lie on the table. "I want you to look at
your mother. I have to give you that shot we talked about.
It will only hurt for a second. It's important you be really
still. After that, you can watch if you wish. If not, then look
at your mom."

Drake handed her the syringe with the local anesthetic.

"Okay, here we go. Stavn, tell me what you like to do."
She inserted the needle. "Do you like to ride a bicycle?"

The boy grunted a positive sound.

"I do too. I like to ride a mountain bike. I was sad when
I couldn't bring one with me on the plane."

"I have a mountain bike too." The boy perked up.

Trice finished deadening the area. She touched around
the spot. "Can you feel this?"

"No." The boy sounded unsure.

"Good. You are being so good. Dr. Stevansson, what kind
of thread would you go with for a boy as strong as Stavn?"

Drake acted as if he were giving the question a great deal
of thought. "I would select the heavier thread. He needs to
have it really strong."

Thankfully Drake caught on to what she was doing. Putting the child at ease. "I agree."

Stavn glanced at his hand, then back at his mother.

Trice went to work stitching first the inside of the wound
and then the outside. "Almost done." Two stitches later, she
rolled back from the table. "You can look now."

The boy lifted his hand for a second, then put it down
again.

Drake stepped forward. "Why don't you sit up while I
bandage that for you?"

Stavn moved to the edge of the table.

Drake removed gauze from a package and made quick work of wrapping it around the boy's hand. He then secured it with plastic-covered tape. "This should keep it dry. I don't want you getting this hand wet. Ask for help when you need it. I would like to see you back tomorrow for a check." Drake looked at her. "Don't you think a day out of school is deserved?"

"I do." Trice smiled at Stavn.

The mother said, "Thank you. Both of you."

"You are welcome, Mary. I'm sorry. In all the excitement, I failed to introduce you to the new doctor. This is Beatrice Shell. Mary Leesdottir."

"Nice to meet you. Please call me Trice. Sorry we had to meet under these circumstances." Trice placed her hand on the boy's shoulder. "You have a brave son. Maybe show him where the scissors are so he can use them to open a package next time."

The mother smiled and nodded as she ushered Stavn out the door.

Drake turned to Trice. "I'm feeling good about leaving the clinic in your hands. You were excellent just now. You put Stavn at ease, and I've not seen better stitching." His grin grew. "Except maybe mine."

"Thank you for the seal of approval." She had to admit she liked having it.

Two evenings later, Drake rested in his recliner, half watching TV and half reading a book. Yet his thoughts were of Trice. She had been amazing with patients young and old over the last few days.

Stavn's injury hadn't been that extensive, but after Trice's help, Drake had complete confidence she would know how to handle whatever came her way. He shouldn't be spending time worrying about the clinic since he was the one who had chosen to leave. Trice had clearly made that point. To his great irritation.

The people in Seydisfjordur were no longer his responsibility. Despite his desire not to feel any responsibility, he did. That's what caused him to agree to step in when Dr. Johannsson passed away. Drake had had no intention of being here this long. He had been on his way to becoming a great surgeon. All his colleagues had said so. He'd done his part to help his home village, but now it was time to go.

With his parents having moved across the island, and his brother and sister there as well, there was no need to remain here. Drake only anticipated returning for short visits to see Luce, but he hoped one day soon she would agree to live with his parents. He could possibly return after completing his training, but that wasn't guaranteed despite the need for a surgeon in Seydisfjordur.

He had learned that quickly. While at university, he had enjoyed much of what a larger city offered. Returning to Seydisfjordur had been more difficult than he anticipated. Finding a wife, having a family were more problematic in the remote area. And even if he did find a wife in the city and wanted to move back, she might not agree.

He'd learned that the hard way when he brought a woman he was serious about home. At the time he had been considering returning. Dr. Johannsson had been encouraging him to take over the practice. His girlfriend hadn't enjoyed the flight, didn't like that there were no serious shopping places, and hated the outdoors. That was all before she saw the area in the dead of winter. Their relationship soon ended with her red-faced, snarled remark: "Nothing would entice me to ever live here!"

The subtext was, she didn't love him enough to consider

it. That mistake he had no intention of repeating. He would take no chances. In London he could be a part of a practice, find a wife and settle down and be able to do surgery. He wanted to fulfill his dream, honor his grandfather, yet Seydisfjordur still pulled at him.

When the town needed the medical care he could provide, he had put his life on hold for them. Now that Trice was there, it was time for him to return to his training. Something that would give him a chance to help a larger number of people. Still, guilt ate at him when he thought of leaving.

He couldn't have it both ways. The discussion had been made. He would leave in little more than a week.

The next morning at the clinic, he called, "Trice, come up front when you're finished. I'll show you how to access charts on the computer. I also need to take you out back and show you how to handle the generator. It can be temperamental."

"Be right there." A few minutes later she approached the desk.

He stood and started toward the door. "We need to go outside to the back of the building."

She joined him.

They exited into the bright mid-day sunlight. The sight of the fjord and the mountain surrounding him always grabbed his attention. To Trice he said, "Tell me how you are planning to go about this research you have in mind."

"Is there a problem with me doing so?" Her tone had an edge to it as she stepped over the uneven ground.

"No, I was just curious."

"I'm particularly interested in the long-term effects HEP has on people. Studies have been done, but I believe there is more to learn. While I am here, it's the perfect opportunity to do research and write a paper. I would like to start by looking at files and then interviewing people."

He stepped up beside her and took the lead. "Files shouldn't be a problem. People might be more of one. I could help with that. Pave the way a little. Maybe I can get them to open up to you some. I know a few people who have had HEP and a couple of children. I'll need to speak to them before I share their names with you."

Her eyes brightened. "I understand. I appreciate any help you can give me before you go."

He stopped in front of the generator. "Come to think of it, there's a community event tonight. It would be a good way to meet people, to get to know them before you start asking them questions. If they interact with you some socially, then they'll be more likely to share."

Her look met his. "Is that how you are too?"

"I can be. Is there something you want to know?" He had the feeling she saw more of him than he wished.

She eyes narrowed when she angled her head to the side in thought. "I'm good for right now, but maybe I'll have something later."

"Okay. I'll honor that." Enough about him. They needed to get back to what they were doing here. "About the generator."

Fifteen minutes later after he'd explained the work of the machinery they head inside. "About tonight. Do you want to go?"

Trice smiled as if pleased with the idea She pushed the door open. "Of course. This will be my home for at least a year."

"If not more." She could get stuck here just as he had. Another doctor might not agree to take her place.

"Like you did?"

"Yes. If you are called to medicine, it is hard to pull away when you are needed." *Especially when you know the people. When it is home.*

Trice met his look. "You're doing it."

He followed her inside. There was a note of accusation in her voice. He didn't like it. "I am, but I put my surgery career on hold for two years."

She looked over her shoulder. "Why is doing surgery day in and day out so important? You already have the skills. A practice. I bet you have gotten to use your skills here."

His jaw ticked like it had earlier. Who did she think she was, questioning his decisions? "I have, but mostly I've done general medicine stuff. Earaches, gout, and stitches, as you know. If I finish my fellowship, I can return to Reykjavík if there is a position in the hospital. Most of my family is on that side of the island now. Except for Luce. At least it is less than an hour away. I need to go if I'm going to, because they aren't going to hold my spot in London forever."

"Then I guess you have to go."

"You make that sound like a bad thing."

She shook her head. "It isn't bad. I just think you don't know your value here. But I shouldn't be convincing you to stay." She huffed. "If you did, I would lose my job."

He closed the door with a thud.

"So, are we on for the community center tonight?" Drake hoped she said yes. For some reason, he wanted to escort her.

She turned to face him. "I understand communities here are big on the folk arts."

"We aren't so much this time of the year. Tonight is a special occasion, but in the winter months, when it stays dark for so long and snow is falling and the cruise ships don't come, it's our opportunity for some culture and just getting together."

"Sounds like fun." Trice smiled.

"I'll pick you and Luce up at seven then."

"We could just meet you there."

He shook his head. "Not on your life. Luce would have my hide if I didn't escort you both."

"I wouldn't want to be the cause of that. I wasn't planning on working tonight, so I'd best let you walk us over." Trice had a grin on her lips as she headed down the hall.

Drake chuckled.

Trice turned the corner of Luce's house just as Drake did.

"Oof."

Strong hands cupped her upper arms, holding her in place. "Sorry to almost bowl you over. I was afraid I was running late."

Her heart jumped just being close to Drake. Why did he appeal to her so? It couldn't possibly be the fact he was good-looking, strong, intelligent and likable.

"Good evening," he said in a low, sexy drawl. "Are you ready for this?"

She backed away, smiling. "I'm not only ready. I'm looking forward to it."

"You're a brave woman. That Nordic blood in you is coming out."

Trice searched his face. "Are you talking about the town scaring me off?"

His face turned serious. "Maybe it should."

What did he mean by that?

He stepped back. "You look nice."

She couldn't help but blush. Her effort to impress him hadn't failed. The dress she had picked out was a lime color and went almost to her ankles. A tie of the same color encircled her waist. Dress boots in tan covered her feet.

"Different boots, I see."

She put out her foot and turned it one way, then another. "These are broken in."

"Good to hear." He pursed his lips and nodded.

"I'll have you know I'm wearing my other ones every night to break them in too." She threw her shoulders back proudly. "With heavy socks."

"I'm surprised you even put them back on your feet."

She met his gaze. "I'm not easily defeated."

"I'm learning that." Drake looked rather pleased with her statement.

"I want to get them wearable so I can explore some more. I haven't really had a chance to do much of that. A good hiking trip would be fun."

"You should take some time while I am still here. You have been staying close to the clinic. We have been pretty busy, but I think most of the people who have come by the last couple of days weren't as sick as they were interested in meeting you."

Trice met Drake's look. He had such beautiful eyes. "It was nice to meet them. I hope to meet more tonight."

"Are you two going to the meeting or standing there all evening?" Luce's gravelly voice said from behind Drake.

Trice and Drake stepped back from each other.

Drake spoke first. "We were just on our way to get you."

The older woman harrumphed. She stood there with her purse on her arm, a little hat on her head and a shawl across her shoulders.

"You look lovely, Luce." Drake kissed her cheek.

"Don't you start trying to flatter me, boy," the older woman said, but she grinned.

He put his hands over his heart. "I wasn't trying to flatter you, Luce. I was telling you the truth."

"Let's go before all the good chairs are taken," the woman grumbled.

"Come on." Drake offered his arm to his grandmother. "Let's get you to the community center."

A number of people entered the low block building ahead of them. They trailed behind them. Luce left them to join a friend. She and Drake found seats on a row about halfway up. Trice couldn't help but be excited about the coming program. This was a new adventure as far as she was concerned. She had a sense of being part of the community.

After all, she would be living here. This would be her world for the next year. She was already starting to fall in love with the place. It would be different in the winter months, but something deep down in her felt like it didn't matter what the weather was. She had found her place. This might be home. Was she jumping on the idea too soon?

She glanced at Drake. Or could it be someone who made her feel that way?

Trice enjoyed working with him. He was methodical and thorough, doing his job with a smile on his face, which indicated he loved his profession. She could see Drake's skills as he took care of his patients. He had capable hands. Drake would make an excellent surgeon.

But she would miss him. She suspected the entire town would. Those weren't emotions she should be having or encouraging.

CHAPTER THREE

TRICE SAT STRAIGHTER at the sound of the guitar tuning. A group of people had settled on the stage. They looked as if they might be a family. The children were around the ages of ten and twelve. Everyone clapped, then quieted.

Trice shifted in her seat and clasped her hands in her lap. She must calm her nerves. Her hands trembled slightly. Oddly she felt a part of these people, included. Something that had rarely happened while she was growing up. She'd been lucky if she had spent over a year with a family until she was fifteen. Even with her last family, she had always been an outsider.

Drake leaned toward her. "Everything all right?"

She nodded. "Everything is wonderful."

He studied her a moment, then smiled.

She needed to appear confident in front of him. His support would be needed to get the village behind her.

"Hey." Drake placed a hand over hers for a moment.

"Yeah?"

"You'll be fine tonight."

For the next hour, they listened to the group play. The notes they could coax from their instruments were amazing. Their fingers would fly over the strings at times. Trice sat enthralled. More than once, she found herself tapping a toe.

When the concert was over, the crowd stayed for a pot-luck dinner.

Drake stood. "Let's have something to eat before they push back the chairs and tables to dance."

Dance. She hadn't expected that. Trice didn't consider herself a dancer.

They filled their plates with food stationed on two long tables.

"I didn't bring anything." Trice didn't want to look to the town as if she wasn't the type to do her share.

"Don't worry about it this time," a woman behind them said. "We will expect you to bring food next time. By the way, I'm Birta Atlasson. I heard how good you were with Stavn. I'm his aunt."

Trice said with true pleasure, "It's nice to meet you."

The line moved, and the woman's attention was caught by someone else.

Trice and Drake returned to where they had been sitting to eat. He went to get them drinks.

Returning, Drake handed her a cup. "Did you enjoy the music?"

"I did. I've never really done anything like this before. I'm enjoying it." She was too aware of him sitting close to her. The amount of attention Drake gave her both thrilled and disturbed her. Did the others notice? Maybe he was just being nice because she was new to town?

With everyone finished with their meal, the tables were pushed to the walls. Chairs circled the room. The family who played earlier returned to the stage. The rest of the crowd was invited to dance.

Trice touched Drake's arm. "I see Stavn and his mother over there." She indicated across the room. "I'm going to check on how his hand is doing."

Drake nodded and turned to speak to a man who had walked up.

Trice crossed the room, smiling at people as she went. Many returned her smile, but no one stepped out to introduce themselves. "Hey, Stavn. How's your hand today?"

He grinned when he saw her. "Look, I can move it now."

She went down on one knee, making sure her dress was tucked in at the right places. "Yes, you can. Don't get too sure of yourself until those stitches come out."

Trice stood and faced Stavn's mother. "Hi."

"Hi, Dr. Shell."

"Remember, it's Trice."

"Yes, that's right. Trice, I would like you to meet my friends." She introduced the three ladies standing nearby.

Trice had no hope of remembering their names, but she nodded and smiled. She would learn them all one day. She had been nervous earlier, but that had settled down. After a short conversation with the women, she looked over her shoulder to see Drake dancing with a young, slim, dark-haired woman almost his height. They were laughing as they moved.

"It didn't take Marie long to get Drake to dance with her," one of the women said.

"Nope. She will miss him when he's gone," said another.

"I hope he makes it out of town without her following him," the other commented.

Trice chest tightened. Her look stayed with the couple. Why did the women's words bother her? There wasn't anything going on between her and Drake. Trice had no right to feel concern. Yet she still wanted to know if Drake was involved with the pretty woman.

At the end of the song, Drake stepped away from the

woman and headed toward their group. "Ladies, do you mind if I have a dance with Trice?"

"You might want to ask her," Stavn's mom snapped.

Drake's brows rose. "You are correct. Trice, would you care to dance?"

Trice took a step back. "I'm sorry. I don't really dance."

Stavn's mom's hand on her back stopped her movement and gave her a nudge. "Go on. You'll be fine. Drake will show you what to do."

Drake offered his hand. A new tune started, and the floor began to fill up. "Join me."

Still she hesitated. Stavn's mother nudged her again before Trice placed her hand in his. "You better take care of me."

Drake looked her in the eyes. His hand squeezed hers. "I will."

Something about the statement went straight to her heart. She could fall hard for his man who was going a different direction from her. She shouldn't let that happen. No scenario made that look like a good idea. But wouldn't it be okay to act on her daydreams, just for a little while?

Drake placed his arms around her but held her at a distance. "This is an Icelandic folk song. Follow my steps."

She put a foot out when he did. He turned her and she followed. There were awkward steps, but they continued around the floor.

"You are a natural." Drake grinned at her.

"Thanks. I don't feel like one." She worked to follow his movements.

"You'll catch on after you do it a few more times." He turned her and brought her to him.

"I hope so." She missed a step and caught up.

"There will be plenty of men to show you while you are here." His words were flat as he made a move.

Trice wasn't sure she liked that idea any more than the look on his face implied he did.

When the song ended, they went right into a slow song. Drake pulled her closer. She could feel his heat. Her hand lay lightly on his shoulder and was held securely in one of his hands. His other hand lay at her waist. It almost spanned the expanse of it. They swayed to the music.

"You looked pretty popular over there talking to Stavn's mother. Here I was thinking you were nervous about being in Iceland. You have been busy winning friends and influencing people."

"Stavn's mom was kind enough to introduce me around. That was nice of her."

"Did you ask about them knowing anyone with HEP?" He led her to the right.

"No, I figured I'd wait until they got to know me better."

He gave her waist a gentle squeeze. "Smart move. I think you'll do just fine here."

"I already know I like it here." She leaned closer. "That woman you were dancing with is glaring at us."

He started to turn his head.

"No, don't look," she hissed. "I don't want her to know we're talking about her."

"It's just Marie. She's one of the nurses who comes in to help." His tone was dismissive.

She didn't look like she liked Trice much. "I'm going to have to work with her. By the look on her face, I don't think that will be much fun."

Drake shook his head. "You're being silly."

"You aren't the one she's glaring at."

Drake spun her. "You're right. She doesn't look happy."

"I think I'd better go. I don't need any drama in my days or nights. I don't need to step where I shouldn't since I'm new to town."

His grip tightened. "We've gone out a few times, but I have no claim on her or her on me."

"That's an interesting, old-fashioned way of putting things." Trice was trying to make a good impression, not become part of a soap opera.

"But it's true." Drake sounded anxious to have her believe him.

"Still, there's nothing between you and me, and I don't want her thinking there is. I better leave."

He let her hand go, and they walked off the floor.

Marie glided up to them. "Drake, aren't you going to introduce me to the new doctor?"

"Sure. Trice, I would like you to meet Marie Laxness. She will be helping you on clinic days."

Trice offered her hand. The woman took it after a moment of hesitation. "It's nice to meet you," Trice said.

Marie offered Trice a smile that didn't reach her eyes. "You too. I look forward to working with you."

Luce walked up with shawl in place, hat on her head and purse in hand. "Time to go."

"I'll get our coats." Drake left.

"Marie, how are you?" the older woman asked.

"Fine." Marie appeared unsure about Luce singling her out.

Luce's eyes narrowed. "Aren't you here a little early for a clinic next week?"

The other woman looked uncomfortable. "I came early to spend a long weekend with a friend"

"Mmm." There was no doubt from Luce's response she didn't believe that.

Drake returned, handing Trice her jacket. He pulled his on while she donned hers.Soon, she, Luce and Drake were outside in the cool air. They made their way home in silence.

At Luce's door, Trice said, "Good night."

"Give me a sec with Luce, and then I'll walk you to your door."

"That's not necessary." Trice continued on. As she turned the corner, she heard Luce say, "Don't you hurt that girl, boy. You're leaving here."

It had only been daylight two hours when Drake knocked on Trice's door. No sound. She must sleep like the dead. This time he banged on the door loud enough that he was afraid he might wake Luce. If Trice didn't answer soon, he would have to leave her. Relief washed through him at the rattle of the door handle.

Trice opened the door a crack. "Drake, what's wrong?"

"We've got an emergency. Get dressed and bring those boots you've been breaking in. You will need them. Also, the heaviest jacket you have. You got five minutes while I get supplies from at the clinic."

"I'll be ready in four." She slammed the door.

He shook his head in amazement. Trice was tough as nails. He rarely drove his truck, but he didn't have time to walk the distance to the airport. Trice hurried up as he came out of the clinic. She had a black bag with a red cross on the side in her hands.

"Let me have that." He reached for her bag. "Hop in." She did as he requested, and he placed their bags in the back of the truck.

"What happened?"

"There was an accident at Fjaroara Falls. A hiker slipped and fell. Rescue was called. As the rescuer and the hiker were being pulled up, there was a rockfall. They are both injured now. One hanging and unconscious. The other stuck on a small ledge. We are the medical care who could get there the fastest." He pulled into the airport.

"What're we doing here?" Trice tried to keep her voice even.

"We're flying there. That's why we can get there so fast." He hopped out of the truck, going around to retrieve their bags.

Trice climbed out slower.

Drake was halfway to the plane before he realized she wasn't with him. He turned to find her still beside the truck, staring at the plane. "Is something wrong?"

"I don't really do planes, and not small ones." Her voice was so low he had to strain to hear her.

He didn't have time for this. "If you are going, then you'll have to this time."

She looked around. "Where is the pilot?"

"Right here." He touched his chest.

Her voice rose an octave. "You have a pilot license?"

"I do." He started for the plane once more.

She hustled after him. "You really know what you're doing?"

He opened a storage door on the side of the aircraft and placed their bags inside, then closed the compartment. "Yes, I know what I'm doing. You better get in. I'll take care of you."

When she didn't move right away, he said, "Well?"

"I'll go," she announced, sounding braver than she felt.

Drake opened the passenger door and helped her up on the wing so she could climb in. The woman was feather-light but had a will of iron. "Get in and buckle up. I'll close the door for you."

He did so. On his way to the other side, he checked the plane and soon settled in his seat. Minutes after going through the checklist, he had them rolling down the runway.

Trice hadn't said a word or moved the entire time. He'd not had a chance to reassure her, and he felt the tension rising off her in the cockpit. They were in the air and flying steady when he glanced at her. "You know if you open your eyes, you can see this beautiful morning. You don't want to miss this view."

"If I do open my eyes, I'll also see us crash."

He chuckled. "You don't have much faith in me, do you?"

"I didn't mean for it to sound like that." She still had her eyes closed tight, and her hands clutched the edge of her seat.

"I know."

"But I'm scared."

He grinned. "That's obvious. How about trying to open one eye?"

"Oh, my." Her soft sigh a few seconds later had him thinking he would like to do something to her that would elicit that reaction.

"It gets me every time too. Keep your focus eye-level. Don't look down. But look at this land. It's beautiful."

"It is lovely. I don't see how you can leave it." As she became caught up in their conversation, she had eased her fingers off the console and relaxed in the seat.

"You would if you had planned and worked toward being a surgeon most of your life. If you wanted to live where people like Luce didn't have an opinion about what you do. If you would like to buy something and not wait a month for it to come."

"I would love to have people who cared like that about me."

He glanced at her. The vulnerability on her face pulled

at his heart. What he had, she wanted. She had a way of making him see what he would be missing when he left. "I can understand that, but it can get to be a bit much sometimes. Often."

"It's hard for me to even imagine that. Growing up as a foster kid, I never had anyone who really cared enough to offer much advice." A few minutes of silence passed before she asked, "How long have you been flying?"

"Most of my life. My father is a pilot. I learned from him but also took flying lessons. Somebody in town needs to know how to fly. I wanted to learn."

She looked around the cockpit. "Does the plane belong to you?"

"It does." He was proud of the airplane.

Trice relaxed some in her seat. "What will you do with it when you leave?"

"I'll fly to Reykjavík. John, the pilot who brought you in, will bring it back when he can."

"But doesn't it need somebody to fly it once in a while?" Her attention stayed on the view ahead.

"John will use it when he needs it. When you need him to fly somewhere, he'll take you."

"Not in my game plan to do this too often. If you weren't staying and I didn't come here, what would happen with the medical service up here?"

"A traveling doctor would come once a week. There's always somebody in a community who rises to be the go-to person for medical care. Or a nurse might even be persuaded to take the job. Just stay here full-time."

"Like Marie?"

He didn't miss the tight note in Trice's voice at Marie's name. Was she jealous despite him saying there was nothing between him and Marie? He liked the idea. It meant Trice might care. "Yes, like Marie. But she will not stay. She has already been asked." He dropped altitude.

Trice grabbed the seat. "Why're we going down?"

"Because we're almost there." He went to work landing them.

"That didn't take long."

"It never does if you fly, but it would've been a long walk and a longer drive. The roads between here and Seydisfjordur are not that well cared for. There's a short airstrip here. It's the only reason I was called. They knew I could get here."

"I won't be much help in cases like this if I'm not able to fly."

"This trip is an anomaly. You won't be called on for something this far away." He pushed and pulled a few knobs. Then adjusted the flaps.

Soon they were scooting along the runway to a stop. Drake looked at Trice. "I'm proud of you. At least you kept your eyes open."

She glared at him. "You should've been watching what you were doing instead of me."

"You were much more entertaining, and I could land the plane with my eyes closed."

"I'm glad you didn't." She unbuckled. "This was a good lesson. I'm learning to focus on things like the morning sunrise or what I want to do bad enough to try something that scares me."

"You have a point there."

Before he had turned the engines off, a truck had pulled up nearby. Drake climbed out of the plane and went around to help Trice down. She'd managed to open and close the door. Their bags were sitting on the wing. Apparently, she was determined she would be of help and not a hindrance. He liked that.

He offered his hand, and she jumped down to stand beside him.

"Stevansson?" asked the truck driver.

"Yep. And this is Dr. Shell."

"They're waiting on you up at the falls." The man pointed up the valley.

"We're ready when you are." Drake threw the bags in the back seat of the heavy-duty truck. Tricc took a seat beside them, and he climbed in the front.

"Tell us what's going on. All the information I got was I was needed for backup. That a rescuer was injured along with a hiker."

"The hiker stepped over the rail before daylight, as they do when they want to get the just-right sunrise picture, and hit a slick spot and went down. Thankful he hit a ledge. Rescue was called. They went after him. On his way down, his large body caused a rockfall. Now there are two injured men. One with a head injury and the other with a broken leg. We need to get them both up. Let you do what you can before we get them out of here. A storm is coming in, and we're not sure a helicopter will make it in time. Your accessibility to a plane was why we called you. There was no time to wait. We've got to get these men out."

Relief washed through Trice as her feet settled back on the ground. When Drake had driven up to the plane, she'd thought her body would refuse to get in it. She had barely made it flying into Seydisfjordur. But she had to go. She and Drake had people needing their help waiting on them. If this was the best way to get there, then she'd have to make it work. It would have been nice if she could have kept her fear from Drake, but he'd seen it right away. He'd left her no choice but to admit to it.

He had managed to coax her to open her eyes and control her breathing.

After she had gotten over her initial fear of flying and being in such a small plane, she'd started to enjoy it. It had been reassuring being in Drake's hands. It calmed her nerves enough to at least enjoy part of the view. The beauty of the countryside in the early morning took her breath away.

This was a lifestyle she would have to get used to during the year ahead. She had wanted to come to Iceland, to find herself and her heritage. She couldn't close her eyes to that or her job responsibilities. She had to step up and do what must be done.

Now they were barreling down a narrow paved road. Ten minutes later, the man driving came to a neck-jerking stop and hopped out. She and Drake followed after grabbing their bags. He took hers from her as they started toward the group standing near the edge of the falls. Water rushed nearby with a deafening roar, creating a mist that filled the air and blew toward them.

Trice shivered. This wouldn't be much fun. But staying warm and dry would be a problem for later. Right now, the injured men were the worry.

The driver joined the group of other official-looking people. The circle opened when she and Drake approached.

Now it was time for a serious discussion. The hiker and the EMT had already been in the ravine for hours. Not only the injuries but the elements were working against them. Daylight helped, but the dark clouds gathering would not. They must be brought to safety right away.

"I'm Dr. Stevansson, and this is Dr. Shell. What can we do to help?" Drake asked.

"Glad to have you here." The man looked at her. "Both of you. We have one with a head injury hanging nine meters down, dangling from a line, and another with a possible broken leg. The rescuer, the best we can tell, is unconscious, and the one with the broken leg is another eight meters below him on a ledge. He has little mobility. We have to get some medical help down there, but the space is small. We need no more rockfalls. The conditions are wet and slippery. We're trying to work out the logistics now."

Trice said without thinking, "I'll go."

CHAPTER FOUR

DRAKE COULDN'T BELIEVE what he'd just heard. He along with the group turned and looked at her.

"Trice, I can't let you do that."

"It's not for you to say. I have some rock-climbing experience. I have the medical knowledge, and I am the smallest person here. I have to go."

Drake could do nothing but glare at her with his heart in his throat.

"Are you sure about this?" one of the men asked.

Trice squared her shoulders. "No, but I don't think there's a choice. I can do some quick triage easement and treatment if necessary, and then you can bring them up."

One of the rescue men, after crossing his arms on his chest, said, "I do appreciate your offer, but I don't think you are qualified, and we certainly don't need a third party down there making matters worse."

Drake watched in bemusement as Trice crossed her arms over her chest, too, and glared at the man. "And if you had a better plan, I think you would be executing it by now."

The man closed his mouth with surprise as if dumbfounded. He blinked.

Drake decided to intervene. "She has a point. We need to get these men up and to help before this storm rolls in."

The man shook his head. "Okay. I don't know that I have a choice. I'll get the harness."

Drake turned his back to the others and pulled her around to face him. "Are you absolutely sure? You've only been in Iceland for a week."

"I'm sure. If I don't do it, who will?" She met his look.

Drake didn't have an answer.

"I know rock climbing. I'm not afraid of heights, and I certainly know medicine. More importantly, I'm the smallest and lightest person here. That makes me the most qualified."

She had a point, but he didn't like it. "But you don't like flying."

"That's different. But we can argue about that later. Don't we want to get these people out of there safely and with as little additional injury as possible?"

Drake shook his head. "I still don't like the plan."

The mountain rescuer returned with harness and rope in hand.

"You don't have to like it to go along with it." She turned to the man.

As the rescuer rigged her up, Trice said to Drake, "Talk this through with me."

That statement told him Trice didn't feel as much bravado as she tried to show.

She didn't wait on him to begin. Her look implored him. A flash of fear went through her eyes. "Explain exactly what I need to do. I can perform the medical assessment with no problem, but what else should I look for? If those guys have been down there for hours, they'll need blankets, even heat packets to put inside their jackets to warm their cores."

"Are you finished?" Drake asked the rescuer doing her harness.

He nodded.

"Give us a minute, please?"

The man walked away.

Drake's hands went to her shoulders, and his look met hers. "You've got this. You'll be lowered slowly. Keep your feet and hands against the rock. I'll make sure you have some gloves. You will assess the injured rescuer, then see that he gets up to the top safely. Then you'll have to go back after the man with the broken leg."

"I'll need my bag."

"I will see that it is sent down to you. Along with splints and supplies." He placed a small earpiece in her ear. "Through this, you can talk to me the entire time Tell me what you need. You'll be able to hear me too. Now, how are you doing?"

"You will be there with me?"

"I'll never leave you." That wasn't exactly true. He would be leaving her in a few days. But for now, he was here for her.

Trice walked toward the edge of the cliff with Drake beside her.

She put out a hand, stopping him. "Don't go any closer. I don't want you to slip. You need to be tied off." She had been secured to a truck winch. The rope stretched across the ground.

"I don't like this plan at all." Drake's mouth went into a tight line.

"I'll have this over and done before you come up with another way, and you know it." She reassured him as well as herself.

His look bore into hers. "You be careful. I'll be right here waiting."

Trice stood in front of Drake as he switched on the light attached to her helmet. "You are going to need this."

"Step back a little bit," one of the rescuers called. "You're getting mighty close. We don't need to have another person down there."

Trice nudged him back. "He's right. It's slippery here. If people—" she gave him a pointed look with a forced grin "—would read the posted rules, then there would be no need for us to do this."

He returned her smile. "Point taken." He walked to a safe distance from the edge.

She looked at him. "Any other ideas or suggestions?"

"Other than I wish it was me going?"

Was he really that worried about her? "I'll be as quick as I can. I promise."

All her worries and fears went out of her head when he approached again, cupped her cheek and gave her a long look. For a moment, it crossed her mind he might kiss her. Then he said, "Be careful."

She blinked. "I will be."

Two of the rescue team who were tied off joined them. She gave Drake a last look and walked to the edge with the men.

Trice leaned back, holding the rope between her legs with one hand behind her back and the upper part of the same rope with her other hand, bracing with her feet against the stone wall to rappel down the cliff. She glanced below at the boulders and water rushing over them. This was nothing like rock climbing in a gym. She swallowed hard.

Drake's voice came in her ear. "You got this. Slow and easy."

It was good to hear his voice. He had a nice one. She let out the breath she had been holding. "Okay."

"How far away are you from the first man?"

"You can hear me?"

"Yes. The radio has an automatic mic."

"Oh, okay. He is about twelve feet from me…uh… I mean four meters from me now. He's just hanging there. I see no movement."

"Trice, where did you learn to rock climb?"

She moved slowly down. "In the gym of the university. I did it for exercise. Who would have thought it would have paid off like this?"

"You keep surprising me."

A few minutes later, she said, "I've reached him. He's unconscious." She hung there, balancing herself to stay upright. Then she looked down. The man with a broken leg was on the other side of the crevice. "Hey, can you hear me?"

"I hear you, Trice."

"Sorry. I'm calling to the man with the bad leg."

A man below her groaned. Then she heard a weak, "Yes."

"I'm here to help. Stay put. I have to get this man out of the way before I can come after you. But I promise I am coming."

"Hurry," came the man's low response.

"I'll be there as soon as I can." She couldn't afford to hurry. Haste could create mistakes. She fought to turn the man so she could see his face. "Drake, I'm doing the assessment on the first man now."

She pulled the digital thermometer from where it hung on her vest. Running it over the man's forehead, she read the numbers. "He has a low-grade fever. Pulse eighty over sixty. Breathing slow but pathway clear."

Wrapping her legs around the man's knees and locking her heels, she held him close enough that she could lift one eyelid. She shined her light in his face. "Pupils are fixed and dilated."

"Roger that," Drake's voice came back.

"He has a crack in his helmet, but it's still secure to his head. He took a good hit. He's too heavy for me to do much with. Tell the guys to start pulling him up. I'm coming too to guide him between the rocks. I need to stay between him and the sides so he doesn't have further injury."

"But Trice—"

"Drake, there isn't time to argue. Just don't let our ropes get tangled, and pull them at the same speed." Trice turned so her back was to the rock face. She held the man with her legs and arms. "Go slow."

With a tiny jerk, she started moving up. The man moved as well. When she could, she used a hand to push off the wall in an effort to protect her back. She misjudged an outcropping and took a long drag over a sharp rock.

"Ouch."

"Trice?" Drake's panic-stricken voice came over the radio.

"I'm fine. Let's get this man up." She couldn't worry about her back now.

"Take care of yourself first. You're no help to that guy or the other one if you get hurt. I see you. You're almost here. Slow and easy."

"You shouldn't be so close to the edge." She didn't need Drake falling.

"I'm tied off and lying on the ground. Okay, let go of the man. We can take him from here."

She released the man, and he was slowly lifted past her until he disappeared over the top.

Drake said, "I'm going to leave you to see about this

man. I'll be back soon. One of the rescue people is going to be here with you."

Trice couldn't deny she hated to lose Drake's reassuring voice. She could get used to it. And she shouldn't.

"Hello, Dr. Shell. This is Sunna. I'll be with you until Dr. Stevansson can return. Are you going down again?"

"Please call me Trice. Send me down before I back out."

"Trice, your rope has been released to you. You are free to rappel," the woman's voice assured her.

Once again placing her hands in the correct position, Trice started down the wall again. "Please talk to me, Sunna. Are you from around here?"

"Born and raised. I understand you are from America. Heck of an introduction to Iceland being part of this show."

Trice had made it to where the first man had been. "Mister, I'm coming," she called to the injured man. Her back screamed with pain, but she kept moving. "Sunna, I'm going to have to swing over to the edge in a moment."

"I'm glad you let me know. Dr. Stevansson threatened my life if I let anything happen to you."

Warmth washed through Trice. "Nothing is going to happen to me. Okay, here I go. My rope may go slack. I'll try to sit on the edge." Trice pushed off the wall and almost made the edge.

The man half lay and half sat, his legs stretched in front of him.

Trice spoke to Sunna. "I'm too high. I'm going down a few feet and trying again." This time she was successful. She managed to reach the ledge and sit on it near the man's feet. "Made it."

Trice went to work immediately, telling the man, "We're going to get you out of here as soon as possible. What's your name?"

"Mark Richards."

"I'm Trice. I'm a doctor. Tell me where you hurt." Trice did a visual assessment using her headlamp.

"My left leg. Just below the knee."

"I need to touch it. It may hurt." Trice gently probed the man's leg from above the knee down, until the man winced. "I feel the break. It'll need to be splinted before you can be moved. I want you to lie back and take deep breaths. Sunna, are you still there?"

"Right here."

"Please send down my med bag, a blanket and the splints. Dr. Stevansson should have gotten everything ready. Also send some drinking water. You will need to swing the rope if you can in order for me to reach it."

Sunna responded immediately. "I'll have it down in a moment."

Trice turned back to the man. "I need to get your vitals. Just lie still. This shouldn't take but a few minutes." She quickly went about getting his heart rate, respiration rate and temperature. "Other than a broken leg and being stuck down here, I would say you are a lucky man."

The man grunted, clearly not impressed with her appraisal.

Sunna's voice filled the air. "Trice, the supplies you requested are coming down."

Trice looked up. The light landed on the stuff hanging from the end of a rope. "I see it. Swing it."

She missed the first pass. On the second she managed to snatch the edge of the bag and bring it in. "Got it. Don't move."

The rope slackened. Trice quickly removed the rope and set the bag and splints between the man and the wall, making sure they wouldn't be lost to the rocks and water below.

"Mark, I'm going to splint your leg. Before I do that, I'm going to give you a pain pill, because you'll need it on the way up." She located the pill bottle in her bag and was pleased to find two bottles of water tucked in the bag as well.

She handed both to the man.

"Trice?" Sunna's voice.

"Yes?"

"Everything okay? Dr. Stevansson wants to know."

"All is well. I'm getting ready to put the splints on now." She wasn't used to this much concern from one person. It would be easy to get used to. Especially when it was from Drake.

After placing the splints on either side of Mark's leg, she began to secure them with a flexible bandage. Wrapping the leg until it would not move, she soon had Mark ready to transport.

"Sunna, what is the plan for bringing him up?"

"We're sending down a harness. You'll need to strap him in."

Trice packed the leftover supplies into her bag. "Send it down. I'll need instructions. I'm getting a little punchy, and my fingers are cold. I don't want to make a mistake."

"Harness is on the way down. I'll talk you through it."

A minute later, the harness was in Trice's hands. "I'm ready when you are."

"Here we go," Sunna said. "Hold the harness by the D-ring. Shake it out so all the straps fall. Unbuckle any buckles."

"Done."

"Put the shoulder straps on first," Sunna continued.

"Hold on a sec, Sunna." Trice spoke to Mark. "You'll need to sit up as much as you can." She helped Mark with the straps while making sure she didn't go off the edge. "Legs straps next. Right, Sunna?"

"Yes."

"Mark, this is where we're going to have to be careful. You'll need to lift yourself with your arms so I can reach under you for the straps. Tell me when you're ready."

The man lifted his back and hips. Trice ran her hands beneath him until she found the straps, pulling them out between his legs. He quickly lowered his hips with a loud sigh. Trice secured the lock on one leg and then the other.

"Trice?"

The sound of Drake's voice vibrated through her. "Hey. How's the other patient doing?"

"He should be fine with time. He's off in a helicopter." His voice dropped lower as if they were alone. "Are you all right?"

"I'm fine. Will you help me lift this man up? I'm ready to get out of here."

"I'll be glad to see you." There was a pause as if he might be collecting his emotions. "So, where are you with the harness?"

"I'm locking the breast strap now." Her cold fingers worked with the metal.

"Be sure to pull out any excess in the shoulder straps. They need to be snug." Drake's voice had turned anxious-sounding.

"Done."

"Good. The rope is coming down with the caliper. Clip it on the D-ring. Make sure it closes."

"You have to swing the rope for me to reach it." She caught it on the first arc. "Got it. Clipping it on now."

With the caliper firmly closed, she said, "We're ready down here. Tell them to go slow and easy."

"Will do."

"Mark, I'll be going up with you. Making sure you don't hit the wall. Help me by keeping yourself off the wall using your hands. I'll be between you and the rock."

Mark nodded.

Trice studied him a moment. He wouldn't be the help she hoped for. He'd been through as much as his body and mind could stand. "Mark, give me five more minutes before you pass out if you can."

He muttered something unintelligible.

She was losing him quickly. Scooting along the edge as far as she could, Trice used her hand to steady his leg as he was lifted into the air. "Hold him there. Now bring me up." She swung out to take the man by the arms, making sure she was between him and the rock face. "Okay, we're ready."

They move slowly up. She said nothing for a few minutes.

"Trice? Talk to me."

"We are fine. We'll be there in a minute." She winced as her back brushed the wall.

"You okay down there? That sounded like pain."

"All's good. Just ready to be on firm ground again." She checked her patient. He had passed out. All the while, she could hear Drake giving instructions on what would be needed for the incoming patient.

"I see you."

Trice looked up. She focused on Drake's handsome face. "Hold me here and bring Mark on up. He has passed out, so he won't be any help."

Mark moved above her and was pulled over the side.

She held the man's good leg so he wouldn't swing more than necessary. "Careful of that leg. I did the best I could in the cramped space."

"Looks good to me." Drake sounded impressed.

Seconds later she was lifted over the side and drawn to a safe place away from the cliff.

A woman stood in front of her. "Nice to meet you, Trice. I'm Sunna. Dr. Stevansson is with the patient. He told me in no uncertain terms to help you and see that you were taken care of."

"I don't think that's necessary. I'm fine." Trice's fingers fumbled with the lock on her harness.

"Let me help you with that." Sunna came to stand in front of her.

Trice flexed her fingers back and forth. "My fingers seem incapable of moving all of a sudden."

Sunna reached for the breast lock. "I'm sure they are cold. We'll get you over to the truck and warm you up."

Trice was amazed at how she had managed to go from doing research to rescue work. "I should check on the patient."

Sunna held the harness in one hand and took Trice's arm in the other. "Dr. Stevansson said you would say that, but he wants you checked out, and I am to take you to the truck. Please don't get me in trouble."

Drake's heart had thumped against his chest as Trice came over the side. He only had time to glance at her to make sure she was really there before his attention returned to their patient. He hated that he couldn't go to her, but the man needed to be readied for travel.

He didn't know why he was so concerned about Trice. She wasn't anyone to him, yet the anxiety that ran through his veins screamed something different. His heart had only started to truly beat again when she had safely been pulled out of the falls.

He had instructed Sunna to care for Trice, but he was still anxious to check on her himself.

Moments later he heard her voice beside him. "What can I do to help?"

His head jerked up. "What are you doing here? I've got this." He looked beyond Trice to Sunna, who threw her hands in the air as if she had tried to stop Trice. "You did a good job down there. Go take care of yourself."

"But—"

"He's almost ready to go. I'll give you a full report in a few minutes. I don't need another patient today. Please do as I ask. If not for your sake, then mine."

Trice didn't look happy, but she joined Sunna, and they walked toward the truck he and Trice had arrived in.

Goodness, what had happened to make Trice so resilient? To think he had been worried about her being able to handle the conditions during the winter. She was more than up to it and anything else Iceland dished out. She certainly had more backbone than the other women he'd been interested in. Interested in? Yes, he was attracted to her.

He finished giving his report to the ambulance EMT. The injured man had a long, uncomfortable ride ahead of him. A big, fat raindrop landed square on top of Drake's head. It was time for them to get out of there. "He's all yours, fellows. Good luck on the drive down to the hospital. Be careful."

Drake waited until the man was loaded safely in the ambulance, then jogged to the truck just as it began to rain in earnest. A roll of thunder and a flash of lightning went across the sky as he reached for the back seat door handle.

As he climbed in beside Trice, Sunna climbed out the driver's seat. She had the truck running, and it was warm inside. "I need to go help wrap up and make a report."

"Thanks, Sunna. I owe you one." Drake climbed in beside Trice.

"Me too," Trice said.

Sunna smiled. "You are both welcome. See you around."

Trice sat with her arms across her chest, shaking.

"You need to get those wet clothes off." He shifted to look at her.

Trice glared. "Don't you get in and start giving orders. Especially when you're telling me to take off my clothes."

Drake couldn't help but grin. "There's my Trice."

Her fingers went to the zipper of her jacket but failed to bend enough to hold it. "I'm not your Trice."

Drake studied her a second. He wasn't sure that was true. "Let me help with that." He reached for the zipper pull and opened her coat, then helped her remove the wet material, dropping it on the floor.

Trice picked up a blanket from the seat.

Drake adjusted it around her shoulders. He was as damp from the mist, the rain and lying on the ground as she was, but he didn't acknowledge it. His concern remained on her.

The driver who had brought them to the site climbed in the driver's seat. "I'll see you get to some warmth and food. We really appreciate your help today." He drove along the road they had come on. "The rescue leader has already made arrangements for a room at a resort not far from here where you can warm up and rest."

Trice gave Drake a questioning look.

"There is no flying out of here today." Drake observed the pouring down rain.

Ten minutes later, the driver pulled into a gravel parking lot in front of a small cabin and handed Drake a key.

Drake climbed out and offered his hand to Trice to help her down. "I'll carry you in."

"No, you won't. I've got this."

"You don't even have shoes on." She had taken them off before he'd climbed in the truck. "It'll be much faster my way."

"No."

Drake gave up arguing. "Then I'll get your clothes and boots. Run for the porch."

She hurried away.

Drake grabbed their belongings, thanked the driver, and stalked up the steps to join Trice. "Get the door." He nudged her with a hand to her back. "We need to get in out of this."

Trice yelped.

His look searched her. "What's wrong? Are you hurt?"

"Just a scrape."

"Go inside. I need to have a look." Drake followed her, dropping her wet coat and boots in the floor along with their bags.

"Turn around and let me see your back." He reached for her.

She took a step out of reach. "I'm sure it will be fine. I'll shower and clean it well."

"Like you can take care of something on your back. I'm a professional. Let me judge." He came toward her.

"And I'm not?"

"Trice, I'm too tired and my nerves have been stretched too far for you to be so difficult. Let me see. I can take care of it easier than you can. If you could reach it."

She was impossibly independent. "Let me get out of these wet clothes first. But I don't have anything else to put on."

He pulled a blanket off the back of the sofa and handed

it to her. "Go to the bedroom and take them off, wrap up in this, lie on the bed and call me."

"Do you always make such demands on women?"

He looked at her and quirked his mouth. "You choose now to try to be funny." He took her by the shoulders and turned her in the direction of an open door. "I don't have to make demands to get a woman into bed. Now go do as I say. I'll get a fire started."

Trice disappeared into the bedroom. He went about finding a match to light the fire, which had already been laid. With that done, he removed his boots and stripped off as many clothes as possible while leaving enough to remain decent.

"Trice? Are you ready yet?"

"Yes."

Drake picked up his medical bag and headed for the bedroom. Trice lay on the bed on her stomach just as he had directed her to.

She shivered. "I don't know if I'll ever be warm again."

"You will," he assured her. "Promise. I'll try to be as fast as I can with this. Then you can get in a warm shower. Then come sit by the fire." He sat on the edge of the bed. "I'm going to bring the blanket down just low enough for me to see your injury."

She said nothing as he pulled the blanket away from her body and lowered it. He winced when he saw the angry bruised line down her back, thankful there were no abrasions or open wounds. At least her clothes had protected her some.

"When did this happen?"

"When I was bringing the first man up." Her voice was muffled against the bed.

"Oh, Trice. You should have said something. We could have figured out another way."

"There wasn't one. They were depending on me."

He knew that feeling well. Hadn't he been living that for the last two years? He pulled the blanket up, covering her to the neck, not allowing himself to step out of doctor mode no matter how much he might want to. "You don't have any broken skin. Which is good. I'll let you get a shower. Then I'll put some cream on it that Luce swears by. It has always helped my aches and pains."

Trice said nothing. The soft sound of even breathing was all he heard. She was asleep. Trice was exhausted after her heroic work. He couldn't blame her.

Drake pulled the corner of the bedcover over her, making sure her feet were tucked under. Unable to resist, he brushed her hair away from her face. "That Viking blood served you well."

CHAPTER FIVE

TRICE ENTERED THE toasty warm living room. A fire blazed in the fireplace. She pulled the blanket tighter around her. Her clothes were hung on chairs circling the fire. Drake had been busy and thoughtful.

He wasn't there, but he lingered everywhere, especially in her thoughts. He had shown such tenderness before she'd gone down over the cliff. His voice had held concern when he had spoken to her, reassuring her he was there with her. Rarely had she had that in her life.

The bravado she had shown him had been forced. She had been terrified. Relief had swept through her, and adrenaline had washed her energy away after she reached the truck. She'd done what must be done and hoped it didn't happen again. She had lived much of her life that way. The exception was that this morning, it had affected others' lives. They had needed her assistance, or they might have died.

She fingered her clothes, but they were still damp. Her boots lay on their sides with the mouths open as wide as possible. Drake had thought of everything. Taking a seat on the sofa, she brought her feet up under her. If she was this cold this time of year, how was she going to handle the winter?

A sound at the door drew her attention. Drake entered with a bag in his hand and kicked the door closed with his foot. "Well, hey. I hope you're hungry. I have some soup and sandwiches here."

"I am. Where did you get those?"

"I've been over to the main office and then to the restaurant. I have coffee going here, but would you rather have something else?"

"Hot tea would be nice."

He set the bag down on the table. "It just so happens there's some tea bags here as well, and one electric burner. I'll heat some water. How are you feeling?"

"Better now with sleep and a shower. Have you had either?" She turned to see him better.

"I took a shower. My morning wasn't as physically demanding as yours. You earned the rest." His eyes focused just below her face.

Trice glanced down. The blanket had slipped, showing a generous portion of her shoulder and the rise of one breast. She met his glaze and pulled the material back into place. The look of disappointment in his eyes satisfied in a way she hadn't expected.

He blinked, then turned to the electric eye. "I'll have this ready in a minute."

Drake acted as if he were a little uncomfortable. "Is there something I can do to help?"

"No, I've got it."

She stood and adjusted the blanket, tucking it in so it stayed in place, then pulled a throw off the sofa over her shoulders. She wasn't a fashion statement, but she was covered and warm.

"Take a seat at the table." Drake set out the food from the bag. His attention remained on his actions.

She joined him, taking one of the two wooden chairs at the small table. "Have you heard how our patients are doing?"

"The helicopter landed just before the storm broke. The man with the head injury is conscious but has a banging headache. He should completely recover. The one with the leg injury is still on his way. It takes four hours to get him to the nearest hospital, but at least he could go by ambulance."

"Sorry I fell asleep on you."

"Understandable. Your back thankfully isn't too bad. You will be sore more than anything. I need to put that cream on it before you go to bed tonight to help with the ache in the morning. How are you feeling now?"

"Like I've done all the climbing I want to for some time." She grinned.

He glanced up. "I would imagine. All of that was pretty intense."

"It was. Does the practice take part in stuff like that often?" She took the top off the bowl of soup.

"Today was more the exception than the rule."

"That's good to know. I'm not sure I could take it on if I thought it happened regularly."

Especially if he wasn't there to work with her.

"You certainly impressed the rescue squad. They couldn't praise you enough. I know of two men who were glad you were there."

"And you as well. I can't take much credit for my size, how my mom and dad created me." She hadn't thought of her mom and dad in a long time. Who they were. Where her father was. If he was alive or dead. Even what he looked like.

"Do you know anything about them?" he asked quietly.

"No. You know about my mother. I don't even have an idea who my father was or is." She didn't want to stay on this subject. "I'm hungry. Let's eat before the soup gets cold."

He took the chair across from her. Both started eating with gusto.

"This soup is really good. I was starving. I missed two meals today. One from when some crazy man woke me up before the birds to force me to fly around in an airplane, then stood around looking down as I went into a hole."

He grinned. "I might know that person."

"I thought you might." She enjoyed recovering in this cozy cabin with Drake, a flickering fire, and hot soup that filled her stomach and mellowed her mood. She liked being with him. Too much.

"We're socked in for a while. I found a few board games in the back if you want to play."

She looked at the window. Rain still came down. It only made matters worse, forcing them closer together.

"Will Seydisfjordur be okay without us?"

"I'm sure they are. You do know you won't have to be glued to the place. You can have a life too. Even be gone overnight."

She propped her elbows on the table and studied him. "What do you do with your free time?"

"I go hiking in the mountains. Even in a quiet place, you need to get away sometimes."

"Is that why you want to leave so badly?"

His eyes held a defiant look. "No, it's because I want to use my surgery skills. There isn't enough going on in Seydisfjordur for that to happen. If you haven't noticed, there is no operating theater attached to the clinic."

"Seems to me that based on today's activities, there is plenty to keep you busy. Maybe not with surgery, but certainly being needed."

"Being needed is important to you, isn't it?"

She shrugged. "It is better than no one knowing you are alive."

* * *

Drake averted his eyes. Had she really lived like that? He couldn't imagine not having someone who really cared. Seeing what it meant to her made him appreciate it more.

He had actually noticed how much he was needed. For the first time in a long time, he was rethinking his decision to leave. But he feared that had more to do with Trice than it did with the medical practice or Luce.

Still, he had made his plans, and he wouldn't let a woman he had just met derail them. Dr. Johannsson's death had done that once. Drake had no intention of letting that happen again.

"Will you tell me what it was like growing up here? Do you have brothers and sisters?" Trice watched him with expectation.

"I do. My sister lives in Reykjavík, and I have a brother who lives across the island in a small village. My parents moved a couple of years ago when my father was transferred to Reykjavík. That's when Luce became my responsibility. We've always been close. I do hate the idea of leaving her."

"It's nice to know you have a family. Everyone should have someone." She couldn't keep the sadness out of her voice.

Drake looked at her with sympathy. "You have no sense of what that is like, do you?"

"No, not really. Friendships and working relationships but no true connection."

"As much as I might complain, I'm glad to have my family, here. So many of us from Iceland are connected." He was quiet for a moment. "You know, it just occurs to me there is someone I've heard of living up here that you might like to interview for your research project. Let me make a few contacts, and we can possibly visit her before we leave." His gaze met hers. "If you'd like to? It looks as if we're going to be stuck here for the night. Maybe this evening, we could go do an interview."

"That would be wonderful." She sat straighter. The blanket slipped.

Drake took the chance to enjoy the view. He couldn't help but be disappointed when she adjusted it and curtained his show. The eagerness in Trice's eyes made his heart expand with pleasure. He had put that look on her face. "Let me make some calls, and I'll let you know if we can make the trip. I will also see if one of the women on the rescue squad has any spare pants. I have a shirt you can wear, but the pants, I'm afraid, will swallow you whole. You hang out here, and I'll be back with clothes and information." He grabbed his coat and started for the door.

Trice still sat on the sofa warming herself when Drake reentered with the damp wind and rain behind him. He quickly closed the door. "I wish I could say the weather is better, but it doesn't feel like it. We are a go, and I had good luck with clothes." He held up a bag.

"Thanks for thinking of everything."

"Before you dress, we need to get some cream on your back. I saw you wince a moment ago."

She looked at him. "Are you sure I can't handle it on my own?"

"Please just let me see to it." Drake went to his pack and removed a small jar. He sat beside her. "Let the blanket down." He tugged the material out of the way. This time he did take a moment to admire her lovely back. The urge to kiss the ridge of her shoulder almost overcame him. He closed his eyes, refocused his thoughts. This wasn't the time or the place.

"Hey, what's taking so long?"

"Just opening the jar." He lifted the cream with his index finger and slowly ran it over her spine. Trice's muscles rippled. Her skin was like touching velvet, warm, plush and elegant.

"That feels good." Trice's voice held a deep, sexy timbre that didn't encourage his control.

This was a worse idea than he had feared it might be. He took another moment to gather himself. He would and could get through this.

"All done." With a sigh, he covered her back with the blanket. He quickly stood, moving away. "Go get dressed. We must leave soon to be there on time."

That was all it took to get Trice moving. "Give me five minutes."

She returned wearing a T-shirt with his shirt buttoned over it and tied at her waist. The jeans he had borrowed from the female EMT were snug and hugged Trice's curves in a provocative way.

Drake swallowed hard. He could do this. Luce was right. Trice deserved better than being pursued by someone who had no intention of being around next week. Based on what she'd said, she had experienced more than her fair share of that in life already.

"Let me get my boots on and I'll be ready to go," she said.

"By the way, I was very impressed with your professionalism and your abilities today. Not everyone would've done what you did."

"Sometimes we have to do what scares us because it has to be done."

"Like flying?" He grinned.

"Yeah. And other things."

Was she trying to make a point? "You understand that better than most."

"I guess I do."

"That doesn't make you any less amazing." He stepped toward the door.

"Thank you. Enough about that. Who is this person we are going to see?" She followed him out, grabbing her coat on the way.

"An elder woman. She knows Luce. I visited her when I was a child. She is related to almost everyone around here. She might give you some names of people who have had HEP. Her seal of approval will take you a long way in gaining information."

"She does sound like an excellent person to get to know." Trice pulled on her coat.

He shrugged into his jacket. "Hallveig said she'd be glad to see us in about an hour. I made arrangements for us to borrow one of the rescue trucks."

"You think of everything, don't you?"

"Not everything, but I try to be thorough." That was one of the skills he had been told made him a good surgeon.

"That's what makes you such a good doctor." Trice had recognized it, and she hadn't even seen him with a scalpel.

"Thank you. You are starting to embarrass me. We've had an emotional day, so I guess we're going to brag to each other for the rest of it."

Trice laughed as she ran for the truck. She called over the hood as she climbed in, grinning, "If we don't, who's going to?"

He like the sound of her laugh. It made him want to join her in the humor. "On that note, let's get going. We have a drive ahead of us."

"Is it a long way?"

He settled behind the steering wheel. "Not so much distance. More like windy, steep roads. It just takes time to maneuver."

Half an hour later, Drake drove around another switchback. "I have only been this way once, and it was a long time ago."

"I am not complaining. I'm just glad for this opportunity. Is there anything I should know about Hallveig?"

"She's not exactly the spiritual leader of the area, but she's right up there. She's around ninety years old but doesn't know for sure how old she is. She knows most people around here, and she keeps the old Icelandic ways that have been handed down."

Another half an hour later with it still raining and the wind whipping around them, Drake pulled onto a narrow path and parked on the side of the road. "We have to walk from here."

"How did you even know where to pull over?" She looked around with eyes wide and mouth open.

He enjoyed looking at Trice when she had that bright-eyed, anything-is-possible look on her face. It made him want to see things the same way. "I got very specific instructions. Large tree with rocks in the curve."

"Interesting road signs." Trice climbed out of the truck and closed the door.

He met her at the front of the truck. "They aren't that unusual around here."

"Those I'll have to get used to. So, Hallveig lives all the way out here by herself."

"She does, which makes her that much more interesting. Despite where she lives, she knows everything going on for miles." He caught her elbow when she slipped.

"She must be fascinating."

They made their way down a single-file path with only a few trees.

"Why aren't there more trees?" Trice asked.

"Because they were all cut down and used for building houses and keeping warm through the years of settlement. Now we have a program to plant trees. It's working, but it's a slow process. It will take time to correct what we did in the past. Now we're looking for other ways to have what we need without cutting down trees."

"That makes sense."

They navigated the narrow path between two large boulders. A small house came into view. One that was little more than a shack. No light shone from within.

"I thought you said she is expecting us." She looked at him with a wrinkled brow of concern.

"She is." Drake stood before the door, giving it a light knock. He didn't want to disappoint Trice. The idea of being her hero appealed.

Time passed to the point he feared either Hallveig wasn't home or something was wrong. As he had made the decision to enter to check on her, the door was opened. A twisted, stoop-shouldered woman he hardly recognized stood there.

"I was expecting you." She didn't wait for them to respond. Instead, she turned and started back into the dim room.

The house held only a few pieces of furniture. Just the necessities. The glow from the fire gave off light along with one oil lamp sitting in the middle of a table in the center of the room. The bed was located on one side of the house and the kitchen on the other.

"Close the door and sit." The command came as little more than a growl.

"I'm Dr. Drake Stevansson. Years ago I came to see you with my grandmother, Luce."

"I remember you." She studied Trice as if she were something interesting under a microscope. "And you are?"

Trice stepped forward. "I'm Dr. Beatrice Shell."

"The new doctor."

Trice held eye contact. "Yes."

"Sit." Hallveig waved a gnarled hand up and down. She sat in a well-worn chair near the fire.

"Thank you for seeing us," Trice said. She pulled a wooden chair from the table, faced the woman and lowered herself into it.

Drake chose to stand on the other side of the fireplace from Hallveig.

Trice didn't appear taken aback by the woman's abrupt manner. "The reason I am here is that I am doing a medical study on people carrying the HEP gene. Are you familiar with the genetic disorder?"

Hallveig nodded.

"I understand you know everything that happens around here and everyone." Trice watched Hallveig intently.

She nodded but offered no encouragement to talk.

Trice moved to the edge of her seat. "Do you know anyone who has HEP or has been diagnosed with it?"

The question hung in the air for a minute. "I had it as a child. I recovered with a few scars. My brother had many."

"May I ask you some more questions and draw a small amount of blood?" Trice pulled a notebook out of the pocket of her coat.

Apparently, she had taken a few minutes while he was gone earlier to prepare for the meeting. Trice continued to impress him.

"Questions, yes. Blood, I'm not sure." Hallveig leaned back in her chair and picked up her knitting.

Trice leaned forward, looking earnest. "I could make it just a finger stick, if you would allow?"

Hallveig took so long to nod, Drake worried she might not.

"I would also like to talk to members of your family if I may. I would ask them the same questions I am going to ask you." Trice almost vibrated with her excitement.

Hallveig looked at Drake.

He nodded. "You can trust her, Hallveig."

The woman nodded too. "I heard what she did at the falls."

Drake smiled. How it had reached the old woman all the way up here so fast, he might never understand. "Yes, she was impressive."

Hallveig's attention returned to Trice. "I will agree. But I must ask my family if they agree."

"Will you tell them to contact me at the clinic?"

"I will."

Over the next few minutes, Drake stood quietly by while Trice conducted her interview. Once again, he was impressed by her consideration and scholarly manner. More than that, she was patient and kind with the older woman. Where had Trice been all his life?

"That's it for the questions," Trice announced. "Thank you so much, Hallveig. I only need one more thing. Just a little bit of blood." She pulled a blood sample kit out of her pocket.

Drake grinned. Trice used that pocket like a magician used a hat to do a trick. What else did she have in there?

"Hallveig, may I see your finger?"

The older woman offered her hand.

"There will be a little prick and squeeze." Trice suctioned the drop of blood into a small plastic tube and closed the top. It went into the pocket. She then carefully placed a Band-Aid over the spot. "That's it."

With the efficiency he had come to expect from Trice, she finished with Hallveig. "Thank you so much for doing this."

The woman nodded.

Now it was his turn. "Hallveig, when was the last time you had a checkup?"

"I don't know." She continued with her knitting.

"That long. Would you mind if I had a look at you since I am here?"

"I don't need one." The woman's hands didn't slow down. She wasn't going to agree without some coaxing.

"Would you please do it for me? It won't take but a minute. It will not hurt at all. I'll just have a quick listen to you."

She considered him long and hard, then nodded.

Drake smiled. He looked at Trice. "May I borrow your stethoscope?"

She reached in her pocket, found the instrument and handed it to him.

Minutes later he pronounced, "Hallveig, you are in remarkable health. May we all be doing as well as you."

Hallveig gave him a toothless grin. "I knew as much."

Drake returned her smile, then winked at Trice before handing back her stethoscope. "I bet you did. We must go now."

Trice stood.

"Dr. Stevansson leaves soon," Hallveig stated more than questioned.

"I do." Drake placed his hand on the woman's shoulder briefly. He was no longer saying that with the confidence he once had.

"Hallveig, do you ever come to Seydisfjordur?" Trice asked quietly.

"Once a year. It is a long way for me."

"I understand. I hope you come while I am still there. It would be lovely to see you again. You will talk to your family?"

"I will." Hallveig narrowed her eyes as she looked at Trice once more. "You have the Viking ancestry."

Trice smiled. "I do. Somewhere. Sometime."

"Come closer," Hallveig demanded. The woman took her chin, gripped it, then moved it back and forth. "You are a Bjonsson."

"What?"

Drake said, "That's a last name. We put *daughter* or *son* on the end of the father's name. The Bjonssons are well known in this area. There's even one in Seydisfjordur."

"I am a Bjonsson." The pleasure in Trice's voice said it all. Her world had been made complete. In an odd way, he wished he had been the one to put that pleased look on her face.

"Are you sure?" Trice asked with tears forming in her eyes.

The woman nodded.

"I would never doubt Hallveig," Drake assured Trice with a squeeze on her shoulder.

Hallveig looked perplexed. "She did not know?"

He smiled at the old woman. "No, she did not know. You have made her very happy."

Trice gave the fragile woman a gentle hug. "Thank you."

Hallveig put her hands on Trice's shoulders and looked into her face. "You are good. We will be glad you are one of us."

Drake let Trice exit before him. "Thank you, Hallveig."

"Young man." She stopped him.

Fear washed through him at her tone.

"You do not know your heart or your place. You think on that before you make a mistake."

CHAPTER SIX

TRICE STOOD IN dumbfounded silence outside Hallveig's house. She couldn't believe it. She was a Bjonsson. She had family. No matter how distant. Roots. A history.

Hallveig pronounced it with such confidence. Could it be true?

Drake stood close beside her. "Are you okay?"

She looked into his concerned eyes and gave him a huge smile. "I'm better than okay." She wrapped her arms around his neck. "I have family. Real, breathing family."

His hands came to her waist. "Yes, you do."

"I'm so excited. I can't believe it." She hugged him tighter, then pulled away.

"Isn't that part of why you wanted to come to Iceland, to find family?"

She liked being held by Drake. In fact, she wanted him to hold her more. "It is, but I never really thought I would find anyone that might belong to me."

He chuckled. "We better get out of this weather and back to the truck or you may be too sick to find them."

"Never." She started down the path. "This has been the best day. Do you know the Bjonsson who lives in Seydis-fjordur?"

"I have met him." His tone was flat and dry.

She stopped walking and studied Drake. "That didn't sound very encouraging."

Drake twisted his mouth. "He isn't the most approachable person."

All the air went out of her lungs. "Oh. You don't think he will speak to me?"

"I'm just afraid you might not get a very warm welcome." Drake took her elbow and directed her on down the path.

"I'll take my chances." She would get the man to at least see her. Make him understand how important to her it was to meet him.

They reached the truck. Trice climbed in, shivering.

Drake slid behind the steering wheel, then turned a knob. "It'll be warm in here in a few minutes."

Trice huddled close to the warm air coming out of the vent. "By the by, I'm sorry I didn't even think about giving Hallveig a checkup. All I was concerned about was what I wanted."

"That's what we went for. I just thought since we were there, she needed to be seen. We've had more than a big day. Let's go back to the cabin and get some rest. We'll leave at daylight if the weather will let us. I'll see about us visiting old man Bjonsson when we get home."

That's what he thought of Seydisfjordur. As home. Soon he would have a new home. A new life. A new career. He would prove to himself and anyone else watching that was where he belonged. He would keep his promise to himself and his grandfather to help people. But wasn't he helping people here? Hallveig's words came to mind. *You do not know your heart or your place.*

Trice rubbed her hands together. "You know you don't have to take what little time you have left in town seeing about me. Give me some directions and I will go see him."

Drake looked at her. "I like spending time with you."

"OK, thank you."

"After we get back and see things settled around the clinic, we'll drive up the valley to visit him. I just don't want you to get your hopes up. He's not what you would call a family man. In fact, he has run all of them off that I know of."

"Oh, then he may not welcome me." The idea made her sad.

He glanced at her, then returned his attention to the road.

Less than an hour later and not soon enough for her aching back, Drake pulled into the road by the cabin. "I sure would like to know how our two patients are doing."

"So would I. Would you like to go to the restaurant for dinner and see what we can find out?"

"That sounds good."

Drake drove along a road she didn't recognize, then parked in front of a long building. "Since there's only light rain, we'll leave the truck here and take the path back to the cabin."

"If anybody's learned their lesson about the importance of staying on a path, that's me." She climbed out of the truck, taking a moment to stretch her back.

"I can't say it enough. You did impressive work this morning. Far above what you were expected to do." He held the door for her to enter the building.

"I think it was more about me being scared than anything." She stepped by him to stop in what was obviously the lobby of the resort.

"Many people don't do things because they're scared." A low fire burned in a rock fireplace. He started down a hall.

She joined him. "Are you scared of something?"

"Yeah. I'm afraid of never having the chance to do what I love."

Trice regarded him. "Surgery?"

"Yeah. I am so close to finishing my training." He stopped at the door of a room filled with tables and chairs.

"Why did you go into medicine?"

"Because my grandfather died when there wasn't someone close who could perform surgery. He was too sick to fly, and the road would have taken too long. I watched him suffer. I made up my mind then that I'd become a surgeon so others wouldn't have to watch their loved ones die."

A woman came to show them to a table.

"But if you leave, won't the people around here be in the same situation?" She weaved between tables of people to their spot.

When they had settled in their chairs, Drake leaned over the table toward her. "Leave it to you to ask the difficult questions. No, because I have no place to do surgery, no theater. The clinic would need to be enlarged. There's no money for that."

"I can understand that, but I can also understand the significance of what you do here."

Drake had obviously made up his mind about leaving. It wasn't her place to try to change it. Even if she could. He deserved his chance at his dream just as she was getting hers. Yet it still made her sad to think of him leaving. She would miss him. Too much.

The woman taking their order brought her attention back to the here and now. Their discussion went to subjects more general over dinner. They strolled back to the cabin.

Trice pulled her coat off and hung it up before turning her back to the smoldering fire. "I'm glad our patients are doing so well."

"I am as well. I just wish you hadn't gotten hurt in the process."

She twisted her back. It had eased since they got out of the truck. "It's not that bad, but I know I'll be sleeping on my stomach."

Drake made a noise that sounded like a groan.

She considered him, eyes narrowed. "Are you okay?"

"Yeah. Fine." He didn't look at her. "I should put some more cream on your back. Otherwise, you'll have a difficult time sleeping the night through. I'll build the fire while you get ready for me to do that."

"Are you planning to stay here tonight?"

"I was. Unless you have a problem with it. We are lucky to get this cabin. All of them are taken with the rescue crew and tourists. I can see if I can bunk with someone else if you aren't comfortable with me being here. I promise to be a perfect gentleman."

"What if I don't want you to be a gentleman?" That popped out. Was her subconscious speaking for her now? What would be wrong with them enjoying each other while they could? Would that be so awful? He would be gone soon. She gave him a sideways look to see what his reaction was to that. Had she shocked him?

Drake stopped midmovement to look at her. "Trice, you need to think carefully about what you are saying."

She faced him. "I know what I'm saying. I'm attracted to you. I thought maybe you were to me too."

He looked at her for a moment. Saying nothing.

That was a gamble that didn't pay off. She started toward the bedroom. "I'm sorry. Am I being too blunt? Just forget I said anything."

"Trice."

"Yes." She glanced back.

His voice dropped low. "You didn't misread anything."

She continued into the bedroom with a smile on her lips. A few minutes later she called, "Ready." Trice had slid under the covers to her waist, her back bare. She hurt and looked forward to having Drake's fingers moving across her in a gentle glide. A creak in the floor told her Drake had entered.

"Scoot to the middle some."

She did as he requested, being careful not to show more of herself than necessary.

The bed dipped. Drake sat on the edge of the mattress. "This still looks painful."

"Yes, Mother Hen," she grumbled.

"There's nothing wrong with being careful." He smoothed cream over her skin.

She shivered from the coolness of the cream, or Drake's touch, she wasn't sure which. "Never said there was."

"Yet you're making fun of me."

She considered him over her shoulder. "I do appreciate your concern."

His gaze met hers. It was soft, caressing and enquiring. His fingers journeyed down her back. She quaked. He blinked, and the look disappeared. He quickly stood. "You need to get some good rest. I'll see you in the morning."

She held the blanket to her as she rolled so she could see him. "Where are you planning to sleep?"

"I'll take the sofa. You are in pain."

"But there's plenty of room in this bed."

"You do know what will happen if I do that, and you are in no shape for that amount of activity."

She couldn't let him sleep on an uncomfortable sofa. "Don't make me feel guilty about sleeping in this comfortable bed. You've had a hard day, and you need your rest too." Why was she pushing this? "Look, there's plenty of room for both of us. We're adults. I believe we can control our actions." She hoped she spoke for them both, especially herself. "Don't we have to be up early?"

Drake looked at her long enough that she had become convinced he wasn't going to take her up on the invitation.

"All right. I will, but if I disrupt your sleep or hurt your back for some reason, then I'm off to the sofa."

He headed for the bathroom.

By the time Drake returned, she'd pulled on a T-shirt and settled on her stomach. She was aware of the dip in the mattress as he climbed in beside her.

Drake faced away from Trice, trying not to move until his muscles had locked into place. He would be sore in the morning from trying not to touch her. Sleeping on the floor might have been more comfortable than having a warm woman next to him and being unable to touch her. His life kept taking turns he hadn't expected. And currently didn't enjoy.

You do not know your heart or your place. Those words echoed again. "Trice, about what we were talking about earlier."

"Mmm."

"What do you think we should do about it?" He sure knew what he wanted to do. But he wanted to hear her say it.

"I thought a hot no-strings fling as long as you are here would be superb."

Drake's stomach muscles tightened at the idea. His manhood twitched in anticipation.

"We aren't going the same direction in life," she said. "I don't see either one of us settling down anytime soon. We have plans we want to accomplish. Let's make it clean and simple so that when you leave, we part as friends."

He winced. Had she been so hurt in the past that she didn't want any strings? Her background had made her that way. She had no ties to anything, and his entire life was filled with strings. He had to give her credit. Her fortitude impressed him.

If she could put what she wanted ahead of everything, then he could too. "I like that plan. But not tonight. I want you feeling better and in no pain."

She rolled, and her fingertips brushed along his bicep.

His hand stopped hers. "You rest, and we will talk about it more tomorrow."

"Promise?"

"You can count on it."

Minutes later, he heard her even breathing. She was asleep.

A groan awakened him. There was movement from Trice's side of the bed. She rolled to her back, yelped, then returned to where she had been, releasing another groan.

His hand hadn't touched her skin before he felt the heat. Trice had a fever. He rested the back of his hand on her forehead. It was a high one.

She relaxed for a moment.

Drake turned on the bedside lamp, then went to the main room and retrieved his medical backpack. After finding his thermometer, he ran it over her head from ear to ear. The reading flashing in the tiny screen was one hundred two degrees. He searched for the fever-reducing medicine and shook out a couple of tablets before he filled a glass with water.

Placing the glass on the table beside the bed, he took a seat beside Trice. "Trice, you have a fever. Can you sit up and take some medicine?"

She rolled her head back and forth.

He slipped an arm under her shoulders, being careful not to touch her injury, and lifted her forward.

She moaned and opened her red, glassy eyes. "I was having a wonderful dream. You were kissing me."

He wished he had been. Trying to ignore her statement and his urge to do just that, he said, "You need to sit up and take these. Open your mouth."

She did.

He quickly brought the water to her lips. She eagerly drank. Some of it dribbled down her chin and dropped on her chest. "Finish the water, sweetheart."

Trice did as he instructed.

He dabbed the stray water from her chin with the sheet. "Now, lie back. I'm going to get a cool compress for your head. You'll be fine in the morning."

"Don't go." Her eyelids slowly closed.

"I'll be right back." He hurried to the bathroom, found a washcloth, wet it and returned to Trice.

She lay back on the pillow, her eyes still closed.

Drake placed the cloth across her forehead.

Trice sighed. "Feels good. Back hurts."

"I know, sweetheart. I know. I need to have a look at it. Can you roll over?"

"I don't want to." Her eyes fluttered open.

"Your back won't hurt as bad if you get off it." She muttered something he couldn't understand. "I'll help you." He pulled at the blankets. All she wore was the T-shirt and light pink panties, but he wouldn't allow himself to dwell on that fact. He raised one shoulder and pushed her hip, encouraging her to shift. She moved to her stomach without a noise.

Drake lifted her shirt and winced. The bruises had turned darker. Trice said nothing and didn't move.

"I'll need to check things in the morning. Try to get some sleep." He carefully lowered her shirt. Taking the rag to the bath once more, he ran it under cool water and placed it on her forehead. Trice felt cooler now. Turning off the bedside lamp, he lay down.

Trice took his hand. Her hot breath flowed over his arm. "You're a nice man."

Drake couldn't see her clearly in the dim light. He smiled. Had there been no one who took care of her when she was sick?

"Sorry I woke you." She wiggled next to him.

"Not a problem. Hush now. You need to sleep."

She pushed into his side. "You do too. I'm cold."

Her fever was breaking. He put his arm beneath her neck. She rested her head on his chest. He was careful not to touch her back.

Her lips touched his chest. "Thank you for taking care of me. I wish I felt better."

He groaned. "Trice, don't do that. You are not up to it, and I can't resist you if you don't help me."

She wiggled against his side again and sighed.

Trice had fallen asleep, but that wouldn't be happening for him for a long time to come. He had been trying to keep some space between them, but that wasn't working. Trice had a way of pulling him closer. His fingertips brushed the top of the curve of her hip. He hadn't anticipated being shaken by the instantaneous combustion between them in such a short period of time.

He wanted her. It was time for him to accept that, but he didn't have any business letting himself fall for her. Her back hurt, and he planned to leave in five days. His thoughts had gone crazy since Trice had arrived. No matter what he did, they circled around to her.

That would end when he left. His emotions would settle down again. He'd get involved in his work and adjust to life in London. Would she even want him to stay? If she did, would he be just another person on the long list of people who had let her down?

Drake reminded himself of that idea throughout the night while he held Trice. Somehow, he didn't think it would be that easy anymore. He didn't want to leave Trice alone. And oddly, leaving Seydisfjordur didn't have the same appeal. Luce was right. It didn't seem fair to Trice. Yet he had to. There were commitments to honor. His dream to pursue. Returning to Seydisfjordur had only been a detour.

Trice woke to the warm reality of a hard body next to hers. She lay on her side, and a heavy arm rested across her waist.

A soft snore came from above her head.

She opened her eyelids just enough to look over the plane of Drake's chest covered by material.

Another snore made her grin. She looked up, seeing the dark shadow along his jaw. She really liked his jaw. Her fingers twitched to trace that dark line, but she stopped them. She shouldn't start anything that she wasn't physically capable of carrying through with.

She needed her life to move forward. There was a chance she might find a family member, a distant one, but family none the less. She couldn't become wrapped up in a man who would leave and never look back. That wasn't the type of relationship she wanted or needed. She wanted a sturdy and healthy one. There had been enough partial relationships in her life already. But to spend a few lovely hours in his arms with no strings attached would make for nice memories. "Drake."

His eyelids fluttered. His fingertips brushed the curve

of her breast as he removed his arm. Looking at her, he said, "Hey."

The temptation to kiss him right then grabbed her when his sexy morning voice flowed over her.

"Did you sleep any last night?" He studied her.

She yawned. "Best ever. How about you?"

Drake's warm, caressing look found and held hers. "Best ever. How's the back?"

"Hurts."

"Roll and let me have a look." He shifted, making the mattress dip.

"I don't think this—"

"Trice, let me see."

She did as he said. Satisfaction went through her when she heard the tight intake of his breath. She hadn't bothered to pull the covers up. Her bikini underwear was clearly in view.

Drake pushed her T-shirt up her back in a slow, revealing way. The sizzle in the air made her breath catch. She remained still.

"Trice." His voice sounded hoarse.

She said softly, "Yes?"

"You may want to breathe. I don't want you to pass out." A teasing note surrounded the words.

She rolled enough that she could see his face. "I'm breathing." She took a deep breath, letting it out slowly. Drake's eyes widened and focused on her breasts.

"Trice." His tone matched a father disciplining a child. "I'm trying very hard to remain a doctor here. You are not making it easy. Now stop playing and let me see your back."

She settled on her stomach again, pleasure filling her. Drake struggled with their attraction as much as she did.

"This looks better than it did last night." The tip of a finger ran down the length of her back to the dip of her waist. Cool, dry lips rested a second on the back of her shoulder. In a low voice Drake said, "Two can play the same game."

She rolled to her side. Her gaze locked with his. "Do you really want to play?"

Drake climbed out of bed and regarded her. "I'm leaving. You're staying."

"You didn't answer my question."

"Which one? Do I want you? Yes. You are the sexiest woman I've ever seen. The most amazing one. The bravest. The most beautiful. Hell yeah, I want you."

"You mean that?" Did he really feel that way?

He looked into her eyes. "Every word of it."

Trice slipped from the bed, not caring about the skimpy clothing she wore. Walking to Drake, she put her arms around his neck and kissed him. "Thank you for that. No one has ever said anything like that to me."

Drake gently placed his hands on her waist, but the tension in his body said he held himself under control. His mouth found hers. He pulled her secure against him. His manhood stood strong and thick between them. His tongue ran along the seam of her lips. That was all the encouragement she needed to open for him. Drake invaded with the eagerness of a person thirsty for water. Their tongues tangled. She gripped his shoulders. His hands remained on her waist, but his fingers tightened. How like him to always be mindful of her injury.

She'd been kissed before, but none had been like this one. This went to her soul, captured her.

Drake cupped her butt and lifted. She wrapped her legs around his waist. Her center rested against the stiffness of him, making her tingle with desire. She whimpered. His thumbs slid beneath the elastic of her panties.

A knock on the door stopped any further exploration. Drake's mouth left hers. His heated eyes held want, disappointment and something she couldn't define. He let her deliberately slide down his body.

"I should get that." He stepped away, jerked on his jeans, and headed for the door.

She heard Drake talking to another man but couldn't make out the words. Quickly she pulled on her clothes, taking special care with her shirt, not applying too much pressure to her back.

Drake returned. "We need to get moving. That was one of the rescue squad. They are leaving and wanted to know if we needed a ride to the plane. I told them we would appreciate one. We shouldn't make them wait."

"I'll be ready in ten minutes. Will that do?"

He didn't look at her as he spoke. "That will do. The sky looks nice and clear. The flight home should be smooth."

She shuddered.

Drake narrowed his eyes. "What was that for?"

"The thought of going up in an airplane again." She pulled on her pants.

He pulled on his shirt. "You know, you could hurt my feelings."

She wasn't clear if he was teasing or not. "I don't mean to. It's just that I'm not a big fan of flying in general."

"Or my plane in particular. Yet you jumped at the chance to hang ten meters above roaring water and rocks."

"I didn't jump at the idea. I did what had to be done." Why did she feel the need to defend herself? He'd been there. Knew the situation.

He stepped to her, his eyes predatory.

Would he kiss her again? She would like it if he did.

"And you were magnificent. I was proud of you." He

placed his hands on her shoulders and gave her a kiss on the forehead. "Now to see if you do as well getting home."

She sagged with disappointment when he moved away.

"Do you have everything?" He looked around the room.

"Yep. I didn't come with much."

"You will need your jacket." He pulled it off the back of a chair and handed it to her. "It's time to go home."

She hadn't thought about it, but she was going home. Seydisfjordur was as much her home in a little over a week as any other place she had ever been. "Yes, let's go home."

An hour later, Drake had the engine warmed up and prepared for takeoff. He pushed the throttle forward, and the plane ran down the runway.

As he made movements with his hands and feet that were now second nature to him, he was aware of Trice trying to cover her anxiety. It wasn't working. She held her breath, and her fingers bit into the seat cushion.

"I wish you'd settle back over there. It's a beautiful day for flying." He turned the plane toward the east.

"So you say," she grumbled.

"Look out at how beautiful it is." For some reason he wanted her to enjoy flying.

"I can't yet."

"For a woman who hung over the side of a cliff for hours yesterday, I can't understand why you're so scared being in an airplane with me."

"It's not your flying."

"Thank goodness. Would you like to fly over the waterfall where we were yesterday?"

It took her a moment, but she said, "Yes. I would like to see it."

He made a turn.

"Wow, I didn't mean for you to do that." Her hand gripped his arm.

His look met hers. "I'll take care of you. Now, be looking down, because here it comes."

"Oh, wow."

She let go of him. He missed her touch immediately. "This is one of the most beautiful waterfalls in Iceland."

"Look at those boulders below. I'm glad I didn't know of their size yesterday. You might have had to push me over the side."

He had known. That had been one of the reasons he'd not wanted her to go. "It is deep. This is a wonderful tourist spot, but it has to be respected. It's also dangerous."

"I'm going to read up on it when we get home."

At least she no longer looked terrified and was speaking to him normally. "You might enjoy a book I have about Iceland's history and special sights. You need to visit some of these places if and when you have a chance."

Her face turned eager, eyes bright. "I'd love to read the book. I promise to leave it with Luce to return to you, or I could even mail it."

"You don't have to do either of those. I would like to give it to you." He made a banking turn to the left, leaving the falls behind them. He loved seeing her enthusiasm about what he considered commonplace. It made him see the sights in a different light. With wonder and anticipation. Being with Trice had him experiencing what he'd always known but with renewed pleasure.

"Thank you. That's nice of you. I will cherish it."

He like the idea of her having something that had been his.

They continued toward Seydisfjordur. Drake did a few subtle dips and turns so Trice could see the mountains.

"I love the snow-tipped mountains," she said as much to herself as him.

Drake chuckled. "After six months or more, you may not see them the same way. You'll be looking for spring like everyone else around here."

"But not you. You will be in England with rain."

They had reached the fjord. He flew over the water. Trice's fingers turned white as she held the door handle. The tires touched the runway with a screech, and they rolled toward the building.

Trice released her grip and breathed a sigh of relief. "Were you trying to impress me just now with those maneuvers?"

"What if I was?" He pulled the plane to a stop.

"Why would you?"

He looked at her. "Isn't that what a guy does when he likes a girl?"

Pink spotted her cheeks. "Drake, are you flirting with me?"

He grinned. "About ninety percent of the time."

CHAPTER SEVEN

TRICE CLIMBED FROM the plane as Drake exited the other side. Relieved to have her feet back on the ground, she had still enjoyed being with Drake. She especially enjoyed him flirting with her. And most of all his kiss.

"I know you must be tired. I'll drop you by Luce's and head over to the clinic to see if there's anything I need to do."

"I work there. I should be there as well." She pulled her bag out of the storage compartment.

He grabbed his too and closed the door. "You are a tough person to be nice to. I might have made a few more dips and turns if I had known you could be so contrary."

"You would have done that?" She looked at him with a mock shocked face that included an open mouth.

He shrugged. "Sure. I have already admitted I was showing off some."

She glared at him. "If you were trying to impress me, that wasn't the way."

He stepped closer, watching her. "If I wanted to impress you, how would I go about doing that?"

"I don't know. Maybe by taking me out for a nighttime picnic to watch the stars. Something that was less likely to make my stomach roll."

"Then how about joining me tonight? I know just the

place. And just the sky to find them in. Wear warm clothes and the socks I loaned you."

"Okay. I'll take that dare, or date, whichever you're making it." They started toward his truck.

"I like the idea of a date." A look of satisfaction came across his face.

They climbed into his truck.

She smiled. "I like the idea of a date as well."

Excitement he'd not experienced in a long time ran through him. Just the idea of spending time with Trice had a way of doing that. He made the short drive to the clinic.

They were only there five minutes before they had three patients. They were simple matters of a child with an upset stomach, an older woman complaining of a bad cold, and a man who had a bunion that needed attention. They divided the cases between the two of them and soon finished.

After yesterday's adventure, every problem seemed easier.

Trice hadn't complained of her back hurting despite her discomfort in the plane. When she returned home, she would give it some attention. She had almost finished cleaning the exam room when Drake came to the door.

"Your turn."

"What?" She faced him.

"It's time for me to give your back a look. I saw the way you shifted in the plane seat. You were in pain." He entered the room.

"Not pain. Uncomfortable. I'll look at it when I get home."

"You know you can't reach it if you need to care for it. Now stop arguing and let me see." He stood beside the gurney.

She huffed. "I think you're enjoying this."

He grinned. "I think you might be right. I do like looking at your lovely back, but right now I'll focus on giving a medical evaluation."

She turned her back to him and lifted her shirt.

"You will be glad to know it's much improved. You have a rainbow of colors. You can pull your shirt down now." He stepped away from her.

She did and turned to face him. "Satisfied?"

"With your recovery, yes." He walked toward the door. "I think we have everything settled here if you want to go home. I'll be leaving in a half an hour as soon as I put in the reports."

"I can do those and close up." She didn't want him to see her as a slacker.

"Trice, wouldn't you like to get out of those clothes?"

She looked down at what she'd been wearing for the better part of two days. "Are you saying you would like me to freshen up before you see me again tonight?"

His look remained on her. "I don't think it would hurt either one of us to clean up."

"Okay. I'll go. What time should I expect you?"

He stopped on the way to the office. "Eleven o'clock too early?"

"Wow, that late?"

"It takes a long time to get dark here this time of year."

"I will be ready." The idea of seeing him again made her giddy.

"You sure you're up to it tonight? It can wait until tomorrow."

She was eager to spend as much time with him as she could. "If you're up to it, I'm up to it. I might have another social engagement if we wait."

They both laughed.

"This isn't a place where there's a nightclub on every corner or even a movie theater."

Like he would have in London. "I'd rather look at the stars anyway."

"Then I'll see you in a few hours. Don't forget to wear warm clothes."

She was curious now. "Where're we going?"

"That's my surprise."

Drake was astonished he hadn't seen Luce. He expected her there with her disapproving look. A tinge of guilt filled him. But he was an adult and so was Trice. They didn't need Luce to make their decisions for them.

Still, he suspected she was right. This probably wouldn't end well for one or both of them. He held his head high and walked to Trice's door. Knocking, he waited until she opened it.

"You still feel up to an evening out?"

"You bet. Let me get my coat." She went back into the house and returned with the coat in hand.

He led her to the truck and helped her in. Five minutes later, they were on the road leading into the valley.

"Shouldn't we be going up the mountain?" Trice looked ahead of them.

"You just sit back. I'll do the driving. We're higher than you think."

After another two miles, he turned off the paved road and drove along a gravel one. A few minutes later, she realized how high they had gone, causing her to hold on to the door handle.

Drake glanced at her. "High enough for you?"

She continued to focus on the outside view. "I'd have to say yes."

Drake chuckled, pulling to the side of the road and parking the truck.

"We're stopping here?" She looked around them as if expecting more.

He opened the door and hopped out. "This is where we're going."

"Oh."

He wanted to show her the best of Iceland. She said she loved the stars, and there was no better place to see them than here. The sky would be a regular festival of lights tonight. This was the perfect place to see the show. Once again, he had to remind himself this wasn't some relationship where he had to impress the girl. Yet he wanted Trice to remember him well. Why was it so important that she did?

She climbed down from the truck to meet him. "This view is amazing without stars."

"I think so." He reached in the back for the picnic basket, blanket and plastic ground cover. Closing the door, he said, "This way."

"Can I help you carry something?"

He handed her the blanket. "Up for a little stroll?"

"Sure."

He led the way up a path. They walked for ten minutes until they came to an open field. By this time, it was dusk. They were surrounded by nothing but sky.

"I didn't think it could get any better, but it has."

Drake knew from the sound of Trice's voice he'd impressed her. He liked that idea. What would her reaction be in a little while? It was fun showing his homeland to someone who appreciated it.

"How did you find this place?" she asked.

"It wasn't too hard. My house is just right over there." He pointed behind him toward a rise.

She gave him a suspicious look. "So what was all the driving and walking about, then, if your house is right over there?"

Drake shrugged. "Because it was the easiest way to get to this spot." He kicked a couple of rocks out of the way, then flipped the plastic sheet out, laying it on the ground. Taking the blanket from her, he positioned it over the plastic. In the middle, he placed the picnic basket. From the basket he pulled a candle in a glass. He lit it and set it to the side.

"Join me? The light show will start in a few minutes." He sat with his legs crossed.

Trice joined him on the blanket, a grin on her face. "Why, Doctor, this is impressive."

"I'm glad you like it." He opened the basket and removed food containers, placing them within reach. Last he took out plates, utensils, wine and glasses.

"You thought of everything."

"I tried." He served their plates, handing her one.

She tasted each item. "This is wonderful."

"Thank you." He bowed his head.

She took another bite. "Did you make it?"

"No, I asked Marta at the café to put something together, so I can't take credit for it." He opened a container.

"It's a relief to know you aren't perfect at everything." She ate a spoonful of pasta salad.

"I had no idea you thought I was." He rather liked the idea she believed that. "Now you know my secret." He grinned. "Eat up. We'll need to blow out the candle to really appreciate what we see."

She took a large bite. "I've lived in cities all my life. Until I came here, I'd never really seen stars without some light. I've heard people talk about them but have never seen them myself. I'm so excited."

With their meal finished, Drake took a few minutes to pack their leftovers away in the bag, leaving the wine out. He blew out the candle and lay back on the blanket with his hand beneath his head and legs stretched out and ankles crossed. "Come join me. This is the best way to see the sky."

Trice lay beside him in the same manner. "Oh, wow. I had no idea the sky could be so big."

"Yeah, this I will miss living in the city," he said softly.

"It's just beautiful." She continued to look up.

He admired Trice. "It's not the only thing."

Trice glanced at him to find him watching her. Her skin heated. She looked back at the sky. A pink wave of light emerged. Then a green one. They appeared to dance with each other. A vivid blue joined them.

"Oh, wow. The aurora borealis. I never thought I would ever see it." She couldn't take her eyes off the show in the sky. "I love it." She would remember this forever. She couldn't believe the colors. The view was everything she ever thought it might be. It went on forever.

She grabbed Drake's hand. "You knew, didn't you? Of course you did."

Drake held her hand. "The lights are a regular this time of year when it is clear."

"They look like they are dancing. Or fabric flowing across a black backdrop. Oh, I know. Like those trapeze artists who wrap themselves in silks and twist and turn."

Drake laughed. "And the list goes on."

"I can't help it. They are amazing."

He couldn't stop grinning. "I love watching you. Hearing you express your pleasure."

"Thank you so much for bringing me here. Next to finding out I might have real family here, this is the best." She wrapped her arms around his neck, kissing him. Just as quickly, she pulled away, and her attention returned to the sky.

He nudged her back to him. "Come lie beside me. Rest your head on my shoulder. Get comfortable."

Trice did what he suggested with a sigh and snuggled close. He was warm and hard and felt like security. This she could do for the rest of her life. Except they didn't have that long. And she refused to get attached.

They said nothing for a long time.

"Drake, are you asleep?" She placed a hand on his chest.

"No." The word brushed her ear. "I was just enjoying knowing you were beside me, sharing this beautiful sky."

"We didn't have to do this tonight if you were tired." Still, she was glad they came.

His hand ran up and down her arm. "There's not too many more nights left to do it."

He sounded as sad as she felt. "I don't want to think about that."

Drake didn't respond. Had she said the wrong thing? Yet it was the truth. She should've kept the thought to herself. Now that she had said it, she had no choice but to speak. "I will miss you."

In the dark, she felt more than saw him roll toward her. Her heart plummeted.

Drake placed his large hand on her stomach.

Her muscles rippled. Her nerves shot like live wires in response. "It's been fun getting to know you," she said.

"How's your back feeling?"

Even in the poor light, she could tell his face hovered over hers. "It aches a little bit."

With a minimum of movement, he pulled her on top of him. "Is this better?"

"Much."

"Trice, may I kiss you?"

"Why don't I kiss you instead?" Unable to make out his features clearly, she still knew every dip and rise, curve and angle of his face. Her lips found his without searching. As if pulled to them by a string.

His mouth was firm, warm and welcoming. He took. He gave. He suggested. He accepted.

She'd found heaven.

The tip of his tongue ran the width of her lips. She opened for him. Their tongues danced like the colors in the sky. Blending, meeting and swaying to each other and then away. The heat between them built.

His hand moved to her back. She winced.

His head jerked back. "I'm so sorry. I didn't mean to hurt you."

Trice planned to kiss his lips, but her mouth landed on his nose. "I'm fine."

"I just got caught up—" His voice sounded anxious.

"I can't think of anything more flattering. Kiss me again." She leaned down.

His hands came to her shoulders. "Not until I've checked your back. I would never forgive myself if I hurt you."

She sighed and crawled off him. "You're making too much of it."

"Maybe so, but that's the way it's going to be. I'm going to need good light. Do you mind if we go to my place? There are pillows and a big porch with rocking chairs where you can sit in comfort for as long as you like without your back hurting."

She wanted to go with him to his home, to his bed if he wanted her. She wanted to know all there was about Drake, see how he lived, feel his arms around her again. "Okay, my back would appreciate that."

He flipped on a flashlight.

"You think of everything."

"Experience."

She didn't like the idea. "Do you bring women up here often?"

"Why Trice, are you fishing for information about my love life?"

She was confident that his teasing tone was meant to ease her thoughts, but it didn't. She might have been concerned, but she would never admit it. "Dr. Stevansson, don't let your ego get ahead of you."

"To keep the peace, I can say I have never brought another woman to this spot. Now, does that calm your ruffled feathers?"

"My feathers aren't ruffled." They were though. She didn't like the idea of him sharing something as special as the last hour with anyone else.

"It didn't sound that way to me." He returned to putting the wine and glasses away.

She stood out of the way, holding the flashlight as he folded the blanket.

"I'm flattered you wanted to know." He gave her the blanket, then turned his attention to the plastic sheet. "The question you really want the answer to is, do I think you are special?"

"You are so…egotistical." He was making her mad now. Maybe that was the plan. It would put some space between them. She had to remind herself not to let emotions get involved.

He stepped to her, into her personal space. "That may be true, but it's also true that I do think you're special. Very special. I would like to show you how much if you will let me. But no pressure. I'll only go as far as you wish."

Drake pulled up his drive. Trice hadn't said a word since leaving their picnic spot. He wasn't sure if this was a good or bad thing. Worry had started to nag at him. Had he come on too strong? He only had a few more days with Trice and didn't have the time to miss out on a minute of them.

He had left one interior light on, which made the A-frame house glow on the high hill.

"Drake, what a wonderful place. I can imagine the view during the day."

"It's a nice one. You can see almost the entire fjord." One he would miss when he moved away. He drove to the house and around to the back and pulled under a carport. He turned to her. "Still want to come in?"

"Of course I do." Trice grabbed the door handle and got out. She walked round to his side of the truck. "Let me help carry stuff in."

"I've got it. Just the food bag. The blanket and the plastic sheet I'll leave for later."

Drake went ahead of her, flipping on the light switch. He set the bag on the kitchen counter.

Trice entered more slowly. "What a kitchen. I might learn to cook if I had one like this."

"You are welcome to use it anytime." He moved further into the one large room, kicking off his shoes near the sofa. "Come on out to the porch. I'll get you a pillow for your back."

She wandered in his direction as if taking it all in.

"You are thinking mighty hard over there."

"This place is amazing." Trice trailed a finger along his leather sofa.

"I'm glad you like it. Make yourself at home. I'll be right back." Drake soon returned with a pillow. He offered his hand, and Trice took it. After leading her outside to the front porch, he settled her in a rocker with the pillow behind her back. "You enjoy the lights while I get us something hot to drink."

Drake quickly put together hot chocolates from supplies his mother had left behind the last time she had visited. He hadn't had it since he was a child, but he thought Trice might enjoy it. She seemed like that type. He soon returned to her with mugs in hand.

She took hers with a smile on her face. "Hot chocolate. With a marshmallow even." Lifting the mug to her lips, she took a sip. "Perfect."

He sat in the rocker next to hers. "I'm glad you like it."

"Do the lights go on like this all night?" She looked out beyond them.

"They do. They lengthen and get thinner with the season. Then leave to return." Was that what he would do? His grandmother lived here. He would be back, but would Trice be here? She could come and go, but for him it was more complicated.

"With time everything changes." Melancholy hung in her voice.

"It does." Drake didn't want to talk about him leaving. He wanted to live in the here and now. With Trice.

They sat in silence for a while.

Drake liked that. It was rare to find someone he felt comfortable enough to just find pleasure in just being with. "Trice?"

"Mmm?" She sipped her hot chocolate.

"I know the timing is all wrong. I'm going away, and

you are staying here. There are only four days left before I leave."

"Are you trying to depress me?"

"No. What I'm trying to say, poorly obviously, is that I don't want to waste what little time we have together by pretending I don't want you in my bed."

Trice looked at him. She stood and offered her hand. "I'm getting cold, and I haven't had a tour of your house yet."

This wasn't going the way he had hoped. After baring his soul, he hadn't expected she'd ask for a tour. He wasn't sure whether to laugh or be insulted.

She walked around him and headed inside.

He picked up the mugs and followed. Trice wasn't in the living room where he thought she would be waiting. He took the dirty dishes to the kitchen sink. "Trice?"

"Up here."

He tracked her voice up the stairs to the loft master bedroom. What was going on?

"Drake? Are you coming?"

He stopped in the bedroom doorway. His heartbeat bumped up three paces. Trice wore one of his dress shirts and stood in the middle of the room. Sexiest sight he'd ever seen. He hoped he wasn't reading this view wrong.

"I thought we could start the tour here. If you don't mind?" Her sweet voice pulled him to her.

He looked at her from head to toe. His gaze captured hers, held as he deliberately walked her direction. "You better not be teasing me, Trice."

A Mona Lisa smile graced her lips. She placed a hand on his chest over his heart. "I would never tease about something so important."

Drake's anticipation went up. Being with him was important to her. One of his hands went to the hem of his shirt, his fingertips brushing the smooth skin of her outer thigh.

Trice's intake of breath told him she was as aware of the sexual tension in the room as he was. Yet she didn't move. Instead, her expression dared him. "I don't think my shirt ever looked this good on me."

She stepped back a couple of paces. "This old thing?"

He moved toward her. "That happens to be my newest shirt."

"That must be why it was hanging on the closet door." She took another step back.

"I was planning to pack it." He moved forward.

That took some of the light out of her eyes. "Let's not talk about that."

"Agreed. What would you like to talk about?"

"I'd rather you kiss me. I like your kisses."

Drake reached for her. His mouth found hers. Trice's arms circled his neck. His hands at her waist pulled her to him. She used her fingers on his shoulders to come up on her toes to reach his lips.

This time he made sure his hands stayed on her hips, not touching her back. Trice didn't make him request she open her mouth. She invited and welcomed him. He might combust right then if he wasn't careful. She never stopped surprising him.

Trice ran her fingers through the hair at the nape of his neck, urging him to deepen the kiss. He didn't disappoint her. His tongue twirled with hers. She pressed against him. His manhood throbbed with desire.

His hand slid over her hip to her thigh. He ran his palm along it, then up and down again to return. The last time he stopped at the elastic of her panties. His index finger nudged under the panty line.

Trice moaned and shifted her hips, her lips placing kisses along his jaw.

His finger moved lower toward the junction of her legs. Heat dwelled there. She shifted, opening her legs. An encouragement. One he didn't need but appreciated. He retreated. This time her moan was more of a complaint.

"Patience, my eager lovely." He went down on a knee and reached under her shirt until he found the top of her panties.

Trice's hands came to rest on his shoulders for support. He slowly removed the material as if revealing a present at Christmas. A perfect present. One he had asked for.

She shimmied and the panties fell to her feet. He had to focus on a spot beyond her for fear he might explode right then. Trice had him thinking and acting like a man starved for a woman. He was. For her. Hooking the tiny piece of clothing on her foot, she lifted it and flung it across the room.

He captured a thigh with a hand.

"Drake." His name was nothing more than a whisper.

He kissed the inside of her thigh. "Sweet."

Trice quivered. Her fingers brushed the hair at the top of his head.

"Liked that, did you?"

She tugged on his hair.

He stood. Her lips found his. Her hands went under his shirt and lifted it. He stepped back and scooped it off, letting it drop to the floor. Trice's palms rested on his pectorals. She ran her hands up and along his shoulders. He remained still, soaking in the pleasure of her touch. His hands rested on her hips. He was ever mindful of her back.

"This is nice," she murmured across his chest before she kissed him just below his neck.

His lips found hers. Tasted and absorbed the brilliance

of her. The feel of her against him. Drake wanted this to go on forever. He paused. But it couldn't.

Trice studied him a moment. "Everything okay? Did I do something wrong? You want me to go?"

She acted so secure, yet with the slightest suggestion she might not be wanted, she overcompensated. He forgot how vulnerable her background made her. "Sweetheart, if you left now, I would have to follow you."

A soft smile formed on her lips. "Would you?"

"All the way to your front door, begging you to come back."

She grinned. "I like the idea of seeing the whole town watching you."

His gaze fixed on hers. "I'm not ashamed of everyone knowing I'm crazy about you."

Trice's smile grew wider. "I'm crazy about you too. Please kiss me again. I like it when you kiss me."

He cupped her face. His lips touched hers, wanting her to know he meant everything he had said. Her arms came around him, and she hugged him as if he were her lifeline. Her hands roamed his chest, then his back. He loved being in her arms. Couldn't get enough of it. Drake wanted to trace her smooth, hot skin once more. Running his hands down her neck, over the ridge of her shoulders, he then moved them to her waist. There he gathered the shirt until his fingers found what he searched for. His hands traveled over the spheres of her butt, pulling her to him, raising her to her toes.

She brushed her center against his solid length. It strained, held in check by his jeans. He lowered her along him. She kissed his neck, then nibbled at the same spot. Holding her with a hand at the waist, he eased his other hand to her center. Wet heat waited for him. Heated his blood. Thrilled him.

Trice's breath caught. She widened her stance, giving clear access. He accepted it. Slipping his finger inside, he felt her tighten around him. She stilled, gripping his shoulders. He pulled his finger from her and entered again.

Trice leaned against him. He held her low on the waist, still aware of her injury. She lowered against his finger and rose again. He gave her what she wanted, pushed upward.

Finding her small nub, he teased her with the tip of his finger. She tensed and groaned, wiggling against his manipulations. After three quick inhales, she ground out, "Drake, please."

Picking up the speed of the movement of his finger, he held her pressed against him. With a sound of joy, she plummeted over the edge to her release.

Drake grinned when her knees buckled and she went limp against him. He swept her into his arms and carried her to the bed. Laying her carefully on it, he came down beside her.

CHAPTER EIGHT

TRICE BASKED IN the gratification of Drake's lovemaking. She lay on the bed with her eyes closed, regaining her breath and composure. Her dazed look met Drake's. A grin rode his lips. The man was pleased with himself. He should be.

She reached for him. He came to her. "It's time I return the favor."

"That sounds nice."

"Lie back." He did. She kissed him. Her hands roamed his chest and stopped to remove his belt. She released it and tugged it from the belt loops, dropping it to the floor.

"Let me help." Drake sat up beside her, then quickly removed his socks before standing to take off the rest of his clothes. They were dropped to the floor.

She watched with appreciation. His body was well taken care of. Drake stood in front of her in all his bare splendor, then came down beside her. Trice sucked in a breath. She'd seen many male bodies, but none were as magnificent as Drake's. The thought that he wanted her humbled Trice. He looked into her eyes as if he really saw her.

Trice shifted. "You are staring. You're starting to embarrass me."

Drake cupped her cheek. "I was just marking you in my memory, thinking how beautiful you look." His finger drifted away from her face to travel along her neck to the first button of the shirt. He flipped it open.

Trice's breath came faster with every movement of his fingers. She squirmed.

"Please don't move." His focus shifted lower. With each empty buttonhole, the shirt revealed more of her to his view. Drake's eyes burned bright with desire, which fueled her own.

Drake stopped the descent just below her belly button. He ran the back of his hand slowly back up, ending between her breasts. Using only a finger, he pushed the shirt away enough to reveal a breast.

Her center throbbed as Drake lowered his mouth to cover her nipple. Heat flooded her. Her breath came in jerks. Could she stand much more of this? Could she live without it?

Drake nudged her gently to her back, shifting the shirt to reveal both her breasts. His mouth moved to her other breast. Could anything feel so wonderful as having Drake's lips on her? Her fingers played in his hair as he teased and lavished attention on her nipples.

His hand rested on her middle. He found the last two buttons on the shirt and released them, leaving her completely exposed.

"You're so amazing." Drake kissed her belly button. His mouth whispered over her skin until his lips found hers. His hand dipped lower to tease her center.

Two could play that game. Trice's hand wrapped his solid length.

Drake stilled. A moment later, he removed her hand. He looked at her. "Trice, I want you and can't wait any longer to have you. Say you want me too."

"I want you."

Drake rolled away and pulled out the bedside table

drawer. He removed a square package, covered himself and turned to her. Reaching beyond her, he placed a pillow beside her. "I don't want to be responsible for hurting you further. Let's put the pillow behind your back."

"I have a better idea." She tugged on his hand. "You lie down."

He did. She straddled him. Drake's eyes widened a second before a wicked gleam entered them. She leaned down to kiss him, her hair creating a curtain. His hands found her waist and skimmed upward until he held a breast in each hand.

Trice lifted on her knees, bringing her center over the tip of his manhood. Slowly she lowered herself down on him. With a sharp lift of his hips, she captured all of him. She moved in a steady up-and-down motion.

She looked at Drake. His eyes were closed, and his face was twisted in a look of unspoiled pleasure. Suddenly he flipped her, braced on his hands he rose over her and re-entered with gentleness. Even during his fierce desire, he showed concerned for her injury. He plunged full-hilt and sent her spiraling into the clouds. She hung there, absorbing the bliss and slowly floating back to reality.

Drake's look locked with hers. He retreated and returned, as he drove toward his release. He groaned her name long and reverently before he fell to the bed beside her. With his breathing still deep and quick, he pulled her close and kissed the top of her ear.

Trice smiled and placed her hand over his resting on her stomach.

Drake woke in a panic in the middle of the night. He was in trouble. Big trouble. Like nothing he had ever known. Worse than the fifth grade when he had two girlfriends at the same time. He cared for Trice, far more than he should. This time he couldn't just break up with her and move on. Trice wouldn't be easily pushed away or dismissed.

He had plans. Plans he needed to keep. Important plans. But he couldn't have it both ways. Trice wanted what he was leaving. More than that, he needed to use his skills. He needed to finish his training. That would never happen in Seydisfjordur. There just wasn't the population to give him enough experience.

Could he ask her to come with him? Would she? Did she care for him enough to do that?

"Hey," Trice said from where she slept curled against his side. "Something wrong?"

"Nothing." And everything. "Except I'm not making love to you."

Her hand ran across his chest and back, caressing him, encouraging. "You can remedy that, Doc."

He rolled toward her. "You think I'm just the medicine you need."

She kissed him. "I know you are."

He groaned when she ran a finger along his already hardening manhood. "You keep that up and I'll be the answer to all your problems."

Her look turned sassy. "Who says you aren't already?"

Drake wished he was. He feared he had created more problems, but he couldn't have stop himself. Trice made his heart swell and his body hum. "Back okay?"

"I'll be fine. Just kiss me."

He would take the here and now and worry about later—later.

That morning, he slipped out of bed, leaving a soft, warm Trice behind. Maybe if he went into another room, he could think clearer. Figure out how to complete his surgery training and have Trice at the same time.

In the kitchen he prepared a light breakfast. He had his head straightened out by then. His determination was back in place. He would be leaving in a few days. He had his spot waiting on him in London. If he didn't take it, then it might be years before he had another chance. Trice would be a wonderful memory. With that decided, he would make the most of the time he had with her.

He jerked to a stop in the doorway. She still lay facedown on his sheets. The sun streaming across Trice's bare skin made it glow. The sight had him filing it away in his memory.

Drake recognized the moment Trice woke. She stretched like a feline, coming up on her hands and lifting her behind in the air, and then bringing her abdomen to the sheets again. His manhood shot to ready in seconds, watching her erotic movements. His flannel sleep pants did little to cover his reaction. The tray in his hand shook. He carried it with the steaming mugs of coffee, boiled eggs and toast to the bedside table. "Good morning, sleepyhead. I was starting to think you were never going to wake."

"Good morning. What have you been up to?"

"I thought you might like something to eat." He placed the tray on the bedside table before he dropped it.

"You are always so considerate." Her hand brushed his arm from elbow to wrist. "Where's my…uh…your shirt?"

"Don't feel like you need to put something on for me." Drake found the shirt and handed it to her.

She turned her back to him, slipping her arms in the sleeves, then buttoning it. "What time is it?"

Disappointment filled him, but it was probably just as well. He needed the distraction. "It's still early."

"We should be at the clinic on time since we were gone a day and a half. I still have to prove myself. I want the town to know I'll be there for them."

Unlike what he would be for his grandmother. Still, she was the one pushing him to go. Trice would be here. She would be here to see to Luce. But it was his responsibility. He had to move past this. Up until ten days ago, he'd had it all settled in his mind. Now uncertainly had creeped in. Slowly Trice had become the center of his world. That had to end.

Trice raised her arms in the air for another big stretch. She looked at the tray. "What do you have here?"

"Our breakfast." He picked up the tray and set it in the center of the bed.

"Looks good. We'll get food all over your sheets." She picked up a napkin.

"Like I care about that."

She grinned. "You might not until you wake with crumbs all over you." She took a bite of toast, making sure to keep it over the tray.

Drake enjoyed a nice view of her breasts in the gaping shirt.

She looked toward the window. "This I could get used to, waking up to this green valley with the ice blue of the fjord surrounded by the snow-tipped mountains. I can imagine watching a storm coming is magnificent."

He knew all the views well. But he must give those and other things up to reach his goal. "Almost as magnificent as the view I have now."

Trice followed the direction on his look. She sat straighter. "I don't see how you can leave this house either. Are you going to sell it?"

"No. My family will come here for holidays and visits.

My parents built this house. For the view. I bought it when they moved." He took a bite out of a boiled egg.

She added butter to her bread. "I've seen nothing in the village like it."

"No, all the materials had to be shipped in. It took a couple years before we could move in. Everyone said Dad was crazy to put all the glass in the house since it's so cold here, but my parents wanted to feel like a part of nature. They felt like the view was worth it. There is special wire in the glass to warm it. They also added special insulation and thick drapes that disappear into a wall pocket that are used for heat and light control on the long days."

Trice shook her head. "I don't see how you can leave it."

"You're not making this any easier."

"I'm sorry. That isn't my intent." She took a sip of coffee looking at him over the rim. "Do you think you will have a chance today to call Mr. Bjonsson?"

"For you I will make a point to. I'd like to be the one to introduce you."

She put her mug down on the tray. "I better get dressed so you can take me home to get changed." She moved to get off the bed.

"Before you do that, let me check your back." He went to her side of the bed.

"You're still worried about my back?"

"I hope I didn't make it worse."

She looked directly at him. "It is fine. If it weren't, it would have been worth it."

"I'll take that as a compliment." He grinned. "You'll have to take the shirt off."

She looked over her shoulder with a teasing grin. "Are you sure you're not just doing this to get me to undressed?"

"I can't deny the idea has appeal. But I actually want to

have a look at your back." He moved the tray back to the bedside table.

"You didn't hurt me, I promise." She lowered the shirt over her shoulders while looking back at him.

"Quit arguing. I would like to see for myself." He kissed her shoulder and down her back. "I think you'll recover nicely." He reached around her to cup her breasts.

She leaned against him. Her warmth met his heat. "How much time do we have?"

He turned her to face him. "Enough."

Trice watched Drake put the last stitch in the nine-year-old boy's head. The child had fallen and busted his head open. Drake had great surgery skills. He hadn't hesitated about handling the emergency. He had swiftly and confidently prepared the area while at the same time putting the boy and his mother at ease.

As much as Trice hated to see him leave, she understood he had commitments he must honor. His skills were too great for a small clinic that would see little need. Still, she dreaded the time she had to watch him go. She had made a deal with herself not to think about how many days Drake had left. Her plan was to make the most out of the time they had together.

She had to remain strong and detached if she wanted to survive.

That morning after breakfast, they had made love in the sunshine. Never had she been quite as free or bold in her lovemaking, confident in her body. She spent most of her life insecure in her personal relationships because she had had so few, but with Drake she had opened up and given her all. He had given her that security and confidence. For that she would always be grateful.

The next man in her life would have a lot to live up to after Drake. As if by a silent mutual agreement, they had decided not to discuss him leaving, as if they were going to pretend he would always be there.

She stood there and watched Drake tie off the last stitch and snip off the thread like a lovesick teen. Love? Was she in love with him? She had only known him a little over a week. She couldn't be. Love took longer than that to develop. Yet the moments they had shared had been more intense than any she had ever felt.

The bell ringing on the door of the clinic refocused her attention. She stepped out of the exam room and walked down the short hall to the front. "Can I help you?"

"We are here to see Dr. Stevansson." A middle-aged woman stood there with a preteen girl beside her.

"I'll be taking over for Dr. Stevansson." Trice didn't like the taste of those words on her tongue. She wished Drake would be here tomorrow, the next day and all those that would fellow. "I'm Dr. Shell."

"You're the woman who saved those two men's lives," the preteen stated.

"That was more of a team effort." Trice looked between the woman and the girl. "Now, what can I do for you?"

The woman lifted her foot. "I have foot pain. I thought it was getting better, but this morning I could hardly stand."

"Come back this way." Trice turned toward the examination room.

The woman hobbled across the floor, supported by the girl.

Trice pointed to the examination room. "Please have a seat in the chair. What's your name?"

"Maude Traustason. This is my daughter, Lula."

The girl stood beside the woman.

"Nice to meet you both. Well, Maude, can you tell me what's going on with your foot?" Trice pulled the stool forward and took a seat.

"Drake says I have plantar fasciitis. He told me to soak it, but I don't have time. I have to work at the cannery and take care of my kids. Is there something else I can do?"

"Please take your shoe and sock off and let me have a look." While the woman removed them, Trice continued, "Do you stand on cement all day? Or sit at a desk?"

"I walk on cement most of the time." The woman dropped a shoe to the floor.

"Have you been taking an anti-inflammatory?"

She peeled off her sock. "I did for a while."

"Did it help?" Trice looked at the woman.

"It did."

"May I see your foot?" Trice rolled the stool closer and placed the lifted heel across her legs. The red angry skin made her flinch. It had to hurt. "I'm going to touch it." She looked at Maude. "Please don't kick me."

"It really hurts." Maude's face twisted up.

"I don't doubt it." Trice examined the foot with a gentle hand, then lowered it to the floor. She picked up the woman's shoe. "Is this what you wear to work?"

"Yes."

"Then I would suggest you get a pair with more support. Especially in the heel area. Did Dr. Stevansson give you some exercises to do?"

"He did."

"Good. Be creative about when you do them. At work when you have a moment, do just one or two at a time. At night I want you to soak your feet. Others will have to help—" she looked at the girl "—or you'll just have to let something go, or this won't get better. I also want you to take an anti-inflammatory on the days you work, and come back to see me if you aren't better in two weeks. I can't stress enough that soaking your feet is important."

The woman nodded. "Okay."

"And you really should buy some better shoes."

"All right."

She glanced at Drake standing at the door. He had been listening. She felt him come up a few minutes earlier. Her body had a way of knowing he was around. He had a way of muddling her mind as well. She needed to concentrate on what she was there for and not Drake.

Trice placed Maude's foot on the floor. "May I ask you a medical history question?"

"Okay." Maude looked at her.

"Do you or any of the members of your family have HEP? I'm doing a research project on HEP and would like to interview anyone who has it."

Maude looked at her, not saying anything for a moment, as if deciding if she would offer any help. "I carry the gene. My sister does too."

Trice worked at containing her joy. "Would you be willing to answer a list of questions and allow me to view your medical records?"

Maude appeared unsure but said, "I guess so."

"I'll let you put on your sock and shoe while I go get the questions." Trice hurried toward the door.

Drake stepped out of the doorway to let her pass.

She returned with her electronic pad. Drake ended his conversation with Maude's daughter and left the room. Trice handed the pad to Maude. "Here, if you would answer these, it would be wonderful. Do you mind if I take Lula for a soda while you're working?"

"That's fine." The woman went to work on the questions.

Trice led Lula toward the back of the building. "I know where Dr. Stevansson hides his soda."

They went to the kitchen area. Trice handed the girl a can of drink. In a falsetto high voice she said, "Don't tell Dr. Stevansson. It's our secret."

"What's going on in here?" Drake popped out from behind the doorframe.

Trice and Lula jumped.

"Caught you. Are you in my snacks again?" He looked from one to the other, then grinned. "Help yourself." He looked directly at Trice. "Since you already have."

"Lula, let's go see if your mother is finished." Trice ushered the girl out of the room as if they had gotten away with a crime.

Lula laughed.

Her mother handed the electronic pad to Trice when they entered. "All done."

Trice took the pad. "Thanks so much, Maude. I really appreciate it. Would you mind letting your sister know about my research and ask her if she would participate?"

Maude's lips thinned. "She doesn't come to town often."

"Do you happen to know any other people who might have the syndrome?" Trice needed to move forward with her project.

"I can ask at my knitting circle tonight. Maybe somebody there does or knows of somebody who does." Maude stood to leave.

Lula headed out the door with soda in hand.

"I would appreciate that." Trice smiled. "Come by and let me know how your foot is doing."

Maude stopped at the door. "Do you knit?"

Trice shook her head. "No, but I've always wanted to learn."

"Why don't you come to our circle tonight? You can meet everyone and give it a try."

Trice looked at Drake, who leaned against the doorframe, talking to Lula. She had planned to spend the evening with him.

He gave her a smile that didn't reach his eyes. "You should go. You will have fun."

She wasn't sure if she was disappointed he didn't discourage her or glad he was unselfish enough not to say anything. She needed to move beyond him anyway. What they had now wouldn't last. She had her future to consider.

Trice's attention returned to Maude. "Thanks. I'd love to come."

Maude smiled. "Good. We meet at Unndis Hanson's house. See you there."

"I don't have any supplies." Where would she find needles and yarn on such short notice?

Drake volunteered, "My mom left some of hers. They're at the house. I'll get them for you."

Trice could have kissed him. "Thanks, Drake. That would be nice."

Maude moved toward the door. "I'll call my sister on my way home. Thanks for your help."

"Come back if the foot doesn't get better. I'll be here to help." Trice saw her out the door. "I look forward to seeing you this evening."

Drake wanted to disagree with the evening plans, but he had no right. Trice needed to become a part of the community, find her own way, one that didn't involve him. He had made the choice to leave town. He shouldn't, wouldn't hold her back. Asking her to forgo the knitting group to spend time with him would be selfish. Her research was important to Trice, and more than, that it was important to people who had the disease. Yet he wanted Trice with him as much as possible.

After Maude and Lula had left, Trice kissed him, her eyes bright. "I am making progress. I'm so excited."

"I never doubted you. I think you can do anything you put your mind to."

She wrapped her hands around his bicep and pressed against him. "You're just being nice because you like me."

"True." He gave her an indulgent look.

"I'm going to clean up the examination room, then log in Maude's answers and get ready for tonight."

Trice sound so happy, he couldn't bring himself to complain about the plans. "I have some paperwork to do as well if I don't want to stay late tonight. I better get busy."

She gave him a searching look. "You're not angry, are you, about me going to the knitting meeting instead of spending the time with you?"

"No, no. You need to go to the knitting meeting. I understand that."

"I hope so. My research is really important to me. And I want to fit in here."

"I know." He did. What he'd taken for granted all these years, she desperately craved. "You should go."

She kissed him again. "I'm glad you understand."

He pulled her close. "I would understand better with another kiss."

For the next hour, they worked without interruption. Then Drake knocked on the office door where Trice worked. "How about having lunch with me?"

She looked up. "Shouldn't one of us be here?"

"I'll put a note on the door about where we are."

"Okay then." Trice stood.

Before they went out the door, he pulled her into his arms and kissed her. She wrapped her arms around his waist and returned his kiss.

Drake pulled away, looking into her eyes. "Let's forget lunch and lock the door."

Trice giggled, which only made him want to really do what he'd suggested.

She pulled away from him. "That wouldn't do much to instill faith in me. I need to make a good impression on the town."

"I believe you have that covered already." She'd proved her abilities more than once. Luce would be in good hands.

"I can't take any chances on messing that up. And I fear once I get started kissing you, I won't stop."

"Mmm. I like that idea." He gave her another quick but heated kiss.

She placed her hands on his chest. "We better have some lunch and stay out of trouble."

He opened the door. "It's too late for that."

Trice grinned, her look warm. "Maybe."

They headed down the street. Drake was tempted to take her hand but resisted doing so. He didn't know if Trice would appreciate everyone knowing something was happening between them. He was confident that if anyone saw him looking at Trice, they would know right away he was crazy about her.

"Where are we going?"

He pointed down the street. "To the diner for a sandwich."

"We could go to my place. I'll fix you a sandwich." Her eyes held a mischievous light.

"Dr. Shell, are you trying to lure me into bed in the middle of the day?"

"I was just trying to offer you lunch. No agenda." She stopped and fixed him with a twinkling look. "Unlike you, who had me come look at the stars, then lured me to your house to take advantage of me."

His look locked with hers. "I lured you? If I remember correctly, it was you waiting in my bedroom."

Her face pinked sweetly. "I hope I wasn't too bold."

Heat from the memory covered his body. "I couldn't have asked for a nicer welcome."

They continued walking. At the café, he held the door open. The noisy place went quiet. Everyone stopped what they were doing and clapped.

Trice looked at him, perplexed.

He said just for her ears, "They appreciated your work the other day. Come on, let's find a table." He directed her to one in a back corner. Trice took a chair on one side, and he took a chair on the other. He would have liked to have sat next to her, but that would have made his feelings too obvious.

A waitress came from the bar to take their order.

"I'm really looking forward to learning to knit. I'm amazed at all the community activities the town has." Trice was almost buzzing with excitement.

"In the dead of winter, we have to make our own enter-tainment. We have something almost nightly. In the nice months, we still like to get together. We especially enjoy our folk dancing and singing."

Trice sat forward. "You sing? I know you can dance."

"It's folk dancing. And yes, I do both well enough." He would miss that comradery when he moved to the large city.

"I'd like to hear you sing."

The eagerness in her eyes made him smile. "Maybe I'll

sing for you sometime." He looked around, "But it won't be in the middle of lunch."

"And I had so hoped…"

He laughed. "Trice, I think you could get me in trouble."

"Maybe you could teach me a folk dance."

He was impressed with her efforts to acclimatize to the town. He wasn't sure someone else would make the effort. He shouldn't have been surprised. She gave all of herself, and people responded to that. She certainly had to him last night. Like no one else ever had. His greatest fear was that he might not find someone who would ever give so freely again.

How could somebody possibly not want her in their life? He wanted her badly. The problem was, he had made plans that didn't include her. If he did stay, having Trice beside him would make it easier.

The waitress brought their meals, stopping his out-of-control thoughts.

"I meant to tell you on the way over here that I called Bjonsson."

She sat forward. "You did?"

"I didn't get to talk to him, but I left him a message with a woman who answered. She told me she would see to it that he got my message. I will try again before I leave, maybe drive up there."

"Hopefully he will contact you. I won't give up. I'll keep trying even after you are gone."

"I never doubted you would for a minute." He put his sandwich down. "Tomorrow night the town is throwing me a going-away party. Would you like to come?"

The light went out of her eyes. She raised her chin. "I've already been invited. Luce said something about it a few days ago."

"I should've known. It's hard to get ahead of her. Are you planning to come?"

She shook her head. "I don't think so."

He met Trice's eyes. "I'd like for you to be there."

Trice said nothing for a long minute. "I will come if you really want me there."

He moved his legs so hers fit between them and gave them a gentle squeeze.

"You know," she said, "I'm starting to have a very busy social life. I may get busy at the last minute."

"My party is going to be the event of the year, so I don't think I need to worry." At least her good humor had returned.

"It will be another good opportunity for me to meet people."

"I agree. And I promise to help you in that area." He leaned forward so only she would hear him. "Now, how do you plan to repay me?"

She put a finger to her chin as if considering. "I haven't thought about it."

He leaned forward. "Maybe an early thank-you?"

"Like?" She acted innocent.

"I was thinking I could come by after the knitting meeting." Dared he hope she would agree?

"It'll be kind of late."

He crossed his arms and laid them on the table, putting him that much closer to her. "Are you trying to get rid of me already?" He was half teasing and half serious.

"No, I'm trying to figure out how to live without you."

Those words were like a punch in the chest. He hadn't meant to hurt her. Had tried not to. Luce had been right. He should have stayed away.

"I've been thinking maybe we shouldn't see each other

again. I'll be alone in a couple nights anyway." Her eyes remained downcast.

"I'm sorry. I just made this assumption that we would see each other every night until I left. My apologies. I shouldn't have done that. I know this isn't easy for you."

"I should be used to it. It has happened enough in my life."

"It wasn't my intention to hurt you." His hand covered hers. He no longer cared what others saw or thought. Trice was hurting because of him.

Trice pulled her hand away and put a smile on her face. "Enough of this. I knew the score when I arrived. After all, I came here to take your place." She shook her head. "Let's enjoy what time we have and not talk about the future."

They both returned to their meal.

He gave a curt nod. Despite the pleasant conversation he tried to participate in, the food in his stomach had soured.

CHAPTER NINE

AFTER THEIR LUNCH, she and Drake strolled back to the clinic. There he left her to oversee the clinic while working on her research. He drove home, returning with a cloth bag containing two knitting needles and a skein of navy yarn.

"This is wonderful. Thank you so much. Are you sure your mother won't mind?"

"Positive. Now you're all set for this evening."

She wished his support reached his eyes. "I have to say I'm looking forward to it."

"Mind if I walk you to the Hansons' later?" He looked like a puppy left behind.

Trice had to give him something. "Oh, course not."

That brightened his face. She would miss him tonight. Still, she didn't enjoy being a foregone conclusion for the next few nights. Maybe it was just as well they let things stay at a one-night event. Still, she hated seeing Drake look disappointed. "I'm actually nervous about this. I've never had a chance to socialize with a bunch of women. What if they don't like me?"

He roared with laughter. "Like that's going to happen. Everyone you meet likes you."

At the knock on her door, she opened it to Drake. She grabbed her sweater and the knitting bag and stepped outside.

He grinned. "You are excited about this evening."

"I am." She headed toward the street.

His hand on her arm stopped her. "Hold on a minute. I have something I need to do."

Drake's gaze held hers before his face came down to hers. The kiss was sweet, tender. Unlike any other kiss they had shared. With this one, he was trying to tell her something. Did she dare believe he really cared?

He pulled away and rested his forehead against hers. Her breathing had increased. She placed a hand over his heart. The rapid thump there matched hers. "Luce is going to be watching."

"I have no doubt. Luce knows exactly what we've been doing. She knows everything. She'll have something to say about it. She has already gotten on to me."

"For what?"

"She told me not to hurt you."

Trice straightened. "I'm tougher than that."

"I wish I could say the same."

She studied him a moment. "What do you mean by that?"

He met her look. "I'm going to miss you, Beatrice Shell. A lot."

"I will miss you too." She hurt at the thought.

"Maybe our paths will cross again one day."

Many families and temporary friends had said the same to her over the years. None of them had she ever seen again. People got busy. They didn't care enough. She was just forgotten. "Let's enjoy knowing each other now." She stepped out of his reach. "I need to go. I don't want to be late."

A few minutes' walk later, she hesitated at the Hansons' front door.

Drake's hand on her waist was warm and reassuring. He

gave her a nudge. "Go on. They will love you. You will have a good time. I'll see you in the morning."

She wanted to turn and walk away with him, but she didn't. Drake didn't even look back to see if she had gone inside. If he had, she would have run to him. Bracing herself, she knocked on the door.

A woman opened the door and invited her in. The living area was bright. Women stood around in groups talking. She moved further into the room without anyone making eye contact or speaking. Worry started to creep in.

Some people could be reserved about talking to anyone new. Trice understood that well. She had hoped tonight would be different. A moment later, Maude hurried toward her.

"Come sit beside me." Maude returned to a chair across the room. "I see you brought something to work with. Good."

The other women in the room moved to their chairs as well.

Trice waited, watching the other women remove their needles and yarn. As if in unison, they began moving their needles, creating a click-click sound while looping yarn. Moments later, they were in conversation about someone she didn't know.

Maude said, "Let me show you."

Trice removed her materials.

Maude said, "Take the needles and hold them in your fingers like this. Attach the yarn."

Trice followed the instructions the best she could. After a couple of false starts, she managed the basics. Soon she had created a row of stitches.

"Now you have to go back the other way."

Trice almost groaned, but she made the effort. Minutes

later, she had another row, but with a number of uneven loops. Still, she was proud of her efforts.

While knitting, she listened to the conversations about who was pregnant, who was sick and who would be marrying soon. These were all parts of life within a community. People she would be caring for over the next year, the baby she would help deliver. Her eyes watered. This was part of belonging. A life she had never known. But might have found.

"Dr. Shell, did you really climb down and save two men?" one of the younger women asked.

Trice laid her knitting in her lap. She wouldn't be able to concentrate and talk at the same time. There had been medical problems to solve that had been less frustrating than figuring out how to make identical loops. "I wouldn't exactly put it that way, but yeah. I was the one who climbed down, only because I was the smallest. I could fit in the crevice. And please call me Trice."

She had the entire room's attention. Someone said, "That must've been scary."

Another lady said, "I couldn't have done it."

Trice gave them an indulgent smile. "It was scary more after the fact than at the time. I just did what needed to be done."

"That's pretty impressive," someone else said.

The entire time, their needles never stopped.

Trice cleared her throat, hoping it wasn't too early for this conversation. "As I'm sure you know, I'm taking Dr. Stevansson's place for the next year. While I'm doing that, I will also be doing some research work." This was her chance to say something about HEP. "My research is studying HEP."

The blank faces of the women told her more explanation would be needed. Trice took a moment to explain the disorder. A number of the women nodded, now understanding what she was referring to.

Trice leaned forward. "In fact, I could use your help. I need to speak to anyone who has had HEP or is willing to be tested for it. If you have had it or know someone who has been tested for it, I would really appreciate you letting me know. I promise there will be nothing or very little that is painful involved."

The room went quiet. The circle just looked at her, saying nothing. Watching.

Trice broke the silence. "I have it. I learned about it when I became sick. That's when I became interested in the disorder. I want to learn more about the disease. I can do that by talking to people."

Suspicion filled the women's eyes. Maybe Trice should have waited on Drake to say something about it. But he had his own life to worry about. He was packing to leave and tying up business. She couldn't depend on him. He would soon be gone.

A woman shifted in her chair. "I was sick with it as a child, and my daughter as well."

Excitement filled Trice's chest. Maybe this would work. "Will you come to see me one day next week? Bring your daughter as well."

The mother nodded.

"Thank you. That would be wonderful."

Another said, "I think my neighbor had it. I'll tell her to come see you."

"I would appreciate it." Trice couldn't help the thrill going through her. She had made progress. Picking up her knitting again, she tried to get in the groove.

Nobody else said anything for a couple of minutes as they returned to their work. Finally, one of the older women said with a sly grin, "What do you think of Drake? He seems to like you."

Each woman eagerly watched her. Their hands automatically moved the needles, but their looks stayed with her. Trice's body warmed. Her hands shook, causing her to drop a loop. "I think he is a great doctor. I know you will miss him."

"He seems smitten with you," a woman with a toothless grin said.

"We are friends." Trice should have expected this. Prepared herself for it.

A giggle went around the room.

"Maybe she could get him to stay," a woman on the other side of Maude said.

Trice looked at each of the women. "I won't be doing that."

Maude took pity on Trice and asked one of the women a question, moving the attention away from her and Drake. Trice wasn't interested in sharing what was happening between them. It was too new and was going to be too short.

The meeting broke up. Trice packed her knitting carefully away. She would continue to practice. Maybe make something for Drake and send it to him. No. They had agreed their fling would end when he left. That would mean no contact.

Trice stepped out into the dim light, fully expecting to find Drake waiting for her. He wasn't. She couldn't help but be disappointed. He was doing as she'd asked. She started home. This time she wished he hadn't abided by her request.

It didn't take her long to walk past Luce's front door and round the corner toward her own home. Her home. She liked the sound of that. It was a small space, but she'd never had a spot all her own. She had always shared with someone else. All her personal belongs could fill her suitcase, but here she had more. It was a place that needed her and where she could belong.

Trice opened her door to the lone light she'd left on. Again a sense of disappointment went through her. Drake wasn't there. She had to move past this expectation. He would be in a matter of days. She had to learn to do without him.

She went about getting ready for bed, and still there was no knock on the door. Wearing her warm pajamas, she climbed under the covers, then turned off the light. She tossed and turned, thinking of how little time she had to spend with Drake. Worse, she had told him she wouldn't see him personally again. Why had she insisted on doing that? To protect herself.

She was only hurting herself. Early in her life, she had learned not to let anyone close because she would soon leave, but this time she wanted as much of Drake as she could get. They had so little time. She wanted to create more happy memories.

At the tap on her window, she jerked straight up. Another tap. She walked to the window. A face was pressed against it. Drake.

He pointed toward the door.

She hurried to it. "What are you doing here in the middle of the night? Is something wrong?"

He stepped into her personal space, far enough that she stepped back. He kept coming, closing the door behind him. "Yes, there is."

"I'll get dressed."

"I was thinking you need to get undressed."

Trice met his look. His eyes held a predatory gleam. "What are you up to?"

"I came to see you. I missed you. I couldn't sleep." He sounded pitiful.

She liked the idea of him needing her. "Why were you tapping on the window instead of knocking on the door?"

"I was trying to be quiet." He moved toward her again. This time her back came up against the wall. "Luce has ears like a twenty-year-old." His lips brushed hers. His cool hands came to rest under her pajama top at her waist.

She shuddered. "Your hands are freezing."

"How about warming them up?" He nuzzled her neck.

She gave him a light slap on the shoulder. "You're crazy. People are already talking about us."

"So? We're adults." His lips found hers before they traveled down her neck, leaving kisses along the way. "You will let me stay the night, won't you?"

She couldn't resist him. "What kind of doctor would I be if I didn't take care of a man in need of warming?"

"My thoughts exactly." His lips met hers as he brought her against him. He began walking her backwards towards the bed.

Sometime later, Trice lay beside Drake, her head resting on his shoulder and her hand tracing circles on his chest. Why couldn't she have this all the time? Life seemed to always be shoving her out of the way.

"You know, I could do this forever." Drake gave her a gentle squeeze.

"It is nice."

"I wish we had longer. We only have tomorrow night left, and part of that will be taken up with my going-away party." He sounded as if he'd like to forget about the party.

She kissed the side of his jaw. "We agreed not to talk about you leaving."

"I know, but I think we should." He rolled so he could see her face.

"And accomplish what?" She didn't want to go down this road. It was too muddy, sticky.

"I was hoping for a compromise. Will you come visit me? I could come here some." Even he didn't sound confident about how that would work.

Her hand fell away from his chest. "I would like that. But soon it would become difficult for us to get away. Then slowly we would get too busy to see each other at all. We would just be prolonging the inevitable. I've lived it all my life."

Drake's face turned to one of hurt and disappointment. "You don't even want to try?"

"I have tried—before. Everyone says they will stay in touch, but no one does. It's a lot more painful to let things drag on. To hope for a phone call. To look for a letter. To make plans that must be canceled. You need to leave here and embrace your new life. It's what you want. I need to find my place in the world. Let's make the most of the here and now." She brushed her fingertip across his chest.

"You don't have much faith in people, do you? I'm not one of those who will forget you. You don't have to be alone all your life. Have you ever thought it was a two-way street? That you could have tried to stay in contact as well?"

"I was a child—"

"But what about those you went to medical school with? How many of those people have you tried to stay in touch with? Or your last foster mother?"

"I…uh…"

"Exactly. I think we have something worth trying to build on. But both of us have to want it. To work at it. Have faith that we can do it. I know your past tells you that there are no lasting relationships, but I care about you. I won't let you go."

She shook her head.

A deep sadness filled his eyes. "You won't even try, will you?"

"You have an intense year ahead of you. You won't have time to come here. You shouldn't have distractions. I'm not going anywhere at least for a year. I can't just leave anytime I want, and neither will you be able to."

A stream of anger went through Drake. "I have agreements and obligations as well. I've been trying to get back to my surgery training for two years. If I don't go now, I might never get to go. Space may not open up at another time. What I learn could make the difference in someone's life. Even my grandmother's. She isn't getting any younger. Now is my chance to get that training."

Trice pushed up on an elbow so their looks met. "I don't blame you. Your skills are needed. That's how I felt about coming here. It was something I had to do."

"It would be too difficult to get another placement." He needed the training to bring it home to Iceland.

"Hey, I'm not asking you to stay for me. I would never do that no matter how tempted I am to do so. We need to face it. The time just isn't right for us."

He wanted to shake her. "I don't want to accept that. You're too important to me."

She lay beside him again. "You can't accept it because you've never had to live it."

"I'm not one of those who will forget you when I'm gone. You don't give me enough credit."

Trice offered him a wry smile. "I have to go with what I know."

"I can and will prove you wrong. What will you do when you leave here?"

"I don't know. I'll be trying to get my research paper published. Then find a place to practice medicine. If they will have me, I might stay here."

She wanted what he was giving up. Why had he found her now? "Why here?"

"I really like it. I feel at home."

Just as it had been to him. "You wait until you spend a winter here. You might change your mind. I was hoping you might come to London. We could come back to Iceland when the time was right."

"You know that isn't easy for an American."

"Could we at least stay in contact? Online. Write."

She sighed and rolled over on him. "Why don't we concentrate on another form of communication right now?"

He ran his hands gently up her smooth back while she gave him a wet, hot kiss. He must find a way to keep her in his arms.

Trice woke when Drake left her bed early, before daylight, with a sweet kiss that had her reaching to hold him to her. How would she survive when he left? She didn't want to consider it, but that was all she could think about. She wanted to forget about their conversation. It had hurt too much to tell him no. To discourage him. Some of what Drake had said was true. That wasn't what really bothered her. The problem was, she had been left after promises had been made to keep in contact. Too many times that had failed.

All she said was true. In time they would get too busy for each other. Distance would kill what they had. It was easier just to shut it down now. She had never intended for it to get this complicated.

In fact, it should've been only for one night and that's it. They had both known the score going in. The plan had been for their relationship to remain short and sweet. They should have kept it that way, but she couldn't. She wanted Drake too badly. Now she would put it all behind her. Her life had given her plenty of experience in how to do that.

He would be gone in little more than twenty-four hours. After that, she would figure out how to survive. If he managed to return for a visit or they had a chance to see each other, she would make the most of that as well. She had no doubt he would soon find somebody in the big city of London. It wouldn't take much for him to forget her. Of this she was confident.

Drake's surgery training should take priority. He had made it clear what his dream was. That meant he needed to leave Seydisfjordur. She wouldn't be a part of making him unhappy. That she promised herself and him as well.

Not a person to scare easily, she was terrified now. With knowledge of a few relationships, and none of those ending well, she had no doubt she and Drake would end the same way. Yet she dared to dream they could be different. That they might really have something worth fighting for.

He'd been more than a wonderful distraction. This was the first time she'd been in love. Drake's leaving would hurt. Deeply.

Entering the clinic, she found Drake in the storage room with his iPad in hand. "Hey."

His face lit up. He set his pad down and wrapped his arms around her. His lips found hers. She clung to him. He kissed her breathless. Her knees had gone weak by the time he let her go. "Will you come to my house after the party tonight? I still have that book to give you."

"How could I say no after that kiss? And I do want to read that book."

He grinned. "You are going to miss me."

Heaven help her, she was.

The rest of the day, she vacillated between walking on air and deep depression. She could hardly concentrate on her patients. To her great delight, two people came in to help with her research.

"You must have won them over last night," Drake commented after a man left.

Trice sat in the office. "I don't know about that."

"I've never known them to open up to a stranger like they have you. But you do have a way of bringing that out in people." He sounded proud of her, and she liked that idea.

"I wouldn't have thought that. It hasn't happened before." How many homes had she been in where she'd just blended into the background? They had decided she wasn't a good fit for them. In Seydisfjordur, she seemed to have blossomed.

"Will you be going back to the knitting circle?" He continued to lean against the doorframe.

"I think I will. I started a project, and I would like to try to finish it." She would return to the circle if for no other reason than being part of the group.

"And what is your project?"

She grinned "I hope it's the beginning of a hat."

"I'm impressed. I look forward to seeing it finished."

A hush filled the air. They both knew that wouldn't happen.

Trice quickly tried to cover up the heavy moment. "My knitting leaves a lot to be desired. I just have never been asked to be a part of something."

His brows rose. "Never? How could somebody not notice you are amazing?"

"Maybe a study group, but come to think of it, I asked them. It doesn't matter. It's just nice to have a place to belong."

Drake placed his arm around her shoulders, held her tight and kissed her temple. "Seydisfjordur is lucky they have you."

What had she done to deserve Drake? She was in trouble.

CHAPTER TEN

IT HAD BEEN a long time since Drake had been nervous before any event, especially one taking place in his hometown. Yet here he was, getting ready to face his family and friends, and tonight his hands were damp.

He couldn't believe he was this close to getting what he'd been dreaming of for so long. But the gloss was off because of Trice. How was he going to leave her? Her hand holding his bicep only reminded him of how much he wanted her close.

Drake opened the door to the community center. The group gathered must have been the entire town and surrounding area. The clapping started and continued to the point that he hung his head and shook it with embarrassment.

Trice moved off to the side, leaving him standing in the middle of a horseshoe of smiling people.

The longer he looked into the smiling faces of people he'd known all his life, the more overwhelmed he became.

The mayor stepped forward and commanded everyone's attention. It took a moment for the noise to die down. "We're going to have our meal and then the program."

Program? He hadn't expected that. The meal, yes, but that was all. He looked at Trice to see if she knew anything about that.

She pursed her lips and shrugged her shoulders. He wasn't getting any help there. Then Trice's mouth formed a smile. She apparently liked seeing him unsure. His grandmother proved even less help.

The mayor said to him, "Now, you and the new doctor go first. We have a place for you right up front at the main table."

He and Trice moved to the table that had so much food on it, he feared he heard it groan. He asked into Trice's ear, "Do you know what's going on?"

Over her shoulder, she said sweetly, "I have no idea. I believe most of this must've been planned a long time before I came. Here you had me believing you were a man who had his ear to the ground and knew everything going on in town."

The smile left his face. "Apparently not. Because I haven't heard a word about this."

"Just sit back and enjoy it. They're only showing you how valuable you have been to the community."

Why hadn't he put more value on that? He'd certainly known it where Dr. Johannsson had been concerned. He just had never thought of himself in the same terms.

Trice went about filling her plate. She stopped and looked at him. "Are you okay?"

"Yeah, yeah, I'm fine."

With food in hand, they were directed to the front table. Trice hesitated. "I shouldn't be seated up here."

"You're with me. My guest sits beside me." He needed her there.

People began filling the other tables. A number of them approached him to share how much they had appreciated him. Helga Olafsdottir told him thanks for taking care of her broken arm. Einar Abelsson said thanks for stitching up his hand. Lydia Einarsson, with her daughter on her hip, voiced her appreciation for delivering her baby. Mr. Jonsson hobbled up with his gout. Drake couldn't eat for the interruptions. Almost everyone in the room was a patient he had seen at one time or another.

A grizzly-looking man came to stand in front of Trice. He watched her. Said nothing. It took Drake a moment to recognize him. Drake had last seen him when he was a teenager. Even then it hadn't been but for a moment or two when Drake helped him out of the clinic.

She glanced at Drake, then looked at the man again. "Can I help you? Is there a problem?"

"I am Olafur Bjonsson."

Trice went statue-still, then jumped up and cut around the table. Drake hurried after her. He feared she might scare the man off.

Drake came to stand beside her, putting out his hand. "Mr. Bjonsson. Thank you for coming. I would like you to meet Dr. Beatrice Shell. As I said in my message, there is a chance you are related to each other."

Trice looked as if she wanted to throw her arms around the man. Her eyes glistened. Was she going to cry?

Olafur continued to study Trice. Then he grunted. "She looks like my aunt, Lilja Andresson, who ran off to America when I was a child."

Trice stared at the man. Her mouth opened, closed and opened again. Finally, she found her voice. "Can we talk sometime? Please. I would really like to get to know you. Learn about your family. Possibly mine."

He nodded.

"Thank you so much. I promise to call you."

Olafur nodded again, then walked away.

Trice hugged Drake. "Can you believe it? I really might have family."

He smiled indulgently. "It is wonderful. I wasn't sure he even got my message. I hated to leave when you had not made contact with him. I never imagined he would show up here."

"I can hardly wait to talk to him. I'll call him tomorrow. Do you think he has any pictures?" Her words were tumbling over each other.

"May I make a suggestion?"

"Sure." She watched him, all smiles.

Drake gave her an earnest look. "I would be careful not to overwhelm him. Go slow and easy."

She took a moment before she spoke. "You're right. I'll be careful. And go slow."

Another person came to speak to him. When that person left, he and Trice returned to their seats. People continued to stop and speak to him, give their thanks.

Trice said, "It must be gratifying to know you have meant so much to so many people."

"It is."

The mayor joined them on the other side of Drake and drew his attention away from Trice. Drake would have rather spent his time with Trice. This would be their last night together. He was too aware of time slipping away. If he wasn't careful, he would become melancholy.

He had spoken to the surgery program leader in London that afternoon. They were expecting him in three days. He had just enough time to get settled in a leased flat.

Drake had eaten little of his food when the mayor stood and tapped on his glass, calling the place to order. "Quiet, please. I have a few words. Drake Stevansson was born and raised here. He went off to college and medical school and returned to help us when we were in desperate need of a doctor. Now it's his turn to go off again and succeed in his training as a surgeon." He looked at Drake. "We are thankful you put your life on hold for these past two years for Seydisfjordur. I don't know what we would have done without you.

"In appreciation, we've all contributed to this gift wishing you the very best." The mayor handed Drake a thick envelope. "Use this to help with whatever you need."

Drake's throat had a knot in it. He worked to swallow. He was overwhelmed with the generosity. He stood. "I don't know what to say. This wasn't necessary. It's too kind. I've enjoyed being your doctor. I will be leaving you in good hands with Dr. Shell."

The entrance door burst open. In a frantic voice, a man yelled, "There's been an explosion at the cannery!"

Trice was right behind Drake as they exited the door. As he passed the mayor, he thrust the envelope back into the man's hand for safe keeping. He called over his shoulder, "Trice, go to the clinic and bring anything you think would be needed in an emergency. Just fill any bags you can find. We can send others after them. Then bring my bag." With that, he picked up his pace, leaving her behind.

Ahead of them, gray smoke billowed from the cannery located on the fjord on the other side of the airport. The blue sky framed the plume of smoke.

She ran to the clinic, wishing for more stable shoes than the ones she wore. Throwing open the door, she hurried down the hall to the supply room. She picked up a large duffel bag and began dumping gauze, antiseptic and tape into it. Soon she had almost cleaned out the supply bins.

She took a moment to pull on Drake's shoes, which she

had already borrowed once. With as much weight as she could carry, she started toward the door.

A man entered. "Drake said to come help you. I have a truck."

She thrust the bags at him. "Take these. I'll get the others. We're going to need blankets."

"People are gathering them. We should have some when we get to the cannery." The man headed out the door.

She returned to the supply room and picked up more supplies. With those in the truck, she climbed in the passenger seat.

The driver sped around the harbor. He honked the horn, clearing the people so they could get past. Three minutes later, they were traveling through the iron gates of the long red building.

Before the truck driver could pull to a complete stop at the front door, Trice had opened her door. She yelled, "Drake."

Another man loped up to them. "He's around this way."

"Hey, I need those two black bags on top," Trice stated.

The man reached over the side of the truck and grabbed the bags. Seconds later she was following him into the dim light of the building.

People were running around every which way.

"He'll be up these stairs in the boiler room." The man indicated the metal steps, and putting down the bags. "I'll go back for the supplies."

Trice hurried up the stairs. The area was almost dark. "Drake?"

"Here."

Relief filled her at the reassuring sound of his voice. She hurried forward.

"Trice, be careful. There is debris on the floor."

Her toe caught on a piece of metal. With luck, she remained upright. She kept moving. Finally she just made out the shape of Drake.

She dropped their bags beside him, then joined him on her knees. "How many people injured?"

"Ten that I know of. There are still eight missing." The pain of loss rang clearly in his voice.

She gave him an anxious look, grateful he was still in town for this event. She could have handled it, but she was glad to have his help. "What do you need me to do?"

"I need you to organize triage. Send four men to me with blankets. I'll have them carry some people out and lead the others. Set up triage as far away from the building as possible in case something is unsteady. So far, I've seen mostly minor things and breathing difficulties."

Trice stood. "I'll get started now." She turned away, then back again. "Drake. Be careful."

"I will." He refocused his attention on the man he cared for.

Trice hurried back outside. She found the man who had driven her. "I need you and three more men to go to Drake. He needs you to bring patients out here. I'll be setting up the triage area." She looked around her. "Over there in the parking lot for the injured. Bring them to me."

"Will do." The man called other men's names and headed inside.

A group of women came up to her. One said, "What can we do to help?"

"I'm setting up a triage station in the parking lot. I need the supplies in the back of that white truck and all the blankets you can find." Trice went to work seeing about the men and women Drake sent to her.

Marie, the nurse from the night of the dance, came to Trice. "What do I need to do to help?"

"See this patient gets oxygen." Trice moved on to the next patient. "This one needs stitches." She called to Marie. "Those—" she pointed to the patient's right side "—will have to wait. She will need to be moved to the clinic."

"A hospital has been set up in the community center. There are a few who live here with some basic medical skills. They are working there. She will be well taken care of until you or Drake can see her again." One of the women who had been helping Trice waved a man over. He loaded the patient in the back of a truck.

Trice liked being a part of a community who came together during a disaster, no matter how large it was. The people didn't wait on one person to make all the decisions. They saw a need and jumped in to fill it. This was the type of place she would like to call home.

Trice quickly assessed the next man's broken hand. Marie joined her. "This one needs his hand wrapped until we can x-ray it and set it."

The next man lay on a blanket.

"Where does it hurt?" Trice asked.

"My foot. Part of the tank fell on it."

Trice pulled his pants leg up to see the man's calf, which had started to swell. "Your foot is most likely broken. Leave it in the boot, which will give it support. We will set it later." She waved to one of the men helping. "Over here." The man stood above her and the patient. "This man needs to be put with the group who need an X-ray. Do not remove his boot. Understood?"

The man nodded.

Trice returned to see patients. The next had a superficial injury to the ankle. She left him for Marie to bandage. Thankfully the patients coming in were slowing. Since they had eased, Trice sent Marie to the community center to organize it and listed who needed to have care first. She also made lists of those who should be sent home after she or Drake saw them and people who needed attention overnight.

One of the men who had been helping Drake hurried up to Trice. "Drake needs your help inside. Can you come now?"

Fear went to her throat. "Is he okay?"

"Yes. He has a patient he needs help with."

Trice snatched up her bag. "Show me."

Drake hated to call Trice into such a dangerous situation, but he had no choice. He needed her assistance. He couldn't do this without her. Even then he wasn't sure they would manage to save the man's life.

"Drake. I'm here. What can I do?" She moved as fast as safety would allow.

He turned the flashlight on the man crushed between a large boiler and a beam.

"Oh, Drake. Is he still alive?"

"He is. I'm treating him for shock. He needs a blood transfusion." His voice held concern.

"Do you know his blood type? I'll start typing blood and getting more donated." She would see to that as soon as she returned to the outside.

"I'm going with O. I already have some of the men rounding up people."

"Send them to the clinic. I'll see about it," Trice assured him.

"The problem remains that if moved, he may bleed out. He would never make it to Reykjavík. He needs an exploratory laparotomy immediately if he even has a chance to survive. It needs to be done here and soon."

She placed her hand on his arm. "You can do it."

"There is no theater. No one to put him to sleep. No recovery."

"We'll use one of the exam rooms. I'll assist along with Marie."

"Marie?"

"She's at the community center, overseeing it. You have the skills. Use them."

Drake didn't have a response to that statement. Wasn't surgery what he had been wanting to do? But under these conditions?

"You stay with him." She placed her hand on his shoulder. "I'll go to the clinic and get things ready. I'll let you know when to bring him."

"There isn't much time." His look met hers.

"We'll hurry."

Time flew by and crawled at the same time as Drake waited to hear from Trice. His patience was almost gone by the time the blood came. He had spent the time regularly checking vital signs and rigging a system to deliver the blood along with helping the cannery workers form a plan to move the huge boiler.

When a man arrived with two pints of blood Drake immediately went to work administering it. It would be too little too late if Trice didn't hurry.

His phone rang. He put it on speaker, needing both his hands for his patient.

Trice's voice said, "Drake, we'll be ready for you when you get here."

"We're on our way." He hung up the phone. "Okay, guys. Let's go to work." With two men on each side of him to lift his patient, he directed the man on the crane. "Lift slow and easy."

The groan of metal made him fear they might be damaging the man further, but they had to get him out. Not soon enough, the space opened so the men could pull the injured man out.

"Slowly. Lay him on the blanket." Drake managed the blood still flowing. Trice had better have plenty of blood waiting at the clinic. They would need it.

They made it out of the building without a mishap. Waiting near the door sat a truck with the motor running and padding for the patient in the back. The men placed the patient on the bedding, and Drake climbed in beside him. To the driver he said, "Keep it slow and steady."

Trice was waiting for him at the clinic door. She rushed to meet him when the truck stopped. "How is he doing?"

"Just hanging on." Drake jumped from the back of the truck.

"You go get scrubbed in, and I'll see about prepping him. Everything you need is lying out in the restroom." She went to work overseeing the unloading of the patient.

Drake glanced into the first examination room. It was filled with furniture. The next one had the door closed. He continued to the restroom. Just as Trice had said, a gown, surgical hat and gloves waited.

Minutes later, he opened the door to the examination room. It had undergone an obvious makeover. Everything that was unnecessary had been removed. He could smell a hint of disinfectant. No doubt Trice had made sure the walls and equipment had been sanitized.

A gurney sat in the middle of the room with his patient on it. A tray with instruments stood beside it. The examination light had been positioned near the bed. With two swift steps, he stood beside the man. He pulled on his headlamp. It felt good to have it on again.

"I located what gas I could find to use to put him to sleep." Trice wore surgical gear as well. "I went through your office and found your surgical headlamp."

Behind her stood Marie.

"We are ready when you are, Doctor," Trice announced, taking her position on the other side of the patient from him. Marie stepped up beside him.

"Vitals, please," he said.

Trice rattled them off. "He's being given blood now."

"We need to get him to sleep." Drake picked up the gas mask and placed it over their patient's face. "Trice, monitor vitals."

Her gaze met his. She nodded.

Confidence he wouldn't have said he possessed filled him. He could do this in this makeshift theater. He had excellent support.

"BP is ninety over sixty," Trice announced.

"That's to be expected with internal bleeding. But it's time to stop that. Let's find those bleeders. Scalpel."

Marie placed it in his palm.

Slowly and carefully, he made a midline incision in the man's abdomen.

"Suction?" What were they going to do for suction?

Marie handed him the end of the tube to the stomach pump machine. He looked at her. "It was Trice's idea."

His gaze met Trice's. The woman never ceased to amaze him. He went to work removing the blood pooled in the man's middle section. "We're going to need more blood."

"It's on the way. People all over town are giving." Trice moved to check the transfusion site.

There was knock at the door. A voice called, "Blood is here."

Trice went to the door to take it. She returned to hook it up to the man after checking the IV.

Drake searched the internal organs. "I wished we had a way of taking X-rays."

"You don't need them." Trice's voice held complete confidence. "You'll find the problem."

He suctioned the area as well as he could. "Sponge."

Maria handed him one. "Keep count. We don't want to leave one lying around somewhere. In fact, keep a written tally."

"There's a pad and pen in that drawer." Trice point to the small cabinet in the corner.

Maria found it and made a notation.

Drake couldn't believe what Trice had managed to pull off in less than an hour.

She had created a full operating theater. He couldn't think of many situations more dire than doing surgery with rudimentary equipment in an examination room turned theater in a remote area.

"We need to find the bleeders or bleeder and get him closed. The helicopter will be here in a few hours after we know he is stable enough to move to Reykjavík. Suction." He cleaned the area as well as possible once more. "Sponge. Trice, vitals."

She rattled off precise and to-the-point numbers.

"Now move the spleen aside and let me see if the bleeding is from there." He searched the area. "There is one. Clamp."

Maria handed him something close to what looked like a surgical clamp.

"What is this?"

Trice spoke up. "A hair clamp. I couldn't find any surgical clamps anywhere. I had to improvise."

"Nicely done." She was wonderful.

She had a smile in her eyes.

"Let's get this stitched up and look for more. Marie, you handle suction. Trice, you help with holding the two sections together while I stitch."

Both women went to work.

It felt good to command a theater. There was no room to argue with the man's life in the balance.

Marie opened a suture kit and handed him the needle already pre-threaded. She suctioned. With the area clear, he carefully joined the two ends of the vessel. "Hold it right there, Marie. Almost done. Suction."

"Excellent. Got it." He nodded to Marie.

Blood still pooled in the man's cavity.

"We've got another somewhere." He went looking, gently moving organs around in a mythical order. He lifted a lobe of the liver. "There it is. This is going to be tricky. Vitals."

Trice gave him the numbers.

"Okay. He's holding his own. Marie, I want you to hold the liver like this." He positioned it where he wanted it. "Trice, I need you to clamp this off the best you can." He held the vessel. "Then help keep the area clear so I can see and get it attached. We're going to have a devil of a time because of the angle."

They all took their positions, and Drake went to work. It might have been the most rudimentary of theaters and the job the most difficult he'd had to perform, but he did some of his finest work.

He stepped back. "Suction one last time. Marie, count those sponges. We can't afford an infection or left behind sponge."

Trice and Marie followed his directions while he searched for further issues.

"Well done. Let's close. Any broken bones will have to

wait until he can be x-rayed." Drake checked his watch. "The evacuation helicopter should be here in an hour. We couldn't ask for better timing."

In a silent room, he closed the man's abdomen.

While Marie covered the man in blankets and checked his vitals every fifteen minutes, Trice and Drake cleaned the room.

Trice said, "You've got some skills with stitches."

"I practiced long enough." He grinned behind the mask. "Marie, thanks for your help. You go get some rest. You've done a night's worth of work," Drake said.

"It was amazing to watch you. Both of you. Trice will make a great local doctor. I'm glad I'll be working with her. I going to check on those injured at the community center before I get some rest."

Trice pulled off her gown and hat. "Thanks for your help. You were amazing. You've earned a rest. I'll see about the community center."

"But—"

"I've got it. If you want to, you can come in later today and oversee what's going on. And Marie, thank you. I wouldn't have wanted anyone else's help."

"Thanks. I feel the same about you." Marie smiled and headed for the door.

With her gone, Drake said, "Apparently Marie has become one of your fans as well."

"An emergency helps people see others in a different light. Plus, I think she knows something is going on between us."

Drake would agree with that.

Trice finished putting away supplies. "I've got to go now. I need to check on things at the community center. I'll have work to do in the morning."

"I'll be right here until the evac arrives." He stood over the patient.

She hesitated at the door. "Don't you have to leave this morning?"

Her sad eyes were almost his undoing. "I'm postponing for at least twenty-four hours. I can't leave you with all this to do by yourself. You've got your hands full."

"We had some last night together."

It wasn't what he had planned. "Story of my life. There's always something getting in the way of my plans."

Trice gave him a quick kiss on the lips. "I'll check the other patients. After you see this patient off, why don't you go to my place and get some sleep? It's closer than yours, and you'll be nearby in case you're needed."

"You'll join me?"

His hopeful look warmed her heart. She nodded. "As soon as I can."

Trice trudged to the community center. Exhausted, she still had work to do. In the two weeks she'd been in Seydisfjordur, she'd done more, felt more than she had in her entire life. She wasn't sure she could keep up this pace, but she was exhilarated by the idea of seeing if she could.

Here in this remote place, she'd found herself. A place to belong, a place to grow, and place she could call hers. If only Drake stayed…

At the center, she entered to find patients lined up in orderly rows. One wall was a food area. "Good morning."

The women working there greeted her with tired looks.

"Would you mind fixin' a plate for Drake? I'm going to check on the patients here. Then I'll take it over to him."

"You have done enough. I'll see about that," the older

of the two women said. "Thank you for all you have done for us."

"You are welcome. And thanks for taking a meal to Drake. I'm sure he'll be happy to see it."

Over the next hour, Trice reviewed charts and ate a bite herself. She heard the whirl of the helicopter approaching. Her and Drake's patient would be leaving soon. They had done good work together. Pretty amazing stuff in fact.

And the town. They had come together and organized as if they had practiced it. They knew each other so well, they knew whose skills to call on. Those who had some medical experience led those willing to help.

Trice told the lady who came in for her shift of overseeing care that she was leaving to get some rest. "Call me or send someone after me if there's the slightest problem. When I return, we'll see about discharging patients."

In the early sunlight, she walked home. The lights were off in the homes, and a few businesses were opening.

She was turning the corner of Luce's house when her door opened. "You did good last night. You okay?"

"I'm fine."

"You need to rest. He is already doing so." The old woman carried no censure in her voice.

"He'll leave tomorrow." Trice wasn't as good at removing emotion from her voice.

The old woman looked sad but resigned. "It has to be."

"I know."

"One must learn what they really want." Luce stepped inside her house and closed the door.

Trice had found what she wanted. Caring, support, and a place where she gave and got it in return. She'd found those here with or without Drake. She had also found love despite the fact it was leaving her. Her heart squeezed at the idea of losing him. Yet he had to go, just as she had to stay. He needed a chance to find what he wanted.

She opened the door of her home to find Drake sound asleep on his stomach in her bed. He snored softly. She went to the bath and showered. Pulling on an oversize shirt, she headed for the bed as well.

Giving him a shake, she said, "Scoot over." She wiggled in next to him, pushing him to give her room using her behind.

Drake rolled to his side and pulled her to him. He murmured next to her ear, "Everything okay at the center?"

"Under control."

"Mmm."

A soft snore filled her ear. She snuggled into him. He would be gone in less than twenty-four hours. She would take what she could get for as long as she could get it.

Hours later, she woke to Drake nuzzling her neck while his hand under her shirt fondled her breast. "I'm sorry. I can't help myself." He nuzzled her ear again. "Reconsider us staying in contact."

Trice was flattered. She snuggled closer. She would miss this time and intended to absorb as much of it as possible. Trice didn't want to have this discussion now. She wanted him to make love to her. "We've already talked about that. I have responsibilities here, and you have training in London."

"I'll come here when I can. You come to me when you can. We can talk and write, call often."

She hated being the one to voice reality. "It won't work."

His lips followed her brow. "You won't even try?"

Trice kissed his chest. "It's not that."

"Then what?" He looked at her.

"I'm tired of having only half of what I want. I don't want crumbs. It's time I demand to have the whole cake. To be the center of someone's attention. To come first. You can't do that in London, and I won't ask you to stay here."

"Come on, Trice. It'll only be for a little while. If we both work at it, we can make it work. We can get through the year, and then we can be together."

Would that be what she wanted to do? She already knew what it was like to be anonymous. She liked being included in a knitting circle. The fact that people helped others without question. She had no desire to return to what she had before. No longer would she settle for part-time. Trice looked away.

"You think you belong here?" He pulled away and lay back on the pillows.

"I don't know for sure, but I believe so. But it's not all about Seydisfjordur. It's about me." She pointed to her chest. "Me standing up for what I want. Finding my place in the world."

"You don't think you can do that with me?" Drake growled.

"Not in London. Not when you are focused on surgery." She raised a hand before he could speak. "Which you should be. This was supposed to be a fling for a reason. I care too much for you to hold you back. I would never want that. You need to go. I won't hold you here. I can't."

"You sound like Luce. She pushes me to go, yet she knows I worry about her."

"I will take care of her. You need to go. If you don't, think of all the people who might not get the care they need. You owe it to yourself, and your future patients to finish your training."

All Drake's hurt showed in his eyes. Her heart broke. She hadn't wanted it to end this way.

He threw the covers back. "You finish getting some sleep.

I'll go check on the community center and see if I can send some of the patients home. I'll be busy the rest of the afternoon tying up business and packing. Bye, Trice."

Through tear-filled eyes, she watched him dress, then walk out the door and out of her life.

CHAPTER ELEVEN

TRICE DIDN'T SEE Drake for the rest of the day. She stayed busy at the clinic and then later at the community center. He had discharged a number of the patients at the center, but there were still others that needed to stay at least another day.

Day turned into night, and she returned home lonely and sad. She'd been both of those before. She would survive. She would work through them again.

By the time she went to bed, there had still been no word from Drake. More than once, she had thought of going to him. What would she say? That she had changed her mind. But she hadn't. She couldn't lead him on to believe that.

She wasn't surprised he was hurt, even understood it, but she knew what it was like to have promises made to stay in touch and then there be nothing. She didn't want that. Refused to live like that ever again. It was better to cut it off clean and remember each other well.

Trice wanted him to concentrate on his surgery. Getting his career started. To have his dream. Worrying about her wouldn't make that happen. He wouldn't intend to hurt her, but it would happen. Not once had they discussed forever. Had he even considered that?

Returning to her house, she tried to get some rest, but it never came. In a short amount of time, she had become used to sleeping next to Drake. Even that she would have to adjust to, and it might be the hardest to accomplish.

She couldn't figure out a way to make their situation different. For them to have a future, one of them would have to give up their dream. She wouldn't ask Drake to do that. His skills were needed. But she also couldn't agree to give up what she'd finally found—a community. Exhausted, she walked from the clinic to her house.

The next morning, Trice strolled to the front of Luce's house on her way to the clinic. Luce's front door opened, and the old woman stepped out. "He came by earlier to say goodbye. He left you this." She handed Trice a paperback book. "He said for you to keep it."

Trice had heard the plane taking off. She had hurried outside and watched as he circled over the town and headed south.

The older woman said quietly, "Drake needed to go so he can know his mind. His heart is here. He must learn that. Then he will come home."

"I'm sure he'll come back for a visit."

The way Luce looked at Trice told her the woman's words had another meaning. "You must work to stay busy. Time will go by."

Not fast enough to heal her heart.

"That way you will not notice him being gone." Luce patted Trice's arm.

Trice would notice Drake being gone no matter what she did. "Thanks. That's good advice." She would start today. Determined, she squared her shoulders. She walked to the clinic, went in and proceeded with business. She was here to do a job, and she would do it and do it well. She had her research to review and a call to Olafur to make.

Yet that heavy block of sadness and loneliness weighed her down.

Over the next week, he didn't call, nor did she receive a letter. She didn't like being cut off any more than she had the times it had happened before. Yet Drake was doing as she had asked.

Trice worked to fill her days, but her nights were long and sleepless. As the hours crawled into days and those into weeks, it didn't get any easier. She just pushed forward. Every time she heard the engine of a plane, her heart palpitated with the possibility it was Drake, then crashed when it wasn't.

Drake had circled Seydisfjordur the day he left.

Had Trice looked up, hoping to see him one more time? Had she been as disturbed by him leaving her behind as he was by doing it?

He had studied the little town nestled on the water below him. It had been his home forever. He had gone knowing he had left part of himself behind. Trice might not still be in town when he did return, but he knew well the others who made up Seydisfjordur would be there just as they always were.

He hadn't liked the way he and Trice had parted, but he couldn't help his anger. She didn't even want to try to work out something between them. It wouldn't have been easy, but they could have tried. Her problem was she had no faith in anyone wanting her.

If they both wanted the relationship, they could have figured out how to make it work and overcome the complications. They didn't have to become part of the negative statistics that said it was next to impossible. She wanted stability. To be the center of someone's world.

Had he made her think she could be? No, he hadn't offered her that. Not once had he offered her anything permanent, especially with him. Drake blinked. Was that what he wanted? Trice in his life forever?

He had been gone for three weeks. He wished he could say he was happy and had adjusted well to returning to the structure of hospital schedules and the requirements of surgery. But that wasn't the case. Thankfully, his skills weren't lacking.

He disliked the noise and lights of the city. They were nothing like he remembered. Now they irritated him. He missed the quiet of a starry night. The peace of the wind.

To make matters worse, he longed for Trice. He couldn't get beyond that. Or that he had all but demanded everything be his way. That she come to London. That she work there. She would have been giving up everything for him. He'd been unfair to even think she might follow him when he'd seen how happy she was in Iceland. Above all, he wanted to see her happy. Yet what he'd asked for wouldn't have done that.

He had been so confident that when he reached London, he would be so caught up in his work that the pain of losing Trice would ease. That hadn't been the case. He had planned this move for so long, had looked forward to returning to surgery so much, that he shouldn't be this miserable. He was horribly lonely for Trice. And he missed Seydisfjordur.

He recognized happiness. He had it with Trice. What he felt now wasn't it. Still, this was what he needed to do, to hone his surgical skills. Then he could return to Iceland prepared to do more for his homeland than he had been doing. He just had to give his feelings time. To hope that it worked. He had made a commitment, and he would stick with it.

He had just finished his third surgery of the day. He

had seen inside three humans' bodies, yet he couldn't say what they looked like or their names. He couldn't say what they did for a living, or how they had come to get a scar on their hand or what nickname their mother called them or what their favorite folk dance was. All of that he knew about most of the people in Seydisfjordur. His patients in the hospital were just people passing through the OR who he would never really know. He missed the personal connection of working in a small clinic.

You do not know your heart or your place. Hallveig's words marched through his head.

He did know now where his heart was, and his place as well. It was time he went home to Trice and Seydisfjordur. With that decision made, the weight he had carried on his shoulders fell to his feet. Finally, the center of his back relaxed for the first time since circling Seydisfjordur the last time.

An hour later, Drake said to the balding, stern-looking man standing beside him as they scrubbed their hands, "Dr. March, may I speak to you in your office after this procedure?"

The man observed him a moment and nodded. "That will be fine."

Drake sat in the chair across the desk from the older surgeon. "How can I help you, Stevansson?"

"Sir, I'm sorry to tell you this, but I will not be staying with the program."

The man sat forward. "And why not? We held a place for you. Why would you leave us after only three weeks?"

"Thank you, sir, for doing what you did, but the two years I've been gone have changed things. I've learned to appreciate knowing my patients. By name, not as a number. I love surgery, I do, but I need more. More interaction."

The older man leaned back in his chair. "Your work is impeccable, but I have to admit I've been unsure about your happiness with working in a hospital."

Drake wasn't sure how to respond, so he remained quiet.

"I realized how much you wanted to rejoin the program and how patiently you waited until you could, but you seem to go through the motions, which are better than par, but your heart doesn't seem to be in your work."

Drake sat straighter. "I assure you—"

The man held up his hand. "This is not a criticism but an observation. Please speak freely."

"Working in a large city just isn't for me anymore. I belong in Seydisfjordur." And with Trice.

"You're going to give up surgery to return to your small-town clinic? It will be a waste of talent."

"I'm sorry you feel that way, sir. But this isn't the right place for me. I'm sorry to have taken your time and a space, then let you down."

"There is no way to change your mind?"

"No sir, there isn't." On that Drake had no doubt. He was going back to Seydisfjordur and begging Trice to have him.

"Then I guess all I can do is wish you well." The man stood and offered his hand. Drake shook it. "I hope you aren't making a mistake."

Drake squared his shoulders. With complete confidence he said, "I am not."

As the days went by, Trice became less confident about having made the right decision regarding Drake. What she had was nothing. No phone calls, no notes, no interaction. She'd requested it be that way. He was honoring his word.

Yet everything in her mind, body and soul clambered to hear his voice, to know how he was doing.

Maybe he was right. They could compromise. She had only a year's commitment to Seydisfjordur. The town hadn't asked her to stay longer, and if they did, she didn't have to agree. Yet by then, how she and Drake felt could be completely different. Only she knew it wouldn't be for her.

Was he as lonely as she? She felt like Seydisfjordur was home, but without Drake, she wasn't as sure as she had once been. She should be with him.

The only true bright moment in her life was when she had spoken to her potential cousin, Olafur Bjonsson, at length and requested a DNA test. She was waiting for it to return. Still, she felt deep in her soul it would be positive. He was her family. He had a sister who had three daughters, but they lived on the other side of the island. Trice hoped to meet them one day. Just knowing they existed filled her heart. She had blood connections in a world where she had never had anyone. Yet something was missing. Drake was the connection her heart longed for.

Would he even respond to her if she called? He'd been angry with her when he had left. How would he react if she dared to call him? Would he be glad she did?

One afternoon, she dared to call his number. Her heart almost beat out of her chest. Would he answer? Her heart settled into its place when the call went to voicemail. She sank to the chair while she listened to his voice. At the beep, she hung up. Tears flowed like they never had before. Maybe it was best to leave well enough alone.

Three days later, the sound of a plane made her head pop up from where she worked at her desk. Would she ever move beyond that reaction to a plane engine?

Since she didn't have any patients, she walked outside

to the front steps. The sun shone brightly. She watched the plane circle, then line up for landing. The plane had markings like Drake's, but she knew that was just wishful hoping. The plane came to a stop near the terminal.

A man came around the front of the plane. His mannerisms reminded her of Drake. Hope had her imagining things. But the idea it might be him pulled at her enough to keep her standing there. The pilot looked her direction, but the distance was too far to really make out who he was. Still she stared.

The man walked toward the terminal. John, who ran the airport, met him and shook his hand. The man slapped him on the shoulder just like Drake would have. Trice slowly went down the steps and started walking toward the airport. She wanted to run, but controlled her actions, not wanting to embarrass herself if it wasn't Drake. Her heart quickened. What if it was him?

She started down the road. He moved so much like Drake, but he was in London doing surgery. Her feet kept moving of their own accord. Her pulse ran wild in anticipation. He walked toward her along the road around the harbor. The closer he came, the more he looked like Drake. She picked up her pace. His strides lengthened.

It was Drake!

She broke into a run. He loped toward her. He was close enough now for her to clearly see him.

He dropped the pack from his back and opened his arms. She ran as fast as she could the last few yards, not stopping until she slammed into his chest. Drake rocked back with the force of her reaching him. His arms tightened around her. Her arms went around his neck, and she clung to him. He squeezed her tighter. If it was up to her, she would never let him go.

They remained wrapped in each other's arms for a few

minutes. Trice fought the moisture filling her eyes. She focused on absorbing the fact that Drake's heat warmed her, and he was there with her again.

"I've missed you." Her voice was gruff with emotion.

"I've missed you too." He sounded as if he were having a difficult time controlling his emotions as well.

She pulled away enough to see his handsome face. "I'm sorry I was so stubborn about us not having anything to do with each other."

"I'm the one who should apologize to you. I wanted everything to go my way." His look held nothing but sincerity.

She cupped his cheek. "I wanted you to have your dream."

"Honey, when you're in my arms, I have my real dream. I love you."

"Drake, I love you."

He kissed her, long and sweet and perfect. Her heart swelled. All her life she'd been looking for connection, roots, love. This man in her arms gave her all of that and more.

Drake picked up his pack and pulled it over one shoulder. He put an arm around her waist and directed her toward the clinic.

Trice slipped her arm around his waist, too, laying her head against his shoulder. "Luce said you would be back."

"Somehow Luce always knows."

"She seems to. Why are you here? How long can you stay?"

"Can't a guy say hi before you start grilling him?" He grinned. "Can't I just come visit you?"

She gave him a sheepish look. "I'm so excited you are here."

"Why don't we ride up to my house, where we can talk uninterrupted?"

She stopped and studied him a moment. "Because I don't think you have talk on your mind when we're at your house."

His grin turned wolfish, predatory. "Well, you might be right about that, but I'd like for you to come with me anyway."

"Let me close the clinic and put out the sign about where to find me." Trice hurried ahead.

A few minutes later, they climbed into his truck, which had remained parked behind the clinic. He had left it for her to use when needed. Drake drove up the steep, winding road to his house. He opened the front door, letting Trice enter first. He closed the door behind him, grabbed her and kissed her so tenderly she came close to crying.

He rested his forehead against hers. "I didn't want us to be interrupted at the clinic. Sometimes the town doesn't know boundaries."

"Drake, shouldn't you be in London? Is something wrong?"

He gave her another deep kiss. "Everything was wrong. You weren't there. I came home for you."

Her eyes narrowed. "For me?"

He cupped her cheek. "Yes, for you. Sit. I'll explain."

Trice wasn't confident she would like what was to come, but she did as he requested. "I need to say something."

He sat beside her, but not close enough for her to touch him. His look turned earnest. "I gave up my surgery fellowship. I want us to be together. I'll do whatever it takes to make that happen."

Trice wanted to wrap her arms around him but remained where she was, her hands tightly clasped together. Her voice turned stern. "Drake, I won't let you give up your dream. You are a surgeon. You should be doing surgery. What you love."

"I love you more." He pulled her into his lap.

Placing her hands on his chest, she pushed back so she could see his face. "I don't want you to one day resent me because you gave up something you love for me."

"That will never happen. You are the most important thing in my life."

She searched his face. "We can make it for a year writing, seeing each other over the internet, visits."

"I want more than that. I want us to really be together. Right here." His eyes were bright with the possibility.

"How?" Her brows rose.

"I'm back here to stay." He grinned.

"But Drake, you can't to that. You were born to be a surgeon. I hope you didn't leave for me."

"I left for me. And because what we have together is more important to me."

"I can come to London after I finish here. We can find a place outside of the city where we can have the best of both worlds."

He studied her with a look of amazement on his face. "That's not what you want. I know you well enough to know that."

"I would do it for you. I could make it work."

"I don't want you to make it work. I want you happy. This is your happy place. It is mine as well. I have found it has a hold on me no matter how much I might try to say it doesn't. No matter where I am, it will always be here, calling me. With you here, it screams, *I belong here.* One of many things I have learned lately is that I can be invaluable wherever I am. It just may not take the same form."

She kissed him. "It took you long enough to figure that out."

He smirked. "Some of us are slow to get the idea."

Trice cupped his cheek. "Yes, they are." She dropped her hand. "If you come back here, I will need to find a job elsewhere. I won't be needed."

"I'm not coming back to take your job. I was already

packed and ready to head this way when a representative of the Reykjavík Hospital phoned. He wants me to start a pilot program for local surgical clinics. The first one would be right here. I would handle the simple surgeries and emergencies as needed in the surrounding area. I also discussed it with the town council through the mayor. I want to use the money they gifted me to help buy a small CT machine. They agreed. Iceland's medical commission hopes you would be willing to stay and oversee the clinic and continue to help me when your year is over. They heard how efficient you were when we did surgery."

It was almost too perfect. Trice appreciated the excitement on Drake's face and how animated he was talking about the plan.

"We can be together. Right here where you want to be and where I have realized I belong."

Trice didn't know what to say, she was so overwhelmed.

Drake took both her hands. "What do you think? Would that make you happy?"

"That would be wonderful. I can't think of anything more wonderful."

"Nothing?" He watched her with a smile on his face.

"What's going on, Drake?"

He continued to look into her eyes. "This is a personal matter, not a medical issue."

"Are you sick?" She looked at him, suddenly concerned.

"I'm fine except for one thing. My heart hurts."

She sat forward. "What's wrong with your heart?"

"It hurts for you. I've missed you. I love you, Trice." He went down on one knee. "I love you so much. I know we haven't known each other long, but I also know I love you and I want to marry you as soon as possible."

She threw her arms around his neck, squeezing him tightly. "I love you too. I always will."

"So, what do you say?"

Drake looked so unsure, she had to take pity on him. "Yes, yes, yes, yes, yes, yes, yes! A million times yes!"

He kissed her with such tenderness that expressed his love clearly. She sighed when he released her.

"I can get my family here in a couple of weeks," he said. "Do you think you could be ready to marry me by then?"

She grinned. "I bet I can call a meeting of the knitting circle and have it done in no time."

He threw back his head and laughed. "I'm sure you're right."

Her gaze locked with his. "One more thing. Having a family is important to me. I know you are good with children, but how do you feel about having some of your own?"

"If they're with you, I want them. In fact, I think we should start practicing right away." He took her hand and tugged.

In the doorway of his bedroom, she stopped him. She met his questioning look. "I came here hoping to find blood family, and I found so much more. You are the real family I've been looking for. Thank you for that."

"Honey, I'll always be here for you. Seydisfjordur has always been my home, but with you here, it's where I belong."

* * * * *

HEALING THE BABY SURGEON'S HEART

TESSA SCOTT

MILLS & BOON

In memory of my mom,
who always encouraged me to follow my dreams.

CHAPTER ONE

CLAIRE DELANEY PULLED her soft cardigan tight around her chest as a breeze rose off the Atlantic Ocean and flitted through her thick chestnut hair. She was walking along a paved path at least one hundred feet inland from the rocky coastline, so the chilled wind caught her by surprise. Still, she welcomed its invigorating caress against her skin.

Two days ago, she had arrived in the small town of Ballyledge on the West Coast of Ireland for a month of...well, she still wasn't quite sure what to call it. Rest and relaxation? Not exactly, given that she had taken an extended leave of absence from Boston General Hospital in order to reevaluate her career as an obstetrician and gynecologist.

It was a chosen profession that meant the world to her. That was until one day seven months ago, when she had lost her own baby daughter as a stillbirth at thirty-two weeks along.

Claire winced as emotions flooded through her, still as raw now as ever. And the words that she had once used to counsel and reassure her own patients who had suffered a miscarriage or stillbirth? Turned inwardly, they brought little comfort as she tried to make sense of her loss.

As a highly regarded double board-certified ob-gyn at the top of her field, Claire knew that it wasn't always possible to pinpoint the reason why a pregnancy ended in miscarriage or stillbirth. An autopsy might have provided some answers, but she hadn't been able to bear to have Ariana's tiny body cut open like that. And she didn't need conclusive evidence to know deep in her heart that her loss had been triggered at least in part by the stress and shock of her then husband Mark walking out on their marriage six months into her pregnancy.

She could deal with the end of her marriage. But the loss of her unborn child? The pain and devastation were so profound that they had extinguished the joy and passion she had once felt for her profession.

You just need some time, everyone had said.

And yet here she was, many months later and seemingly no further along in the healing process. How could she be, when every day in her life as an ob-gyn was a reminder of her loss?

Almost instinctively, Claire touched her lower abdomen, her right hand lingering there for several seconds until she forced herself to lift it away.

Quickening her step along the path, she spotted a smattering of people partaking in various activities on a gently sloping carpet of rich green grass to her left.

It really does look like the color of emeralds, she mused to herself, once again glad that she had chosen Ireland as her getaway destination on not much more than a moment's notice.

It made sense, given that as a proud Irish American, visiting the country had always been on her bucket list. Although she had certainly never imagined that it would be under such trying circumstances.

A smile formed over Claire's lips as she watched a man with two young children—presumably their father—trot across the field as he struggled to control a fluttering kite that was caught in a rip-roaring wind. When he slid on the grass and the kite escaped his grip, twirling upwards until it was little more than a tiny diamond-shaped spot in the sky, she cupped a hand over her mouth as her smile gave way to a chuckle.

It felt good to laugh, to feel the warmth of the sun on her

face as the late-morning clouds began to drift further apart. Maybe she'd get through this after all. Maybe she would still find happiness somehow, some way. Perhaps she could take up another area of medicine that wouldn't be a constant reminder of her loss.

Yes, I could do that, she told herself, pushing aside her doubts that she had it in her to start all over again.

Or maybe there was another profession calling to her, outside of the medical field—a previously unfathomable proposition.

She turned to view the coastline, and the small slice of pale blue water that peeked through the gap between the cliff bluffs and the horizon.

I'll become a painter.

She envisioned herself perched in front of an outdoor easel in a flowing silk scarf and red beret, conveniently ignoring the fact that she could barely draw stick figures.

Or maybe I could try—

Claire's thoughts—and her body—suddenly froze as a woman's agonized shriek reverberated through the air. Catching her breath, she scanned the several small groups of people in the field to her left, her eyes locking in place as they fell upon a woman lying on her back in the grass. A kneeling man hovered over her.

The sight sent a current of ice through Claire's veins. Was he attacking her in broad daylight? And, if so, why was no one rushing to her defense? The kite man was slowly making his way over with his kids, as were several other people who had been walking nearby. But there was no attempt to tackle the man. Something wasn't right.

Wait.

Claire squinted, and then took a deep breath. Even from a distance, there was no mistaking the woman's hugely swollen belly. She was pregnant. And as another guttural scream punctured the otherwise quiet morning, Claire knew one thing for certain.

She's in trouble. I have to help.

It wasn't until she was halfway to the unfolding scene that Claire realized she was running—and fast. It was as if her legs had a mind of their own and her "off" doctor button had been switched back on.

Dropping to her knees beside the woman, she turned to the ashen-faced man who was clutching her hand, his eyes wild with fear. They were both young, quite possibly first-time parents, Claire surmised.

"It's okay," she said breathlessly, her lungs still reeling from her no-holds-barred sprint. "I'm a doctor."

She turned to the woman, equally as pale as her partner, but drenched in sweat, her long dark hair nearly as soaked as if she had just stepped out of the shower. Her light peach cotton maternity top clung to her damp chest. During her quick scan of the woman's body, Claire observed the growing patch of wetness on the inseam of her gray sweatpants. It was all the confirmation she needed that her water had broken.

"I'm Claire," she said, in the soothing tone that was her go-to voice for nervous moms-to-be—and often more so their partners. "What's your name?"

"Margaret," she said in a near-whisper. "And this is my husband, Ted. We were out having a picnic and—" She gasped, grabbing her lower belly, pain gripping her face like a vice.

"Our baby… S-Sam," Ted stuttered. "He's breech."

Two words that cut through the air like a knife.

Claire's throat clamped shut, but he wasn't about to let on that her concern had instantly shifted from medium range to glaring red warning lights.

"We…she has a C-section scheduled in…in…" Ted stammered, unable to say more.

"Three weeks," Margaret managed to say through clenched

teeth. "My doctor said this could happen, but I…" She paused to release a barely controlled yelp as another contraction grabbed hold of her.

"But he said it most likely wouldn't," Ted said, finishing his wife's sentence.

Claire tried to piece together the bits of information being volleyed around. "You mean an early labor?"

"Right," Ted replied, nodding vigorously. "He told Margaret to have an overnight bag at the ready, because if her waters broke before the scheduled C-section it would be an emergency situation. Oh, God. What have I done?" Clasping his forehead with jittery hands, he slowly rocked his upper body back and forth. "It was my idea to have a picnic today. I thought the fresh air would do us both some good—"

Claire grabbed Ted's forearm and squeezed it just tightly enough to pull him back into the present. "Ted, I want you to focus, okay? You need to be strong for Margaret. I know you can do this."

He straightened up, the panic in his eyes giving way to resolve. "Right. You're right. Um…um…what can I do?"

Claire glanced at his phone on the ground next to his knee. "Did you call nine-one-one?" It wasn't until she saw the perplexed look on his face that she realized it might not be the same number in Ireland as in the US. "Emergency. Did you call for help?"

"Yes. They said they were sending the nearest ambulance… about ten minutes out."

No sooner had the pronouncement left his mouth than the sound of an approaching siren pierced the air.

Claire turned to Margaret, clasping her free hand with her own. "You're going to be okay, Margaret."

Margaret's gray eyes were clouded with fear. "Sam…"

"Sam is going to be okay, too."

Don't make promises you can't keep.

Reassuring smile still in place, Claire inwardly winced as the obvious crossed her mind. Breech births *were* safe—in a hospital setting. But the chances of them getting to a hospital in time was iffy at best.

"I told you earlier I was a doctor, but I left out an important detail. I'm an ob-gyn, so delivering babies is my specialty."

By now, a small crowd of about a dozen people had gathered around.

"Oh, thank goodness," an older woman said as she puffed out a sigh of relief.

"What are the chances?" a male voice murmured.

What are the chances, indeed? Claire thought.

"Have you delivered breech babies before?" Ted asked anxiously.

"I have. Many times."

Claire's calm voice and reassuring words masked her significant concern. As the ambulance siren grew louder, she forced her mind to filter out the noise so she could be fully present in the moment.

"Did your doctor ever say what type of breech position Sam is in?"

"Um…uh…frank—is that right?" Ted asked, and Margaret replied with a tight squeeze of Claire's hand.

This was slightly better news than a transverse breech, in which the baby was positioned horizontally across the uterus, but dangers still abounded.

"Margaret, I'm just going to feel on your abdomen now," Claire said as she gently pulled her hand away from Margaret's grip. "It's possible Sam has turned on his own, so what I'm trying to determine is the placement of his head."

"I tried everything," Margaret said through gritted teeth as she bit down on her pain. "Acupuncture, chiropractor, tilt exercises…"

"Our doctor tried to turn the baby as well," Ted said. "He wouldn't budge."

It only took several light-pressure pushes on Margaret's abdomen for Claire to confirm that Sam's head was just under her ribcage. *Damn.* She had witnessed many babies flipping into a head-first position in the final days of pregnancy—sometimes just hours before birth—but it was not to be in this instance.

"Is this your first baby?" Claire asked.

Though she was fishing for critical information, she posed the question as casually as possible, so as not to set off further alarms.

"Yes," Margaret replied, smiling weakly as rivulets of sweat rolled down her cheeks.

"We've been over the moon, waiting for Sam to arrive and starting our family," Ted added.

"That's wonderful," Claire said.

She meant it…but the unspoken flipside of this acknowledgement was that a first-time vaginal birth was riskier, especially with a late preterm baby. Sam's small body pushing through the cervix first meant the opening could still be too narrow by the time his head was ready to pass through. If his head were to become stuck before they could reach the hospital, Claire would need to act without delay, flexing and maneuvering it to help bring him into the world as quickly as possible so that he could take that critically important first breath.

Though her intensive training and expert skillset were made for moments like this, Claire couldn't pretend that her nerves weren't on edge. But, as was always the case in a medical emergency, she knew how to fully suppress her fight-or-flight response while staying fully—and calmly—engaged in the moment.

"Thank God! The ambulance is here," a female voice within the small gathering announced.

Claire looked up. The yellow and red box-shaped vehicle

slowed to a stop on the road that ran parallel to the walking path, but it was a good five hundred feet or more away. She wondered if it would remain there, which meant the EMTs would have to cover a lot of ground on foot to retrieve Margaret on a stretcher, but seconds later the ambulance pulled off the road and slowly rambled down the green field.

Claire discreetly breathed a sigh of relief—then tensed up as a pair of muscular legs in maroon running shorts appeared just inches away. Her line of vision followed them upwards, settling on a rugged, dark-haired man who looked like he had stepped—or jogged—off the set of a commercial after playing the role of "quintessential Irish hunk."

"I'm a doctor," he said as he kneeled down beside Claire.

Claire did a double-take. He could easily pass for a professional rugby player—but a doctor? It most certainly would not have been her first guess. Still, she was grateful that he had chosen this particular morning and pathway to go for a run. She could use all the help she could get to ensure a safe birth delivery for Margaret and Sam.

"I'm an ob-gyn," she said. "Claire Delaney."

He nodded, thick, tousled hair bobbing as he did. "Kiernan O'Rourke."

"The baby is in a frank breech position," Claire said, her eyes meeting his to silently convey the gravity of the situation. "It's her first pregnancy and she has a C-section scheduled in three weeks."

He pursed his lips together, and Claire felt an unspoken understanding pass between them.

This could be serious. Their lives could be in danger.

"They're probably taking her to West Mercy Hospital in Galway. I'm chief of surgery there." He extracted a phone out of the athletic carry belt around his waist. "I'll call my team to make sure they're on standby."

Claire thought he looked too young to be a chief of surgery, but maybe the climb up the surgical hierarchal ladder proceeded at a quicker pace in Ireland than in the US.

As the ambulance pulled up and came to a stop, the back doors flew open and two EMTs emerged. Kiernan stood up to greet them, pulling a hospital ID badge from the wallet in his belt, which he quietly showed to the pair. Claire observed a subtle shift in the demeanor of both EMTs as they glanced at the badge, then looked up and nodded respectfully.

"I've been in touch with my team at West Mercy and they're awaiting our arrival," Kiernan said.

"Got it," said the young female EMT.

"It's a good thing you came out for a run today, eh?" said the other EMT, a thin man in his fifties with a salt-and-pepper goatee.

"Yes, but she was already in good hands when I arrived." Kiernan nodded toward Claire. "She's a doctor as well."

"Wow!" the female EMT exclaimed as she and her partner set the stretcher next to Margaret. "That's one heck of a coincidence."

It was all hands on deck as Claire, Kiernan and the EMTs carefully helped Margaret onto the stretcher.

"You're doing great, Margaret," Claire said as she squeezed her hand.

"I don't know if he's going to wait," Margaret said in a near-whisper.

"We're going to get you to the hospital as soon as possible," Claire said.

As the stretcher was loaded into the ambulance and secured into place, both EMTs stepped back outside.

"I'm going to ride in the back with you," Kiernan said, and the male EMT nodded.

"Me, too," Claire quickly added.

The EMT looked at Claire, his expression hesitant. "Are you a doctor at West Mercy as well?"

"No," Claire replied, "I'm a doctor in Boston." She paused, thinking perhaps she shouldn't assume they knew it was a large city on the East Coast of the United States. "It's in—"

"Boston!" The EMT cut her off. "I've got some cousins living there. Nice city. Cold, but nice."

"Go Celtics!" the female EMT said enthusiastically as she referenced the world-famous basketball team that called Boston home.

Her fervent cheer startled Ted, who had been standing several feet away. "Shouldn't I be with my wife?" he asked, his face dazed and his voice equally shaky.

"You can ride with me in the front," the female EMT replied.

He turned to Claire, wide-eyed with worry, and she nodded reassuringly. "It's okay. We'll be watching Margaret closely."

As Ted followed the EMT to the front of the ambulance, her partner gestured to Claire. "I'm sorry, but only authorized medical personnel are allowed to ride in the back."

"Seriously?" Claire asked, unable to hide her displeasure. She looked at Kiernan, waiting for him to overrule the EMT's well-meaning but—in her opinion—misguided decision.

"I'm sorry, but he's right," Kiernan replied, his honey-brown eyes conveying that he wished it were otherwise. "There was an incident a few years back… A man at the scene with a heart attack victim claimed he was a doctor, so they let him on the ambulance while they transported the patient to West Mercy. Turns out he was an imposter."

"That's putting it mildly," the male EMT said as he raised a squirrelly eyebrow. "One of my colleagues was on that run. The guy went berserk inside the ambulance and the patient almost died because of the ruckus."

"That's terrible," Claire conceded. "But I can assure you I'm a real doctor." She paused, her mind racing. "You can look up my name on your phone. I'm an ob-gyn at Boston General."

Kiernan stepped up into the back of the ambulance, turning to face Claire as the male EMT hopped inside and disappeared from view. "I'm sorry," Kiernan said as Margaret screamed through another contraction. "I really am. But we need to leave *now*."

As he shut the left-side ambulance door and started to close the right, Claire's arm shot out, pulling the door open again.

Kiernan's startled look matched her own.

Did I just do that?

She blinked and swallowed hard. Defying orders was so not her thing, but saving lives *was*. And that took precedence over everything.

"Look," she said in a barely controlled low voice. "I get that you're a chief of surgery. But have you ever delivered a frank breech baby? And I don't mean by C-section. Her water broke and she's having contractions. Maybe you'll get to the hospital before the baby enters the birth canal, but you can't guarantee it. And, depending on how he presents, it might take the two of us to turn and maneuver him safely out."

Claire thought she could actually hear the seconds tick by as her stalemate with the handsome chief of surgery continued.

"Well?" she finally asked, rising adrenaline creating an even louder buzz in her head.

Kiernan stood immobile as he stared at the American doctor who stood just inches away from him. With wavy reddish-brown hair that bounced past her shoulders, porcelain skin and the palest green eyes he had ever seen, she was, without question, one of the most beautiful women he had laid eyes upon. But it wasn't her striking appearance that had frozen him in place. Rather, he had a split-second decision to make—and, in full contrast to his normally resolute, take-charge nature, he wasn't sure what to do.

If he allowed her to accompany this patient and himself to

the hospital—potentially assisting in a breech delivery on the way—he would be violating medical emergency transportation laws. And hospital protocol as well. For a chief of surgery, that could have all sorts of repercussions, and none of them good.

Another second passed and Margaret cried out in the throes of a contraction. It was more than enough to jolt him into action.

"Come on," he said, reaching out and pulling Claire up into the ambulance.

She brushed past him, her silky, fruit-scented hair swiping him on the cheek. As the ambulance suddenly took off and began to roll up the grassy field Claire's knees buckled, and she struggled to regain her balance. Kiernan quickly grabbed her arm and pulled her up, her face just inches away from his own.

"Uh…we have a situation here," the EMT announced loudly as Margaret wailed and called out Sam's name.

Kiernan locked eyes with Claire, but only for a second. Rushing over to Margaret, she pulled away from him with such force that it nearly pushed him into the ambulance doors.

"I need gloves," she said to the EMT, her voice growing sharper as she called, "Doctor? I need you over here."

Kiernan was at her side before the words were fully out of her mouth. Snapping on the gloves handed to him by the EMT, he moved in closer and lowered himself while still giving Claire the room she needed to assist with the delivery.

And then he spotted it. Margaret's umbilical cord was protruding, trapped between her pelvic bone and Sam's buttocks, which were lodged in the vaginal opening. He knew that Claire had to find a way to quickly release the pressure on the prolapsed cord, or the baby would be starved of oxygen and blood.

Kiernan took a deep breath and held it in. Standing idly by while another doctor took action was foreign to him, but for once he had to concede that doing so was in the patient's best interest. He barely knew Claire, yet something told him she was an exceptionally gifted ob-gyn. But were they intervening in time? Had the umbilical cord been compressed before they'd loaded Margaret onto the ambulance?

As Claire briefly turned and looked up at him, concern clouding her light green eyes, he couldn't help but think she was silently asking the very same questions.

CHAPTER TWO

"I'll take full responsibility," Kiernan said as the EMT looked wide-eyed at Claire, his lips slightly parted as though he was about to launch a protest.

Eventually he nodded and said, "Just let me know what you need."

"Can you stay close to Margaret, monitor her vitals and coach her breathing?" Claire said.

As the EMT quickly moved toward the front of the stretcher, Claire slid her gloved hand under the baby's partially exposed buttocks, effectively lifting him off the umbilical cord.

She turned to Kiernan, her voice calm and a steely determination in her eyes. "I need you to replace my hand with your own so that I can free his legs."

Kiernan did as instructed, his gloved hand at the ready as Claire slowly slid hers out. "Got it," he said, as he carefully but swiftly lifted the front of Sam's lower torso upwards.

With hands that were considerably larger than Claire's, it was an even tighter squeeze as he concentrated on maintaining the slight yet still sufficient space that would release pressure from the umbilical cord.

With his right shoulder pointed downward at an uncomfortable angle, and Claire pushing up against his stomach as she moved in closer for better positioning, he felt like he was in a medical practitioners' version of the game Twister. A cramp caught him hard in the side, and he cursed under his breath.

Claire looked up at him, her forehead creased as if to say, *What are you bellyaching about?*

"Sorry, I just... I moved the wrong way."

Her face softened slightly, and she nodded before getting back to the task at hand. With her palm pressing down on Sam's lower back, Claire rotated his trunk to the left, then slid her right hand into the vaginal opening, gently looping her fingers around his right leg and pulling it through. Without pause, she moved to the left side and repeated the action with his left leg.

It wasn't until Kiernan saw both legs freed and the rest of Sam's body beginning to inch out that he realized he had been holding his breath the whole time.

"You're doing great, Margaret," Claire called out. Moving her hand next to Kiernan's forearm, she quietly added, "Okay, I'll take it from here."

The exchange of hands was seamless—a feat in itself, given the circumstances, Kiernan thought. He stepped back slightly to give Claire more room. Another contraction sent Sam further out into the world.

"Here come his arms and shoulders," Claire said.

Knowing that they, too, could have become trapped like Sam's legs, Kiernan felt relief that another hurdle had been cleared. All that was left was for his head to emerge.

Clenching his jaw, Kiernan silently encouraged Sam.

You can do it. You're almost there.

It seemed like many minutes passed while Kiernan repeated the silent mantra, though he knew it couldn't have been more than thirty seconds.

From her crouched position, Claire looked up at him. "His head is trapped," she said in a low voice, so as not to alarm

Margaret. "I'm going to need a towel...something that I can fold and wrap around his torso."

Kiernan quickly scanned the ambulance interior, then rifled through several supply bins on the left. "Okay, ready when you are," he said, stepping back with a folded towel in his hand.

After placing her right forearm underneath the length of Sam's body, Claire looked up at him. It was the only cue he needed to slide the folded towel between her arm and Sam's torso, lifting him up at an angle that allowed Claire to slide her hand in further.

"I have his jaw..."

Several seconds ticked by. Kiernan knew that she was attempting to place her fingers in Sam's mouth, so that she could better position his head for the next step of the procedure.

"I got it," Claire said, an expression of relief flooding over her face. She slid her left hand over Sam's back and into the vaginal opening, nodding as she said, "I'm flexing his head downwards. It's coming..."

Without looking up, she instructed Kiernan to push above Margaret's pubic bone with his free hand.

As Sam's head emerged, Kiernan wondered if he had ever witnessed a more wondrous sight. Yes, he was a surgeon. The jack-of-all-trades type, as he was fond of saying whenever anyone asked if he had a specialty. With advanced training and certifications there weren't many surgical areas that he hadn't delved into. Heart bypasses, cancer surgery, joint replacements—he'd done it all. But he had to admit there was something especially poignant about bringing a new life into the world.

Kiernan watched closely, still sending words of encouragement to Sam in his thoughts. The baby boy had officially arrived, but he wasn't fully out of the woods yet. At least not until he took that crucial first breath on his own.

"Betadine," Claire said, her left arm outstretched as Kiernan once again began searching through the supply bins.

"The one on top," the EMT called out.

"Left or right?" Kiernan asked.

"Left."

Kiernan quickly extracted the antibacterial solution and some gauze. Anticipating that Claire would next be asking for clamps and scissors, he grabbed those as well.

Claire wiped the cord with Betadine, then placed two clamps several inches apart. She turned to Kiernan, meeting his eyes. "Do you want to cut the cord?"

She didn't have to ask twice. Snipping the section between the clamps, Kiernan held his own breath as he waited for Sam to take his first. His eyes met Claire's once again, and though no words were said, he knew she was thinking the same dreaded thought.

Had they delivered Sam in time?

"Can I have another towel?" Claire asked urgently.

Kiernan quickly complied, and Claire began vigorously rubbing it over Sam's body.

And then the most glorious sound that Kiernan could ever imagine filled the ambulance.

"I never thought I would be so happy to hear a baby cry," Kiernan said quietly.

A wistful smile crossed Claire's face. "Welcome to the world of obstetrics, where every day is a miracle."

Kiernan couldn't help but notice how she seemed to have momentarily stepped into another time and place, her eyes unblinking, yet focused on nothing in particular, until another surge of sound caused her to snap out of it.

"Sam!" Margaret called out, her voice shaky but unmistakably joyous.

"He's beautiful, Margaret," Claire said, taking the stethoscope that Kiernan had just handed to her.

She placed it over his tiny chest, then looked up at Kiernan and smiled as she nodded. Wrapping Sam in the towel, she lifted him up to Margaret.

"He has a great set of lungs on him, that's for sure," she said as Sam wailed even louder. But once placed in Margaret's arms, he immediately stopped crying.

"He knows where he belongs," the EMT said.

Claire looked up from the mother and baby, nodding to Kiernan with the hint of a smile. It was as if she was silently acknowledging that the two of them had helped make this moment a reality. He smiled and nodded back.

Ten minutes later, the ambulance pulled up to the emergency entrance at West Mercy Hospital. Kiernan hopped out of the vehicle, then turned and offered his hand to Claire as she was about to disembark. She glanced at it before meeting his eyes momentarily. He tried to read the expression on her face. Surprise? Hesitancy? A little of both?

"Thanks," she said, but instead she braced her hand against the open door before stepping carefully out onto the pavement. Given that she hadn't accepted his assistance, he couldn't be sure what she was thanking him for.

As the EMTs rolled the stretcher holding Margaret and Sam toward the entrance, Ted bounded out of the passenger side of the ambulance and ran toward them. Seeing Margaret clutching their tiny newborn son in her arms, he froze in place.

"Oh, my God. Oh, my God. *Oh, my God!*" he exclaimed, his body unlocking as he ran over to the stretcher. "He's beautiful," he said quietly with awe as he beamed down at Sam.

"He certainly is," Margaret said, mustering up the strength to turn her head toward Kiernan and Claire. "And these wonderful doctors saved his life."

Ted turned to Kiernan and Claire. "I don't know how to thank you. This is just…this is the happiest day of my life."

Kiernan smiled and reached out to shake Ted's hand. "Congratulations."

The poor guy is a bundle of nerves, Kiernan thought as Ted continued to shake his hand vigorously, like a wind-up doll with no "off" button.

As smoothly as possible, Kiernan pulled back his hand. He looked over at Claire, knowing that she, too, must be beaming with joy over such a hard-earned happy ending.

Except…she wasn't. Kiernan's own smile faltered as he saw the angst etched on her face. But why? Was it a delayed reaction to the heightened adrenaline and uncertainty that had earlier prevailed, up until the very moment that Sam had been safely delivered? He had seen that sort of thing before with colleagues, after a particularly grueling surgery—even those with miraculous outcomes.

But this felt different.

As though suddenly realizing she was being watched, Claire looked over at him, her eyes meeting his for only a few seconds before she looked away.

Any further contemplation of her strange reaction was cut short by a *swoosh* as the large glass entrance doors swung open. Out strode Lucy, head nurse at West Mercy and Kiernan's right-hand…well, *everything*, given her uncanny ability to stay two steps ahead of his packed daily agenda. And today's unpredictable rollercoaster was no exception.

With a small team of medical professionals behind her, Lucy looked down at the stretcher, her eyes popping open when they landed upon not one, but two occupants.

"We had a bit of an eventful drive on our way over here," Kiernan said, in what he knew could be construed as the understatement of the year.

"I guess so," Lucy said wholeheartedly, a deep smile forming on her lips as she peered down at the new mother and baby. "I would imagine this is one ambulance ride you'll remember for the rest of your life," she said to Margaret.

"I definitely will," Margaret replied with a smile.

"Lucy," Kiernan began, "I'd like you to meet Dr. Claire Delaney. She's visiting from the US and, luckily for Margaret and Sam, she was in the right place at the right time when Margaret went into labor."

"So nice to meet you," Lucy said as she extended her hand.

Claire shook her hand and smiled graciously. "Same here."

Lucy rested both hands on her hips as she turned back to Margaret. "Well, Dr. Preshad is scrubbing in as we speak, expecting that he was going to be performing an emergency C-section. But I'm sure he'll be delighted to know that nature took its course on the way here, and both of you came through with flying colors."

A low rumble of laughter emanated from her team, with Kiernan adding a subdued grin. He wasn't quite at the point where he could look back on the stressful events of the morning and chuckle, but maybe with time. A *lot* of time.

"You've no doubt been through a lot," Lucy continued, "so let's get you inside and settled in."

"Thank you, Doctors," Margaret called out to Kiernan and Claire as two staff members began to wheel the stretcher toward the hospital doors, with Ted close behind.

"Yes, thank you again," Ted called out, before disappearing with the others from view.

Kiernan turned to Claire. "I need to chime in with my huge thanks as well. You truly saved their lives."

"I couldn't have done it without your help."

Though he was tempted to point out that he'd done little more than hand her medical supplies, Kiernan instead smiled and accepted the compliment. "I'm just glad we were both at the right place, at the right time."

"Me too."

"Say, while you're here, I'd love to show you around our new neonatal wing. It's scheduled to be fully up and running in another month. It might not have all the bells and whistles that you're used to at a big-city hospital like Boston General, but it's close. In fact, one of our longer-range goals is to offer cutting-edge neonatal care and the latest treatment options that aren't widely available. And I don't just mean for this region, but for the entire country."

Claire smiled.

Finally, Kiernan thought.

"That's sounds wonderful. And certainly ambitious." She paused, and there was a distinct look of pain in her eyes. "But I have to leave now."

It was not the answer Kiernan had expected, and he wasn't prepared to reply. Finally, he managed to utter, "Oh?"

"Yes, sorry. I have to…there's…um… I have to be somewhere."

Kiernan studied the stunning but increasingly mysterious woman before him. He didn't believe for a second that she had to be somewhere else. An incredibly talented doctor? Yes. But a convincing actress? Not so much.

"Well, I'm not sure how long you're staying in Ireland, but I'd be happy to give you a tour another time."

Kiernan creased his brow as he waited for her reply.

Why is she looking at me like I'm asking her to tour a room full of rattlesnakes and tarantulas?

"That's nice of you to offer. But I'm not sure I'll have time while I'm here."

"I understand," Kiernan said, although nothing could be further from the truth. "No problem."

Claire slid her phone from the back pocket of her jeans and tapped on the screen. "I did a search before coming here about whether there are Ubers in Ireland…" She looked up at Kiernan. "The answer was yes, but they're actual taxis—not drivers in their personal cars. Kind of defeats the purpose of an Uber," she added with a nervous laugh.

"Look, I'm heading back to Ballyledge myself. Why don't you ride with me? It's the least I can do after you saved the day like you did. The hospital has a small fleet of cars that are used for patient transport. I'll have one of my staff take us back."

Claire's smile vanished faster than the flipping of a light switch. She looked down at her phone. "Actually, it looks like I have a ride that's two minutes out."

Kiernan forced a smile. There was no point suggesting that she cancel the taxi and ride back with him instead. For whatever reason—despite what he felt had been a connection between them as they'd worked together to save Margaret and Sam—she wanted nothing more to do with him.

"That was fast," Claire said just over a minute and a half later as she waved to a taxi heading toward them. As the taxi came to a stop, she turned to Kiernan. "It was nice meeting you. And thank you for helping me with the delivery. I really couldn't have done it without you."

Kiernan was about to insist otherwise, but stopped himself. She was merely trying to be polite, so no need to point out that he'd done little more than hold a folded towel and grab some supplies. Not when she had made it clear that she wanted to leave as soon as possible.

Opening the taxi passenger door, he waited for her to be seated before saying, "Take care of yourself. And enjoy your stay in Ireland."

Another skittish smile. "I will. Thank you."

As Kiernan watched the taxi drive away, he heard footsteps approach from behind. Dr. Sebastian Kincaid, an anesthesiologist and one of Kiernan's best friends since medical school, swaggered up to him.

"*Who* was *that*?"

Kiernan rolled his eyes—a reaction he didn't in the least

bit bother to hide from Sebastian. Known as a real-life Dr. McDreamy by half of the female staff at West Mercy who regularly ogled him for his perpetually tanned skin, thick sandy-blonde hair and gym-aficionado physique, he had also earned the moniker of Dr. McDouchebag from the other half who'd had the misfortune of actually dating him at one time or another.

"That's Claire Delaney. She's an American doctor who happened to be walking nearby when the patient we just brought in went into labor. And a breech presentation, no less. She was pretty amazing delivering the baby. I'll tell you that."

"Pretty amazing, huh? I'm sure she was," Sebastian noted with his usual lack of subtlety. A pained grunt followed as Kiernan elbowed him sharply in the ribs. "What's that for?"

Kiernan grinned. "For you being you."

Sebastian straightened himself up, still rubbing his side. "So, how long is she here for?"

"I have no idea."

"Seriously? You didn't get her number or anything? What— are you losing your touch?"

Kiernan sighed exasperatedly as he raised an eyebrow. "Yes, well… I decided to hold off hitting on her while she was delivering a breech baby in the back of a bumpy ambulance." He paused for full dramatic effect. "I'm silly like that."

Sebastian shook his head, but with a smirk and a twinkle in his eyes. "You know, I really thought once you made chief of surgery you'd finally loosen up and realize that there's more to life than work."

"And why would you think that?"

"You're at the top of the food chain now. Which means it's time to enjoy some of the fruits of your labor. So to speak."

As Sebastian winked and wiggled his eyebrows, Kiernan reluctantly grinned.

"You've got the goods, mate," Sebastian continued. "You just need to show more of your authentic self, that's all."

Kiernan was beginning to lose patience. Fast. *"What?"*

"Remember that speaker we had here a few months ago, who talked about how to avoid career burnout? She mentioned the importance of bringing our authentic selves to work. You know—being real human beings and not just the series of medical credentials after our names. No one—besides myself, of course—feels like they really know you. That's all. A little banter here and there, some joking around, sharing your weekend plans—or at least pretending you have some… Things like that could go a long way."

Kiernan stared at him hard. "Remind me again why we're friends?"

Sebastian smiled, revealing teeth so white that Kiernan wondered if he should don sunglasses.

"Because you need me. I'm the best wingman you'll ever have—even though you refuse to take advantage of my services."

"I'm head of the surgery department. I see people whose lives are at stake, day in and day out. I don't have time to mollycoddle my colleagues."

Sebastian stared at him, his mouth twisted to one side. "Right. If you say so," he finally said, this time slapping Kiernan on the other shoulder. He looked at his watch. "Well, I'm off to prep for a gallbladder removal."

He took a few steps in the direction of the hospital entrance, and then he stopped and swiveled around.

"And by the way… No one says 'mollycoddle' anymore. Other than time travelers from the nineteenth century."

He flashed a smile and gave a thumbs-up before turning on his heels and continuing on his way.

Kiernan sighed, then shook his head and managed a weary smile.

Bring your authentic self to work. Who comes up with this stuff, anyway?

And yet…

His thoughts turned to Claire, and the incredibly intense turn of events that had brought them so briefly together. Two complete strangers, working in tandem to save the lives of a mother and her newborn baby.

It doesn't get any more real than that, he thought.

But as he replayed their parting of ways in his mind, he was faced with another reality, and this one left a sting in its wake.

She couldn't get away from me fast enough.

Claire watched silently from the back passenger window of the taxi as rolling green fields, stone walls and the occasional grazing sheep whizzed past. Ten minutes ago they had left the city limits of Galway, and viewing the quiet countryside was like a calming elixir for her soul. Which was something she certainly needed right now.

Another patchwork of green fields, this time grazing goats, and Claire turned away from the window, leaning back against the headrest. She closed her eyes and breathed in deeply, feeling as though it was her first full breath since the moment she had knelt down on the ground beside Margaret.

Slowly, she shook her head. Was the universe trying to mess with her mind? She had come to Ireland for a reprieve from her life as a baby doctor, and only days in she'd been thrown back into it in the most unexpected and harrowing way.

Dabbing at her moist eyes with the sleeve of her cardigan, she caught the driver glancing at her through the rearview mirror. She hoped he would look away, and was relieved when he finally did.

It will pass, she told herself.

Not the pain that she still felt from losing Ariana, but the tears that flowed every time a situation triggered her emotions into overdrive.

Still… As she thought of the exhausted but overjoyed Margaret, holding tiny Sam in her arms, she couldn't help but think that maybe the universe knew what it was doing after all. Yes, a yet to be fully healed wound in her heart had been tugged open. But now there was a very happy new mom and a healthy baby boy who might not have had the same outcome if it hadn't been for her and a chief of surgery who had also been in the right place at the right time.

Her mind wandered again. And this time she didn't call it back. Not when it had settled upon a handsome doctor with a rugged build and kind brown eyes. Kiernan O'Rourke. Now, *that* was an Irish name, she mused to herself. Her emerging smile halted as she thought about how earlier she had cut him off at the knees. He was just trying to be friendly by offering a hospital tour, one doctor to another, and she had abruptly declined.

I have to be somewhere.

She rolled her eyes at what must have come across as the lamest excuse ever.

In another day or two he'll forget all about it, Claire told herself.

At least that was what she hoped. The last thing she would ever want to do was hurt another person's feelings. And something told her that was especially true of the attractive Irish doctor who had just helped her bring a new life into the world.

CHAPTER THREE

CLAIRE PLOPPED DOWN on the small couch with its lopsided cushions in her quaint two-room rental cottage. It was early Tuesday evening, three days since that whirlwind of medical drama had left her spinning on every level.

She had arrived in Ireland with no game plan other than to engage in some much-needed soul-searching. But, even so, she recognized that her tendency to withdraw from others when dealing with a personal issue was not doing her any favors right now. Perhaps it was time to switch things up. No one had to know the real reason she was in Ireland for an extended stay. So why not seek out some group activities…like a guided tour of castles?

Great idea, she thought as she proceeded to search for local attractions on her phone.

A notification icon popped up on her screen and she stared at it for several seconds. If there was one sound piece of advice that had come out of her therapy sessions, it was to stay off social media as much as possible. The algorithms had a way of knowing what was on your mind and only feeding you more of it—whether "it" was something good or bad. She had long ago removed her ex-husband Mark from any social media friends list but, both being doctors, they had so many mutual acquaintances in the medical world that she couldn't be certain he wouldn't pop up in someone else's post when least expected.

Still, what was the harm in tapping on one update? Maybe it would be a fun kitten or puppy video—always guaranteed to bring a smile.

She opened the notification…and her heart stopped.

Staring back at her was a photo of Mark, cradling an infant in his arms. *Daddy celebrates three months of diaper duty and butterfly kisses with his little girl!* the caption read, followed by hearts and smiles emojis.

Furiously scanning the post, Claire quickly discovered it had originated on the page of Christine White, a physician assistant at Mark's internal medicine practice. Just as she had been warned, Christine's post had found its way onto her phone as a "people you may know" notification.

She closed her eyes, somehow managing to do the math in her head that confirmed Christine had been pregnant with Mark's child when he had walked out on her and Ariana. She shouldn't be surprised. She *wasn't* surprised. And yet the revelation still cut like a knife.

The blade went even deeper as she recalled how Mark had been contacted by the hospital when she was about to have labor induced for the stillbirth of Ariana. He couldn't be bothered to come. The depths of his cold indifference to his own flesh and blood were almost inconceivable…but he had started a new family, and had already rendered her and Ariana inconsequential.

A few more moments of pained disbelief and then Claire shook her head, as though she could physically dislodge all of the distressing thoughts.

Time to pull yourself up by the bootstraps, she instructed herself.

She hadn't traveled three thousand miles just to sit in a

small cottage and brood, now, had she? Well, maybe she had, but that was about to change.

When in Rome...

Okay, she was in Ballyledge, which most certainly wasn't Rome, but it had more than its share of charm and possibilities.

Rising from the couch and walking several steps to a side window, she looked out onto the purplish-orange sky as dusk set in. Her mind flashed back to a cute little pub that had caught her eye the previous day, while she'd been picking up groceries in the village. Overlooking the water, and with an outdoor terrace softly lit by string lights, it had just the right vibe to help ease her out of her slump. Or so she hoped.

Before she had a chance to talk herself out of her sudden plan, Claire headed to the bathroom to brush her hair, put on some clear lip gloss, then stare in the mirror as she declared, "You. Can. Do. This."

Twenty minutes later she was seated at a small wooden table on the outside terrace of Gilroy's Pub, watching the rising moon cast an ethereal glow over the inland bay. The low hum of conversation around her was just enough of a reminder that she was not alone. But that all changed in an instant as a loud, rambunctious group of men tumbled onto the terrace.

I might as well be in an American sports bar, Claire thought as she turned to look at the sweaty, disheveled men.

Their blue and white shorts and matching shirts were streaked with dirt and mud, and their metal-cleated shoes sounded like a herd of horses galloping to the barn for their oats. Not exactly the ambiance she was expecting at the pub, but then again, was it really so bad to witness a group of guys having some rabble-rousing fun?

Nope, Claire concluded, but she still turned away and refocused her gaze on the shimmering bay.

"Dr. Delaney?"

Claire swung her head around, then did a double-take as her eyes landed on Dr. Kiernan O'Rourke.

"I thought that was you," he said, briefly glancing at the chair across from her.

It was more than enough of a cue for her to ask him to have a seat. As he pulled up the chair, Claire's mouth was still slightly agape. Whether it was from the overall surprise of seeing him again, or the fact that West Mercy's chief of surgery was now sitting across from her with a patch of dirt caked on one cheek and a nasty scratch etched across the other, she couldn't be sure.

"This is quite the surprise, Dr. O— Mr. O'Rourke." Suddenly remembering that Irish surgeons use honorific titles, Claire caught herself just in time.

"Please, call me Kiernan. With all we went through the other day, at the very least we should be on a first-name basis."

Claire dipped her head as she smiled, then added, "Claire. Nice to meet you—again." After a slight pause, she shook her head and laughed quietly.

Kiernan cocked his head. "I'd ask if you were laughing *with* me, except I haven't told a joke."

"I'm sorry. It's just that… Well, the first time I saw you, I thought you looked like a professional rugby player."

"Ahh." Kiernan appeared almost relieved. "And then you discovered I'm just the boring chief of surgery at West Mercy Hospital."

Claire smirked. "No—it's not like that at all. More like, what are the chances that I'd see you again and you really *do* play rugby. At least I think that's a rugby uniform you're wearing. Or is it soccer?" She tapped her hand to her mouth. "Oops, I mean football."

"You saved yourself just in time," Kiernan joked. "In fact, I'm not sure if the word 'soccer' is officially banned from Ireland, but it should be."

Claire chuckled. "Point taken."

"But, yes, I play in a local rugby league. We usually have a match every Tuesday night from spring to late autumn."

"So you live in the area?"

"I do. I have a house about five miles from here. Up on a high bluff and overlooking the ocean—just in case I ever decide to take up cliff-diving in the spare time that I don't have." He paused. "You look surprised."

"That you might take up cliff-diving?" Claire replied, gamely playing along.

He grinned. "That I live in town."

"I guess I am…sort of. Working at the hospital in Galway— I would have figured you lived in the city."

Kiernan nodded his head from side to side, as though weighing her observation, his thick dark hair bobbing back and forth in unison. "That's a reasonable assumption. And I did live there for a few years."

"Oh?"

"I came back because I grew up in Ballyledge, and I may be biased, but I don't think there are many more pristine spots in the country."

"The scenery is breathtaking, that's for sure," Claire agreed.

"Plus, it helps keep me grounded. I'm sure I don't have to tell you that working in a hospital—especially on difficult cases when lives are in the balance—is like a constant adrenaline rush that can be hard to come down from. But here…" he nodded toward the water "…the sound of the waves crashing up against the rocks, with no one around other than some egrets and a few seals—it helps put things in perspective."

Claire gestured appreciatively. "Poetically said."

Kiernan took a sizeable sip of beer. "I kind of surprised myself with that one." As Claire laughed, he added, "Okay, now it's your turn."

Claire's laughter quickly petered out. "My turn?" she asked, wide-eyed. Her mind raced as she tried to think of what to say.

Keep it light. And happy. And...

"I didn't mean to put you on the spot," Kiernan said, viewing her through perplexed eyes.

It took some effort, but Claire found her smile once more. "No—that's fine. I was just trying to think of something that might be remotely interesting."

Kiernan raised an eyebrow, his expression equal parts surprised and amused. "I just spent two hours on a muddy field listening to nothing but grunts, burps and the splat of projectile spits. So trust me when I say *anything* you'd like to share about yourself right now will be infinitely more fascinating by comparison."

Claire snickered, feeling her guard drop a notch, not just emotionally, but physically as well. The release of tension in her neck and shoulders was a welcome respite. "Okay, well... I always wanted to visit Ireland, and here I am." She paused, debating whether to go one step further. "For a month."

Slow down there, girl, she chided herself inwardly.

"Now, see? *That* was interesting." Kiernan studied her closely, as if trying to discern more through sheer will.

Good luck with that, she thought.

"Did you come here with others?"

As Claire shook her head, she could almost see the intrigue growing in his eyes.

"Did you come here to visit someone, then?"

"Nope."

Kiernan sat back in his chair, crossing his arms and grinning at the same time, as though relishing the challenge before him. "So, why Ireland?"

"It's an Irish American thing, I guess. We all want to visit the motherland, so to speak, at some point in our lives."

"Delaney," Kiernan said with a nod. "Of course. And the hospital is okay with you being away for a whole month?"

Claire swallowed hard, her heart momentarily surging in her chest before quieting down. She needed to steer the conversation away from her career—which ultimately led back to babies—and fast.

"Boston General's good about encouraging us to take time off as needed."

"I see. That's great." He paused, another grin emerging. "I feel like I'm on one of those game shows where I'm trying to guess someone's back story with limited clues."

Claire smirked, realizing she was about to let her guard down a teeny-weeny bit more, but was surprisingly okay with that. "Go ahead—give it your best shot."

"All right, then." Kiernan glanced down at her unadorned wedding ring finger, then back up at her, his warm brown eyes latching onto her own. "You're here alone, so either there's no husband or kids at home, or you decided you needed a bit of a break from them, too."

Her smile faltered for a fraction of a second, but she managed to recover it. "No husband or kids."

He cocked his head to the side. "Hmm…the plot thickens. So you came here in the hopes of meeting some strapping Irishman who looks like he stepped off the set of a commercial?"

Claire had just taken a sip of wine, and in short order choked on it as Kiernan unknowingly voiced her silent assessment of him at their first meeting.

Kiernan chuckled. "I think I'm on to something. Ten points for contestant number three."

Claire waved him away as she coughed some more. "I just swallowed the wrong way, that's all."

"Right…" he said, clearly unconvinced.

She laughed, perplexed at the high level of comfort she felt around Kiernan, but determined to go with the flow.

"Okay," Kiernan began. "I've put you on the hot seat long enough. Now it's your turn to ask me a question."

Claire ran her index finger over the rim of her wine glass as she stalled for time. So many possible questions, but best to keep it light. "Did the hospital make you take out an insurance policy on your hands when they heard you were playing a rough contact sport on the side?"

Kiernan laughed, then held up his hands in mock examination. Claire felt a swish of butterflies in her stomach as she admired their obvious strength and masculinity. Not what she would normally picture as "surgeon's hands," but she certainly had no complaints about the view.

"No, but they did suggest I trade in rugby for badminton."

Claire chuckled. "Somehow I can't picture you daintily prancing up to a badminton net."

Kiernan laughed heartily. "You got that right."

"Let's see… You live high up on a bluff, but no cliff-diving as of yet?"

"Correct. I'm waiting for the cliffs to shrink to the size of ant hills."

Claire grinned. "Do you live alone?"

"I do."

"Is that a good thing or a bad thing?"

Kiernan teetered his head back and forth, as though weighing his answer. "I would say it's a good thing."

"Just a man in his castle?"

Kiernan looked amused. "Something like that."

"So, no wife and kids in your future, or you just haven't met the right woman?"

Careful, Claire…

"I suppose the latter—although some might say I'm married to my profession."

There were so many possible replies to that—some humorous, some cutting—but Claire chose instead to safely change the subject. Except that no alternative subject immediately came to mind.

Keep it happy, she reminded herself once again. *Nothing too deep...*

"Which is probably just as well," he went on. "Since I don't foresee any children in my future."

It took a few moments for Claire to realize that her face must have frozen into a mask of shock. How else to explain why Kiernan's smile had instantly faded, and his forehead visibly tensed as he attempted to explain himself further.

"I only mention that because you asked."

"Yes... Right... Not everyone wants kids. Nor should everyone have them, based on some of the horrors I've seen as a doctor. And you, too, I'm sure."

"Unfortunately, yes. But for me personally, it's more like I've learned from the mistakes of my own father. He was a surgeon, too. A *brilliant* surgeon, I should add. He helped pioneer some of the first organ laparoscopic surgeries. But he was a lousy father. I know it sounds crass to say that about one's own parent, but he'd probably be the first to admit it himself if he were still here."

"He's passed away?" Claire asked as delicately as possible, still reeling from Kiernan's unexpected revelation, but doing her best to hide that fact.

Kiernan nodded. "Three years ago. In the last five years of his life, we actually forged some semblance of a relationship. Although it was more like a friendship based on a shared interest in medicine rather than a father-and-son kind of thing. He did finally acknowledge that he'd been an absentee father for most of my life. I think that's why he felt it important to advise me not to have kids if I truly wanted to be the best surgeon I could possibly be."

"Hmm… That's interesting."

Kiernan cocked his head slightly to one side, a look of curiosity in his eyes. "What's interesting?"

"That instead of telling you not to make the mistake of putting career over family, he essentially told you the opposite."

Kiernan was silent for a moment. "I never really looked at it like that, but I suppose you're right."

"And your mom?"

Kiernan's face brightened. "My mum is doing great. She lives about a half-hour from here in an independent living community. I don't think she realized how much she was living in my dad's shadow until he passed away. Now, she's made new friends, has taken up gardening as a hobby, and to be honest, I don't think I've ever seen her happier."

"Well, I've obviously never met your mom, but I'm glad to hear that."

She had never met his father, either, but she sure was getting a picture of an overbearing man who may have been a genius with a scalpel, but couldn't quite cut it as a father or a husband.

"And what about your family?" Kiernan asked.

"I lost my dad, too, also three years ago. We were very close, so it was hard. Still is, some days. My mom lives in one of those nice little New England towns outside of Boston. You know—the kind that have old historical houses with placards that say, *Paul Revere rode past here to warn colonists about approaching British troops*."

That observation elicited a chuckle from Kiernan, prompting Claire to laugh as well.

"I have a younger brother who works in finance and lives in New York, still doing the bachelor thing despite my mom's matchmaking attempts. And I have a sister, Grace, who works in real estate and is two years older than me. She moved to Pennsylvania recently, when my brother-in-law relocated for a job promotion, and she has two young sons. They're great kids and I love being an aunt."

Kiernan smiled. "Well, I think I know you better now than I know most of my colleagues."

Was he joking? Claire couldn't be sure. She had certainly known her share of doctors who were all business while on duty, but Kiernan didn't strike her as the uptight, humorless type. Then again, they weren't in a hospital environment at the moment. Perhaps he felt the need to maintain a measure of personal detachment from his colleagues as chief of surgery—and, given the monumental responsibility of the role, that was understandable.

But before she could contemplate things further, Kiernan's rugby teammates came barreling over, surrounding their table and kicking up an aromatic cloud of sweat, dirt and beer.

"Is he bothering you?" a gargantuan man with hands the size of baseball mitts slurred, as he tried to focus through red-tinged eyes.

"Not at all," Claire replied with a wink in Kiernan's direction.

"He's a great catch, this one, you know," another teammate said with a wallop on Kiernan's back that nearly shook the table. "He's a surgery bigwig. Which is good—because he'd never make it as a professional rugby player."

As the teammate topped off this observation with a hard knock of his knuckles on Kiernan's skull, Claire winced. "Oh…careful! That had to hurt."

Kiernan chuckled—but not before slugging his buddy hard in the thigh from where he sat.

"Eh… I've been punched harder by my ninety-year-old grandmother," the teammate said, though his bulging eyes and creased forehead suggested otherwise.

Kiernan backed up his chair a bit. "Well, I'd love to continue this scintillating conversation with you brutes, but...*no.* You can leave now."

He pointed to the terrace bar—not that they needed directions on how to return to their temporary watering hole.

After some good-natured grumblings and a few rounds of friendly slaps and punches, the group retreated to the other side of the pub.

"Wow!" Claire exclaimed, before breaking into laughter.

"Not the most subtle bunch, huh?" Kiernan replied as he shook his head, a half-smile on his lips.

"Last orders!" the bartender boomed from behind the counter.

Claire glanced at her watch. "Geez, that went by fast."

"Can I get you another glass of wine?" Kiernan asked as he nodded toward her empty glass.

The word "sure" was about to roll off her lips. And then... reality set in, bringing with it a slew of blinking red caution lights. She would be leaving Ireland in less than a month.

He doesn't want kids!

Even though she knew he was simply being polite in asking if she wanted a drink at last call, she couldn't deny that she felt a growing attraction to him. So why tempt herself with a situation that could never be? She might be putting the cart before the horse, but it was for her own good. She had come to Ireland to find clarity and to heal—not to muddy the waters with a strong but dead-end attraction.

Claire slowly pushed back her chair and stood up. "Thanks, but I think I'm going to head back to my cottage now. I must still be grappling with some jet lag, because I feel like it's three in the morning!"

Really, Claire, another lame excuse?

She could tell by his pinched expression that Kiernan wasn't buying her explanation for a second. And the fact that this pinched face was still one of the most handsome she had ever encountered… Well, that was reason alone to conclude that she was doing the right thing.

Kiernan stood up from his chair. "Did you walk here?"

"I did. It only took me fifteen minutes. I'm staying at one of the pink cottages about a mile that way," she said, pointing west.

"Ah, the pink cottages—which used to be white, by the way," Kiernan noted. "There's a rumor that the owner refurbished them while on an acid trip, but you didn't hear that from me."

Claire snickered. "I did wonder about the color…not going to lie. But they're cute, and it's sort of the perfect little home-away-from-home while I'm here."

"Well, let me at least walk you back."

Claire forced a smile to mask the discomfort that was expanding inside. "I'm fine, really. It's not like walking back through some dark Boston alley. In fact, I went for a walk last night along the pier and it was really quite beautiful." She looked up at the sky. "The moon and stars were out in full force, just like tonight."

Kiernan watched her silently for several moments, his lips pressed tightly together. Finally, he nodded and managed a smile. "Well, if you get bored and want someone to talk to over the next few weeks I'm here every Tuesday evening with my fellow louts. I'm occasionally here on late Sunday afternoons, too. There's a team practice that I join when I can, and we usually wind down afterwards with a pint or two."

"I'll keep that in mind," Claire said, truly appreciative of his offer.

Kiernan's lips curved into a slight grin. "Oh—and one more thing. If you decide to hit up the usual tourist spots, you might want to spray the Blarney Stone with a strong antiseptic before kissing it. Just saying…"

Claire chuckled quietly. "That's good advice."

"By the way, how are you getting around? Do you have a car?"

"I rented a Mini. A little red one. Goes perfectly with the pink house."

Kiernan smiled and nodded. "Good choice. Well, you take care."

"You, too."

As Claire walked past him, unable to fully divert her eyes away from his muscular body as it pressed against his taut athletic shirt, it was as if something grabbed hard at her stomach.

Once outside, she took a deep breath and allowed the cool night air to seep into her lungs. For a split second she questioned her decision to close the door—no, make that *slam* the door—on any further interaction with Kiernan. But she had no choice. She had come to Ireland to make a difficult decision that could potentially alter the course of her life from hereon in. The last thing she needed was to tempt another complication that would only create more heartache. She had had enough of that for a lifetime already.

Kiernan walked into the still-dark kitchen of his home and tossed his keys onto the counter. Switching on the light, he felt as though he could hear the emptiness that surrounded him. There were plenty of inanimate objects in view, of course, and some, like the refrigerator, emitted a low-level hum that could pass for a sign of life, albeit an electronic one.

But no human voices. No greeting from a loving partner, no joyful screeches of an excited child.

Not even a bark or a meow.

And although he had once toyed with the idea of getting a couple of goldfish, even that had fallen by the wayside when he'd considered the possibility that his fairly frequent one, two or even three-nighters at the hospital meant potentially coming home to fish that were floating belly-up in a tank.

The irony that he could save lives in the direst of situations as a surgeon but couldn't sustain a pet goldfish—or even a companion plant—was not lost on Kiernan.

He grimaced as he opened a bottle of electrolyte-infused water, staring blankly at the bland, cream-colored wall as he took several long sips. He was used to being met by silence upon returning home—found comfort in it, actually—but tonight something felt different.

He wondered if his reaction had been spawned by the look on Claire's face when he had mentioned his intention to live a child-free life. She had seemed surprised by his revelation, if not momentarily disturbed, but should she have been? How could any doctor at the top of their game feel differently?

He placed the bottle on the counter and sighed, knowing well the answer to his own question.

Because not every doctor had a father like you.

Which, depending on how he looked at it, was both a blessing and a curse.

The blessing was that he'd inherited his father's innate ability to excel as a surgeon—a combination of empirical knowledge, think-outside-the-box innovation and exceptional dexterity that had turned his hands into lifesaving instruments.

The curse was…well, it was the very same thing. Because— just like his father—he had an unrelenting desire to constantly improve. And continually expanding his skillset and saving more lives didn't just happen on its own. It required devotion to a singular purpose. Day in and day out. *Year* in and *year* out.

His father had made the mistake of thinking that if he cut back from one hundred percent devotion to his career to ninety-five percent, and directed the remaining five percent to his family, it would be enough. How wrong he had been. Those sparse breadcrumbs had been no substitute for his presence at the primary school play or the secondary school rugby game.

Even career advice had been more aptly dispensed by the

school's advisor than his own father. When Kiernan had told his father that he was applying to the School of Medicine at Trinity College—his father's alma mater—the detached reply had been: "Don't expect to coast on my coattails if you get in." Not *I'm so proud of you* or *You'll make a great surgeon*.

His dad had relayed one more nugget of advice that Kiernan had taken to heart, though: "You'd better not entertain trying out for the Trinity rugby team if you do get in. You need to devote one thousand percent to your studies, otherwise you'll never make it."

Kiernan smiled wistfully as he recalled one of his first actions upon starting his freshers year. Not only had he tried out for Trinity's football team, but he'd been the star inside center up until graduation. Had it been a safe act of rebellion on his part? Perhaps. But he couldn't have rebelled by choosing an alternative profession—that would have only hurt him, not his dad.

He was doing what he was meant to do. And he had learned from his father's mistakes. He would forgo having a family of his own not because he was cold inside, or because he had no affinity for children, but because he *did*. And he would never want them to suffer the loneliness and insecurity that he had felt as a young boy, growing up with a father who was a parent in name only.

Kiernan shuddered as he pulled himself back to the present. That was then, and this was now. Yes, there had been more than a few romantic relationships that had skidded to a halt once the topic of children had been broached, but better to know upfront that his priorities were a deal-breaker for someone. The simple fact was that most women wanted a family of their own—and he would never want to deny them that source of joy and fulfillment.

Perhaps he was destined to sail through life unattached, and he was okay with that. Well, it was more like he had come to accept that this was his fate. It was a choice he'd made knowingly and willingly—career over commitment—and he had yet to regret his decision.

His thoughts turned to Claire, her face coming into sharp focus in his mind. The pale but piercing green eyes, the full, pillowy lips and rich chestnut hair. What was her real story, anyway? Why was she taking a whole month off from her critical role as an ob-gyn at a major Boston hospital? Why had she come to Ireland all alone? Was it some sort of American thing? She certainly didn't strike him as the flighty type— quite the opposite, actually—but something just didn't add up.

Not that he would ever get answers to his questions. Unless Claire decided to deliberately show up at the pub when he was there—and he highly doubted she would—he was never going to see her again. She had disappeared into the darkness of the night like Cinderella, leaving him with no means to contact her. Instead of a glass slipper, he needed…what? A hospital-grade clog to try and track her down?

Perhaps it was just as well, Kiernan thought. Something told him he could fall hard for the intriguing American doctor who had suddenly appeared in his life. And that, quite simply, did not fit in with his ultimate plan.

CHAPTER FOUR

"THERE YOU ARE," Lucy said to Kiernan as he looked up from his tablet.

Though he would admit it to no one, he sometimes longed for the days—not so far in the past—when he could rifle through physical charts rather than be tapping ad nauseam on a digital screen.

"What is it with this thing?" Kiernan said impatiently as he pressed on "lab results" and up popped a list of the patient's current medications instead. "Are my fingers too fat or something?"

Lucy twisted her mouth to one side. "No, I'm sure it's just that the tabs are too small."

Placing the tablet onto the nurses' station counter with an exasperated sigh, he turned to Lucy. "Nice try."

"I do my best."

"Were you looking for me?"

"I was. It's about Jan Reddy—her ultrasound last week showed fetal spina bifida."

"Yes…right. I haven't met with her personally, but her case came up in the weekly staff meeting."

Lucy nodded. "She's here for more tests this morning, and I was wondering if maybe you'd be able to talk to her. She's having a hard time dealing with the diagnosis, especially since her surgery options are still up in the air."

"Of course. I'll swing by and see her. I thought we had our scheduling staff looking into fetal surgery availability at other hospitals?"

"They are, but no luck as of yet."

Kiernan grimaced. It was not the news he wanted to hear. Fetal surgery for spina bifida offered hope for babies that were developing in the womb with an open gap in their spinal cord. But it was an extremely complex surgery that only certain hospitals were equipped to offer, and West Mercy wasn't one of them.

Kiernan hoped that this would change once the new neonatal wing was up and running, but even then it would most likely be some way down the road. It took a very gifted surgeon to perform this delicate operation, and although he had many exceptional surgeons on his staff, none were trained in this type of procedure. All of which meant Jan would have to find another hospital that could schedule the surgery in time, and even if that was possible it would mean significant personal expense and possibly traveling away from her two young children.

"Okay, keep me posted. I'll probably touch base with Dr. Fleming first," he said, referring to Jan's obstetrician, "but I'll check in on Jan right after."

"Great, thanks," Lucy replied. She nodded toward the tablet on the counter. "Don't forget to take your friend with you on your travels. As of last count, it's been brought to a nurses' station on every floor and designated as 'lost' no less than a dozen times."

Kiernan shot an annoyed glance at the device. "Yeah, well... I guess subconsciously I keep hoping that it won't find its way back to me."

Lucy smirked. "Progress, Mr. O'Rourke. It's a good thing, I promise."

Once Lucy had departed, Kiernan took a moment to organize his thoughts. Per usual, he had a busy day ahead, but he preferred to map it out in his mind rather than record it on the tablet.

"Hey, hey, hey, my man!" Sebastian exclaimed as he suddenly inserted himself in front of Kiernan like a photo-bombing squirrel.

"Not you again," Kiernan replied with a mixture of annoyance and friendly affection.

"Listen, that hot American doctor from the other day... I got the goods on her."

Now *this* had Kiernan's attention. "What do you mean?"

"I discovered she's got quite the resume back at Boston General."

Kiernan's voice grew sharper. "And how exactly did you find this out?"

Sebastian let loose with a crocodile smile. "Simple. You told me her name..." The smile grew impossibly wider. "And Google is my friend."

Kiernan slid the tablet off the counter and tucked it under his arm. "Good, because you don't have any others."

Like all of Kiernan's pretend insults, this one rolled off Sebastian like water off a duck. "My, my, we're touchy today. I was certain you'd want to know that she's considered an expert in high-risk pregnancies and cutting-edge fetal surgery. And she's got quite the list of awards and distinctions."

"I'm not surprised," Kiernan said. "I saw firsthand what she's capable of."

Sebastian ran his fingers through his perfectly coiffed hair, then leaned his elbow on the counter. "You think she's still in the area? I bet I could find out where she's staying. I've never played tour guide before, but for her I'd make an exception."

Kiernan viewed him through narrowed eyes. "And I've never punched a colleague before, but I'm about to make an exception as well."

Sebastian raised his hands in mock surrender. "Take it easy, sunshine. I was just joking around."

Kiernan swung his arm in Sebastian's direction, prompting him to lurch back from the counter with a high-pitched yelp.

Instead of landing a punch, Kiernan patted him on the shoulder. "You're awfully jumpy today. Might want to cut back on your morning caffeine fix."

With a wink, Kiernan headed off for a quick chat with Dr. Fleming.

Jan Reddy was lying down on the treatment table when Kiernan entered the room. Her face was turned away as she stared at the far wall, but upon hearing the door swing open, she immediately looked over.

"Hello, Jan, I'm Mr. O'Rourke," Kiernan said as he walked up to her and shook her hand. "I'm the chief of surgery here at West Mercy." He pulled up a chair and seated himself close to the head of the table. "My staff have been keeping me up to date on your case, but I wanted to meet and talk to you personally, if that's okay."

Her tense face softened into a smile. "Yes, of course."

"I know these past few days since the spina bifida diagnosis haven't been easy."

She shook her head. "They haven't. You read about this sort of thing happening to other women, and you never think it's going to happen to you. Especially since my other two pregnancies were perfectly healthy."

"Unfortunately, that's how it is sometimes with birth defects. There's no rhyme or reason to it. I reviewed your case history, and you have none of the risk factors."

"That's what Dr. Fleming said. She's so nice… But things like diabetes, and I think she said folate deficiency was another factor—they don't apply to me."

Kiernan pressed his lips together and nodded. At times

like this, when there was nothing he could do in the moment to instantly fix something, he could only offer a genuine gesture of understanding.

"So, I know Dr. Fleming has talked to you about fetal surgery to repair the spinal opening…"

"She has. And I know the surgery can't be done here."

"Believe me when I say I wish that weren't the case. We're working hard to get to a point where we can offer fetal surgeries for spina bifida and other congenital anomalies. In the meantime, we're hoping we can find a spot for you at another hospital that can perform this procedure. I spoke to Dr. Fleming a little while ago, and she said that even if we can, you have some concerns about whether to move forward with the surgery."

"I do. And I know this probably won't make any sense, but when I found out that I was a candidate for fetal surgery, I wished for a second that I wasn't. Because that way I wouldn't have to make a decision that could possibly lead to the death of my baby." She paused and swallowed hard. "Or me. And I want you to know that I would do anything to save my baby's life—even if it meant losing mine. But I have two other children who need me. And a husband, too." She rolled her eyes, topped off with a half-smile. "You know how most men are just big babies themselves."

Kiernan laughed quietly. "So I've heard."

He truly felt for Jan. She was facing a dilemma that he wouldn't wish on anyone. It was true that not all mothers-to-be facing her predicament fulfilled the criteria needed to move forward with the surgery. From the mother's past medical history to a current BMI, and even the presence of a support person, there were a number of boxes that needed to be checked off before the green light could be given for the procedure. Additionally, the anomaly had to be discovered early enough for the surgery to be performed—in the twenty-second to twenty-fifth week of pregnancy. In Jan's case, it had been discovered during her second trimester scan at twenty-one weeks. Which meant the clock was ticking…and the pressure was on.

As a surgeon, Kiernan didn't believe in sugarcoating the risks to a patient. In his mind, it was ultimately a disservice to them. Instead, he believed they should have all the facts they needed to make an informed decision, and he would always fully support them in whatever they chose to do.

"Jan, I know this is not an easy decision. I'm sure Dr. Fleming went over this with you, but there's always the option of post-delivery surgery. This would typically be within the first twenty-four to forty-eight hours after birth. It's less risky but, since spina bifida is a progressive condition, it won't halt progression within the womb like fetal surgery can do, so your baby will most likely experience more complications down the road. That being said, I've seen it lessen considerably the severity of spina bifida in the handful of patients that we've treated here."

"And you can perform this surgery here?"

"Yes."

"But it won't fix the defect to the same degree that fetal surgery can?"

"Unfortunately, no."

Jan stared up at the ceiling and sighed. "I wish I could talk to someone who's actually performed fetal surgery for spina bifida and can personally share with me the good and bad of how it turned out." She gasped, then sat up on her elbows. "I'm sorry, Mr. O'Rourke! I didn't mean to imply that talking to you isn't helpful, because it is…"

Kiernan smiled. "No need to apologize. I totally understand where you're coming from. I'm still hopeful that we'll be able to line you up with a surgeon at another hospital, and once we do, I'm sure they'll be more than happy to answer any of your questions."

She squeezed her lips together as though doing her best to smile through her anxious thoughts. "Thank you for coming by."

"Of course." Kiernan stood up. "And I know you're in good hands with Dr. Fleming and the rest of her team, but I'm here if you need anything."

This time her smile was full width. "I appreciate that."

As Kiernan started down the hospital corridor, he tried to organize the tidal wave of thoughts that were cresting all at once in his mind. Hearing Jan speak firsthand about the treatment options for her baby's condition only strengthened his resolve to ensure West Mercy's new neonatal wing would one day be fully equipped to offer cutting-edge fetal surgery—and more.

But that wasn't going to help Jan now. His temples throbbed with the realization that, no matter how lofty his ambitions to go all in and give one hundred and ten percent on behalf of his patients, there were still obstacles that he had no control over. All he could do was plow ahead, knowing that progress was inevitable, but often on its own timetable.

And then another thought hit him like a bolt of lightning. He paused and rifled through the pocket of his lab coat, extracting his phone and instantly initiating a search. Tapping on a search results link, his eyes widened…and then widened some more.

"Thank you, Sebastian," he said under his breath. "You're a pain in the ass, but sometimes a *helpful* pain in the ass."

Claire tossed some breadcrumbs into the water and laughed as a small flock of ducks pounced on the treats, slurping them up within seconds. She threw out another handful, then announced, "That's all I got, guys!"

Yesterday, she had followed the path from her cottage down over a slight hill, through thickened brush and finally an opening that revealed the shallow, rocky shoreline of the bay. She had been instantly captivated by the colorful waterfowl, chirping birds and myriad wildflowers, and today was no different.

Despite her vow a few days ago to get out and mingle with other people, she was finding the quiet serenity of nature to be a much greater draw. Spotting a large boulder to sit on, she pulled up her knees and rested her forearms and chin on top of them. There was no doubt in her mind that this peaceful solitude would be a better facilitator than loud tourist spots for the monumental career decision that she needed to make. And yet she felt no closer to a resolution than when she had first arrived in the country.

Closing her eyes, she replayed all that had already transpired in less than a week. An emergency breech delivery. An unexpected but powerful attraction to a fellow doctor. No wonder she was no further along in sorting out a difficult professional dilemma.

Reopening her eyes and staring out at the gently shimmering waters, her thoughts were pulled like a magnet back to her encounter with Kiernan at the pub. Since the end of her marriage, and the loss of Ariana, she had not felt even the slightest spark of interest toward another man. Not those who had approached her during occasional social outings with friends, a drink in one hand and a "How *you* doing?" tumbling out of their mouths, nor the male colleagues who had been circling the waters upon news of her divorce.

Her therapist and her friends had more than once suggested that maybe she was protecting her heart after Mark's betrayal and Ariana's death. But if that were true, it was on an unconscious level, rather than a deliberate decision to squash any attraction. She simply hadn't *felt* anything, either physically or emotionally, toward another man. And, given that she hadn't been in the right headspace to open her heart up to someone else, it was probably just as well.

And yet, with seemingly no effort on his part, Kiernan had drawn her in and reawakened a yearning in her that she had come to believe was gone for good. Perhaps it was the easy rapport they shared. The kind brown eyes and disarming smile. The sexily tousled hair—oh, heck, the sexy *everything*. She smiled at the deliciousness of her thoughts—until reminding herself that although daydreaming about Kiernan was an enjoyable pastime, it was also a distraction that she couldn't afford right now. Not when her career hung in the balance, and her time would be best spent engaging in some serious soul-searching.

With that in mind, Claire forced herself to redirect her thoughts. But a sudden, familiar voice stopped them dead in their tracks.

"Claire!"

Swinging her head around, Claire watched, mouth slightly agape, as Kiernan spread aside the end of a thicket patch with both hands and emerged out into the open.

What in the...?

She stood up from the boulder, both happy to see him and wishing she could feel otherwise. "How in the world did you know where to find me?"

Kiernan grinned, the sun catching golden flecks in his brown eyes. "Well, I knocked on every pink cottage door, and only strangers answered. Then I came to your cottage, and no one was home. But I saw fresh footprints that looked to be your size on the path behind the cottage and decided to follow them."

"For real," she insisted, with a *Yeah, right* expression etched across her face.

"Okay, the red Mini parked outside gave it away."

Claire tapped her head with her hand as if to say, *Of course*.

"I know this is a surprise…" Kiernan said, taking a few more steps to close the gap between them.

"You could say that."

Kiernan stared into her eyes. "I have a favor to ask you. Actually, if you could magnify the word 'favor' by about ten thousand, then that's what I'm about to ask."

"Okay, now you're starting to scare me," Claire said, only half kidding.

"I don't mean to scare you," Kiernan said, as he briefly touched her forearm.

Perhaps the gesture was meant to calm her, but the electricity that shot through her had the opposite effect. Coupled with the intense physical attraction she felt for the hunky surgeon just inches away from her, the surge caught her off guard. But as she regained her breath and looked into his eyes, she allowed herself to settle into the feeling his touch provoked. And it felt good.

"I met with a patient today whose unborn baby was recently diagnosed with spina bifida."

Kiernan's words quickly put a damper on the opening she had allowed herself. She wasn't sure if it was her chest or her stomach that tightened first, but either way a sense of dread was building.

"She's been ruled as a candidate for fetal surgery, and we're trying to set her up with a hospital that offers the procedure. But she's worried about the outcome if she goes through with it. She has two young children, and she doesn't want to leave them without a mother if something goes wrong."

"There's always a risk," Claire conceded, "but the odds would still be in her favor."

"I think knowing that would help her make the right decision for her baby and her family."

"You mean no doctors at West Mercy have explained the risks and benefits of the surgery to her?"

"They have. But I really think it would help if she heard it from someone who's actually performed the procedure."

Claire felt her heart quicken—no small feat given that her chest was now tighter than a drum. "Wait—do you mean *me*?"

Kiernan nodded, his eyes eager with anticipation.

"What makes you think I've even performed this surgery?"

"It came up in a Google search."

"You *Googled* me?" Claire asked, her voice rising.

"It's not as bad as it sounds," Kiernan replied, his face tight as though he were talking on eggshells, never mind walking on them.

"After meeting with the patient this morning—her name is Jan—I got to wondering if maybe you'd done this sort of surgery yourself. It was just a hunch. In fact, I wasn't expecting anything to turn up in my search when I entered your name, but quite a bit did." He paused, his face softening as he added, "It's not my fault you're an exceptionally talented doctor."

Claire *almost* smiled.

"You've performed close to a dozen successful spina bifida fetal surgeries. I mean, I can't imagine anyone more qualified to talk to Jan about what to expect if she moves forward with the surgery." He paused, the silence between them peppered with the sound of birdsong and water gently lapping up against rocks. "I know you're here on vacation, and I shouldn't even be asking you. But if you're up for this, it would just be an hour at most of your time. A consultation, that's all."

Claire stared down at the ground as she ran through the scenario in her head.

A woman has discovered she's carrying a baby with a condition that could significantly compromise the quality of his or her life. She's devastated. She's scared. She wants to do the right thing for her unborn baby and the two children she already has. How can I not do what I can to help her make that decision?

Claire knew very well that she couldn't answer this question without first placing it within a greater context. After all, if there were two things that were *not* on her Ireland travel itinerary, they were entering a hospital and meeting with a patient. Especially when her whole reason for being here was to figure out whether she could resume that life. But there was a flipside to every coin, and an argument could just as easily be made that the only way to determine this would be to walk the walk. Which in this case meant meeting Jan and talking through the treatment options that were best for her and her unborn baby.

Trial by fire. Or, better yet, trial by *controlled* fire.

Claire looked back up at Kiernan, silently catching her breath as his handsome face greeted her with a smile. There was something in that moment between them that told her she could do this. Something about *him* that made her feel safe and infused with inner strength.

"Okay," she said, a smile slowly emerging. "I'll do it."

"Thank you," Kiernan said breathlessly. "Thank you so much."

"No need to thank me."

"Would tomorrow work for you?" he asked. "Say at around eleven a.m.?"

"Yes, I can do that."

"Great! I'll pick you up at—"

"I'll drive to the hospital myself," Claire interjected, softening her tone when she noticed how Kiernan flinched at her unintended harshness.

It was difficult enough pushing past her fears and agreeing to the consultation. No need to add to the stomach butterflies she'd be feeling tomorrow by sitting oh-so-close to Kiernan on the drive in.

"After all, I've got this cute little Mini, so I might as well put it to use."

Kiernan chuckled. "Yes, good idea."

Ten silent seconds passed by as slow as molasses. Claire

smiled and widened her eyes—her go-to expression when she was feeling uneasy or awkward. There was a nonverbal exchange of...*something*...between them, and it pulled at every fiber of her being in a way that she hadn't felt in a very long time.

"So I'll see you and Jan tomorrow at eleven?" she asked, feeling the need to fill in the silence.

Kiernan smiled and nodded—then jolted slightly as though suddenly remembering something. He pulled his phone from a side pocket in his scrub pants. "Should we exchange phone numbers? Just in case there's an emergency or I need to adjust the time?"

Claire hesitated momentarily. It was a reasonable request, but also one more swing of the sledgehammer into the barrier she had built around herself. But maybe she should let go of a brick or two. For Kiernan, she could do that.

"My phone is in the cottage, but call my number and I'll have yours as well." She quickly recited the numbers, and he punched them into his phone.

"Great. Well, I've got two surgeries scheduled this afternoon, so I'd better be heading back to the hospital." He started to leave, then stopped. "Oh, and don't forget. We drive on the left side of the road here."

Claire grinned. "Thanks for the reminder."

Trudging through the dense thicket that lined the midsection of the path on the way back to his car, Kiernan felt elated. Not even the thorns that were catching on his shirt or the burrs sticking to his hair were enough to deter his ear-to-ear smile. He had successfully convinced Claire to meet with Jan and fully trusted that she would help Jan better understand the risks and benefits of spina bifida fetal surgery so that she could make the best possible decision for her and her family.

But his smile soon wavered as he replayed the look in

Claire's eyes as he had awaited her answer. Granted, he hadn't expected her to jump for joy at the prospect of taking time out of her vacation to consult on a patient. Or...maybe he kind of had. She was a dedicated doctor and a confident, highly skilled surgeon, and this was an opportunity to weigh in on a potential surgical outcome that could significantly better the lives of a mother and her unborn child. Plus, shouldn't she be even mildly curious to see how West Mercy was positioning itself to eventually offer innovative neonatal surgeries? So why the unmistakable hesitancy on her part?

His hand resting on the door handle of his SUV, Kiernan stood immobile as he pondered the question further. Finally, he shook his head and opened the door. Perhaps he was overthinking things. His question had caught Claire by surprise, and understandably so. Tomorrow it would all work out. Jan would get the consultation she had hoped for. And he would once again have the chance to bask in Claire's presence. And, oh, what a presence it was. Beauty, intelligence, empathy and compassion—all wrapped into one somewhat mysterious but altogether magnetic package.

His thoughts were steamrollering through his head—until an obvious buzzkill slammed on the brakes. In less than a month Claire would be returning to her life in the States. Which meant time was of the essence if he was going to act on his undeniable attraction to her. Perhaps Sebastian was right—painful as that was to admit. He should savor the present moment—nothing more, nothing less. And the good thing about the present moment? It was already here.

CHAPTER FIVE

CLAIRE FELT HER tight grip on the steering wheel relax as late-morning sunshine filtered in through the Mini's windshield and side windows. The fact that she had butterflies in her stomach was more than apropos, given that springtime was on the verge of full bloom in the early-May countryside.

The serene landscape of lush fields and colorful wildflowers helped calm her nerves, but didn't erase them altogether. Not that anything could totally put her at ease. After all, she was on her way to West Mercy Hospital, where she would be meeting with a worried mother to help her make a momentous decision about her unborn baby.

You can do this, Claire told herself, slowly drawing in a breath of air and holding it for several moments as she inwardly repeated the mantra. *It's a one-time consultation, that's all.*

She needed to remind herself of this as well, given that it was a far cry from her normal interaction with patients. She was accustomed to getting to know them and their families well—especially those who were dealing with difficult medical situations.

The importance of maintaining an emotional detachment had been instilled in her since day one of medical school. But even though she had been an overachiever in all of her classes, this was one area where she didn't mind falling short if it meant allowing herself to care about her patients. She celebrated their joys and grieved their losses. Only now did she realize how doing so had made it more difficult to put her own pain aside when she had resumed her physician duties after losing Ariana.

Driving into the West Mercy parking lot, she pulled into the nearest open space, turned off the engine, then closed her eyes and reminded herself that she needed to hide her vulnerability not just from Jan, but from Kiernan, too. Neither of them needed to know that she felt like a walking open wound. Or that just speaking the word "baby" was enough to grab at her gut with a pain that she actually felt on a physical level.

The good news was there could be a happy ending to all of this. As a onetime consultant on Jan's condition, she would be playing the most minor of roles in such a miracle, but it was still something.

Walking up to the main entrance a short time later, Claire suddenly stopped in her tracks and viewed the multi-building complex before her. Seen from the front, the hospital was much larger than she had expected, prompting inevitable reminders of Boston General. Her earlier resolve to push past potential triggers was facing its first severe test, and she had to quickly recover before all was lost.

Deep breaths. Deep breaths.

Pinching her palm with her nails, she temporarily dispersed the distressing thoughts and memories that were tumbling forth. A few more seconds, another deep breath, and she was fully back in the present.

Once inside the entrance, Claire realized she hadn't locked down the details of where exactly to meet Kiernan. But as she approached the main nurses' station, she recognized a familiar friendly face.

"Hello, Dr. Delaney," Lucy said with a warm smile as she walked out from behind the station counter. "Mr. O'Rourke has just finished with a patient and is on his way down." Glancing over her shoulder, she added, "Speak of the devil."

"Are you calling me the devil?" Kiernan asked with amusement as he seemingly materialized from out of the blue.

Or maybe Claire's slightly dizzy reaction upon seeing him once again just made it feel that way. It was a brief but altogether enjoyable distraction from her nerves.

Lucy flashed a side grin. "Of course not. You're nothing short of angelic, Mr. O'Rourke. And I know your patients would all agree."

"Good save." There was a twinkle in Kiernan's eyes that grew in intensity as he shifted his gaze to Claire. "How was the drive in?" he asked, his dark brown hair imperfectly…yet perfectly…tousled.

Claire's next breath caught in her throat. If ever there was an *I'm a brilliant surgeon too busy to brush my hair, but I'm still sexy as heck* vibe, then this had to be it. Not that Kiernan deliberately sent out those signals. Up to this point, everything in his demeanor had convinced Claire that he had no idea how attractive he was. Or, if he did, it fell so low on his list of important virtues that he simply couldn't care less.

She forced herself to exhale, then smiled. "It was fine. I have to say I really like that little Mini. I'm not sure how it would fare during a Boston winter, but I think I'm going to look into getting one when I'm back in the States."

Kiernan's smile momentarily faltered, as though the reminder of the temporary nature of her stay had triggered a somber moment. Or maybe she was just projecting her own suddenly mixed feelings on the subject.

Stepping off the elevator several minutes later, Kiernan turned to Claire. "Before you talk to Jan, I thought you might want to look over her case notes and test results."

Claire nodded. "Sure, that's a good idea."

"My office is just down this hall," he said.

Upon entering the smallish but neat and well-lit room, Claire's eyes were drawn to the barrage of diplomas and certificates, along with a handful of framed photos, that lined the wall behind his desk. "I can see you're quite the under-achiever," she observed wryly.

Kiernan grinned slightly, but said nothing as he rifled through a pile of folders on his expansive desk.

"Wait—is that Bono?" Claire asked incredulously as she homed in on a photo of Kiernan hugging shoulders with the Irish rocker.

Kiernan looked up from a thick folder that he had just ex-tracted from the pile. "Ah, yes. That's from a hospital charity event last year. Quite an interesting chap—and very gener-ous, too."

Claire eyed Kiernan curiously, amused by his rather non-chalant reply.

There was a knock on the partially open door, and she and Kiernan turned as a young male nurse in light green scrubs began to enter the room. Realizing that Kiernan wasn't alone, he stopped mid-step.

"Sorry, I'll come back," he said, slowly retreating back-wards.

"No, come on in," Kiernan said. "Did you hear back from UCLH?"

The man frowned, as though dreading his own reply. "I did. Mr. Ferguson dislocated his shoulder during a golf match over the weekend. He's out of commission for at least the next month."

"Damn," Kiernan muttered under his breath. "We're run-ning out of options. And that one was looking like a sure thing." He sighed heavily, then turned back to the nurse. "What about Manchester General?"

"Still waiting to hear back."

"Okay, keep me posted."

"I will," the nurse said, before exiting the room.

Claire didn't want to pry about what was clearly distressing news for Kiernan, but she did wonder if it could possibly have something to do with Jan. She didn't have to guess for long.

"That was University College Hospital in London," Kiernan explained. "We were told a few days ago that they might be able to do Jan's surgery in two weeks. I haven't told her yet, because we were waiting for final confirmation, and it's a good thing I didn't. And I get grief for risking injury while playing rugby... Who knew putting a tiny white ball around in starched checked trousers was more dangerous than being face-deep in mud at the bottom of a rugby pileup?"

"Wild," Claire said quietly, viscerally feeling Kiernan's frustration. "But fetal surgery is more common now than, say, even ten years ago. Granted, not every hospital is equipped to perform some of the procedures, or has the right team in place, but it seems like there should be more options if you're expanding your search outside the country."

"There are. But one of the issues is red tape—something I'm sure you deal with back in America as well."

Claire rolled her eyes almost instinctively. "I have more experience with that than I'd like to admit. But I thought it would be a bit less so here, given the exchange between countries within Europe. Not that I fully understand how that might work."

"Unfortunately, red tape is red tape—especially when it comes to scheduling a complex surgery in another country at short notice." He grimaced, then gave a slight nod of the head as though trying to snap himself out of negative thoughts. "Here," he said, his voice softening as he handed the folder to Claire. "This should have all of Jan's records."

"Thanks," Claire replied, the hefty stack of papers landing in her hands like a solid brick. Or two. "You don't have digital records here at the hospital?"

"We do. But I like to have a hard copy of cases I'm working on as well." He paused, a half-smirk slowly emerging. "Call me old school."

Claire grinned. "Nothing wrong with that."

She leafed through the numerous documents in the folder, pausing at the ultrasound report. It confirmed what she'd expected with considerable apprehension: Jan's baby had the most severe form of spina bifida, myelomeningocele, in which part of the spine protruded from the back in a fluid-filled sac. It meant the surgery would be that much more difficult—and a positive outcome would be that much more life-enhancing. She then viewed the surgery criteria notes, a checklist of close to two dozen "must-haves" in order for the surgery to move forward. No history of placenta previa or hypertension…ability to adhere to a follow-up requirements…*check, check, check*….

It was only when she was three-quarters through the checklist that she realized she had been reviewing the notes without the stomach-churning anxiety she had tried to prepare for. Could it be because she was in a new hospital, and not at Boston General, which had triggers at every turn? It was a possible revelation that she'd need to ruminate on further. But right now she had to concentrate on Jan's prognosis.

Finishing her review, Claire looked up to find that Kiernan had been watching her intently, as though taking his next breath was contingent upon receiving her thumbs-up. She wasn't about to disappoint him.

"Jan's a textbook candidate for this surgery."

He pursed his lips together and nodded. "That's my team's assessment as well. But I wanted to hear it from the expert."

There was the slightest teasing edge to Kiernan's voice, but Claire didn't mind. She knew he respected her exceptional knowledge and experience on this matter—just as she respected his immense know-how in…well, no doubt in everything related to surgery and hospital leadership.

"Shall we go and talk to Jan?" Kiernan asked as he opened the door to the hallway and gestured for Claire to exit first.

Claire smiled, masking her inner turmoil. As she started down the hallway, with Kiernan by her side, there were only two thoughts in her mind:

Stay strong for Jan. And for her baby.

Kiernan ushered Claire into a tastefully decorated consultation room that more closely resembled a cozy parlor.

A petite woman in a white lab coat with a short black bob and ice-blue eyes immediately stood up from one of several thick-cushioned chairs and came over.

"I'm Dr. Fleming, senior doctor ob-gyn," she said, shaking Claire's hand. "Mr. O'Rourke has filled me in on everything, and I really appreciate you taking the time to talk to Jan about fetal surgery."

"Nice to meet you," Claire said.

As Dr. Fleming resumed her seat, Kiernan introduced Claire to Jan, who sat on the adjacent couch.

"Hi," she said, managing a weak smile. "Thank you for being here. Mr. O'Rourke said you're an expert at spina bifida fetal surgery."

Now seated between Dr. Fleming and Kiernan, Claire silently took note of the dark circles under Jan's eyes, the hollow cheeks and raspy voice. There was no doubt that the immense worry about her unborn baby's condition was taking its toll.

"I'm glad to be here," Claire replied. "I know Mr. O'Rourke and Dr. Fleming have talked to you about the benefits of fetal surgery for your baby, and I'm sure you have lots of questions."

"I do. But the two main ones are, will it work? And is there a possibility I won't survive the surgery?" Jan's voice cracked as she added, "I'm not asking about survival for myself. I'm asking for the sake of my other two children."

Claire gripped the armrest of her chair as the air seemed to suddenly evaporate from the room. She wanted so badly to be fully present for Jan, to calm her fears and help her make the right choice for *all* her children. But first she needed to push past her own lingering trauma.

From the corner of her eye, she could see Kiernan's forehead crease as he glanced down at her white-knuckled grasp of the chair-arm. She had to rein in her emotions, or the situation would quickly spiral downwards.

Focus, Claire, focus...

Pulling herself back to the present, Claire explained to Jan that the rigorous screening process would help ensure the surgery's safety and success. And with each additional question Jan posed, Claire dug deep within herself to stay in the moment. By the time Jan got around to asking whether her previous spina bifida surgeries had been successful nearly twenty minutes had passed, and Claire's anxiety was almost fully in check.

"Here," Claire said after scrolling briefly through her phone and pulling up a picture. She quickly showed the image to Kiernan and Dr. Fleming before walking over to Jan. "This is Samantha. Her mom sent me this picture a few months ago, when Samantha turned five. She was one of my first fetal surgery patients, and she's doing great. Her mom said she started school last fall, and is keeping right up with the other kids."

Jan leaned in further to get a closer look at the young girl with blonde pigtails, freckles and an ear-to-ear smile. "And if she hadn't had the surgery it might have been a different outcome—right?"

Claire reluctantly nodded. Her whole purpose for coming here today was to help steer Jan in the direction that she truly felt was best for her and her unborn child. But if no hospital was available to do the surgery in time, then what was the point? She'd be doing little more than confirming to Jan that her best option was unobtainable. Without the surgery, Jan's unborn baby faced a host of potential health issues, including incontinence, paralysis and cognitive impairment.

Claire turned to Kiernan, meeting his eyes and feeling that he somehow understood her dilemma. He quickly stepped in and reassured Jan that they were doing everything they could to schedule the surgery at an appropriate facility. But would it happen in time? Claire wanted to stay optimistic, but doubt was setting in. She was used to preparing herself for the possibility that a treatment option might fall short of the desired outcome, especially for a high-risk pregnancy. But to not even have the chance to get a life-enhancing surgery off the ground?

That possibility brought with it a new sense of helplessness that she wasn't accustomed to.

"That seemed to go well," Kiernan said later, as he and Claire walked down the hospital corridor after the consultation had ended.

Claire nodded, but couldn't quite muster up a smile.

Kiernan eyed her sideways as they turned onto another corridor. "You're not saying much."

"Sorry. I think it went well, too. But unfortunately, I feel like maybe all I did was get her hopes up for a surgery that she might not be able to get in time."

Kiernan sighed. "I know. I was kind of fighting that thought as well. She did say she'd be willing to travel further than she initially indicated, so I'm going to tell my team to expand their search outside of Ireland and the UK Or I should say outside of the UK It's already been confirmed nothing can be scheduled in time at the few facilities equipped for this surgery in Ireland."

"But it's not just the surgery—there's all the follow-up, too. And it could mean being away from her children for quite some time."

"I thought of that as well. But Dr. Fleming is getting her

team up to speed on post-surgery care for Jan. She thinks it can be handled here, especially with the neonatal unit fully operational."

"I thought you said it wasn't open yet?"

"Not officially. But construction is completed, and the operating theaters and patient wards are equipped and ready to go." He turned to Claire as they continued their walk. "You know how hospital boards are. They want the opening to be big on publicity and fanfare."

"Is that what you want?"

"Personally, I couldn't care less about all that stuff." As they came to a large sliding glass door at the end of the corridor, Kiernan slowed to a halt, with Claire following his lead. "I just want to start offering cutting-edge neonatal care here, so we don't have to scramble to find other options for patients like Jan. But I'm also pragmatic enough to realize that we need to get the word out on as large a scale as possible to make this new undertaking a success. We can't help women with high-risk pregnancies if they're not being sent here for treatment. And that will only happen when we start forging a reputation for top-tier neonatal care."

"Good point."

Claire wondered if the intense effort behind her smile was obvious to Kiernan. She hoped it wasn't. In another time and place she'd be excited to talk about advanced treatment options for high-risk pregnancies. Heck, it was the type of conversation that she herself once typically initiated with colleagues But that had been before the subject matter had become inextricably tied to personal loss and pain.

Kiernan turned and swiped his badge along the reader. The glass doors swiftly opened, and he gestured to Claire to enter first.

She wrinkled her nose slightly as they started down the corridor. "It almost has that new car smell in here."

Kiernan eyed her curiously from the side. "Funny you picked up on that. It's because everything *is* new in here. This is the neonatal wing I've been talking your ear off about."

Claire's breath caught in her throat, her rapid walk quickly decelerating.

Kiernan slowed down with her, his face perplexed. "Are you okay?"

Claire inwardly scrambled to salvage the situation. With every fiber of her being she wanted to avoid being pulled further back into the world of pregnancies and babies. Yes, she was at West Mercy today by choice. But she had never intended for her visit to extend beyond her consultation with Jan.

Still…could she reframe this moment? See it as an opportunity to witness a hospital making major progress for women's health and that of their newborn babies? Confirm to Kiernan that he was doing a commendable thing by driving this progress? He deserved no less. And perhaps at the same time she could begin to see glimpses of the joy and satisfaction she had once derived from playing an integral role in the health and wellness of mothers and their babies.

She looked up at him. His eyes were still searching hers. "I'm okay," she finally replied, conjuring up a smile as she gestured to the corridor before them. "Lead the way."

Kiernan appeared more than happy to oblige. Weaving through the main areas of the wing with Claire at his side, he paused at intervals to get her input on a particular process or piece of medical apparatus, as though wanting to ensure no stone had been left unturned in his quest for the most advanced neonatal center possible.

Entering the neonatal intensive care unit, Claire braced herself for an onslaught of emotion. A startled technician turned from the incubator that he had been testing with a biomedical analyzer. As Kiernan engaged him in a friendly conversation Claire held her breath, wondering if an anxiety episode was about to burst forth. But instead, the tightness in her chest dissipated, and she found herself peering more closely at the state-of-the-art equipment.

Could it be because the memories of her last moments with Ariana were confined to a birthing room and had never progressed to the NICU? Possibly. She only knew that she felt a sense of relief to have made it this far without any significant emotional fallout.

"And that concludes your personalized tour of the new West Mercy neonatal wing," Kiernan said twenty minutes later as they circled back to their starting point. "I hope you've enjoyed this sneak peek of our soon-to-open cutting-edge unit, and please come back again soon."

Her initial raw nerves had now dialed down several notches, and Claire couldn't help but snicker at Kiernan's pitch-perfect flight attendant voice.

"Well done," she conceded. "I can see why you're proud of this unit. Everything is state of the art, and once your team is certified in some of the specialized neonatal and fetal surgery techniques, I can't imagine West Mercy won't make a name for itself in neonatal medicine."

"I'm glad you think so," Kiernan said, looking pleased. "Yours is a highly coveted opinion."

The line was delivered with both sincerity and a touch of humor, and Claire laughed in return.

A door opened behind Kiernan and an electrician emerged, with a flashlight in one hand and a workbag in the other. He pulled the *Do Not Enter* sign off the door, then addressed Kiernan.

"All set, sir. There was some loose wiring in one of the walls, but I reconnected it and everything's good to go."

"Great," Kiernan said, turning to Claire. "The birthing suites are down this way. I didn't think I'd be able to show you, since there's been some electrical issues and we closed off the area out of an abundance of caution, but it looks like we've got the green light."

Before Claire could come up with an excuse to pass on this final and most potentially triggering leg of the tour, Kiernan swung open the door.

"You first."

Moments later they were standing inside a spacious yet cozy birthing suite. Soothing rays of natural light filtered in through floor-to-ceiling windows, dancing off the earth-toned walls and casting an iridescent glow over vast paintings of pastoral landscapes.

The scene was eerily familiar, and as Claire's eyes darted around the room a heavy sadness descended upon her.

Five and a half months into her pregnancy, she and Mark had stood in a nearly identical room during a birthing suite tour at Boston General, admiring the suite's calming color scheme and expansive windows.

Or, at least, *she* had viewed the surroundings with awe. Mark, on the other hand, had seemed distant and distracted. She recalled the unease she had felt at his I-want-to-be-any-where-but-here vibe, chalking it up at the time to the jitters of impending fatherhood.

But even then, something in the pit of her stomach told her there was more at play. Unable to fathom that her suspicions could possibly be true, she had squelched her snowballing doubts.

When they had solidified into reality less than a month later with his abrupt departure, the snowballs had turned into an avalanche of disbelief.

Needing something to grab on to, Claire searched for the nearest solid object. *Kiernan.* No, she was not going to grasp his arm, regardless of how muscular and strong it appeared to be. He might be wearing a lab coat now, but a form-fitting rugby shirt hid no secrets, and she wasn't about to forget *that* earlier image anytime soon.

Really? You're thinking about Kiernan's hunk of a build now?

Mind racing, Claire tried to reason with herself, but crazy thoughts had a way of quickly multiplying. Sweat beads broke out on her forehead. She had almost made it through the tour unscathed. *Almost.* If only the electrician's exit had been delayed a few more minutes. Then she and Kiernan would have moved on from the area and....

"Claire?" Kiernan said, alarm in his voice.

She peered up at him, wondering if she looked like a deer in the headlights, ready to bolt. That was certainly how she felt.

"You're awfully pale. Sit down," he said, nodding to a plump-pillowed chair against the wall. "Let me get you some water."

"I think I... I just need some air."

Making a beeline for the door, Claire was only half aware that Kiernan was right on her heels. But when he jumped in front of her out in the hallway, she could no longer pretend she was unraveling sight unseen. Kiernan had a front row seat to her meltdown, and her humiliation was only equaled by her desire to be instantly transported off the hospital grounds.

Wrapping his arm around her shoulder, Kiernan began to steer her diagonally toward a door on the other side of the corridor. With her fight-or-flight response switched on—emphasis on flight—Claire wanted to run for the nearest exit. But Kiernan's strong, protective grip was like a weighted blanket cocooned around her, and her rapid shallow breathing began to slow down a notch.

Once inside the empty exam room, Kiernan gently helped Claire onto a chair, then pulled another chair up beside her. He placed her hand over the palm side of his wrist, then draped his other hand on top of it.

"Just breathe and feel my pulse, and let yours sync to it."

Thump...thump...thump...

Claire closed her eyes and allowed Kiernan's slow, steady heartbeat to seep deeply into her very being. She felt her shoulders drop, and for the first time became aware that her feet were touching the ground. It was as if his strong but calm heartbeat was telling her own rapid-fire pulse: *Just follow me and everything will be okay.*

When she finally opened her eyes and looked up at Kiernan, she couldn't be sure how much time had passed. She only knew that his kind brown eyes were gazing deeply into own.

"I think we need to trade hearts," she quipped, her weakened voice cracking slightly.

The earlier adrenaline coursing through her body had been the equivalent of running a marathon, but at least she had crossed the finish line—and all thanks to the handsome surgeon just inches away from her.

"There's nothing wrong with your heart at all," Kiernan replied, with such decisiveness that she couldn't help but feel he wasn't just referring to its physical aspects.

Mr. O'Rourke, please report to Room 247 for a consultation.

Claire looked up at the intercom box above the doorway, then back at Kiernan.

He shook his head. "It can wait. You're my patient now."

A smile slowly emerged, and he squeezed her hand just tightly enough for her heart to skip a beat. He sure had a way of making her heart do unexpected things.

"I'm feeling much better," she finally managed to say. "Thank you."

"No need to thank me."

"I should let you get back to work."

"I'm not leaving until I'm certain you're okay." He cocked his head slightly to one side, as if wondering whether to say more. "Is there anything you want to talk about? My colleagues like to call me a grump behind my back—and sometimes to my face, for that matter—but truth be told, I'm a really good listener."

Claire smirked. "I'm sure you are. But I'm okay—really. I should have mentioned that I can be sensitive to a lot of environmental things. I probably just had a reaction to the new paint or the carpets in the suite."

She could tell by Kiernan's narrowed eyes that he wasn't buying her excuse for a second. But that didn't stop her from doubling down.

"Besides, you know how we doctors make the worst patients. Once I'm outside and get some fresh air, I'll be good as new."

"Well, let me at least walk you out to your car."

"That's not necessary—"

"I insist," Kiernan interjected, his sternness offset by the twinkle in his eye. "Besides, I'm going to be checking your stride. Any wobbliness and you'll be confined to quarters."

"Confined to quarters?" Claire repeated with a touch of amusement in her voice. "Is this a hospital or a military institution?"

Kiernan let out a mock sigh. "Sometimes it feels like a little of both."

The rejuvenating midday sun felt good on Claire's face as she walked through the parking lot to her car, with Kiernan close by her side.

"Are you sure you're okay?" he asked as she seated herself in the Mini and rolled down the window.

She smiled. "I'm sure."

"Thank you again for talking to Jan."

"Happy to do so."

After an exchange of goodbyes, Claire watched as Kiernan strode confidently across the parking lot, waiting for him to disappear from view before leaning her head back against the seat and taking a deep breath. She closed her eyes, wishing more than anything that his hand could still be clasping her own as her heartbeat synched with his. How he had turned the feeling of a pulse—normally just a routine diagnostic tool—into something so...*intimate* was something she'd be pondering for days to come.

But it was more than that. He had stayed with her, offering to talk about what had triggered her reaction and refusing to leave her side until he was convinced she was okay. And the kicker to all of this? Not once had he made her feel like he was doing so out of medical obligation.

Compare that to Mark, who hadn't even made the effort to be present during the loss of their daughter....

Claire shook her head. *Don't go there.* A few more deep breaths. *Focus on the positive.*

It was easy enough to do. She just had to think of Kiernan, and the way she was starting to feel whenever he was near.

Up in the third-floor cafeteria, which offered the most expansive view of the parking lot below, Kiernan stared out of the floor-to-ceiling window, his eyes glued to Claire's red Mini. Though ten minutes had passed, it had yet to leave its parking spot, and he decided to give it one more minute before heading back outside to check on her.

Another twenty seconds and the Mini backed out and headed toward the exit. Kiernan stared at the empty spot for several moments, trying to wrap his head around what had just transpired. He had previously toyed with the possibility that there was more to Claire's story than her *I'm just taking a month-long vacation* declaration. But now his suspicions were deepening.

"Mr. O'Rourke to Theater Three, STAT."

The intercom announcement pulled him back to the present. With a possible emergency unfolding, he had to put those thoughts on hold. Although something told him they'd return soon enough…

CHAPTER SIX

KIERNAN KNOCKED BRIEFLY on the hospital room door, then entered while scanning patient notes on his tablet. Yesterday, his concerned speculation over a possible trauma in Claire's past had been cut short when he'd been summoned to the operating theater for a woman—Darla—who had just been admitted with a burst appendix. Always a perilous situation, the risk had been magnified tenfold because Darla was six months pregnant.

Fortunately, Darla's surgery had gone well, and she was now resting comfortably with her husband at her bedside, along with their two adolescent daughters.

"I just wanted to check in to see how you're doing," Kiernan said now, as Darla and her husband smiled appreciatively.

A few more minutes of friendly small talk and then Kiernan wished Darla a speedy recovery back home, knowing she'd be discharged later in the afternoon.

Exiting the room, he glanced back at the family once more, wincing slightly as he tried to suppress the wave of poignancy that descended over him. There was something eerily familiar about the scene, and he didn't have to dig deep within his memories to make the connection.

Twenty years ago, the heavily pregnant woman with a perforated appendix had been none other than his mother. He recalled his aunt bringing him and his younger sister Colleen to visit her during an extended hospital stay due to complications. And his father? He'd been nowhere to be found. Actually… that wasn't true. He'd been in the same hospital as Kiernan's mother, but too tied up with his patients to check in on the most important patient…the most important *person*…of all.

It was probably just as well, Kiernan thought now, eyes narrowing and jaw clenching as he quickened his pace down the corridor. It wasn't like his father had been known for his bedside manner—though for the patients whose lives he had saved, forgoing the warm fuzzies was probably considered a small price to pay.

Still, Kiernan had never forgotten the excuses his mother had made for his father's cruel absence when she'd needed him most. "Your father's busy saving other lives," she had said at the time, struggling to form a smile with parched lips nearly as pale as her anemic skin.

And she had been right. His father *had* been saving other lives. Which would have been all fine and dandy if he'd had no family of his own that needed him, too.

Perhaps that explained Kiernan's actions when his mother had been hospitalized at West Mercy with double pneumonia, just over a year ago. Though she hadn't been a surgical patient, he had popped into her room at every opportunity, plumping up her pillows, double-checking her meds and fussing over her like only a loving son-slash-doctor could.

"I'll say one thing," his mum had said during one such occasion, when his doting had been in full overdrive. "Maybe it's because I'm your mother, but you most definitely have much more of a bedside manner than your father ever did." She had paused, in part to take more air into her healing lungs but also to flash a rueful smile. "Thank goodness for that."

So at least he'd got that part right—and without any real effort, given that he truly cared about his patients. They were actual people, with hopes and dreams and loved ones, not merely a list of symptoms and diagnoses. But sidestepping his father's other major flaw… That required more deliberation on his part.

Throw himself into his career as a surgeon dedicated to saving lives? *Check.* Avoid serious personal relationships that would make that first goal impossible? *Check.* Because the two had to go together—right? Even his mother had seemed to think so. She'd never actually *said* this to him…rather it was more about what she hadn't said.

Once, several years ago, she had asked him when he was planning to settle down and start a family.

"You mean so I can be an absentee husband and father like Dad?" he had replied pointedly.

She had silently looked back at him, understanding and regret in her eyes. And she'd never asked again.

Back in his office, Kiernan stared at the wall as thoughts of Claire incessantly flooded his mind. Ever since they had parted ways yesterday, he had not been able to stop thinking about her. He had texted her last night, to see how she was feeling, and had been at least mildly relieved when she had replied that she was fine. But he wasn't fully convinced.

He closed his eyes, reliving each second that had ticked by when she had tuned in to his pulse, her hand delicately placed on his wrist and her beautiful face just inches away from him. Only now did he realize how lucky he had been that his heart rate hadn't surged with her touch. He had felt it quicken, and only through sheer willpower had he slowed it down so that she, too, would begin to relax.

With a loud sigh, Kiernan swung his chair around to stare at the other equally bland wall. What he wouldn't give to see her again. As in *now.*

Extracting his phone from his white coat, he stared at the screen, then quickly typed out a text before he could talk himself out of it.

There's a great little garden tea shop that serves lunch halfway between the hospital and your cottage. Fancy taking out the Mini to meet me there at noon?

Kiernan wasn't aware that he was holding his breath while waiting for the beep of a text reply from Claire. It was only when his screen lit up with the word Sure that he sputtered and realized he was probably turning blue.

Wonderful. I'll text you the address shortly.

Leaning back in his chair, Kiernan replenished his oxygen supply with some deep breaths, then shook his head slightly, perplexed by his own actions. Lunch—if he even paused long enough to have it—was typically a couple of power bars eaten while on the move from one patient or operating theater to the next. And now he was taking a chunk of time out of his busy schedule to meet Claire? And not just at any restaurant, mind you. By choosing a quaint little tea shop nestled within carefully manicured gardens of tulips, daffodils and roses, he was fully setting the scene for... Well, it couldn't be romance...could it?

"That's crazy talk," he muttered aloud to his own thoughts.

But as he launched himself out of the chair he felt nearly giddy at the thought of soon seeing Claire. It was a state of mind that was new to him. But what the heck.

I might as well go with it.

Kiernan waved to Claire as she approached the small white wrought-iron table on the outside patio of the Gilded Petal Tea Shop. He stood up and pulled out her chair, his nerve-endings on fire as her shiny chestnut hair fluttered against his forearm while he helped push her chair back in.

"You dressed for the occasion," he said, admiring the gauzy flowered dress that clung to her taut curves. Or maybe it was the curves themselves that he was admiring. He cleared his throat at the distinction.

Claire smirked as she nodded toward him. "And I see you didn't."

He glanced down at his green scrubs—an unfashionable necessity given he was squeezing in lunch between surgeries. "You never know when a wilted tulip is going to need medical intervention."

Claire's lilting laughter filtered through him like a soul-soothing elixir. It was a relief to find that the sparkle had returned to her eyes and the peachy glow to her cheeks. Perhaps he had prematurely jumped to conclusions about her puzzling reaction in the birthing suite.

"It's good to see you," he said. "Even though you said you felt okay when you left yesterday, you still had me worried."

Claire twisted her mouth to one side. "Like I said...doctors make the worst patients."

He grinned. "Well, I can't say I disagree with that."

A waitress came by and poured two cups of tea, placing a pot on the table and handing small, folded menus to each of them.

"I should have known this was one of those finger sandwich kinds of places," Kiernan said with mock resignation in his voice as he skimmed the short list of options.

Claire chuckled. "I figured you'd been here before."

Kiernan glanced up from the menu. "To be honest, I've driven by it and admired the flowers, but never stopped in."

"I got to say...you don't strike me as a cucumber sandwich kind of guy."

Kiernan laughed heartily. "Looks like I'm going to have to be today." He perused the limited choices once more. "Or a tomato sandwich guy."

"Let's splurge and get a platter of both."

"Deal."

He placed the menu down and raised a tea toast to Claire, who obliged with a clink of porcelain.

"So, what are some of your favorite spots back home?" Kiernan asked after the waitress had come by to take their order. "There must be an award-winning cucumber sandwich shop back in Boston?"

Claire chuckled. "I'm sure there is. But favorite spots? Hmm... There's a park on the outskirts of the city that I go to whenever I can. It has some nice walking paths. And a pond— with ducks. You might have noticed I really like ducks."

Kiernan laughed as she pondered some more.

"There's also a quirky little bookshop in my town that I really love. It's been family-owned for years—not one of those big chain bookstores. Whenever I go there Marge, one of the owners, will have some hand-picked books put aside for me."

"That sounds wonderful. And what of kind of books do you like to read?"

"Lately, I've been into cozy mysteries."

"Ah, you mean like the little ol' British grandmother who solves crimes while tending to her rose garden?"

Claire snickered. "Sounds like the plot of the last one I read." As Kiernan raised his teacup for another toast, she obliged and said, "Your turn."

"I should have known that was coming..."

"Come on. Favorite places. Spill."

"Well, I think you've already seen both." As Claire raised her eyebrows he added, "The hospital and Gilroy's Pub. Although I guess I should add any rugby field within a sixty-mile radius."

"The hospital is your favorite spot?" she asked curiously.

"Kind of. It's where I spend most of my time."

"All the more reason you need different favorite spots."

"Huh…" Kiernan ruminated on her observation for several moments. "I think I misunderstood the question."

"Nice try."

Kiernan laughed. He was squirming in the hot seat, but just seeing Claire's easy grin was worth the discomfort.

Four finger sandwiches and three cups of sweetened tea later, Kiernan leaned back in his chair and admired the even sweeter view from not so afar. Just across from him, Claire and her serene beauty were nothing short of mesmerizing—and if duty hadn't been calling, he knew he could have got lost in that vision all day. But with a tonsillectomy scheduled for two p.m., he had to get back to the hospital soon.

"Thanks," Kiernan said a few minutes later as the waitress handed him back his bank card. He turned to Claire. "Well, back to the hospital for me—and hopefully back to something enjoyable for you. Have you been doing any fun touristy things?"

"How can I?" Claire replied with a mischievous twinkle in her eye. "You keep interrupting my vacation."

"Ouch." Kiernan chuckled, and when his phone buzzed in his pocket, he was fully prepared to ignore it.

Except medical emergencies had a way of following him.

He pulled out the phone and grimaced. "I'm sorry—this is the hospital."

Silently reading the text message, he felt his jaw and neck instantly tense.

Manchester Gen is out and team confirmed we can't cut thru red tape in time for surgery outside of UK. We're out of options. But wanted to get OK from you before telling Jan.

Kiernan sighed deeply and placed the phone on the table with the screen facing down, unable to pull the trigger that would end Jan's dream of giving birth to a healthy baby.

With a creased forehead and concerned eyes, Claire asked, "Is everything okay?"

"Not really. The last few potential hospitals that could do Jan's surgery in time are no-gos. It looks like we're at the end of the road."

Claire's shoulders dropped, her pale green eyes mirroring the deep disappointment that Kiernan now felt. Silence passed between them, the upbeat atmosphere of a few seconds ago now fully deflated and somber.

Suddenly, a thought sprang into Kiernan's mind. And it was a doozy. As he looked up at Claire she lurched back slightly, as though reverberating with the energy that was bouncing off him.

"I have an idea. A *crazy* idea. But… Okay, just hear me out. If I can get permission from the hospital and make everything else fall into place, would you be able to perform Jan's surgery? The hospital will pay you, of course, and I can't imagine they'd turn down the proposition, knowing how much they want West Mercy to make a name for itself in this sort of surgery. Plus, it would be an amazing experience for my team to learn from someone of your caliber."

Claire appeared stricken as she stared back at him. Her reaction was enough to drop his stomach to his knees.

"Believe me, I know this is a lot to ask." He paused, waiting for her to reply. And waiting some more. "I'm sorry—it was an impulsive thought. I should never have suggested it."

"I… I um…."

Claire's head dropped downwards as she stared at the table. Kiernan didn't need to be a doctor to see that her breathing had accelerated and the color was draining from her face.

Finally, she looked up. "Can I just…? Can I think about it, please? I'll give you an answer by tomorrow. I promise."

"Yes. Yes, of course."

As she started to stand up from the chair, Kiernan stood

up as well, quickly stepping over and gently grabbing her arm as she braced her other arm unsteadily against the table. Her skin was soft, but slightly clammy, and as she locked eyes with him, he saw fear bordering on panic. It was the same look he'd seen yesterday.

But why?

Had something happened back at Boston General? Had there been a failed surgery that had been so devastating she'd taken a leave of absence for a month? Not every surgery was successful—no matter how gifted the surgeon. Or perhaps she had become too emotionally involved in a case and the outcome had pushed her over the edge.

Kiernan tightened his jaw, knowing he needed to reel in his suspicions. He was grasping at straws, wanting to understand. But unless she opened up to him, he was blindly guessing at best.

"Thank you for lunch," Claire said. "If I ever crave a mean cucumber sandwich again, I know where to go."

There was a slight quiver in her smile, and the sheer effort to hide her discomfort was almost palpable.

Kiernan watched as Claire headed out of the dining patio, frozen in place until a wave of heightened resolve swept over him. No. *No!* He was *not* going to let her run off like this in such a clearly distressed state of mind. He pulled his phone out of his pocket and waited for the call to be answered.

"Hello, Mr. O'—"

"Lucy," he urgently interjected. "I have a personal matter to attend to and I need you to put Mr. Ramsey on my two p.m. tonsillectomy."

"Yes, I'll let him know right away." There was a brief pause. Then, "Is everything okay?"

He knew why Lucy was asking. If there were two words she had never heard him utter in succession, they were "personal" and "matter."

"Yes," he said, his voice clipped. "I'll touch base with you when I'm back."

Bounding out to the parking lot, he spotted Claire just as she was about to get into her car. "Claire! Wait!"

She swung around, eyes widened.

She was still holding on to the door handle when he caught up with her. "I can't let you leave like this. Please—can we sit and talk for a bit?"

It took several moments for Claire to find her voice. "I'm not sure what you mean..."

"I've upset you."

"No, I'm fine...really."

Kiernan shook his head. "You're not fine."

Her eyes met his and, surprisingly, she didn't push back on his assessment. He turned and nodded to a cobblestoned path lined with several benches that cut through the flowered grounds.

"Walk with me? Please?"

Perhaps it was the pleading quality to his voice, but Claire slowly closed the car door and together they headed out of the parking lot and onto the path. Several minutes later they were seated on a wooden bench, surrounded by the heady aroma of tulips, daffodils and roses.

"Wait—what about your tonsillectomy?" Claire asked, before Kiernan had a chance to initiate conversation.

"I already called the hospital and another surgeon is filling in for me." He flashed the hint of a smile. "It's one of the advantages of being chief of surgery. I can pass off a procedure to someone else and no one will say anything."

Claire's tense face relaxed slightly as her lips curved upward. But the smile was short-lived. "If this is about Jan's surgery—your question caught me off guard, that's all."

"I don't care about Jan's surgery," Kiernan replied forcefully. He shook his head and looked briefly up at the sky. "That didn't come out right. Of course I care. But right now my concern is you. I don't mean to pry, Claire, and maybe it's none of my business, but I can't help feeling there's something you're not telling me—something that caused you to react the way you did in the birthing suite yesterday, and now this. Whatever it is, you can talk to me. Maybe I can help. Or I'll just be quiet and listen."

She stared intently into his eyes for what seemed like an eternity, as though debating inwardly whether to open up to him.

"You're right," she said finally. "I haven't been entirely upfront with you as to why I took a leave of absence to come here." She paused, her eyes now glossy and pained. "Seven months ago, I gave birth to a stillborn daughter. Her name was Ariana."

Kiernan flinched, feeling as though an unseen hand had slapped him across the cheek. He had not seen this coming. Not by a longshot. "Claire, I'm so sorry."

Claire blinked several times to push back tears. She started to speak again, but nothing came out.

"You don't have to say any more," Kiernan said quietly.

She took in a deep breath, as if re-energized with resolve. "I want to. You see, I came to Ireland for a month to figure out if I can continue in my career as an ob-gyn. I know I'm not the first obstetrician to lose a child, and I really thought I would be able to separate my personal pain from my professional life. But I can't. Every time I witness the birth of a healthy baby, I'm glad for the parents, but I also wonder why I didn't have the same happy ending with Ariana. And every miscarriage or stillbirth…it's like reliving her death all over again." Claire's voice cracked, but she pushed herself to finish. "I'm no good to my patients like this. They deserve better. But I just don't know how to get past it all."

Kiernan looked up at the bright afternoon sky, his chest

tightening as the unintended repercussions of his actions grew clearer. "And then you come here and right from the start…"

He shook his head, unable to say more. An emergency breech delivery. A consultation on fetal surgery for a serious birth defect. And—the ultimate stab in the heart—being asked to perform complex, high-risk surgery to correct that anomaly in an unborn child. Everything she had been trying to get away from he had been unwittingly throwing her way since her arrival.

"Claire, I'm so sorry that I've caused you pain."

She placed a hand over his, and her soft, warm touch momentarily disrupted his focus.

"None of this is your fault. There was no way you could have known."

So many thoughts and emotions were swirling around in Kiernan's mind. Not to mention more questions. Such as who and where was Ariana's father? But he wasn't about to ask. The last thing he wanted to do was potentially add salt to a wound whose depths he could not even begin to imagine.

"In case you're wondering, Ariana's father is no longer in the picture."

Kiernan gulped silently. Had Claire just read his mind? "I'm sorry to hear that."

"It's okay. I mean, better to have found out the kind of person he really is now than even further down the road. The CliffsNotes version is that we met in medical school, married after graduation, and he left when I was six months pregnant with Ariana. It turns out he was having an affair with someone at his practice and she recently gave birth to a daughter."

Kiernan narrowed his eyes. "That's despicable."

He wanted to punch the man, surgeon's hands be damned. The satisfaction of inflicting upon him even a fraction of the pain he had caused Claire would be worth a broken knuckle or two.

"Whew!" Claire exclaimed, dabbing at her moistened eyes. "I'm a real joy to be around, huh?"

"You are—and then some," he said quietly, looking into her eyes. "And I never would have asked you to perform Jan's surgery if I had known what you've been going through."

"Believe me, I know that. But my earlier answer hasn't changed. I just need the rest of the day to think everything over."

Kiernan shook his head. "No, I don't think this is a good idea."

Claire squeezed his hand, her reddened eyes offset by a growing smile. "Too late. You already asked me."

Kiernan clenched his jaw as he tried to wrangle a swirl of conflicting emotions. Maybe *he* needed the day to reexamine his thoughts, too. His first instinct was to protect Claire from further pain and trauma. But at the same time she had come to Ireland to determine whether she could reengage in her profession as an ob-gyn. Could successfully performing Jan's surgery, and at a hospital without all the painful memories of Boston General, provide the definitive answer she needed?

He turned to her, nearly overwhelmed by a sudden desire to lean in and kiss her. She stared into his eyes in a way that made him think she, too, might feel the same. And yet he resisted.

Never had he thought twice about seizing the moment when it came to a kiss. But never had anyone revealed something so deeply personal to him. He had sensed from the get-go that Claire was a private person. You weren't going to find her announcing her every thought and action on social media—if you found her there at all. She had made herself vulnerable by sharing with him her loss of Ariana, and he did not take her trust in him lightly. It was a trust he would safeguard at all costs, and the last thing he wanted to do was misconstrue her willingness to open up to him.

Claire briefly looked out over the flowered landscape, a

kaleidoscope of colors swaying slightly in the breeze, before turning back to him. "I would imagine you need to get back to the hospital soon."

"I'm in no rush," Kiernan replied—an answer that previously would never have left his lips. This was certainly turning out to be a day of firsts for him.

"Do you mind if we just sit here for a bit?" she asked.

That was an easy question to answer.

"I wouldn't want to be anywhere else."

Claire sat on her now favorite rock by the water as she tossed cracked corn onto the ground. In short order, the chopped golden kernels were gobbled up by the boisterous flock of ducks before her.

Quack-quack-quack. Quack-quack-quack.

"Slow down, guys," she said with an affectionate smile as she tossed more corn their way.

It was a brief respite from the whirlwind of emotions that she was still trying to navigate.

After returning home from the tea shop a half-hour ago, Claire had immediately headed down to the water. Mother Nature had an unfailing way of providing clarity when she needed it most, and today that figurative mother had her work cut out for her.

She had been surprised to receive Kiernan's spur-of-the-moment lunch invite, and even more surprised at how readily she had accepted it. But the reasons had been simple—she'd wanted to see him again, her earlier blinking red caution lights be damned, and it would be an opportunity to make up for her skittish behavior the day before. That objective hadn't gone exactly as planned…but maybe that was good thing.

Claire thought back to a nugget of advice dispensed during one of her post-stillbirth therapy sessions. Holding on to a secret gave it power. And if the secret was a source of pain and grief…well, it would only cause more of the same.

Opening up to Kiernan had profoundly changed something inside of her. She could feel it like a heavy weight lifted not only from her shoulders, but from the deepest corners of her mind. His reaction to her revelation had made it clear that he was fully and unequivocally looking out for her. And though he had pulled back on his suggestion that she perform Jan's surgery, they both knew the stakes. There were no more options left for this mother and her unborn child. She was it.

Claire turned her gaze onto several fluffy yellow ducklings as they waddled close behind their mom. When one lost its balance and tumbled over, the mother turned away from the cracked corn she was just about to devour, and used her beak to nudge him back up.

It was a gesture that grabbed at her heart. But that was what all mothers did, regardless of species. They put their children first. And being part of that beautiful dynamic was one of the reasons she loved being an ob-gyn. Or she had.

Claire stood up from the rock and began walking along the water's edge. Could she get that love back again? It was a question she still couldn't answer—although inside she now felt a fluidity where before there had been only rigidness.

But perhaps she was projecting too far ahead. She could make a difference for Jan and her baby *now*. Kiernan had thrown that opportunity into her lap, and she had to…she *wanted* to…give them every chance for the best outcome possible. And with Kiernan by her side, she could do it.

She cupped a hand over her eyes as the afternoon sun glistened on the water. Slowly, a smile emerged. It was accompanied by a flutter of nerves, but that was okay—big decisions could be disconcerting at first. And the fact that this one came easier—and quicker—than expected only solidified to her that it was the right decision to make.

Claire reached into the pocket of her windbreaker to get her phone, then thought better of it. Knowing Kiernan, if she texted him now instead of in the morning, as planned, he'd think she was jumping the gun.

Knowing Kiernan?

Had she really crossed that invisible line from regarding him as a professional associate, kept at arm's length, to someone she was beginning to connect with on a much deeper level?

She closed her eyes, knowing very well the answer to that.

Kiernan entered the kitchen of his home and tossed his keys on the counter. He was greeted by silence save for the hum of the refrigerator.

Nothing he could say to himself—certainly not *What a day!* or similar—could come close to sufficing as a recap of the past twelve hours. His spur-of-the-moment lunch with Claire had set off a chain reaction of events and revelations, all of which he was still trying to process.

As his eyes scanned the room—the spotless counters and perfectly lined-up canisters, the sparkling stainless-steel appliances and the neat stack of mail in its designated tray—one word came to mind: *sterile*. Which, if this were an operating theater, would be more than appropriate.

But this was his home, his personal oasis. And suddenly, it all just seemed…strange.

He shook his head, wondering why he had never really noticed this before. Could it be because there was little, if any, distinction between his professional and personal life? That was a *duh* question, he surmised silently.

An image of Claire flashed in his mind, and he wondered what it would be like to come home to the feeling that he had whenever she was near. It was a feeling that he craved, but one that also scared him. If he gave in to it, then he'd need to reevaluate his whole approach to life—the "must-haves" versus the "can-live-withouts." Full devotion to his career, at the expense of everything else, had always been a must-have. But the more his feelings for Claire were beginning to grow, the more tiny fissures were forming in these notions that had been set in stone.

He'd had a glimpse of one those fissures earlier in the day, when he'd bowed out of performing a surgery so that he could stay with Claire and make sure she was okay. He thought back to the day when his father had passed away. He had been prepping for a coronary artery bypass surgery when he had taken an urgent call from his mother. His father's death from a sudden heart attack had been both unexpected and shocking. But both he and his mother had known the drill all too well. After all, it was his father who had pounded it into him.

Personal matters and relationships came second. *Always*.

And the one thing he had thought that day, as he'd suppressed his emotions and walked into the operating theater without so much as a mention of his loss, feeling the disbelieving eyes of colleagues who had heard the news upon him? *Dad would be proud of me.* Which meant he had been proud of himself.

Only now did he realize how misguided his priorities might have been at that moment.

Realizing he needed some air, Kiernan headed out on the back deck that overlooked the ocean, peering into the darkness. With just a sliver of moonlight, he couldn't see the water, but he could hear every wave that crashed against the cliffs below and smell the brine that brought on an instant head rush.

As a sharp ocean breeze whipped through his hair, Kiernan grabbed the rail of the deck with both hands. He needed to steady himself, because everything around him was churning like a cyclone.

Get a hold of yourself.

He was reeling from Claire's unexpected and deeply personal revelation, and the possibility that she might take on Jan's surgery. That was all this was. *Right?* A lot of raw emotion packed into a short span of time.

Of course, if that was the case, then he'd be on edge every time he came out of a difficult surgery that had been touch-and-go until the final successful moments. He always felt relief for both the patients and their families in those situations, but it had never spurred him to come home and question why the damn refrigerator was the closest thing he had to a significant other after a long day at the hospital.

No, this was about Claire. Of that, he was sure. Seeing her heartache as she'd told him about Ariana...

Could performing Jan's surgery be the catalyst she needed to reengage in her career as an ob-gyn?

The question nearly cut off his air supply, and he took in a deep breath of salty ocean air. He needed to be careful. This was not one medical professional concerned about the career of a peer. For him, at least, it was already so much more. And he couldn't have that in the life he had mapped out for himself.

Unless, of course, he redrew the map.

It was a thought that hit him harder than a tidal wave.

CHAPTER SEVEN

KIERNAN ENTERED THE café on the second floor of the hospital, immediately spotting Claire at a small table in the furthest, most quiet corner. Earlier in the morning she had texted him to say that she wanted to move forward with Jan's surgery, but that alone wasn't enough to convince him. He needed to see her in person, to read her body language and look into her eyes to be certain that *she* was certain.

After all, it was in her nature to want to help others, but he couldn't let that be at the expense of her own well-being.

"Thanks for meeting me here," he said as he sat down next to her.

Dressed in casual jeans and a light pink sweater, she looked downright gorgeous. Then again, Kiernan thought, she could don a burlap sack and still put a designer-clad supermodel to shame. He'd take natural, unfettered beauty over an artificially enhanced appearance any day of the week—and Claire had that in spades.

She smiled, her eyes bright but anxious. "So, you said you wanted to talk to me in person about the surgery. Are you thinking the hospital won't sign off on it?"

"No, that's not why I asked you to come by…" As Claire's smile began to wilt, he knew he couldn't drag out his concerns any longer. "Claire, you don't have to do this."

"I know. But I want to. Look, I don't know what the future

holds for me as far as my career goes. I still have a lot to think through. But one thing I know for sure is that I can make a difference for Jan and her baby. And it's the only chance they have at this point. That alone is enough for me to pull it together. I *want* to do this. Besides, we've already proved that we're a pretty good team in an operating room."

Kiernan grinned. "You mean in the back of a bumpy ambulance?"

"Right." She smirked, but then her face grew more serious. "The thing is, after telling you about Ariana…you know my secret now. And somehow…just opening up to you… I feel like it's lessened its hold on me."

Kiernan wanted to believe she was right. For Jan and her baby, yes. But also for Claire's own healing. Her previous reaction in the birthing suite and at yesterday's lunch clearly indicated she was still in the throes of pain and grief over losing Ariana. Could sharing her loss really have changed all that? Silently, he tossed the question around in his mind, his face tense with concern.

"What's wrong?" Claire asked, picking up on his doubts.

"I'm just worried that you might not be ready to take on this surgery. You've been through so much. How do you know you won't be triggered by something that happens in Theater? I'm afraid it might be too much, too soon."

"Believe me, I've thought about this. I'd never put Jan and her baby at risk. I'm not going into this surgery thinking it will help me decide once and for all what to do about my career. That would be putting too much pressure on myself. But I do know that right here, right now, I'm fully committed to doing everything I can to help them. And knowing you'll be with me in the operating room…"

Her voice trailed off, but Kiernan knew what she was implying—that his presence would have a stabilizing effect on her should a potential trigger arise. He wanted to believe that was true, but wasn't entirely sold on the notion.

Once again, Claire seemed to home in on his doubts.

"You know how people sometimes hold a paper clip when they're giving a speech to calm their nerves? Well, you'll be my paper clip in the operating room."

He raised an amused eyebrow. "You mean like a surgical lucky charm?"

It wasn't his intention to make light of a serious situation, only to help put her at ease. And himself, too, for that matter.

"Something like that, yes." She snickered slightly, then grew more serious. "So, given that Jan's surgery needs to happen very soon, we do need to go over some specifics. I'm sure you already know this, but this is an all hands on deck procedure. I'll need every specialist in every discipline that you've got. Cardiology, neurology, pediatrics—and they'll need to get up to speed on the surgery itself. I mean, is all of that even possible on such short notice?"

"I'll *make* it possible," Kiernan replied, pulling confidence out of thin air given all that needed to fall into place—and fast. "I'm going to call an emergency meeting with the board. It's probably too short notice to get everyone together today, but I should be able to set something up for first thing tomorrow morning. And I'll have my surgery coordinator get to work on putting together a comprehensive team."

"Will you wait to get the okay before telling Jan?"

"I think that would be best. The last thing I want to do is falsely get her hopes up. I don't think there'll be any major roadblocks to moving forward with the surgery, but best to be sure first."

Claire nodded, her face visibly relaxing. "Good."

"So, now that that's settled, I have some doctor's orders for you."

She raised an eyebrow. "Oh?"

Kiernan extracted a prescription pad from the pocket of his white coat, scribbled away for a few moments, then tore off a piece of paper and handed it to her.

Claire twisted her mouth to one side with amusement before reading it out loud: *"You are to spend the next twenty-four hours playing with ducks, reading a cozy mystery, exploring a castle and eating cucumber sandwiches to your heart's desire. Unlimited refills."*

"Don't be one of those patients who refuses to take good advice," Kiernan said with a twinkle in his eyes.

Claire laughed. "I'll do my best."

Claire tapped her fingers on the black-lacquered chair-arm and stared at the TV screen in front of her. A football game was in full swing, and though the half-dozen other occupants in the room sat glued to the action, her eyes—and thoughts—wandered as she waited in vain for time to speed up.

More than twenty-four hours had passed since she had met with Kiernan in the café and, like a *partially* dutiful patient, she had played with the ducks and toured a local castle. But the cozy mystery book would have to wait. And the cucumber sandwiches…? Those would have to wait, too. Perhaps indefinitely.…

With a silent sigh, she once again glanced at the large digital clock on the adjacent wall of one of West Mercy's smaller waiting rooms. The original plan had been for Kiernan to call her as soon as the board meeting ended, but sitting at the cottage to await such a pivotal decision had made her so antsy that she'd been ready to go search for a sand hill.

Instead, she had texted Kiernan to say that she was on her way to the hospital so that she could hear the good news in person. Of course, that presumed that there would *be* good news. But she had to hold on to hope.

Suddenly, she caught a flash of movement out of the corner of her eye. Kiernan swept into the waiting room, his commanding presence prompting those around her to instinctively sit up straighter in their chairs. His serious face was devoid of a smile, and Claire's shoulders sank as her own smile faded in response.

And then a thumb shot up as a Cheshire cat grin spread from ear to ear. "We're on," he said as Claire sprang from her chair.

She caught herself just short of pouncing on him with hug-ready arms. Clearing her throat, she tucked several loose locks of hair behind her ear, dropped her arms woodenly to her sides, and said, in a measured, low-key voice, "That's fantastic news."

Kiernan was still viewing her through widened eyes, as though he was fully prepared for and looking forward to being tackled, and seemed disappointed that she'd reversed course at the last second.

"Did you get any pushback?" Claire asked, hoping the inquiry would erase the awkward moment she had created between them.

"They had a lot of questions, of course. And there are still some logistics to work out. But they also understand that time is of the essence. They're looking at it as a major milestone for West Mercy. But I think you'll agree with me that the biggest win is for Jan and her baby."

"Absolutely. When do you plan to tell her?"

"*We* can tell her right now. She had a follow-up ultrasound appointment today, and I told the technician to let her know that I wanted to touch base with her before she left. I wasn't sure we'd have good news to share, but I hedged my bets and now we actually do."

Twenty minutes later, Claire and Kiernan exited the consultation room after sharing the good news with Jan. As expected, she was equal parts ecstatic and nervous—a completely normal reaction in the face of surgery that held the highest hopes for her unborn baby, yet was far from routine and simple.

At one point, Jan had shared the fact that she and her husband had decided to learn the sex of the baby, and had named their daughter Rhianna. The similar ring to Ariana had caught Claire by surprise, but one glance in Kiernan's direction, his expression both knowing and understanding, and she had quickly been pulled back to the present. That she could acknowledge her pain without being instantly transported back to a very dark place was testament to the healing power of sharing her secret. And not with just anyone, of course, but with Kiernan, whom she was trusting more and more.

As they continued down the corridor a flurry of thoughts vied for Claire's attention. She always felt as though she was balancing on a tightrope when reassuring patients about the outcome of a complex surgery. She believed in her skills, and all of her previous spina bifida fetal surgeries to date had been successful. But that didn't mean complications couldn't arise. And to be performing this procedure at an unfamiliar hospital, with an inexperienced team as far as fetal surgery was concerned... Well, she'd have to be in deep denial not to realize the risk factor was far from non-existent.

"I know it's a lot of pressure to perform this surgery under such unusual circumstances," Kiernan said, perhaps picking up on her concern. "But I want to assure you that we're doing everything at our end to be fully prepared by Monday. You said this is an all hands on deck situation, and I have nearly two dozen surgeons and specialists coming in this weekend to go over everything ahead of time. They might not all need to be present for the surgery on Monday, but we're covering all ground just in case."

"I should be there," Claire said, wondering why she hadn't thought to offer before.

"I don't think that will be necessary. You came to Ireland

to get away from it all, and I don't want you to be pulled back into the medical world any more than necessary."

"I think it's a little too late for that," Claire said, with a touch of humor in her voice.

Kiernan half grinned. "I know. But I've found some great training videos from the hospital that pioneered this procedure, and they're about as thorough as you can get. We'll all study everything over the weekend, and on Monday we'll get an early start so you can address the team and take any last-minute questions. If something comes up during the training this weekend that requires your input, I'll give you a call." He slowed his pace and turned to her. "Does that sound like a plan?"

She smiled. "Yes, that sounds like a plan."

Suddenly, he came to a halt. "Actually, there *is* a bit of bad news that I should have mentioned earlier."

Claire felt her stomach sink.

"The board is haggling about appropriate payment for the surgery and, knowing how slow this sort of thing moves through the system, I think it might be another week or two before the money can be transferred to you."

Claire breathed a sigh of relief. "Oh—that! I should have mentioned this earlier as well. I'm not looking to get paid for the surgery."

Kiernan nearly balked. "That's hugely generous of you, but I can't let you perform such a time-intensive, complex surgery for free. Let the hospital cough something up to compensate you fairly—as well they should."

"How about you let them figure out what they think my services are worth, and whatever it is, I'll donate it to a worthy cause. You can choose what that should be, since I'm not familiar with local organizations. But maybe something like a women's shelter, or a women's health educational program?"

Kiernan stared at her in near-disbelief. "Have I told you lately that you're amazing?"

Claire felt her face flush, and an appreciative smile was the only reply she could manage.

They resumed walking, but took only a few steps before Kiernan stopped and turned to her. "Actually, if you're not going to accept payment, then I have a counteroffer."

"Which is…?" Claire asked, equal parts cautious and intrigued.

"Let me cook dinner for you tomorrow night at my place."

Claire gulped silently. "Dinner?" Another silent gulp. "At your place?"

"It's not a dungeon, I swear," Kiernan replied, prompting a slightly nervous smile from Claire. "Plus, remember how I failed at your question about my favorite spots?"

"Miserably, as I recall."

Kiernan grinned. "Well, this is a chance for me to amend my answer. I have an outdoor deck that virtually dangles over the cliffs and looks out onto the ocean. I might be biased, but it's one of the most magnificent views on the West Coast of Ireland."

Claire grimaced apprehensively. "'Dangles over the cliffs'? You need to work on your sales pitch."

Kiernan laughed. "It's one hundred percent safe and secure, I promise."

"Mr. O'Rourke! Mr. O'Rourke!"

Kiernan and Claire turned in the direction of the eager voice, watching as a young boy ran toward them while his mother tried to keep pace close behind.

"Henry!" Kiernan exclaimed, returning the boy's high five before giving his carrot-red hair an affectionate tousle. "What a wonderful surprise!" He looked up at the boy's mother. "Catherine, how are you?"

"Hello, Mr. O'Rourke. I'm doing great." She smiled from ear to ear. "And, more importantly, *Henry's* doing great."

"I'm on the school rugby team now!" Henry exclaimed.

Kiernan's eyes widened. "Fantastic! What position?"

"Inside center—just like you."

"Best position there is," Kiernan said with a wink.

He turned to Claire and commenced introductions, summing up his history with Henry as being one of many West Mercy doctors who'd banded together to treat the young boy after a life-threatening car accident four years ago.

"Mr. O'Rourke is being far too modest," Catherine said to Claire. "He headed up a team that not only saved Henry's life, but saved his leg—which at one point wasn't a certainty." She looked down at her son, beaming with pride. "And now he's playing rugby on the school team. If that's not a miracle, I don't know what is."

"Were you in today for a recheck?" Kiernan asked.

Catherine nodded. "We had an annual appointment with Mr. O'Leary to make sure everything is working as it should with Henry's leg. Although after Henry bounded into the room and more or less catapulted himself onto the table, Mr. O'Leary said he probably doesn't need to see him again—at least not in an official capacity."

"With an entrance like that, who needs X-rays, right?" Kiernan observed to all-around laughter.

Claire discreetly stepped back. Not only to give Kiernan and Henry some room for their boisterous reunion, but also to make sure her eyes—and ears—weren't playing tricks on her. Because if she hadn't known better, she'd have thought Kiernan—he of the "I don't see children in my future" mantra—was carrying on in a downright paternal manner. Which meant that suddenly, and quite unexpectedly, she could see him as a father. And not just as *any* father, but the kind she would want for her own children.

Whoa, whoa, whoa!

Claire took another step back—but this time because she had just jumped so far out in front of herself. In the span of a few seconds she'd started to see Kiernan in a whole new light—one that made him even more attractive than before, if that was possible. And for the first time since losing Ariana, the thought of having another child had entered her mind.

"Claire?"

Claire jerked her head up just in time to see Henry and his mother departing down the corridor.

"They said goodbye to you, but I don't think you heard them."

Slightly dazed, Claire steadied herself and smiled. "Sorry, I…um… I got distracted."

He cocked his head to one side. "You okay?"

"Yes." Another smile…this time with less effort needed.

"Good. Well, before you head out let's settle on a time for dinner tomorrow. How about if I pick you about seven p.m.?" As Claire's eyes widened, he added, "I know…you love your Mini. But my place is rather remote and tricky to find, and this will just make it easier."

She allowed herself to breathe again. "Yes, of course. That makes sense."

As Claire walked through the parking lot to her car, a short time later, she tried to wrap her head around the dizzying speed at which everything seemed to be swirling around her. Hadn't she come to Ireland to slow things down and mull over her future? Instead, she was about to dive headfirst back into the high-stakes medical world that she had put on hold. And, even more confounding, although romance had been the last thing on her mind when she'd arrived here, the universe seemed to have other ideas.

How else to explain why someone like Kiernan had almost

instantly landed in the midst of everything and every moment spent with him since had been nothing short of magical?

Cupping her hand over her eyes, she looked up at the bright sky, quietly saying out loud, "You're either one very smart universe…" She paused, knowing full well that her time with Kiernan was limited. "Or the joke's on me."

CHAPTER EIGHT

CLAIRE TOOK ONE final look at her reflection in the bathroom mirror, sighed deeply, then headed to the main room in her cottage to wait for Kiernan. The fact that she had changed her outfit three times, segued from a hair-twist to a sleek ponytail and finally loose tresses, told her one thing.

This is not good.

Her attraction to Kiernan had gone beyond the point where she could convince herself that it was simply admiration for his surgical prowess. There was the way he'd been so understanding when she'd opened up to him about Ariana. His supportive concern about her own well-being if she were to perform Jan's high-stakes surgery, which in turn had infused her with the courage she needed to step back into the world of obstetrics.

And can we talk about that thick, run-your-fingers-through-it dark hair and that muscular rugby build?

Claire took a deep breath and reminded herself that this wasn't a date…or was it? Kiernan might have tried to frame the dinner as a substitute payment for her doing the surgery, but she'd have been remiss not to have seen the anticipation in his eyes when he'd made the offer. Especially since it had matched her own.

Just be yourself.

That was all she could do, right? Real date or sort-of date—this was still the first date of *any* kind since her marriage to

Mark had ended. And that alone had her alternating between nervousness and excitement.

A knock at the door brought Claire's racing thoughts to a halt. At least temporarily. They came flooding back as soon as she opened the door.

It should have dawned on her that any man who was a feast for the eyes in drab scrubs would be impossible to look away from in dressier clothes. Which in this case were crisp jeans and a light gray casual sports coat over a form-fitting black T-shirt. Mouth slightly agape, her mind drew a blank as it searched for a standard greeting.

Kiernan smiled, and as his lips curved upwards, her knees buckled downwards. "Hi."

Oh, that's the word.

"Hi," she replied.

"You look beautiful."

"So do you."

As they shared a laugh at her awkward comment, Claire inwardly admonished herself.

Don't be a dork. Please.

A short time later she was seated in the passenger seat of Kiernan's silver hybrid SUV as it effortlessly climbed a steep, winding road framed on both sides by lush green fields.

"I guess you weren't kidding about living in a remote area," Claire observed five more miles into the journey, as the off-the-grid scenery grew increasingly breathtaking.

He turned to her and grinned. "It gets even better."

When she stepped out of the SUV fifteen minutes later, it was with a sense of awe. She walked with Kiernan up the short driveway and viewed the modern, eco-friendly dwelling before her. With more glass than solid walls, its presence was considerable, despite its relatively modest size.

"I was expecting a stone cottage, but this is…wow."

"Thanks. I fell in love with this spot, but there weren't any existing homes. So I bought a parcel of land and had this one built five years ago."

Once inside, Kiernan commenced a brief tour, and Claire couldn't help but notice the tidy, everything-in-its-place décor. She was about to ask jokingly if he sterilized his eating utensils with the same autoclaving method of surgical instrument sanitization, when she spotted a vase of vibrant blue flowers on the kitchen counter that could easily double as a "what doesn't belong here?" picture riddle.

"They're beautiful," she said as she leaned over to smell them. "Did you pick them yourself?"

"I did—from the side of a cliff."

Claire did a double-take. "I never realized flower-gathering could be such a high-risk endeavor."

Kiernan smiled, and when he answered there was a tinge of pride in his voice. "Nothing that some spiked shoes and a sturdy rope couldn't solve. I thought you might like them. It was either the flowers or some ducks, and I figured the flowers would be easier to maintain indoors."

Claire laughed, touched that he'd gone to such extremes on her behalf. She didn't want to read *too* much into the gesture…but it was hard not to conclude that he wouldn't have done this for just anyone.

"Let's head outside."

Kiernan led Claire out to the cedar deck attached to the back of the house.

"Holy moly, Kiernan! This view is unbelievable," Claire said breathlessly as she looked out onto the ocean. "I can see why it's a favorite spot."

"Just don't look down."

"Too late," Claire said as she grasped the deck railing with both hands. "You really *are* dangling off a cliff!"

"More like a highly engineered teetering," Kiernan observed wryly as he opened the bottle of wine that rested in the center of a wrought-iron table, complete with two fancy place settings. He then joined Claire, and together they leaned their folded arms on the railing and looked out onto the waves as they crashed against the cliff.

"Is the water always this turbulent?" Claire asked curiously.

Kiernan nodded. "Enough so that on the rare day when things are relatively still, I start to worry that there's an earthquake or something in store."

They silently appreciated the view for another minute, then Kiernan turned to her.

"I hope you're hungry?"

"That depends on how good the chef is," Claire teased.

"I'll have you know my deep-dish, three-cheese lasagna has been a hit at every West Mercy staff summer picnic for the past six years."

"I'm impressed. So what's on the menu tonight?"

Kiernan's left cheek creased with a one-sided smile. "Deep-dish, three-cheese lasagna."

Claire chuckled. "Ah, so you're a one-trick pony?"

"I beg your pardon?" Kiernan replied, feigning insult. "More like a prize steed that knows enough to stick to a winning formula."

Claire laughed.

"I thought we could dine out here."

Kiernan walked over to a stone-encased fire pit and lit the aromatic wood inside. As if on cue, the string of dusk-to-dawn automatic lights that spanned the surrounding deck rail blinked on.

"Look at this…" Claire scanned the softly glowing deck. "It's like Gilroy's Pub after dark—minus the drunken rugby players and the smell of stale beer."

"My teammates are just a phone call away if you'd prefer the full Gilroy's experience."

Claire grinned. "Thanks, I'm good."

"I was hoping you'd say that." Kiernan pulled out a chair at the table and waited for Claire to be seated. "I was looking forward to dinner just the two of us."

Claire wondered if Kiernan could actually hear her gulp.

Yup, I think this is a date.

With considerable effort, she corralled the butterflies in her stomach that had been set off by a rush of adrenaline.

Just go with the flow, she reminded herself, though it was easier said than done.

"I'm going to go check on my fan favorite lasagna. Be back in a minute."

Claire nodded and smiled. He could serve her a baked hockey puck and she'd probably think it was a culinary masterpiece. Not that he needed to know that, of course.

Twenty minutes later, Claire placed her fork and knife together on her empty plate and pushed it slightly forward, more than pleasantly surprised. "That was delicious. My compliments to the chef."

"You mean the one-trick pony?"

Claire grinned. "All joking aside, you're a great cook. I'm surprised."

Kiernan pretended to choke on her comment. "I'm not *too* insulted."

"Ha! I just mean I'm surprised you find the time to cook with your schedule."

"You did catch the part where I told you I have one recipe in my arsenal, right?"

"Well, it's a winner."

"Glad it wasn't awful. More wine?"

"Please."

Her glass replenished, she glanced over at the fire pit, her eyes lingering on the dancing flames for longer than she had intended. Perhaps because they were a metaphor for the question that was burning inside of her. She turned back to Kiernan. Dare she ask him? A few more seconds of contemplation, and then impulse took over.

"So, I'm curious about something…" she began.

Kiernan cocked his head slightly to one side. "Go on."

"At the hospital yesterday, when you were talking with Henry, I couldn't help but notice how…natural…you were around him. In fact, if I didn't know any better, I'd say you actually *like* children."

Kiernan's expression changed from one of intrigue to confusion. "I *do* like children. What makes you think I don't?"

"Well, you said before that you don't want children."

"I said I don't think I can fully devote myself to my career and children at the same time. One or the other would have to give. It's just the way it is. And my decision to put my career first has nothing to do with any imagined prestige of being chief of surgery. It's that I get to save lives. I mean, *you* know what that feeling is like. It's a huge responsibility and one that I don't take lightly. And it's because I *do* like children that I'd never subject them to the type of childhood I had with an absentee father."

Claire managed a faint nod. "I get it."

She could leave it at that. She *should* leave it at that. Except…

"But on the other hand, I can think of a number of colleagues back home—both men and women—who are very involved with their children and are still top-notch doctors who give one hundred percent to their patients."

Kiernan pursed his lips together and stared at Claire, as though trying to discern why she was grilling him on this matter. "I don't know," he finally replied. "Maybe some doctors can strike that perfect balance. I suppose it depends what field of medicine they're in. Some are more demanding than others." He paused. "And I've never shied away from admitting my views have been shaped in large part by the fact that my father was a very dedicated surgeon, but an incredibly inattentive father."

"And that realization isn't enough to make you wonder if there might be another way?"

As soon as the question left Claire's mouth, she knew she had to stop. She was pushing Kiernan too far—raising questions that might be appropriate if they had just embarked on a relationship, but not as very temporary colleagues. It didn't matter if there was a part of her that yearned for more with him.

Did I just admit that?

It was not something that could ever be. Soon, there would be three thousand miles between them. And did she really need to remind herself about their conflicting views on parenthood yet again?

She could see in Kiernan's eyes that he was struggling to form an answer to her question. So she decided to make it easy for him. Perhaps for them both.

"I don't think we've had an official toast yet." She raised her glass of wine. "Here's to a successful surgery for Jan and Rhianna."

Kiernan's tense face softened, and he raised his glass as well. "I will happily drink to that."

Claire smiled, then took a sip of wine. It was a mellow Merlot that initially tasted sweet on her lips, but quickly morphed into bitterness. Funny how it mirrored her growing feelings for Kiernan, she thought. A dream that was so enticing, and a reality that cut like a knife.

"Hard to believe I'm halfway through my stay here," she said pensively.

Kiernan's smile was cut short, though it soon reemerged with what appeared to be some effort. "It seems like just yesterday we were strangers who met on a hillside during a medical crisis," he said.

"It does…" An uncomfortable silence filled the air, and Claire scrambled to break its hold. "So, I guess I have some catching up to do if I'm going to play tourist for the remainder of my time here. Any suggestions?"

Kiernan's face instantly lit up. "What you really need is a good tourist guide. Someone who knows Ireland like the back of his hand."

"Hmm… Do you have anyone in mind?"

"I do. He's a great conversationalist and he knows all the hidden gems that the big tour companies miss. Plus, I heard that for certain individuals—make that certain *very special* individuals—his services are free."

Claire had been gamely playing along with what she assumed was a playful ruse until she saw the look of earnestness on Kiernan's face. "Wait, you're not serious…are you?"

"That I'm a great conversationalist? Gift of the Blarney here. I just happen to hide it well." He winked. "At least when I'm in surgeon mode."

"But how are you going to get time off from the hospital on such short notice?"

"Leave that up to me. I probably have about five years' worth of unused leave at this point."

"Why do I not find that hard to believe?"

Kiernan smirked. "So, what do you say?"

"Surgeon, restaurateur and now tour guide. You're quite the entrepreneur."

"The day I announce I'm a sheep herder, too—that's when you have to start worrying."

Claire snickered. "Duly noted."

She paused, grappling with a modified version of an angel on one shoulder, a devil on the other. In this instance it consisted of an angel on each side. On the left shoulder, the angel advised her to let down her protective guard and follow her heart. And on the right? Well, that angel had something to say about her heart, too.

This situation can't go anywhere. You'll only be hurt.

Both angels were looking out for her. But though she typically erred on the side of caution—especially with matters of the heart—in this moment, and with this man, she was willing to plunge into the unknown, consequences be damned.

She took a deep breath, silently acknowledging that such a cavalier attitude could come back to bite her. But Kiernan was both smart and perceptive. He had to know as well as she did that there was no future for them beyond the next two weeks. Perhaps he *did* just want to show her some interesting sights off the beaten path. There was no harm in that...right?

"So, when does my personalized tour begin?" Claire asked, her voice a tad too flirty for her own liking. "Given that we first have a very major surgery to get through on Monday."

Kiernan pulled his phone out of his pants pocket and scrolled through his calendar. "How does Tuesday sound? I have a carotid endarterectomy in the morning, and an afternoon of administrative work that I'll be more than happy to push to another day."

"Tuesday works. And is there a particular dress code for whatever you have in store?"

As thoughts of a bare-chested Kiernan in an Irish kilt flooded her mind—a most enticing dress code for *him*—she did her best to keep her eyes from popping out of her head.

"Well, I know you like being outdoors—especially when there are ducks around." As Claire laughed, he added, "So let's plan on a countryside walkabout. I have just the place in mind."

"I'll toast to that," she said, clinking her wine glass against his.

She took a sip and swallowed it down, doing her best to shut out the inner whispers of warning from the angel on her right shoulder.

It was that very same shoulder that Kiernan looked past as he pointed behind her. "The moon's just starting to come up. This is the best time of the night—when it's still partially dusk and the light of the moon hits the water." He stood up and offered his hand. "Let's go take a look."

Claire's breath caught in her throat as he took her hand and helped her up from the chair. As he stared into her eyes she felt as though she might melt into the deck boards. Even the brief stroll to the railing felt like a dream. Had she walked there, or floated? She couldn't be sure…

As they leaned over the railing and looked down onto the foamy waves that shimmered with moonlight, a strong breeze came up from the ocean, whipping Claire's hair around her face and shoulders.

"It's chilly, isn't it?" Kiernan asked, turning to her.

In the diminishing light of dusk, his normally light brown eyes were a shade of dark espresso, but the kindness behind them was unaltered.

Claire crossed her arms tightly in front of her. "Woo! It's like a twenty-degree temperature-drop here."

Wrapping his arm around her side, Kiernan pulled her in close, the warmth of his muscular body seeping into her skin. Now she was *really* melting into the ground… And as he looked into her eyes, she knew he wanted to kiss her. And she wanted to kiss him, too.

He brushed a wayward lock of hair from her cheek, moving his face closer to hers…closer…closer…and then he stopped.

Claire held her breath for several moments. A kiss hadn't passed between them, but in those last seconds, as their eyes locked, an understanding had. Because even though she couldn't imagine a more perfect and atmospheric backdrop to her first kiss with Kiernan, this wasn't the right time.

Her attraction to him was growing exponentially and, as such, it was occupying a huge space in her thoughts and emotions. But right now that space needed to be devoted to one thing above all else: walking back into an operating room on Monday, a path still strewn with trauma from the past, and successfully completing a complex surgery that might also help decide the fate of her career.

And after the surgery? Hopefully there would still be time to pick up where they had just left off. But with her return to Boston imminent, that time was ticking by fast.

No wonder the angel on her right shoulder was whispering in her ear: *Don't get too attached, Claire.*

One, two, three, four, five... Er...yeah, I think that makes six...

Later that night, with his eyes closed, Kiernan counted the number of opportunities he had had over the course of the evening to take Claire into his arms and kiss her. Fully. Passionately. Deeply. There were probably some more adjectives he could add into the mix, but three was enough to get the point across.

He was able to recall each instance with vivid detail, as though they were playing out in real time in his mind.

Leaning closely over her shoulder as he poured her another glass of wine.

Taking her hand and helping her up from her chair.

Standing side by side at the deck railing after dinner as they gazed out into the moonlit sky—*ugh, I really blew that one*—the waves crashing below them.

Walking her up to her cottage door at the end of the evening to make sure she got safely inside.

And not even then?

Truth be told, he couldn't recall ever struggling to get up the nerve to kiss someone when the circumstances seemed right. But the situation with Claire was different. And the reason was simple, really. He didn't want to scare Claire off before he had a chance to show her...well, *what?* That he was the perfect man for her, despite the fact that they lived thousands of miles apart and had incompatible views on children?

And then there was the matter of Monday's surgery. The last thing he'd wanted to do was to complicate things by throwing a kiss into the mix. There was so much riding on this procedure. For Jan and Rhianna, of course. But for Claire as well. In fact, her very future as an ob-gyn might depend on how everything turned out. Which meant it was imperative that extra distractions be barred from the operating room.

Keep it professional.

At least until after the surgery. And then, if he got the chance to kiss her again— No, wait… *When* he got the chance to kiss her again, he would make up for lost time.

Time. That was another complicating factor that he had to push from his mind. Soon—make that *very* soon—Claire would be heading back to the States for good. And his earlier resolve to just enjoy the now?

What had initially been a *problem solved* solution, was now one that filled him with a growing sense of unease.

CHAPTER NINE

CLAIRE'S PHONE ALARM went off at precisely four a.m. on Monday, as planned, but she was already awake, eyes fixated on the dark ceiling above her. Today, she would be altering the course of life for a mother and her unborn child. She wouldn't blame anyone for thinking she was full of herself to reach such a heady conclusion, but it was true. And it had nothing to do with a biased self-assessment of her skills. If everything went as planned, Rhianna would have as normal a life as possible for a child with a spina bifida birth defect. She had seen—and been the catalyst for—such miracles firsthand in the past.

But if complications arose....

Claire sat up in bed and rested on her elbows for several moments. She wasn't going to go there. Only positive thoughts. She was a firm believer that they could make a difference in the operating room and in life in general. But sometimes, in the latter instance, it was easier said than done—especially in light of personal loss.

But today wasn't about her. It was about Jan and Rhianna, about Jan's husband Dave, and their other two children, Melody and Sean. She had to be strong for them.

Claire reminded herself that Kiernan would be by her side throughout the procedure and instantly felt calmer. He had texted her several times to check in and let her know that the weekend-long intense training session with his team had gone well. They were ready to go. And so was she.

The sun was just beginning to rise as she pulled into the West Mercy staff parking lot. The security guards knew to expect her arrival, and ushered her in after viewing her Boston General photo ID. From the side entrance, it was a three-minute walk to the new neonatal wing, but with the weight of what lay ahead, it felt more like thirty.

After Ariana's death, walking to the OR for a scheduled surgery had felt like trudging through a black cloud. But now? She felt a fluttering of nerves mixed with the anticipated joy and relief of a successful outcome. An unsuccessful outcome, and that black cloud would be back and ten times thicker.

Think only good thoughts, Claire inwardly reminded herself. *Just be fully in the moment for Jan and Rhianna.*

Kiernan and a handful of his colleagues were conversing by the nurses' station as she entered the wing. He turned to her as she approached the group and she quietly caught her breath. Could everyone see how she was looking at him not only as a fellow doctor, but also as the man whose desirable lips had nearly touched her own several nights ago?

She hoped not. Just because *she* had thought about that near-kiss all weekend long, it didn't mean anyone else—other than Kiernan, of course—had any inkling of their dinner together. And she preferred it to stay that way. Effectively leading a new team through a complex surgery required being seen as a top-notch professional in their eyes. And fantasizing about locking lips with the hunky chief of surgery didn't exactly cater to that image.

"Good morning, Dr. Delaney."

The smile on Kiernan's face seemed overly calm—and also quite familiar. It was the "pre-surgery smile" that Claire had come to perfect herself over the years, an almost Zen-like state of mind that descended upon her as she readied for a grueling surgery. The only difference was that his smile was accompanied by a twinkle in his eye. Perhaps he was reminiscing about their almost-kiss, too?

Turning back to the small group, Kiernan said, "If you'll excuse me for a few minutes," then gestured to Claire to follow him.

After a short walk down the hall, he opened a door and peered inside, then switched on the lights. Once they were both inside, he closed the door and turned his full attention on Claire.

"How are you feeling?" he asked, eyes gazing steadily into hers.

Over the years, she had been privy to countless one-on-one interactions with fellow doctors in the privacy of a hospital room or staff quarters…and none had ever made her feel weak in the knees like she did at this moment.

It's pre-surgery jitters, that's all.

If ever she'd needed that Zen mindset, it was now. There was so much riding on this surgery—the most obvious being the best possible outcome for Jan and Rhianna. But there was much at stake on a personal level as well. She needed to stay one hundred percent objective before, during and immediately after the complex procedure—a feat that was easier said than done. Letting even a tiny fraction of her personal pain and angst seep into her performance in the operating room could have devastating consequences.

Would she be able to keep a tight lid on her emotions? She wouldn't have agreed to take on the surgery if she hadn't believed that she could. But now that the moment of reckoning was imminent….

"Claire?"

Kiernan's voice cut into her thoughts, and not a moment too soon. It was time to focus on one thing and one thing only: a successful fetal surgery.

"Sorry," she finally managed to say. "I'm okay. Just giving myself an inner pep talk, that's all."

"You've got this, Claire. I know you do."

He reached over and clasped both her hands. His hands were warm and strong, and his touch sent her brain and body to places that they didn't need to go right now.

"You're going to come through this with flying colors. And you know why?"

Claire was too breathless to answer.

"Because once you do, a special outing awaits with a devastatingly handsome surgeon from West Mercy who moonlights as a tour guide. Or so I've heard…"

In an instant, Claire's flailing nerves were flattened on the spot, and she shook her head and grinned. "I'll keep that in mind."

He squeezed her hands tighter. "All kidding aside, I know how strong you are. But I know this surgery is bringing up a lot of personal issues for you as well. Let's just get in that operating theater and give Jan and Rhianna the happy ending they deserve. Then we'll deal with the other stuff."

We? Did he say "we"?

Claire swallowed hard, reminding herself that now was not the time to read too much into anything that Kiernan might say. He was merely helping her double down on her earlier silent pep talk, and for that she was grateful.

Her resolve now cemented, she looked back up into Kiernan's eyes. "Let's do this."

He smiled and slowly let go of her hands, as though reluctant to break the connection, then opened the door and held it for her to pass through.

There was no turning back now.

As promised, Kiernan assembled the large team just outside the OR for a pre-surgery pep talk. With all eyes focused on her—eager eyes, at that—there was little that Claire needed to say. It was clear that everyone understood the gravity of the situation, but also the miraculous possibilities. And they would all be part of that miracle now.

Once in the OR, Jan was wheeled in, groggy from the IV anesthesia medication that had been started in the pre-surgery area, but still cognizant enough to squeeze Claire's hand as she assured her that they were going to take good care of her and Rhianna.

Sebastian placed a face mask over Jan's nose and mouth, administering the gases that would send her into a deep sedation.

Scalpel in hand, Claire briefly looked up at Kiernan where he stood directly across the operating table. With his surgical mask in place, she could only see his eyes, but they spoke volumes.

You can do this. And I'm right here with you.

She waited as one of the OR nurses swabbed Jan's belly with antiseptic, then performed a laparotomy across her abdomen. With Jan's uterus exposed, Dr. Fleming moved in and began performing an ultrasound to determine Rhianna's position. All eyes were on the ultrasound monitor as her tiny body came into view.

"We'll need to rotate her slightly to gain full access to the spinal opening," Claire said, carefully but firmly placing her gloved hands on each side of Rhianna's body and exerting pressure on the left. This prompted Rhianna to roll slightly to the right—enough of a shift to reposition her spinal opening.

Claire looked to her left at Dr. Fleming who, without needing to be asked, stepped over to confirm the repositioning through ultrasound. This seamless communication—with no actual words needed—was so important in a surgery such as this, with so many moving parts, and Claire appreciated the doctor's diligence.

"Perfect," Claire said quietly as she viewed the spinal defect on the monitor, in the exact spot where it needed to be.

A surgical nurse handed her a uterine stapling device.

"You did a great job prepping your team," Claire said as she looked up at Kiernan.

"We had a very productive weekend," he said. "Saturday was chock-full of training videos, and Sunday was a simulated run-through of the surgery. Make that *many* run-throughs."

"It shows."

She nodded her appreciation in every direction, her eyes creased at the corners as her hidden lips curved upwards. Every doctor who had ever donned a surgical mask knew that this was the OR equivalent of a smile. But there was one doctor in particular whose silent encouragement she needed most. Looking across the operating table, she locked eyes with Kiernan and held his gaze for several moments. The exchange was silent, but the message was the same.

You can do this. I'm right here with you.

After a slight nod of acknowledgement, Claire took a deep breath, then cut into Jan's uterus with the stapling device. She flipped the attachment arm of her microscope glasses downward, instantly revealing a detailed closeup of the myelomeningocele sac, a thin, bluish, fluid-containing membrane about an inch and a half long that protruded from the opening in Rhianna's back.

Here we go.

Her breathing calm and her hands steady, she carefully excised the sac and placed it into a pan. A critical part of the surgery was now complete, but the time-intensive delicate closing of the spinal opening remained. Knowing that this multilayer closing was normally performed in tandem by a fetal surgeon and a neurosurgeon, she turned to the neurosurgeon to her left.

"Mr. Siwa, would you like to assist?"

"Absolutely," he declared as he moved in closer.

Once the spinal defect was fully repaired, it was time to close up the uterus. This, too, required the suturing of multiple layers—a more standard procedure than closing the spinal opening, but one that still required intense focus. Claire welcomed the task at hand, for it meant they were that much closer to completing a successful surgery.

There was an air of calmness in the OR as she and Mr. Siwa began stitching up the first uterine layer. It was as if everyone was breathing a collective sigh of relief now that the most critical part of the surgery was now behind them.

Suddenly Dr. McAdams, the cardiologist who had quietly been monitoring Rhianna's heart through echocardiology, called out. "Fetal heart rate is dropping."

Claire jerked her head up as Kiernan asked, "What is it?"

"One-oh-five. Still dropping."

Claire knew that a normal fetal heart rate was one-ten to one-sixty. If it continued to drop steadily, Rhianna would be heading fast to bradycardia. They could lose her.

For a split second, Claire closed her eyes.

"Doctor!" she heard someone exclaim urgently.

Given that the title covered half of the OR team, she couldn't be sure who it was directed to, but it didn't matter at this point. Rhianna's life—perhaps even Jan's—was in her hands now.

"We're in bradycardia," the cardiologist announced, his booming voice momentarily drowning out all the mechanical beeps and hurried voices in the room.

Claire swung her head from the direction of the cardiologist's voice to Kiernan. They locked eyes for a fraction of a second, and in that moment time stood still for Claire. There was no sound, no movement—no anything.

And then…it all came crashing back.

"Increase maternal oxygen," Claire instructed, knowing that doing so would improve Rhianna's oxygen levels as well.

As Sebastian adjusted Jan's oxygen levels, Kiernan asked, "What's her blood pressure?"

"One-ten over eighty," replied the nurse monitoring vital signs.

If the pressure was low, they could increase it through IV fluids and ephedrine, which in turn would improve blood flow to Rhianna. But it was within normal range.

She shared a look with Kiernan, and knew he was thinking the same thing as her. Aggressive intervention was needed to save Rhianna, and they didn't have a boatload of options.

Though fetal surgery had been inching its way into a viable solution for a growing list of congenital disorders, it was—as Claire's fetal surgery mentor at Boston General, Dr. Eugene Martin, would often say—"Still in its infancy, if you'll pardon the pun."

"Start a fetal IV of point-zero-one milligrams epinephrine," Claire said, shutting off the part of her mind that was one step short of inwardly screaming, *Hurry!*

"An IV?" the closest nurse to her asked.

Rather than be annoyed by the question in the midst of an emergency, Claire replied with a simple, "Yes."

She understood the need for confirmation. To say that she was navigating through uncharted waters was an understatement. Fetal bradycardia was a relatively rare complication during open fetal surgery, but it had been known to happen. Still, there was no definitive protocol in place.

Releasing some of the stiches to pull Rhianna's tiny forearm through, Claire inserted the IV needle and held her breath as Dr. Fleming administered the medication through the IV line. Thirty seconds went by—or was it thirty minutes? Claire knew it was the former, but with Rhianna's life in the balance, it felt like an eternity.

She turned to the cardiologist, who shook his head. "Still dropping. Eighty-seven."

"Atropine?" Kiernan suggested, just as Claire was about to call for it.

She nodded. "I need point-zero-zero-five milligrams atropine."

Dr. Fleming quickly administered the medication. Now all they could do was wait an agonizing minute to see if it worked.

Tick-tick-tick...

"No response!" the cardiologist said, just short of a shout.

Kiernan's ability to remain coolly detached through the most dire of surgical circumstances was being severely tested as the unthinkable began to unfold before him.

They couldn't lose Rhianna. They just couldn't.

It had been his idea to do this surgery here, and Rhianna's death would be on him. Not only would he be responsible for Jan losing her baby, but the loss would destroy Claire—a realization that nearly rendered him immobile. But now was not the time to freeze up. If ever he'd needed to shut off his emotions and focus solely on averting disaster, it was now.

"I'm going to start chest compressions," he said as he leaned over Jan's abdomen.

Across the table, Claire squeezed a hand into the reopened uterus and lifted Rhianna up so that her chest was well into view. But it wasn't enough.

"I'm going to lift her out," Claire said as she pulled Rhianna's head and chest through, leaving the rest of her body inside the womb.

Using his forefinger and middle finger, Kiernan began gently but rapidly compressing the center of Rhianna's chest at a rate of one hundred and twenty compressions per minute. At the sixty-second mark, he swung his head in the direction of Dr. McAdams.

Without needing to be asked, the cardiologist blurted out, "Eighty-five."

Kiernan couldn't see Claire's face beneath the mask, but he knew her grave expression matched his.

"Give another point-zero-one milligrams of epinephrine," she said urgently.

Kiernan halted compressions as Dr. Fleming administered the medication.

"We're still at eighty-five," Dr. McAdams called out twenty seconds later.

"Atropine?" Dr. Fleming asked, a syringe at the ready.

"Yes—point-zero-zero-five milligrams."

Tick-tick-tick...

"Eighty!" came the cardiologist's one-word update.

"Start compressions again," Claire said to Kiernan.

He quickly complied, with a laser-sharp focus, as he strived to deliver the precise amount of pressure.

"Heart rate is increasing. Ninety-eight," said the cardiologist.

Another ten compressions.

"One-twenty."

Kiernan's hand froze as he waited, desperately hoping that Rhianna's heart rate would stabilize.

"One-thirty-seven." Another ten seconds passed. "Heart rate is holding."

"Let's give it another minute to be sure before we start re-closing the uterus," Claire said, her voice a steady beacon in the quiet chaos of the operating theater.

Turning back to Kiernan, she gave a brief nod, as if to say, *I think we got through it.*

Forty-five minutes later Jan was wheeled out into Recovery, all of her vital signs, and Rhianna's, holding steady.

Kiernan watched as Claire walked over to the far side of the room, leaning up against the wall and removing her mask to take a deep and unfiltered breath of air.

"You were amazing," Kiernan said as he walked up beside her.

Claire looked up, her expression exhausted and yet exhilarated at the same time. "So were you. You saved Rhianna's life."

"*We* saved her life."

Claire smiled wearily. "Listen to us. We're debating over who did more to save Rhianna. It was a team effort all the way."

Kiernan's smile was as tired as Claire's, but also as genuine. "You're right. What matters most is that Jan and her baby are both safe and it truly was the best possible outcome."

He paused, wanting so badly to brush back the loose lock of silky chestnut hair that had spilled out of Claire's surgeon's cap. Fighting the urge, he forced himself to briefly look away. But wait… It was officially after the surgery, right? Which meant his self-imposed *don't touch* rule had expired.

He turned back to Claire just as she was pulling off her cap, her hair tumbling perfectly around her shoulders. *Really?* Every lock of hair had just fallen into exactly the right place, with nothing for him to brush aside?

She tilted her head, eyes perplexed. "What's wrong?"

Kiernan mustered up a smile. "Nothing. I was just going to suggest we go and talk to Jan's husband."

"Yes—good idea. I'm sure he'll be relieved… I can only imagine how worried he must have been this whole time."

And with good reason, Kiernan wanted to say as the earlier emergency played out in quick snippets in his mind.

After sharing the good news with Dave and Jan's two children in the waiting room, Kiernan escorted Claire back into the corridor.

"That is one happy father-to-be," he noted.

Claire smiled. "It feels good, being part of that happiness."

He wanted to probe further, to ask if the successful surgery had shifted anything for her career-wise, but he knew it was way too soon.

Claire bent her neck from side to side, then rubbed her shoulder. "Well, I think I'm going to head back to the cottage and take a nice, long, celebratory hot shower."

Kiernan was *so* tempted to offer to help loofah her back, and pretty much every other square inch of her beautiful, soft skin... But instead he cleared his throat and looked back at her with widened eyes that he did his best to minimize.

"That sounds like a good idea."

"I'll see you tomorrow for our country walkabout. Oh—and please tell Jan's care team to call me if there are any issues. Everything's looking good, and I'm not expecting any complications to crop up, but just in case."

"Will do."

She started down the corridor, turning back briefly to wave and flash an ear-to-ear smile.

"Enjoy your shower!" Kiernan called out, before cringing to himself.

Geez, did I just say that?

As Claire disappeared from view Kiernan had a sinking feeling in the pit of his stomach. He would see her again—for the time being. But the day was coming fast when that would no longer be the case.

And the feeling that was welling up inside him...the almost desperate realization that one day soon she'd be out of his life... Where was it coming from?

Because it wasn't anything he had ever felt for a woman before.

CHAPTER TEN

CLAIRE GLANCED AT her watch as Kiernan's SUV rolled up to her cottage. It was eleven fifty-nine a.m.

One minute early, she mused to herself as their "country walkabout"—destination still unknown—was about to commence.

The digital screen on her watch flashed as the display shifted to twelve p.m.

Or not.

So now she could add "punctual" to the list of Kiernan's attributes, which so far included "talented, brilliant, handsome, athletic, humorous and caring" among others. Although... could someone who was truly caring opt to live a life with no family of his own?

She frowned at her own line of thinking. It was a silly and unfair question. Some people opted to be married to their job, and in Kiernan's case the job entailed helping others—and often saving lives. So wasn't that a type of extended family? Kind of? Sort of?

"Hi."

Claire closed the cottage door behind her and greeted Kiernan. Standing by the SUV passenger door, a casual smile on his face, he looked both unassuming and ruggedly smoldering at the same time.

Claire's next breath caught in her throat.

Whew! Is it getting hot out here?

"What do you know?" Kiernan said, breaking into a smile. "We're twinning."

Claire's eyes had been so laser-focused on Kiernan that she hadn't seen the forest for the trees. Or, more precisely, she hadn't actually noticed what he was wearing. A closer inspection, and she began to laugh.

"You're right," she said as she took note of his jeans, white T-shirt, navy windbreaker and hiking shoes—all of which matched her own attire. "Great minds think alike."

"And dress alike, too," he said with a wink as he held the passenger door open for her.

As their drive got underway, Claire asked the question that had been uppermost in her mind. "How is Jan doing?"

"I checked in on her before leaving the hospital today. She's doing quite well, all things considered. She said Dave and the kids had come by to see her in the morning and were heading back for evening visiting hours."

"That's great to hear."

"She asked about you."

Claire did a double-take. "She did?"

Kiernan turned to her briefly before focusing back on the road. "You seem surprised. She's very grateful that you took on this surgery and wants to make sure you know this."

Claire was genuinely touched. "Please tell her I'm so happy to hear she and Rhianna are doing well."

Kiernan cleared his throat, hesitating for a moment before continuing, "You could come by the hospital and tell her yourself—if you're comfortable with that. I'm sure she'd be thrilled to see you."

Claire looked out the passenger window to collect her thoughts. "It's not that I don't want to see Jan. But I don't want to encroach on Dr. Fleming and her team. I'm sure they're all doing a wonderful job with postoperative care. They deserve credit, too."

She wondered if Kiernan could see through her explanation, which was half truthful and half flimsy excuse. The half that was truth was that she was afraid to get further involved in Jan's journey. Everything was headed in the right direction, and that was how she wanted to remember the experience. The more positives she could build on, the more she might be willing to fully step back into that world someday.

"Are you sure that's all it is?" Kiernan turned to her, seemingly holding his breath for several moments. "I know you came here to try to figure out if you can recommit to your career. If the reason you don't want to come by to see Jan is because you're still grappling with that, I can understand. Although I'm not going to lie… Seeing how happy you were after the surgery was successful, I just thought…"

His voice trailed off, but Claire knew where he was headed. "I know. You thought I'd finally got over the hurdle that's been holding me back." She paused. "I wish I could say it was that easy. And maybe it did help being in a different hospital and in a whole other country. There are so many memories back in Boston."

"I'm sorry. I shouldn't pressure you like this." Another short but meaningful sideways glance. "It's just that you're such an amazing doctor, and I know you still have so much to give. But ultimately I just want for you whatever will make you happiest."

"Me, too," Claire said quietly. "And I feel like I'm on the cusp of figuring it all out." She conjured up a smile as he briefly turned to her once more, his kind brown eyes locking onto hers. "I'm working on it, I promise."

Twenty-five minutes later, Kiernan pulled into the Connemara National Park visitors' center. "We're not visiting the center," he said with a wink. "We're hiking on the Diamond

Hill Trail. It's one of the most popular hiking spots in the country." As they exited the SUV, he added, "But we'll be veering off the beaten path in pursuit of one of those hidden gems I mentioned earlier."

Claire raised an eyebrow. "A hidden gem? I'm intrigued."

Kiernan grinned, then stepped around the back of the SUV and lifted up the hatch door. He pulled out two walking sticks, handing one to Claire.

"You can't go for a walkabout in Ireland without a shillelagh. I carved it myself."

Claire's eyes lit up as she ran her hand over the smooth exterior. Some women got excited over expensive jewelry, but not her.

Give me a genuine shillelagh, hand-carved by a dreamboat surgeon, and I'm the richest woman on the planet.

Looking up at Kiernan, she asked, "What are you—some kind of Renaissance man?"

He chuckled. "I've been called worse." Reaching again into the back of the SUV, he pulled out a large olive-green backpack. "I forgot to tell you to save room for lunch."

"I ate an energy bar just before you picked me up, but don't worry. I always work up an appetite when I'm out moving around in fresh air."

A thick lock of dark hair tumbled over Kiernan's left eye as he dipped down slightly to strap the backpack in place. "Good," he replied as he straightened back up with a mischievous twinkle in his eye. "That could come in handy."

Did he mean...?

Claire grinned, their earlier near-kiss front and center in her mind.

Ten minutes later they were on their way down a path that twisted and turned like a slate-gray version of the yellow brick road.

"There aren't many people here," Claire observed as she looked as far ahead as her vision allowed.

She could see several moving specks that she assumed were fellow hikers, but other than that they had the wide-open trail to themselves.

"It's a weekday, and still a bit early in the season," Kiernan said. "I've been here on weekends in late June and the trail entrance is like the starting gate at a horse race."

Claire wrinkled her nose. "Nothing against other humans, but I'd rather hike alone. Present company the exception, of course."

Kiernan smirked at her comment, adding, "I second that."

Another thing they had in common, Claire thought as they fell into an easy stride. Though the early-spring air held a faint chill, the afternoon sun was warm on her cheeks. She took a deep breath and soaked in her surroundings, and the panoramic view of gently sloping moors dotted with boulders and low mountains in the distance covered in mist.

Thump, step, thump, step, thump, step....

"You know, I've never actually used a walking stick before, but I have to say this really does help you get into a rhythm."

"And you thought Guinness was Ireland's most coveted contribution to the masses."

Claire chuckled. "You do have a way with words." Anticipating his reply, she beat him to the punch. "I know—it's the Gift of the Blarney."

Amused, Kiernan glanced sideways at her. "Matching outfits and now you're reading my mind. Should I be worried?"

Claire wanted to joke back, except his observation had hit a little too close to the mark. More likely the question was, should *she* be worried that she was enjoying his company so much?

The rapport that she shared with Kiernan was so natural, and so real, that it prompted her to rethink her entire relationship with Mark. Yes, he had turned into someone she no longer recognized, and it still haunted her knowing he had managed to pull the wool over her eyes for so long, shattering her trust in the process. But even before that, back when she'd *thought* they had something good together, it had still never been at this level, nor as easy and effortless.

But soon you'll be out of each other's lives.

The inevitable reminder left a pang in Claire's side, and it was one that she needed to heed. Her mind raced for a way to quickly change the subject, and there was one that was literally in hand.

"What kind of wood is this?" she asked as she held up her shillelagh.

"Blackthorn."

"Sounds prickly."

"It is. The shoots have thorns that can grow up to four inches. Let's just say I practically had to wear an iron hazmat suit when I cut off the branches."

"You definitely are a study in contradictions."

Kiernan glanced at her curiously. "How's that?"

She shrugged. "I haven't known many surgeons who play rugby and carve walking sticks."

"There must be an American equivalent. Surgeons who play tag football and carve pumpkins?"

Claire snickered. "I suppose."

Fifteen minutes later, Kiernan slowed down and pointed to the left. "Here's where we branch off the main path."

Claire cupped her eyes and looked out onto the western landscape. There was nothing obvious that set it apart from the terrain ahead if they stayed on the official trail, but Claire trusted that Kiernan had his reasons for the diversion. Plus, it added to the spirit of adventure, and that could only be a good thing.

They continued on, this time with no words, each taking

in the breathtaking scenery as they navigated the slightly uneven terrain.

Another ten minutes passed before Claire broke the silence. "I can see why you choose to live out here in the country, rather than in the city."

Kiernan turned to her. "What about you? I know you work in Boston, but is that where you live as well?"

"I live in Wayland, which is a suburb just west of Boston. It's pretty built up, but there are some pockets of nature here and there."

"That's good."

The conversation dropped off as they continued their climb, and Claire wondered if it was in part due to the subject matter.

You live here. I live there.

Strip away the niceties, and that was what was left. A reminder that they came from two different worlds. And soon she would be returning to hers.

She winced as this reality sank in. The fact that she'd resume her life in Boston after a month in Ireland had always been a given. But then, she hadn't planned on meeting someone like Kiernan.

She turned to him, wondering if he could possibly know that being in his presence made her feel more blissfully alive... and far less tethered to the hurtful past...than she had in a very long time. His eyes were cast downward as he scanned the uneven ground for safe footing, but when he suddenly looked over at her, she blurted out a question to segue from her own thoughts.

"So, you mentioned you grew up in Ballyledge. Did your dad work at West Mercy as well?"

"No, he worked at St. Joseph's Hospital in Dublin."

"That sounds like quite a commute."

"He had an apartment in Dublin."

"Oh…" Claire grimaced, thinking that something in this equation wasn't adding up.

Kiernan turned to her in mid-stride. "You're wondering if he was living a double life of sorts."

"I am?"

Of course she was—not that it felt appropriate to admit as much.

"Well, that's what I'd be wondering if someone told me their father had his own apartment two hundred kilometers away. Which wouldn't necessarily raise red flags if he was divorced from my mother, but that wasn't the case."

"She didn't mind the arrangement?"

"I don't think she felt like she had a say in the matter."

Claire balked, failing to hide her displeasure at this latest revelation. "Sorry," she said quietly.

"Don't be. My mother deserved better, for sure. As to whether my father had a secret second family in Dublin— I honestly don't think so. At least I hope not, given that he couldn't live up to his responsibilities as a husband and father with his first family. And the crazy part—or maybe not so crazy—was that his father, my grandfather, was cut from the same cloth."

"He was a surgeon, too?"

"Yup. And an absentee husband and father."

Claire slowed to a stop.

It was only when Kiernan was several steps ahead of her that he realized she was no longer by his side. He swiveled around, an expression of slight alarm on his face. "Are you okay?"

"You can break the cycle, you know."

Confusion replaced alarm. "What?"

Claire bit her lower lip.

It's now or never. Say what you need to say.

A few moments passed as she tried to muster up some courage. Scanning the immediate vicinity, her gaze landed on a large, flattish boulder that seemed almost too perfect a find. Perhaps the universe was conspiring with her.

"Come sit with me for a minute," she said to Kiernan, before nodding toward the boulder.

Before he could reply, Claire took a seat, leaving plenty of room for Kiernan to join her. He slowly sat down beside her, leaving only the hint of a gap between them. She could feel the warmth of his body and smell his spicy aftershave. Not exactly helpful as she tried to concentrate on the point she needed to make.

"Thanks," she said. "I needed a break."

"No, you didn't," Kiernan said, squinting as he sized her up with the sun in his eyes. "In fact, I'm beginning to think you might be a secret marathoner. I'm feeling slightly winded climbing this hill, and your respiratory rate is on a par with a sloth's."

"You know, I could take offense at that." Claire laughed nonetheless.

Kiernan grinned. "Don't. I meant it in the best possible way."

A cloud must have covered part of the sun, because suddenly his face was partially shaded. No longer squinting, his eyes now displayed the hint of a twinkle.

"So, you were saying that I could break the cycle. Meaning, I suppose, that I can be the first surgeon in my family to not be a selfish jerk."

Claire was taken aback by his blunt assessment, both figuratively and literally. She pulled her torso forward so that she was once again sitting fully upright. "That's not what I meant at all."

"And, for the record, it's only selfish if a man chooses to have a family knowing that he can't give them what they deserve."

Claire widened her eyes at Kiernan's attempted clarification. He was digging his heels in, that was for sure.

"All I meant was, just because both your father and grandfather took the same approach to career versus family, you might think you can't possibly do things differently. But you can."

Kiernan studied Claire closely, his eyes burning into hers. "The old nature versus nurture argument. Is it something genetic that made them both brilliant surgeons but lousy husbands and fathers? Or did my father learn it from his dad, who learned it from who knows who?" He momentarily looked up at the sky in thought. "Come to think of it, my great-great-grandfather was a doctor, too, although I can't vouch for his parenting skills—or lack thereof."

"I just don't want to see you sell yourself short, that's all. Or go through life settling for less than you can have."

Kiernan nodded, and was silent for several moments. Then, "So you always knew you wanted a family, despite what I would imagine is a fairly grueling career as an ob-gyn at a major hospital like Boston General?"

Claire inwardly winced.

Breathe. You prodded him to get this opening. Now make the most of it.

"Yes and no. As in yes, I knew I wanted a family, but no, I wasn't certain I could be fully engaged in my career and also be there for a child in the way that I'd want to be."

As Kiernan pursed his lips together, Claire could almost see the wheels turning in his mind.

"So what made you decide that you could, in fact, do both?"

"When you work with mothers and babies, you see a lot of miracles. And to be a part of making those miracles happen is just the best feeling in the world. But there were times when I'd watch one of these happy endings play out in front of my eyes and it would suddenly dawn on me... Was it right to deny myself that same kind of happiness in order to help bring it to others? You can't go into medicine at a high level, like we have, and not sacrifice something for your career. But was it too great a sacrifice? That's the question I kept asking myself. And ultimately I decided that it was."

"Did you start to approach your career differently once you'd made that decision?"

"I suppose I did—but not in any way that would negatively impact my patients." A slight smile formed on Claire's lips. "Basically, I learned to say no."

Kiernan raised a curious eyebrow. "Oh?"

"No, I'm not going to be regularly putting in twelve-plus-hour days. No, I'm not going to be answering emails at midnight. No, I'm not going to spend *all* my free time at medical conferences or adding more credentials after my name—unless it's something I specifically need to better treat my patients."

She paused for a moment of self-reflection.

"Maybe I couldn't have taken that stance as a resident. But once I paid my dues, I had to rethink my boundaries. And, truth be told, I'm a better doctor for it."

Kiernan half smiled. "Happy doctor, happy patient?"

Claire grinned. "Exactly."

Kiernan looked out onto the rocky yet still lush landscape, his eyes seemingly fixated on a distant object. Was he weighing her take on balancing career and family? She hoped he was at least considering that there were other possibilities besides the one he was so rigidly holding on to.

"I'm glad you shared this," he said quietly. "And I know you'll have another child when the time is right. You have so much love to give."

"Be sure to mention that to the future father—whoever he may be. I want to make sure I don't unknowingly blow him off before things have a chance to get off the ground."

Claire briefly smirked at her own comment, but it was clear that Kiernan didn't share her amusement. His forehead was creased, his eyes pained. Perhaps he knew her seeming irreverence was an attempt to mask her discomfort.

"That was a stupid thing to say," she said quietly. She waited for his reply, but none was forthcoming. "Well, should we get back on the trail?" she asked, after more silence ensued.

"There's no trail where we're headed, remember?" Kiernan replied with a slight chuckle.

But he had to know that she was deliberately diverting the conversation, and Claire was glad that he knowingly went along with it. As he turned to check his backpack, his shoulder brushed against hers. It felt as strong and as solid as Claire had imagined it would—courtesy, no doubt, of rough-and-tumble rugby rather than the lifting of a scalpel.

"Come on," Kiernan said as he rose from the boulder. "Let's cover some more ground and then we can break for lunch. I have the perfect spot in mind."

No more proselytizing, Claire silently instructed herself.

Today was supposed to be a carefree, take-your-temporary-colleague-on-a-tour day. Couldn't she just go with the flow and enjoy herself?

As she clasped Kiernan's outstretched hand and hopped off the boulder, she had her answer. His grip, firm yet gentle—oxymoron though that might be—was enough to send a jolt through the length of her body. She couldn't be sure what the future held. Not for Kiernan, nor for herself. But she unequivocally knew that in this moment there was no one she would rather be with than the man standing before her now.

You can break the cycle.

Kiernan played the words over again and again in his head, grateful that in a world where it seemed every thought and action were documented in some form of social media, his brain was still a safe haven for every idea and emotion that passed through.

Was he in fact merely repeating what he *assumed* to be true? That dedicated surgeons couldn't successfully split their focus between their career and a family?

Looking back, he couldn't recall a time when he had ever felt differently. And the pushback that had inevitably cropped up in past romantic relationships, the "but of course you can do both" refrains? They had gone in one ear and out the other, accompanied in short order with his own refrain:

I don't think this relationship is going to work.

Done. End of story.

Of course he was exaggerating to himself to think that he had been able to cut all ties so easily. He was human, after all, and he did have a heart—though he sometimes kept that fact well hidden. But what *was* entirely accurate was that no one had ever made him truly question his beliefs. That was until now.

He turned to look at Claire as they forged ahead. With her eyes intently focused on the uneven grassy terrain beneath their feet, she was oblivious to his stare. Which was good. The last thing he wanted to do was unnerve her with his secret rapt attention.

In the late midday sun, Claire's chestnut hair took on redder tones, and her fair complexion was virtually translucent. She possessed a physical beauty that, quite literally, took his breath away. But it was so much more than that. To know everything she had been through, and see her willingness to potentially invite more personal pain through selflessly taking on Jan's surgery...now *that* was a thing of beauty.

"Is something wrong?" Claire asked, startling Kiernan and dismantling his thoughts.

"No—why do you ask?"

She smiled a bit nervously. "You're looking at me like I have two heads."

Kiernan squashed a wide-eyed grimace before it could fully

take hold. "Sorry about that. I was…um…just thinking about something and I guess I was staring without realizing it."

Lame, lame, lame, he silently scolded himself.

"I do the same thing," she said casually, prompting an equally silent *phew.*

"The spot I had in mind for a lunch break is just over that next hill," he said, eager to change the subject.

"Sounds good."

"Your shillelagh holding up okay?"

Claire smiled. "It sure is. In fact, I don't think I'll ever hike again without one."

"Awesome. And, by the way, if you look down near the bottom, you'll see a little something that I carved into the wood for you."

Claire halted and lifted up the bottom of the stick. She twisted it clockwise until the small carved lettering came into view. "'To Claire,'" she read aloud. "'One step at a time. Kiernan.'" She turned to him, momentarily speechless. "Thank you," she said finally, her voice both soft and sincere. "Words to live by, for sure."

Kiernan pursed his lips together and nodded. "You're very welcome."

He had added the message earlier in the morning, before picking up Claire, an idea that had only partially been on a whim. The desire to leave something with Claire that she could always remember him by had been percolating in his mind for several days. That it would be a message on a walking stick had been a last-minute choice, but it had felt so right when it came to him that he hadn't second-guessed the decision.

"Whew!" Claire declared fifteen minutes later, when they had nearly finished descending the final hill before lunch. She removed her windbreaker and tied it around her waist. "The sun is really starting to throw some heat."

"I know," Kiernan agreed. "It feels good."

He scanned the area once they were back on level ground, looking for familiar landmarks. It didn't take long to spot them. A heavy concentration of large boulders lining another hill about one hundred meters ahead and to the left, thick brush to the right, and a narrow grassy passageway in between.

He pointed to a stone ledge at the start of the rocky hill. "We can lunch there."

It was a short climb to the naturally formed perch, and he wasted no time sliding the backpack off his shoulders.

"Heavy?" Claire asked.

"Heavy enough," he replied with a rueful smile, stretching his neck to both sides to work out some of the kinks.

"Let me guess… Deep-dish, three-cheese lasagna?" Claire quipped as he unzipped the backpack.

Kiernan chuckled. "Even better. I decided to ditch my usual lunch of greasy sausage and chips for something healthier."

Claire grimaced. "Sausage and chips? Seriously? That's probably what brought your carotid endarterectomy patient into the OR today."

"Be quiet, you."

Claire smirked. "Just saying. And by the way—how did the surgery go?"

"It was fairly routine and by the book. He'll be back home tomorrow, and hopefully he will start following some of the healthy eating guidelines that one of our dieticians will be going over with him."

"You mean the ones you don't follow yourself?"

Kiernan feigned insult—not easy to do, given that he was actually quite amused. "I don't think I've seen this feisty side to you before."

"That's what happens when I'm hungry. I get a little obnoxious."

"Remind me to carry snacks around at all times," Kiernan quipped as he extracted two brown bags out of the backpack.

"One for me and one for you. Chickpea spread sandwiches with baked—not fried—crisps. And don't blame me if the sandwich tastes like…"

"Chickpeas?" Claire offered teasingly.

"I was going to say chalk."

"I love chickpeas. Good choice. And definitely a step above cucumbers."

Kiernan chuckled as he handed her a bottle of seltzer water and then leaned back, with a boulder behind him doubling as a backrest. He scanned the thicket across the way, looking for any sign that a certain four-legged dweller was still in the area. Suddenly, a swatch of white flashed within the twisted tangles of brown vegetation.

Kiernan gently grabbed Claire's forearm and pointed with his other hand. "There. Do you see her?"

Claire strained to view the area, then gasped. "Yes…yes, I see her! She's beautiful!" She turned to Kiernan, eyes wide with wonder. "I didn't realize there were white foxes in Ireland."

"There aren't. Well, not as a species. She's albino. I first spotted her two springs ago and I thought the same thing, too. White foxes in Ireland? But I did a little research and, though it's extremely rare, there is such a thing as an albino red fox."

As Claire leaned in slightly and squinted, Kiernan quietly pulled a pair of binoculars from the backpack. "I brought them just in case."

Claire peered into them for several moments. "I see two babies with her. Not white."

She handed the binoculars to Kiernan, and he confirmed her observation.

"She has a burrow somewhere in the thicket. To be honest, when I first spotted her two years ago, I never thought I'd see her the following year."

"You mean because she can't blend into her surroundings?"

"Exactly. She's even more vulnerable to predators than a normal fox. But since that first time I've had five sightings in total, the last one being in November."

"Her ears just pricked up," Claire said as she peered through the binoculars. "Oh—she's looking right at me."

"I'd say she can smell the chickpea sandwich, but I'm sure she'd prefer chips and sausages."

Claire smiled at the comment. "She's turning around now. There she goes—back with her babies into the brush."

"Her den's in there and she's being a protective mum."

Claire nodded and rested the binoculars beside her. "Not a bad thing."

"Nope. Safety first."

Claire looked earnestly into his eyes, and this time he held her gaze. "Thank you for bringing me here. You're right—it's a hidden gem."

"I'm glad you think so."

Claire wasn't looking away, and neither was he. His eyes fell to her pillowy lips…those same luscious lips he had come so close to kissing under a moonlit sky as ocean breezes danced around them. He had thought *that* had been the perfect, albeit missed, moment. But being this close to Claire…seeing the desire in her eyes that matched his own…feeling a connection to her that was deeper than he had ever felt for a woman…*this* was the perfect moment. And he was going to make it last.

Every. Spine-tingling. Second.

As he slowly moved in closer, she met him halfway. Their lips touched, and he felt as though he had been waiting for this kiss his whole life. Perhaps he had. Which was why he had no intention of rushing through it. He savored every exquisite sensation: the sweet softness of her lips, the silky luster of her hair as he ran his fingers through it, the warmth of her breath on his cheek as they slowly pulled back, only to reengage…

It was deeper and longer and more satiating than he had

imagined their kiss could be. And he had been imagining it from almost the first time he had laid eyes on Claire.

Moments—no, make that minutes...*many* minutes later, they reluctantly parted lips and leaned back on the rock.

"Wow," Claire said, looking slightly dazed but altogether pleased.

"I second that," Kiernan said.

And third and fourth...

"Are you sure you weren't just trying to get me to work up an appetite for that chickpea sandwich?"

Kiernan chuckled. "Am I that transparent?"

Claire leaned over and grabbed one of the sandwiches, then delicately took a bite as Kiernan watched.

"Well?" he asked.

She shrugged her shoulders. "Eh...maybe I'm just not hungry right now."

An impish grin gave away her ruse, and he placed a hand just above her knee as he pulled himself closer again. "Then you give me no choice but to work more on that appetite."

"If you insist."

As he caressed her back and pulled her close, Kiernan replied, "I most certainly do."

It was still light outside but heading toward dusk as Kiernan pulled up to Claire's cottage. She turned to him while remaining seated. "Thanks. I had a great time. Make that a *really* great time."

"Me, too."

"And I love the shillelagh. I might need to book its own seat on the flight home, but it's well worth it."

Though Kiernan grinned at her joke, this reminder of the transient nature of her stay was anything but amusing.

Seeing her hand on the door handle, he quickly changed the subject. "Despite my insistence that I could take time off during the week, it's not looking like I can break away from the hospital for another outing before the weekend. One of my general surgeons broke his ankle stepping in a rabbit hole."

"Don't tell me—he was playing golf?"

Kiernan rolled his eyes. "He was. And now I have to fill in for some of his surgeries. But I'm free this Saturday, if you're up for another adventure. No chickpea sandwiches, I promise."

"Sounds like a plan." She stepped out of the SUV and turned back. "Call or text me about when you plan to come by, and I'll see you then."

"Wait—I think you're forgetting something."

Her quizzical expression quickly eased into a smile. Leaning back into the car, she readily kissed him before finally pulling away to exit the vehicle once more.

As Kiernan watched her walk to the cottage he briefly closed his eyes. He had never been one to jump on the *life can be so unfair* bandwagon, but it sure as heck felt like the universe was conspiring against him. How else to explain that he had met a woman who took his breath away on every level, but soon she'd be out of his life for good?

He opened his eyes just in time to see Claire wave to him before disappearing into the cottage. With a deep sigh, he put the SUV in "drive." It was equipped with a GPS that had never led him astray. If only he had the equivalent of such a device for his heart. Because that earlier directive of "just enjoy the moment while she's here?" It no longer felt like a viable destination.

CHAPTER ELEVEN

CLAIRE STARED OUT the cottage window as she leaned over the back of the couch, her phone plastered against her ear. Only two rings into the call, her sister promptly answered.

"Claire—it's so good to hear from you! How's it going over there? Meet any hunky Irishmen?"

Claire managed to crack a smile as she shook her head. "No comment."

Her sister was quick to reply. "Whoa—that means yes!"

Claire turned back from the window, her thoughts very much on a particular hunky Irishman. If there were others in existence she didn't know, and quite frankly didn't care.

"Well?" Grace asked, disrupting Claire's *very* enjoyable thoughts.

Grace was not only her sister, but also her best friend. At home, they talked on the phone, often with video, at least four or five times a week. But before coming to Ireland, Claire had made a pledge to herself that she would limit her calls with Grace to no more than a few in total. She had come here to break free of the past and to contemplate her future—and doing so meant uncoupling from reminders of home. Even those reminders that she cared about. Their only previous call had been on the day she'd landed, to say that she had arrived safely. Which meant there was a whole lot of ground to cover.

Taking a deep breath, Claire fully dove in and filled Grace

in on Margaret and Kiernan, and Jan and Kiernan…and Kiernan and Kiernan and Kiernan.

"Oh, my gosh," Grace said breathlessly. "Here I was joking around, but you really *did* meet a hunky Irishman. And another doctor, no less."

"Surgeon," Claire corrected.

"There's a difference?"

Claire smiled ruefully. "According to most surgeons, yes."

"I have so many questions that I don't even know where to begin. Let me start with the obvious one."

"Okay, I'll bite. What's the obvious question?"

"Is he a good kisser?"

Claire laughed while simultaneously feeling her cheeks grow hot. "No."

"Really?"

"He's better than good. But that's all I'm going to tell you."

"Oh, come on, now! I've been married for about a gazillion years—I need some vicarious thrills."

Claire snickered softly, but she was too caught up in her thoughts to answer. Grace's question had sent her right back to that moment when Kiernan had looked deeply into her eyes, pulled her close, and kissed her in a way that had made every previous kiss in her life a pale second at best. Or was it more like a pale tenth? Um…a pale *hundredth*?

"Claire?"

"Huh?"

"I asked you if you thought it was possible that things with Kiernan could develop into something more?"

Claire's smile quickly evaporated. Harsh reality had a way of making smiles doing that. "I don't see how, given that we live in different countries. And I told you he doesn't want to have kids."

"Yeah, that's a deal-breaker, for sure. Although maybe you could change his mind."

"Grace, you know what four words have led to the most disappointment in relationships since the beginning of time? *I can change him.* Or, for that matter, *I can change her.*"

Grace sighed. "I know… I know. It's just that when you talk about him I can hear in your voice how happy you are. And I don't think I've heard that in a very long time."

Claire stared at the floor as she contemplated her sister's observation. It was true that Kiernan had a way of making her feel more alive, and it was a feeling that grew every time she was with him. But that didn't mean they could possibly have a future together. Not when the insurmountable obstacles of living in two different countries, with opposing views on having children, were stacked against them.

"Well, I'm actually on my way to see the man of the hour."

"Kiernan?"

Claire tempered a roll of her eyes with a grin. "No, a leprechaun."

"Ha-ha. Well, good for you. And Claire…?"

After a few moments of silence, Claire spoke. "Were you going to ask me something?"

"I was just wondering if you've made any headway on your decision about your career."

Claire sighed. "Headway, yes. But any definitive game plan of what to do next…not exactly. I came here expecting some quiet time alone to contemplate things. But it's been a crazy whirlwind from the start."

"What about the breech delivery and the fetal surgery, though? You must have felt good about helping those mothers and their babies."

"Of course! I don't think that part of the job ever changes. But it's not always a happy ending like that." She paused. "Maybe I just need to start fresh somewhere else."

"You mean leave Boston General? You love that hospital!"

"I know. I have great colleagues, and I've made some really

good friends over the years. But it's hard to separate that from some of the bad feelings I get when I think about the hospital. There are just so many memories there."

Claire knew she didn't have to point out to her sister exactly what she meant. After graduating medical school, both she and Mark had completed their residency at Boston General, with Mark then moving on to private practice. But it still held three years of memories of one of the most exciting times of her life as she'd fully realized her dream of becoming an ob-gyn.

And then, four years later…in Room 471 on the fourth floor in the obstetrics wing…she'd said goodbye to Ariana.

"Well, if you do decide to move on from Boston General, you'll have no problem landing somewhere else, that's for sure," said Grace. "In fact, they'll be lining up to sign you on."

Claire pulled her lips into a tight smile. "Thanks, Sis. But I'm a long way from making such a big decision. One step at a time, I guess."

Her own words momentarily startled her. Whether consciously or not, she had just repeated the message on her walking stick. As if on cue, she heard Kiernan's SUV roll to a stop outside the cottage.

After promising Grace they'd talk again soon, Claire closed the cottage door behind her, then turned to greet Kiernan as he stood by the passenger door. But instead of saying hi, the only word that came out of her mouth was a loud gasp. It was quickly followed by a blink of her eyes—just to make sure they weren't playing tricks on her.

"That is *not* a kilt you're wearing."

Had he read her mind the other night at his place?

Kiernan peered down at the green and black plaid tartan skirt, then back up at Claire. "Huh. I could have sworn I put trousers on this morning."

Claire's laughter bordered on a giggle.

"Do you like it?" Kiernan asked as he jokingly twirled

around, his rugged body the equivalent of a bull pirouetting in a china shop.

It was a spectacle that promoted even more laughter from Claire.

"I do," she conceded, though she couldn't be sure if she was complimenting the kilt or the black-socked muscular calves that were fully on display. "So, is there a reason for this catchy ensemble?"

"As a matter of fact, there is." He opened the passenger door. "Step inside, lass, and you'll find out soon enough."

Twenty minutes later, the SUV turned off the main road, slowly passed through an open wrought-iron gate, then continued up a narrow paved path. At the top of a hill, a one-tower castle loomed over the lavish landscape.

Claire strained her neck to get a better view from the passenger seat. "What castle is this?"

"Rockminster Castle. Built in 1547 by my great-great-great-great-grandfather on my mother's side. Wait—did I say five greats, or four?"

"I wasn't counting, but I think four."

"Should be five." He turned to Claire, a half-smile on his face. "It was a long time ago."

"Your family has a *castle*? Any other secrets I should know about?"

Kiernan chuckled. "Don't get too excited. It's a small castle. Kind of the equivalent of a studio apartment in the sixteenth century."

"It looks way bigger than a studio apartment," Claire observed as they drew closer to the structure. "Is it open to the public?"

"Not in any official capacity. My uncle, who lives in town, takes care of the upkeep. He'll rent it out for the occasional photo shoot or tea party on the grounds. That sort of thing… There's some interesting history in the walls of this castle, too."

As they exited the SUV, Claire scanned the postcard-worthy grounds with awe. "So, let's hear about some of that interesting history. Ours doesn't go back nearly as far in America."

Kiernan extracted a key from his pocket and unlocked the deadbolt on the large wooden door at the castle entrance. The air was chilled and musty as they made their way inside.

"Better yet, I'll take you right to the scene where it all happened."

As Claire followed Kiernan, she couldn't imagine a sexier history guide. At the top of a short flight of stairs they entered a small room with a wooden bed against one wall, and a dresser with a wash pan on the other side. A single window with metal bars looked out onto the front grounds. It was hard not to feel claustrophobic in such cramped surroundings, although Claire wondered if more was at play.

Kiernan, on the other hand, seemed unfazed as he began to fill her in on some of the castle's secrets. "Legend has it that at the turn of the seventeenth century, during the Nine Years War with England, the daughter of one of my ancestors fell in love with a British soldier."

"Uh-oh…"

Kiernan grimaced. "Exactly. When her father found out, he had her locked up in this very room, fully intending to keep her here until the war ended and the soldier departed. Or died in battle, I suppose—whichever came first."

Whether real or imaginary, Claire felt a sudden breeze rustle past her, and she wrapped her arms close to her chest in a protective stance.

"Am I scaring you?" Kiernan asked, stepping closer until there was little space between them. "I don't mean to."

"More like I'm scaring myself." She forced a brave smile, but the goosebumps on her arms remained. "So what happened?"

"Well, the daughter—her name was Bronagh—didn't take

too well to being locked away. One night, when a castle guard was shoving a plate of food under the door, she asked if she could open the door to speak to him. Of course he said no, but she must have said something to charm him into complying, because he did open the door."

Wide-eyed, Claire blurted out, "And…?"

"She pushed past the guard and ran upstairs onto the watch-tower, where she jumped to her death."

Claire flinched, her breath momentarily caught in her throat. "I think I now have goosebumps on top of my goosebumps."

"You might be feeling the presence of her ghost."

Claire bared her teeth. "Okay, now you're just messing with me."

Kiernan chuckled. "No, it's the truth. Over the years there's been a number of sightings of a young woman in a white frock, gazing out of this window." He pointed just behind Claire. "She stares back…then evaporates into thin air."

"Have you ever seen her?"

"No, but my mum saw her when she was a kid. It scared her so much she's rarely been back here. And my uncle has, on at least half a dozen occasions—including up on the tower where she jumped from. It's up the stairs outside this room. One of the previous groundskeepers saw her there, too."

"Can we go up the tower?" Claire asked, hoping Kiernan would reply quickly, before she lost her nerve.

Kiernan raised an eyebrow. "Are you sure you want to?"

"Are you calling me a scaredy cat?"

Kiernan grinned. "Nope, not me." He nodded to the door.

With Kiernan just behind her, Claire made her way up the narrow stone stairs, which coiled upwards in a clockwise fash-ion like a tightly wound snake.

"I can see why they didn't need elliptical machines back then," Claire said as she felt the lactic acid building up in her leg muscles with each additional step. "They got a workout just from getting from point A to point B in the castle."

"True," Kiernan replied, though Claire was quite certain *his* legs were finding the laborious climb a breeze.

Finally, a ray of sun broke through the darkness and illuminated the stairs just above her. "I think we're almost there."

A few more steps, and they were at the top of the watchtower. Unlike the small, bar-covered window in the previous room, the tower's windows were much larger and free of any hindrance. It made sense, though morbidly so, that Bronagh had chosen this spot to cast herself to the ground.

Kiernan walked up beside Claire, and together they looked out onto the sun-drenched grounds. "It almost looks too idyllic, considering what happened here," she said quietly.

"I know. Although I've been here on overcast days and you really do feel a different energy." Still staring straight ahead, he said, "And by the way…the name Bronagh means sorrow."

"Wow," Claire said softly. "It's like the plot for a tragic romance—except it really happened. I wonder why she felt she had to go to that extreme. The war wasn't going to last forever, so she had to know that someday she'd be free again."

"I don't know…" Kiernan's gaze remained fixed on the horizon. "I guess people do crazy things for love."

He slowly turned to Claire, his dark eyes melting into her own. She felt her breath catch first, and then her heart.

Stepping in closer, he brushed his fingers along her cheek, then pulled her in until their bodies touched. Without hesitation, he caressed her lips with his own, and time seemed to stand still as the kiss grew deeper and more passionate.

Claire no longer needed to fantasize about the rugby-primed chest beneath his shirt. She could feel each taut muscle as it pushed against her breasts, and the friction of their clothing sent waves of pleasure throughout her body. His lingering kisses along the length of her neck made her weak in the knees, and as Kiernan swept her off her feet and up into his powerful arms all she could do…all she *wanted* to do…was fully melt into the moment.

She closed her eyes and tipped back her head, but as Kiernan determinedly strode back to the staircase, like a man on a mission, she reluctantly popped one eye back open.

"Kiernan," she said breathlessly. "You can't carry me down these crazy stairs."

He playfully brushed his lips against her bottom lip. "Aye, I can. Leave it to me, lass."

Claire wasn't sure whether to laugh at his comment, brace herself for a fall, or kiss him passionately for good luck. So she did all three.

With his body of a bull that had somehow merged with the gracefulness of a gazelle, Kiernan descended the twisting staircase in record time. Entering the small room from where they had started their climb, he gently placed Claire on the bed, but there was a fire in his eyes that she knew was about to engulf them both.

Clothing came off…slowly at first, then at a feverish pitch. And as the timeworn wooden bed creaked Claire wondered if it might snap in half.

Go ahead. Break.

It was easy not to have a care in the world when every nerve-ending quivered with desire…

Kiernan was every bit the incredible lover she had imagined he'd be. And, yes, she had been imagining it a *lot* leading up to this moment. He was attentive, generous, and fully attuned to her on a level that seemed to go far beyond the physical. Every kiss, every whisper, every touch seemed solely designed to bring her pleasure, and she fully responded in kind.

As their lovemaking climaxed into a glorious release she felt something deep inside her shift, as though her healing had reached another apex. Lying quietly together, still wrapped in each other's arms, she could only conclude one thing: the power of love was real.

Later, as they walked in the flower-filled castle grounds, Kiernan reached over and took Claire's hand, their fingers effortlessly interlocking.

"How's Jan doing?" she asked suddenly.

The question caught Kiernan by surprise. Was she trying to deflect the conversation away from the two of them, knowing that the closeness and passion they'd just shared had opened an exhilarating door that would soon be slammed shut? It was a sobering realization that hovered in the back of his own mind, so he couldn't blame her for possibly feeling the same.

"She's doing great," he replied. "In fact, she'll be discharged from the hospital on Tuesday. Her C-section has been scheduled, so it's just a matter of her taking it easy at home for the remainder of the pregnancy."

"Do you think I could see her before she leaves?"

Given Claire's previous reluctance to see Jan again, the question shocked Kiernan—but in the best possible way. Still, knowing that literally jumping for joy in his kilt might not only make her change her mind, but also possibly put the family jewels on full display—*ahem*—he tamped down his outward enthusiasm.

"Of course. Do you want to come by on Monday? Say late morning or early afternoon? That way, I'll be able to pop in for the visit as well." He paused. "Unless you'd rather I didn't?"

Claire grinned. "Of course I want you to be there. And Dr. Fleming, too, if she's available. We were all in this together, and it would be nice to have a little reunion post-surgery."

Hoo, boy! This was progress!

Kiernan discreetly took a deep breath, but there was no hiding his ear-to-ear smile. Not only was he basking in the glow of the intimacy they had just shared, but Claire was taking another step in a career-reengaging direction, and he simply couldn't be happier.

Except....

Kiernan clenched his jaw tight as the other half of this equation revealed itself. Resuming her career meant her returning to Boston General. Which certainly was not a new revelation. But now...no, *especially* now, the thought of Claire leaving Ireland stung. And it stung hard.

Be happy for her, he told himself.

And he was. But that didn't mean he wouldn't miss her for the rest of his life.

Claire and Dr. Fleming were standing by Jan's bedside late on Monday morning when Kiernan entered the room. "I'm sorry I'm late. My last surgery went over a bit," he said hurriedly, his rapid breath screeching to a halt as Claire looked up at him, her green eyes sparkling in the brightly lit room.

"No worries," Dr. Fleming replied. "We've just been chatting with Jan about some of the best online stores for baby girls' clothing. My personal favorite is Tiny Frills. And Claire likes the handmade clothes on Etsy."

Uh-oh. Kiernan felt the muscles in his jaw and neck clench. Of course Dr. Fleming could have no idea how much discomfort this discussion would trigger in Claire. Still, though there was a tightness evident in her smile, Claire seemed to be taking it all in stride.

"Jan is being discharged at ten a.m. tomorrow," Dr. Fleming said. "Then it's home to be with her family until her scheduled C-section at thirty-seven weeks."

"Don't forget I have to take bedrest," Jan said, with an understandable lack of enthusiasm in her voice.

"I know it can seem daunting," Claire replied empathetically. "But I have a feeling the time will fly by."

"And then, before you know it," Dr. Fleming added, "you'll be holding Rhianna in your arms."

Seeing Claire's smile waver for a fleeting second, Kiernan quickly jumped in. "So, have you thought about what your first home-cooked meal will be?"

Claire met his eyes, as if silently thanking him for his not so thinly veiled attempt to change the subject.

"That depends on who's doing the cooking," Jan replied wryly. "I assume it won't be me, so that leaves either Dave or my mum, who's going to be staying with us until Rhianna arrives. Let's just say I know who I *hope* will be playing chef. Don't get me wrong—my husband's good at sharing the chores at home. But he can't properly boil an egg, never mind make an edible meal."

Laughter sounded through the room, and after another ten minutes of easy banter between Jan and the doctors the conversation came to a natural standstill. Finally, Claire filled in the silence.

"Well, Jan, I want to wish you the best with everything. I can now leave Ireland knowing you're in good hands here, with Dr. Fleming and her team."

"Thank you for everything," Jan said earnestly. "And I'd love to send you a picture of Rhianna when she's born."

"That would be wonderful."

Ten minutes later, the visit wound down, and Kiernan and Claire exited the room.

"I'm glad I came by," Claire said, in buoyant spirits at least as far as Kiernan could discern.

"I'm glad you did, too. It was good to get that closure with Jan." He slowed to a halt in the corridor, with Claire following suit. "So, have you thought about how you'll spend your last days here?"

He'd dreaded asking the question, but posed it in the hopes that she might say she had extended her leave.

"I'm not sure. Maybe I'll take a drive up the coast…stay in a bed-and-breakfast for a night."

As a sharp pang of disappointment gripped him, he pivoted to the thought of asking if there might be room for two. But before he could get the words out a door several feet away flew open and a young, cherub-faced nurse with reddened eyes nearly stumbled out of the room.

Kiernan froze in his steps. "What's wrong?" he asked urgently.

The nurse glanced at his nametag, her cheeks now reddening as much as her eyes. "I'm sorry, sir," she said, her voice cracking with emotion.

An older nurse exited the room and gently closed the door behind her.

"Is everything okay, Carol?" Kiernan asked.

She nodded, then placed a comforting hand on the younger nurse's shoulder. "This is Amy's first week…she's fresh out of nursing school," she explained. Turning to her younger colleague, she added, "It never gets easy, seeing something like this, but with time you'll be able to keep your emotions in check."

"What happened?" Claire asked, a hint of dread in her voice.

"A stillborn girl at thirty-four weeks. Dr. O'Conner induced labor nearly forty minutes ago, and both parents have been cradling her ever since. It's quite an emotional scene, as you can imagine." She looked back at the closed door, her forehead creased. "I've told them to take all the time they need. Everyone's different. Sometimes, the parents can't bear to do more than kiss their baby goodbye. Others find it hard to let go."

Kiernan turned to Claire, a sense of disbelief seeping into him that such a positive visit with Jan could be instantly counteracted in the worst possible way.

Instead of meeting his eyes, she stared at the door, and all he could do was hold his breath.

* * *

Claire looked at the small square window on the door. Everything told her to remain where she was, that nothing good would come out of peering inside the room. And that was on top of the fact that doing so would be a tremendous invasion of privacy for the grieving parents. But the compulsion building inside her had a mind of its own.

Turning back to Kiernan, she saw the deep concern etched on his face. She smiled and nodded to him as a signal that she was okay, then waited for him to be reluctantly pulled into a conversation with Carol. With his head now turned away from her, Claire discreetly stepped toward the door.

Her glance inside the window could not have lasted more than five seconds. But it was still long enough to imprint the scene on her mind. A couple, presumably husband and wife, clutching each other and sobbing together.

Stepping away from the window, Claire saw Kiernan do a double-take as he glanced back over at her. Had he read the distress on her face? It would have been hard not to at this point. Though she couldn't hear the exact conversation between Kiernan and the two nurses, it was clear from both the inflection of his voice and his fidgety stance that he was trying to wrap things up as quickly as possible.

As the nurses departed, Kiernan was immediately at Claire's side. "Are you okay?"

"Yes. It's just that…" She paused, shaking her head. "I shouldn't have looked in the room."

"I'm sure it brought back painful memories," Kiernan said quietly.

"The husband was holding his wife, and they were both crying. When I lost Ariana, Mark was nowhere to be found. I remember holding her for what seemed like forever, not wanting the doctor to come take her away. And Mark didn't even care."

Kiernan's eyes narrowed, like daggers aimed at an invisible Mark. "Did he know you were in the hospital?"

"I didn't contact him, but one of the nurses did. She really had no right to do that, but she was friends with him. She told me later that he acted all annoyed when she told him that Ariana was about to be stillborn and they were inducing labor. 'Like he couldn't be bothered' was the way she described it to me. She vowed never to talk to him again after that."

Kiernan clenched his jaw. "I'm so sorry you went through this alone. That never should have happened."

Alone. She hadn't really thought much before about how deeply Mark's complete disregard for the loss of their child had affected her, but now she couldn't unsee the connection. Watching that couple grieve together, simultaneously cradling each other and their tiny stillborn daughter—that was how it *should* be. If Mark had been the man she'd initially thought he was—if they'd had a strong marriage and if he had grieved the death of their baby as a loving husband and father should—then perhaps she would have been better equipped to move past the active stage of a trauma that had never fully resolved.

Kiernan wouldn't have left me alone.

That her thoughts had even gone there was almost shocking to Claire. But should it have been, knowing how he had so resolutely stayed by her side through several emotional upheavals?

"Are you okay?" Kiernan asked again, eyeing her intently.

It took several moments for her to nod. "I wasn't expecting this...especially after everything went so well with Jan's visit...but I'm okay. Really."

Less than a month ago she would never have been able to

say this. But that had been before Kiernan. Their time together, though counted only in weeks, had impacted her enough for a lifetime, and given her a renewed strength that she'd thought she had lost forever.

But Kiernan appeared less than convinced by her reply.

"Do you want to go to the café, and we can sit and talk for a bit?"

Claire hesitated as she weighed the offer. Though she had just successfully ridden out the surge of emotions prompted by peering into the stillbirth room, something was still niggling at her.

"I think I'm going to head back to the cottage for some duck therapy," she replied finally.

Kiernan smiled, though it didn't completely erase the concern in his eyes. "Can I see you tonight?"

She held his gaze, unable to answer. There was that niggling again, like a tapping against her brain that said, *Yoo-hoo, there's something we need to discuss.*

"I think I'm just going to lay low tonight. But I'll be in touch."

Kiernan pursed his lips together and nodded. He didn't say anything…nor did he have to. The disappointment in his eyes spoke loud and clear.

Later that night, as she stared up at the dark ceiling from her bed, Claire finally acknowledged what had been chipping away at her subconscious since earlier that day. From their initial chance meeting during a high-stakes baby delivery, and culminating in their better-than-she-could-have-imagined tryst in the castle, she had shared an emotional and physical connection with Kiernan unlike any she had ever known.

But today she'd had an unexpected gut-check. And what

had it taken for the bubble to finally burst? The fantasy to be replaced with reality? It had been seeing the couple at the hospital who had just lost their baby, and knowing that Kiernan would be the kind of husband and father who'd be there for her if she'd been that grieving mother...

Except for one little thing. He wanted nothing to do with either role. Which was his prerogative, right? Just as it was hers to decide to cut her losses before her heart was further crushed. And that meant telling him goodbye. Not on her last day here. Not at the airport. *Now.*

Claire abruptly turned on her side, as though she could dislodge her distressing thoughts, but they clung to her too tightly. She had known from the get-go that her time in Ireland was temporary and any attachment to Kiernan would be a mistake. But somewhere along the way she'd forgotten—or perhaps willfully ignored—her own warning. It was as if she had started to believe that *this* was her life now. Living in the beautiful Irish countryside, working side by side with Kiernan, her love for him growing every second of every day...

Yes... I said it. My love for him.

Never in a million years had she thought she'd fall so head-over-heels in love during her brief stint in Ireland.

But the heart wants what it wants. Even when it can't have what it wants.

Just shy of a week from now she would again be staring at a dark ceiling—but it would be in the bedroom of her condo just outside of Boston. Somehow, some way, she'd resume her previous life—though it now seemed inevitable that Boston General would not be part of that reunion.

It will all work out, she told herself.

More than once in the past those words had gotten her through the toughest of times. But not so much now. Maybe because the mantra implied that something good could come out of saying goodbye to Kiernan forever. And that, quite frankly, just didn't seem possible.

CHAPTER TWELVE

KIERNAN DUCKED AS a sledgehammer swung precariously close to his head. The fact that it came complete with human fingers and was attached to the gargantuan shoulder of a rugby teammate named Angus did little to alter Kiernan's perception that he was being swiped at with a block of iron on a stick.

"Hey, take it easy," he said as Angus swung out again, this time smacking him hard on the shoulder.

In his boisterous teammate's defense, he realized Angus probably thought he was just giving him a friendly post-game pat—not setting him up for future joint replacement surgery.

"Aye! I'm just a little pumped-up about our win."

Angus grabbed Kiernan in a bear hug, landing a couple of knuckle-knocks on the head for good measure. When he finally broke free, Kiernan laughed at his friend's shenanigans, then joined the rest of the rambunctious group as they tumbled into the main room of Gilroy's Pub.

Almost immediately, he spotted Claire sitting alone at a nearby table.

She waved discreetly, and he wasted no time in heading over.

"This is a pleasant surprise," he said as he pulled out a chair, smiling so deeply that he felt his cheeks would burst.

After their downcast parting of ways at the hospital yesterday, this unexpected reunion was a special treat. Actually, that could be said about *any* time he was in her presence. Which begged the question…was it possible he could find a way to stay in her presence more permanently?

I know… I know…she's leaving soon.

Knowing it wasn't the right time to grapple with such thoughts, Kiernan pushed them aside and focused on the beautiful face in front of him.

Claire smiled, but not with her usual verve. "I wasn't sure if you'd still be playing today, with all the rain we had earlier," she said.

"Are you kidding? Rain means mud, and I swear some of the guys—make that most—prefer a soggy field. It's easier to squash someone's face into the ground."

Claire snickered, but her amusement was short-lived. The smile evaporated and her eyes flashed with angst.

"Are you okay?" he asked gingerly.

"I came here hoping that we could talk."

Coupled with her troubled demeanor, the announcement left Kiernan reeling with dread.

"Yes, of course," he managed to say, as evenly as possible.

She scanned the loud and crowded pub. "It was raining pretty hard when I got here a half-hour ago. Is it still raining now?"

"No, just a light mist."

"Can we take a walk on the pier?"

"Sure."

As they walked along the pier several minutes later, Claire stopped abruptly and turned to him. "Kiernan, what I'm about to say is not easy for me. As you know, I came here seeking clarity about my career—something that I felt I was never going to find back home, where there are still so many reminders of painful things. But what I didn't expect to happen…"

She paused, visibly swallowing twice, as though pushing back emotions. "What I didn't expect was meeting someone I'd develop very strong feelings for."

Only the sound of waves lapping against the pier could be heard as she stared into his eyes. Kiernan wanted to stay silent as he waited for her to resume talking, but he couldn't.

"Claire, I wasn't expecting this either. But is it so bad that we *did* meet each other, and that we *do* have these feelings?"

"For me, yes."

Her reply was like a one-two gut-punch. "I see," was all that he could manage to say.

"I can't be the only one realizing that this can't go anywhere. We don't want the same things, Kiernan. I mean, many things, we do—but not the one thing that I can't compromise on."

"A child," he said quietly.

She nodded. "And I know that I'm getting too far ahead of myself here by even bringing this up. It's not like we're even in a relationship—right?"

Kiernan wasn't sure if this was a genuine or rhetorical question, but he was unable to answer either way.

"And you know what kills me about all of this, what I just can't wrap my head around, is how you insist that you're someone you're not."

What?

Kiernan's head was now officially spinning. He had told Claire why he wouldn't put a child in the position his father had put him in. He'd been honest with her about that.

"I'm not sure what you mean."

"Yesterday, when I looked into that room and saw the husband consoling his wife… Mark wasn't that kind of husband and father. But Kiernan, *you* are."

"But—"

"I know," Claire quickly interjected. "What the heck am I talking about, right? You're not a husband or a father, nor do you want to be. But that's what I can't understand. Because the Kiernan I know is kind and compassionate. He's someone who goes the extra mile for his patients, but he also cares about the people in his life. Think about how you cancelled a surgery to stay with me when you knew I was upset. Or how you wouldn't let me leave the hospital and comforted me when I had an anxiety attack after visiting the birthing suite."

Claire's words had nearly knocked Kiernan backwards, but she wasn't finished.

"You're not your father, Kiernan. Yet for some inexplicable reason, you seem convinced that you are. And you know what the saddest part of all this is?"

Kiernan wasn't sure, but he was pretty damn certain that Claire was about to tell him.

"The person you're hurting the most is yourself. Because I *know* you would be an amazing father and husband. And if you could only get past whatever it is that has you convinced otherwise, I know you'd find happiness in committing to more than just your career. And I mean a different kind of happiness—not the one you can find in your work, no matter how dedicated you are or how many lives you save."

It was only the sensation of raindrops on his bottom lip that made Kiernan realize his mouth was slightly agape. He swallowed to close it.

"I think I'm having one of those sorry-not-sorry moments," Claire said sheepishly, as though she, too, was shocked by her own words. "I wasn't actually planning to say all of that. It just kind of came out."

It took several moments for Kiernan to reply, "That's okay." He knew how insufficient those two words were at a moment like this, but was too paralyzed to say anything more.

As Claire reached over and clasped his hand he shuddered at her touch—and at the thought that he might never feel the warmth of her skin again.

"What I *did* come here to say is that I think it's best if we say goodbye now…before it gets even harder to do so. At least harder for me."

"Claire…"

She stared at him, clearly waiting for him to say more. But as the world around him seemingly came to a halt, he could only pose two questions in his mind. Could this be it? Was it the last time he would ever look into her eyes? He'd known this day was coming—but not here…not in this very moment.

Say something!

His directive fell on deaf ears—*his* deaf ears. No, that wasn't quite right. He heard himself, loud and clear, but what could he say? That she was right and he *was* missing out on the joy of having a partner in life and children? *Was* she right?

His breath choked in his throat. It was all too much to take in at this moment. Still, there was something he needed to know.

"Will you be going back to Boston General?"

Claire briefly looked down at the ground, but not before he saw disappointment in her eyes. Was she hoping that he'd tell her she was right, rather than ask about her career decision? He had only asked because he desperately wanted her to continue the work she was meant to do.

Claire looked back up at him. "I might not return to the hospital itself, given that I think a fresh start somewhere else will probably be better for me. But I also think I've come to realize over the last few weeks that making a difference in the lives of mothers and their babies is the work that I'm meant to do." She stared earnestly into Kiernan's eyes. "And I have you to thank for that."

"Claire—"

She squeezed his hand. "I'm not sure what the medical equivalent is of getting back in the saddle…"

A half-smile emerged on Kiernan's lips. "Getting back into the scrubs?"

She grinned. "Something like that. But without your encouragement and support I never would have been able to do it."

"You're an incredible doctor—all I did was open the door. You're the one who willingly walked through it, despite what I know had to be immense difficulty in doing so. I'm just so grateful and proud of you that you did."

With a surge of wind, the drizzle turned into steady rain that began to drum down upon them. Kiernan looked up at the sky, only to be immediately pelted in the eyes.

Claire looked up as well. "Where's an umbrella when you need one?"

Kiernan studied her closely through the raindrops that were pooling on his eyelashes. Even with her hair plastered against the sides of her face and rivulets of water running down her nose and cheeks, she was exquisitely beautiful, both inside and out.

"Come on," he said. "Let's go inside."

"Actually, I think I'll go back to my cottage."

Right, Kiernan thought, his stomach sinking. And it wasn't alone. His heart also plunged as reality set in. *This is the end of the road for us. And it's my doing.*

"Let me at least drive you back."

He hoped beyond hope that she'd take up his offer—if for no other reason than to avoid the rain. At least he would have another ten minutes in her presence.

"No—I'm fine. It's not a long walk. And, believe it or not, I sometimes like being out in the rain."

There it was again. The streak of stubbornness and independence that drove him crazy, but also garnered his admiration.

"Take care of yourself, Kiernan," Claire said, her voice subdued and yet almost echoing against the roar of the rain. "I'll never forget the time that we spent together."

One more long, lingering look his way, and then she turned and walked away from him along the pier. He was still watching intently as she turned left onto the perpendicular portion of the platform that led back to the shore, knowing she would then take the paved path beside the road that led to her cottage.

Soon she disappeared from view. And still, he stayed.

Another ten minutes passed—or was it more like fifteen? Kiernan couldn't be sure. He continued to stare off into the distance, only vaguely aware of the slightly swaying pier beneath his feet as the storm-provoked winds and waves kicked into overdrive.

Apparently he must like the rain, too, he thought. Because here he was, soaked to the bone and then some, and still he couldn't step away from the last spot where he had held Claire's hands and stared into her eyes.

Back at his home, later that night, Kiernan leaned up against the deck railing and stared outwards. He usually did his best thinking when it was just him and the endless expanse of ocean, but now its powers of insight seemed to be on hold. Never in a million years had he thought he'd be facing such a seemingly insurmountable impasse...

But *was* it insurmountable?

Since his early teens, he'd had his whole life mapped out before him. Perhaps it had been a way to assert control when everything else around him at the time had seemed to be about as stable and solid as quicksand. And there was no doubt that this steely resolve had served him well over the years. It had got him through medical school when his own father had cast doubts on his ability to succeed. And it had kept him rising up the ranks as a surgeon, culminating in a position that would allow him to have the greatest impact on patients in need of potentially life-saving care.

But at what cost?

Kiernan shook his head, dumbfounded by his own question. He had never dared ask himself this before—simply because it was a non-issue.

Meeting Claire had changed all of that.

Like a kaleidoscope of images, every moment spent with Claire played out in his mind. From performing a high-risk delivery together, as two strangers in the back of an ambulance, to their passionate encounter in the castle and everything in between... In less than a month she had managed to capture his heart in a way that no other woman ever had. And now he was losing her. Not only to her inevitable return to America, but to his rigid insistence that children were not part of his life plan.

You can break the cycle, you know.

Claire's earlier words echoed in his mind. Was it possible that he had been denying himself the joy and fulfillment of having a family of his own all because of his negative experiences as the son of a negligent father? It couldn't be that simple—a textbook case of unintentionally sabotaging his own ultimate happiness due to the misdeeds of his dad.

It just couldn't.

Or...could it?

"I am not my father," he said quietly into the wind.

It whistled back, as though reassuring him that his thoughts were the key to his salvation.

Nothing would make him happier than seeing Claire with the child that she so desperately wanted. A child that would help heal the wounds of her past loss. A child that she would love with the endless compassion that was so much a part of who she was.

There was only one problem. He couldn't imagine her sharing that joy with anyone but him.

The revelation frightened him—but not because it meant

upending a life plan that up until very recently had been set in immovable stone. No, the fear was that it was too late to reverse course. Claire was leaving the country on Saturday. That gave him three days to do…*something*. And it had to be big.

His mind whirled and whirled and whirled.

Yes…yes…uh-huh…right.

Another nod as a plan emerged out of thin air and began to take shape in his thoughts.

It was crazy. *He* was crazy.

The formerly logical, even-keeled, uber-grounded surgeon was about to go off the deep end, and he had zero regrets. His only regret would be if he waited another second and ended up being too late.

It was time to set his plan in motion.

CHAPTER THIRTEEN

CLAIRE TOSSED SOME cracked corn to the ducks as she walked along the shoreline behind her cottage. Earlier in the day she had started to pack for her inevitable flight home tomorrow, but hadn't got any further than throwing a pair of jeans and two tops into the suitcase.

She didn't have to look deep within herself to know that her heart wasn't fully on board with returning to Boston. Nor did she have to question why. Or, more precisely, the *who* behind the why.

Still, she didn't regret a single second that she had spent with Kiernan. *Not one.* In so many ways he had helped her heal from a loss that had previously seemed insurmountable. She would never, ever forget precious Ariana, but the thoughts were no longer paralyzing to her very soul like they had been before. Plus, she was ready to reengage in her career as an ob-gyn—another step forward that only a month ago had seemed impossible.

And he showed you that you can fall in love again.

Claire winced. If ever there was a positive that came with an equally weighted negative, this had to be it. Yes, she now knew she could love again. But she could love *Kiernan*—a distinction that was non-negotiable. And now, she had to leave him.

Even if you stayed, you'd still have to say goodbye.

Claire pressed her lips together, jaw tightened. Did she really need to remind herself of the obvious?

Just be glad for the time you had together, she told herself.

Not *too* much of cliché, she thought, but it was a notion she was going to hold on to…because right now it was all she had.

"I thought I might find you here."

Claire gasped and whirled around, her eyes wide with disbelief as she saw Kiernan standing barely ten feet away from her. He wore a grin that suited his handsome face in the same way that his dark jeans and long-sleeved burgundy T-shirt suited his muscular body.

It took a few moments for Claire to process what was happening. She had told Kiernan no more goodbyes. But, damn, was she ever happy that he had ignored her request.

"I had to see you again," he said as he walked over and took both her hands in his. "So please don't get mad at me for defying your orders."

She couldn't help but laugh quietly at his cheekiness. "That's okay. I'm supposed to be packing to leave, but as you can see, I've been procrastinating." As he squeezed her hands and pulled her in closer, she could feel the electricity surge between them. "And I can think of worse diversions than seeing you again."

He smiled, but then his face grew serious. "Claire, I couldn't let you leave without telling you something."

She waited for him to continue, suddenly aware that she was holding her breath.

"I love you," he said softly. "And in a way that I've never loved anyone before. You are the most gifted, caring, beautiful…*amazing* woman, and you've made me see things that no one else ever has. Or ever could. Being with you has made me a better person. Which I know probably sounds crazy, given that we've only known each other a month. But it's been a month that's completely changed my life."

Claire caught her breath just in time before it escaped her once more. "I love you, too," she said quietly. "Which is why saying goodbye is so hard…"

"But what if we didn't have to say goodbye?"

Her forehead creased in confusion. They had been over this before. Surely he knew why they had to part ways.

Realizing there was no point in repeating their conflicting views on family, she could only look at him with questioning eyes.

"I've been doing a lot of thinking over the past few days," he said. "*A lot.* You said something to me that day we went hiking. How I could be the one to break the cycle. At the time I knew what you meant on an intellectual level, but I couldn't truly *feel* it, if you know what I mean. But I do now. My desire not to have kids totally stemmed from my father's inadequacies. I thought that being the best surgeon I could be meant forgoing a family, or else being an absentee husband and father like him. But it's simply not true. Being with you…it's made me see what really matters in life. The work that we both do as doctors—yes, that is important. It can even save lives. But it's not the be-all and end-all. I want to spend the rest of my life with you. And to have a family together."

He looked up at the sky, shaking his head and nearly laughing, as though he couldn't comprehend how some of his core beliefs had suddenly been turned upside down.

"All of my life I've wanted to steer clear of anything that remotely hinted at having a family of my own. And now… because of you…it's like I suddenly can't think about anything else."

"Kiernan… I…"

Was this really happening?

She swallowed hard, reminding herself that she needed to stay grounded in reality. "You do know that I'm flying back to Boston tomorrow."

"I know. But I also know that you probably won't be going back to Boston General—at least that's what you shared with me. So I hope you don't mind that I took the liberty of making a few inquiries."

Claire arched an eyebrow. "A few inquiries…?"

"I've been in talks with the hospital board and the CEO, and they all agree. There's no one more qualified to lead West Mercy's new neonatal wing than you. They're still hammering out the fine print, but if you're interested they're prepared to offer you a contract that will give you full control over the direction of this new program. Fetal surgeries, treatments for high-risk mothers—all of it."

Claire didn't think her jaw could fall any further, but with this most unexpected announcement, it found a way. Her mind, though spinning, travelled back to a recent wish…a seemingly *impossible* wish…that she was living in the beautiful Irish countryside and working with the love of her life, who just so happened to be gazing into her eyes at this very moment.

And now Kiernan was pledging his love to her and sharing his desire for them to have a family together. Which meant that in the span of a single minute—two at tops—he had just made all her dreams come true.

"I know this is a lot to throw at you all at once," he said. "And I don't want you to feel in any way pressured to make a decision now. Take whatever time you need. Go home, like you planned, and talk to your family about it if that helps." He paused. "Oh—and I should mention that the contract comes with a very important rider."

Seeing the glint of a twinkle in his eye, Claire grinned cautiously as she asked, "Which is…?"

"Twenty-four-seven access to the chief of surgery, who is fully invested in the goal of making you the happiest woman on earth."

"You've already done that," Claire said softly as Kiernan leaned in and kissed her passionately.

"Like I said before," Kiernan said, once they both had a chance to breathe again. "No pressure… But while you're tossing around the pros and cons of my offer, how about we go inside the cottage and I'll show you some of the exclusive benefits you'll get with that contract rider?"

Claire grinned. She already knew what her answer would be, but there was no need to let the chief of surgery know just yet. "Okay… But just so you know—I'm very much on the fence about this offer, so you'll really need to persuade me."

His eyes flashed with desire as they gazed into hers. "Oh, I will… I can promise you that."

Claire had no doubt Kiernan would keep his promise. He was just that kind of man.

EPILOGUE

CLAIRE PROPPED HERSELF up on both elbows as she lay down on a soft blanket covering an equally cushiony carpet of grass. The early-afternoon sun felt good on her face, and with her eyes closed, she tipped her head back.

"Nothing like getting some vitamin D the good, old-fashioned way."

Kiernan leaned over and kissed her on the forehead. "Hard to believe that exactly one year ago we met at this precise spot."

Claire opened her eyes and smiled. "I know. I sometimes wonder...what if I'd come here for a walk twenty minutes sooner, or you'd gone for a run twenty minutes later. Chances are we never would have met."

"Or been at the right place, at the right time, to help deliver Sam."

"Exactly."

"So, are you saying you believe in fate?" Kiernan asked, with a teasing quality to his voice.

Claire smiled wistfully. "Either that or extremely good luck."

Kiernan scanned the grass that lined the border of the blanket, then plucked a four-leaf clover. He offered it to Claire, placing his other hand on her belly. "Well, I can personally vouch for the fact that I'm the luckiest man alive."

She placed her hand over his. At four and a half months pregnant, she had just started to experience Caitlin's kicks, and her smile widened as one poked her just under her ribcage.

"Did you feel that?" she asked excitedly.

Kiernan nodded, his face beaming with pride. "I think we have a star football player in the making. Or, better yet, a rugby player."

A ringing phone interrupted Claire's laughter.

"Who is it?" she asked as Kiernan glanced down at his phone screen.

"It's Craig," he replied, rolling his eyes.

Two more rings, and the call stopped.

"You can call him back. I don't mind."

"It's nothing that can't wait."

"Are you sure about that? You don't want the hospital CEO labeling you a slacker." She paused. "And I'm only half kidding, by the way, knowing how he expects twenty-four-seven access."

"It's a beautiful Saturday afternoon, and I'm here with my even more beautiful wife. If it were a medical emergency, I'd take the call. But administrative stuff—that can wait until Monday."

"You really have become quite the slouch, Mr. O'Rourke."

Kiernan grinned. "If it means spending more time with you and our daughter, then I'll gladly own up to that."

"I love you," she said, at the exact moment Kiernan uttered the same three words.

They both laughed at the unintended perfect timing.

"And I can't wait to meet you, little Caitlin," Kiernan said as he leaned over and kissed her belly.

Claire lifted the four-leaf clover that she had been twirling between her thumb and forefinger and studied it for a moment. There had to be some truth to its powers of good fortune. Because she was, indeed, the luckiest woman in the world.

* * * * *

MILLS & BOON®

Coming next month

THE SINGLE DAD'S SECRET
Zoey Gomez

Eight patients later, it was lunch time, and Lucien was still seething over Dr Dean Vasquez.

He couldn't get the man out of his head. Lucien couldn't for the life of him think why. Yes, he was very handsome, and his eyes had been a particularly stunning shade of green, but Lucien very rarely found anyone attractive. He barely noticed the way most people looked and almost never got distracted by a handsome face. He usually had to really get to know someone before he could find himself attracted to them. But here he was, unable to get a near stranger out of his head. Or the freckles on Dr Vasquez's nose that were so clear, they'd been visible on a screen. Not to mention the dimple that showed in his cheek when he smiled. It was ridiculous. So what if Dr Vasquez had looked adorably happy hugging his son? The last thing Lucien needed was to have any kind of feelings for a new colleague.

Continue reading

THE SINGLE DAD'S SECRET
Zoey Gomez

Available next month
millsandboon.co.uk

COMING SOON!

We really hope you enjoyed reading this book.
If you're looking for more romance
be sure to head to the shops when
new books are available on

Thursday 27th February

To see which titles are coming soon, please visit
millsandboon.co.uk/nextmonth

MILLS & BOON

LET'S TALK

Romance

For exclusive extracts, competitions and special offers, find us online:

f MillsandBoon

X @MillsandBoon

◉ @MillsandBoonUK

♪ @MillsandBoonUK

Get in touch on 01413 063 232

Afterglow Books is a trend-led, trope-filled list of books with diverse, authentic and relatable characters, a wide array of voices and representations, plus real world trials and tribulations. Featuring all the tropes you could possibly want (think small-town settings, fake relationships, grumpy vs sunshine, enemies to lovers) and all with a generous dose of spice in every story.

♪ @millsandboonuk
⬚ @millsandboonuk
afterglowbooks.co.uk
#AfterglowBooks

For all the latest book news, exclusive content and giveaways scan the QR code below to sign up to the Afterglow newsletter:

SCAN ME

afterglow BOOKS

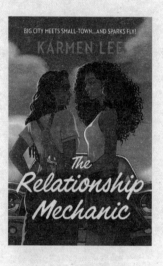

afterglow BOOKS

Looking for more Afterglow Books?

Try the perfect subscription for spicy romance lovers and save 50% on your first parcel.

PLUS receive these additional benefits when you subscribe:

- **FREE** delivery direct to your door
- **EXCLUSIVE** offers every month
- **SAVE** up to 30% on pre-paid subscriptions

SUBSCRIBE AND SAVE

millsandboon.co.uk/Subscribe

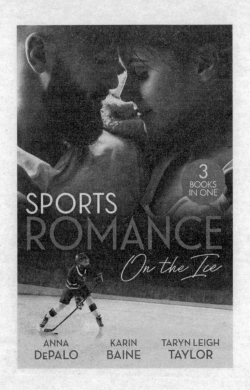